18

EMILY HAINSWORTH

TAKE THE FALL

BALZER + BRAY
An Imprint of HarperCollins*Publishers*

Balzer + Bray is an imprint of HarperCollins Publishers.

Take the Fall

Copyright © 2016 by Emily Hainsworth

All rights reserved. Printed in the United States of America. No part of this book may be used or reproduced in any manner whatsoever without written permission except in the case of brief quotations embodied in critical articles and reviews. For information address HarperCollins Children's Books, a division of HarperCollins Publishers, 195 Broadway, New York, NY 10007.

www.epicreads.com

Library of Congress Cataloging-in-Publication Data

Hainsworth, Emily.

Take the fall / Emily Hainsworth. — First edition.

pages   cm

Summary: "When Sonia's best friend is found murdered, everything she thought she was sure of is turned on its head as the biggest suspect comes to Sonia for help proving his innocence"— Provided by publisher.

ISBN 978-0-06-209422-3 (hardback)

[1. Murder—Fiction.   2. Grief—Fiction.   3. High schools— Fiction.   4. Schools—Fiction.   5. Mystery and detective stories.]   I. Title.

PZ7.H128163Tak   2016   2015015340

[Fic]—dc23   CIP

AC

Typography by Sarah Creech

15 16 17 18 19   PC/RRDH   10 9 8 7 6 5 4 3 2 1

❖

First Edition

For Charlotte—a pretty good sister after all.
And for Mom and Dad, without whom
this book would still be unfinished.

None of them knew just how she fell
Down, down, through the air—
*   and now she'll never tell.*

A scream and a gasp, and then she was gone
From the grass, from the earth,
*   from this side of the dawn.*

PROLOGUE

DON'T THINK, JUST RUN.

Shadows explode across my vision, leaping out at me like specters in a funhouse. My legs can't keep up with my racing heart. They don't even know where to run. There's a snatch of light between the trees, a hint of stars in the sky, and I fix my eyes on these faint promises of—

Someone help me—*please.*

I trip, land on my face. Pain shoots through my lip; there's blood in my mouth. The air leaves my lungs and I just want to lie still, cry, but then a stiff, unforgiving hand wraps around my ankle.

I scream.

It's the twisting hold of a root—not the hands that grabbed me, forced me to the ground. But the memory floods tears down my cheeks. I jerk my foot free, grasping a tree trunk with one hand, plunging the other into a bush. Terror pulls me to my feet. There's no air left to breathe. I trip over rocks and plants I should have memorized, my body drained, threatening to give in.

Don't stop now.

Don't look back.

My knees threaten to buckle. Small creatures shuffle beneath the brush. An owl calls overhead. There's the rush of water, faint, but always there. Then a different noise—and I drop to the earth, flattening myself until my heart hammers like a drum into the leaves.

Because it sounded like a voice.

My head throbs. My ribs scream.

I close my eyes and count.

One.

Two.

Three.

I don't see anyone when I scramble up, but I'm not waiting to figure out where they went. A horn honks faintly in the distance and I rush toward the sound. A minute later my feet thump over a stretch of familiar ground—my heart carries me up the path. I'm going to make it. *Home.*

I burst free of the woods, toward the lights above the Black River Diner, gleaming like a blue neon beacon in the dark. I stumble across First Avenue, afraid to take my eyes off the two figures in the window. The sign says Closed, but I yank the door open so hard the bells above it fall to the floor in a broken jingle. I stand gasping in the security of glaring fluorescent light.

Aunt Dina runs a mop over the checkered linoleum. My mom's behind the register, still laughing at some joke. Her smile fades when she sees me, like she's not sure who I am, and a sob escapes my lips. Minutes ago I was desperate just to see her face again, and now—the thought of telling her—

What just happened to me?

The color drains from her face.

The mop clatters to the floor.

Five minutes later the diner is crawling with cops. The only time I've seen anything like it was when we held a community pie-eating contest to benefit the Officers' Foundation. The deputies wore lobster bibs and poked fun at one another. Now a tense group forms a circle around me and I still feel like I'm running. Blood roars in my ears. I'm aware of Sheriff Wood asking questions. My mom a notch below hysterical. Dina pacing. Deputy Rashid opening and closing the release on his holster. My cheeks are wet, filthy. Tears mixed with dirt mixed with fear. My ribs ache with every sob. My arms sting.

"What happened, Sonia?"

"Who did this?"

"You were attacked? In the woods?"

I can't stop crying long enough to answer every question.

Another call comes in. The sheriff and all but one of the deputies abruptly leave. My uncle shows up. I lie down in a booth. Mom covers me with a blanket. There's some argument about calling a doctor—which I don't need. I'm scraped and bruised, scared to death, but nothing more than that. Deputy Robson gets a call and everyone goes quiet.

People move in the door, then out.

Voices thrum around me.

All I hear is my heart.

Until I realize my name isn't the only one being whispered.

Gretchen. My best friend.

My head is fogged, my arms are lead. I want to sit up, tell them to let her know I'm okay, I made it out. But something's off. I can't get hold of my own thoughts. It takes all the energy I have to lie in this booth and blink. And then I hear:

"Gretchen Meyer—missing."

No.

I grasp the edge of the table, heave myself upright. "What did you just say?"

Everyone stares as if they'd forgotten I was there. My mom slides into the booth, wraps her arms around me, but no one's answering my question.

I pull my phone out of my pocket, dial her number, but it goes straight to voicemail. Of course it does. *I need her to pick up.* My mind weighs possibilities until it's spinning out of control. Maybe somehow, I'll get a text. Maybe she'll be okay.

Hours pass in silence.

The sky brightens, flooding the diner with morning light.

I'm still staring at my phone when the sheriff tells me, "Gretchen's dead."

ONE

"I HEARD THEY HAD BREAKUP sex, then he killed her in a jealous rage."

"You can't have breakup sex after you're already broken up."

"Of course you can, that's the whole—"

"Stop, you guys. I can't believe we're even talking about this."

"I'm just stating the facts. Anyway, the cops know it was him. It's just a matter of time."

"Do you . . . do you think she was scared?"

The coffee filter I'm holding shakes in my hands. I take a sharp breath, aggravating the pain in my left side, and dump in four more scoops of grounds. I grab an order pad and come around the corner into view, not even attempting a smile. "Hey guys, what can I get for you?"

The table falls silent, my friends pointing fingers at one another with their eyes.

"Sonia, what are you doing here?" asks Haley Jacobs.

"We're busy," I murmur, peering at the table of cops by the door. There are only three deputies there now, but if you'd been here this morning you might've thought the sheriff's office had relocated from down the street.

"We heard what happened." Aisha Wallace slides out of the booth and wraps me in a careless hug, setting my bruised ribs and scratched arms alight with pain. I pull back. "Are you okay?"

"I'm . . ."

I'm alive. But maybe I shouldn't be.

"You're at *work*, are you insane?" Haley exchanges a look with Aisha. "I can't believe your family's okay with this."

They're not. I glance at the door to the kitchen. "I just kind of need to be here right now."

"You poor thing, of course you do," Aisha says, sitting close to her boyfriend, Derek. "You must've been so scared."

"Seriously, after what you've been through," Haley says. "You could've been—"

Aisha kicks her under the table.

I support myself on the edge of the booth and nod slowly. My uncle Noah took one look at my face this morning and insisted I go straight back upstairs, but the idea of staring at my bedroom ceiling for a second day while everyone in town debates how my best friend died made me sicker than I already felt. I'm not supposed to be waiting tables, but my thoughts were getting way too loud back in the kitchen. And since my family has lost it and won't tell me anything, snatches of random conversations have become the only way for me to guess what's going on.

Derek clears his throat, eyeing the cops across the room. "This is probably the safest place in town right now anyway."

"Have you guys heard anything?" I ask, trying to keep my voice steady.

Haley leans forward. "They arrested Marcus Perez."

My stomach knots. I should be glad about this. Gretchen's recent ex would be the most likely suspect, and it's not like Marcus and I ever got along. But deep in my heart, I'll admit . . . I don't want it to be him.

"They didn't arrest him," Derek says. "They just brought him in for questioning."

"I—I'd heard that." The whole diner has been buzzing about it.

"Her car is still missing," Aisha adds. "And they found signs of a struggle at the top of the falls."

Haley's eyes go wide. "Did you get a look at the guy who attacked you? Do you think it was—"

The bells above the front door jingle and my head jerks up, but it's just another news crew. My mom comes out of the kitchen, her eyes darting around the diner until she finds me. The alarm on her face dissipates, but her mouth pulls into a frown. I sink in my shoes.

"Be back in a sec, you guys—two Diet Cokes and a Sprite, right?" I don't wait for an answer. One of several talents I've cultivated growing up in the diner is an ability to remember the food and drink preferences of just about every person in town. I can hardly grasp everything that's happened to me the last two days—most of it I'd desperately like to forget—but when I come back, I know Haley and Aisha will still order grilled cheese and Derek will go for a burger with extra pickles.

These little details are all that's holding me together right now.

My aunt Dina is busy cleaning up a spilled milk shake, so I grab a couple of menus and scan the room for a table to seat the reporters, but my mom heads me off before I get to them.

"Honey, what are you doing?"

I avoid her eyes. "Seating the people who just walked in."

"I thought the agreement was—"

"I can't sit back there and roll silverware for eight hours." I clutch the menus to my chest.

"You could go upstairs." She reaches out to tuck a loose curl behind my ear. "I'd feel better if you were resting anyway. You must be exhausted."

"I rested all day yesterday. I need to know what's happening."

"Sheriff Wood said he'd give us an update when he knows more—everything you're going to hear will be gossip and rumors."

"Look, Mom, I just—" I take a deep breath, but my jaw starts to tremble. "I just want to be here, close to everyone."

My mom presses her lips together, her eyes shining like she might start crying again, and I'm afraid if she does, I will too. "Oh, Sonia—" The bells above the door jingle a second time and she stops, looks carefully at my face, then wipes her cheeks. "You can take some of my tables, but come get me if you need me and don't push yourself too hard. The sheriff's coming by soon with more questions."

I nod, trying to pull myself together as I approach a woman in a coral suit and heels standing by the door with a guy lugging a TV camera. Hidden Falls is a small town and doesn't see a lot of reporters, but they're easy enough to spot when they come in. Their colorful outfits stand out against the diner's dark wood paneling and faded turquoise booths. "Hi. Just the two of you?"

The woman smiles and nods, though her blond made-for-TV hair doesn't move.

I spot an open table in the far corner and lead them past a

booth of sophomore girls whose voices dip to whispers as I walk by.

". . . so scary . . . can't believe they're not canceling school tomorrow . . ."

I clear a couple of mugs, wipe down the tabletop, and grab two new place settings.

"Sorry, it's been a zoo here today. What can I get you to drink?"

"Two coffees with cream, please," the woman says, sitting. I imagine her name is Elizabeth or maybe Tina. "You must go to Hurlburt High. Were you friends with Gretchen Meyer?"

I drop a fork on the floor, caught off guard by the question, and it's a long moment before that "were" sinks into my heart—that Gretchen's past tense now. I understand that's the whole reason the reporters are here. The beautiful daughter of a local tech mogul died mysteriously, and the press is having a field day speculating about whodunit. I can ignore the TV repeating the same five tired facts over and over. But I can't take this woman asking me if I *knew* her when I can't even process the fact that she's gone.

"Everyone knew Gretchen," I say quickly.

Tina/Elizabeth ignores the change in my tone and leans closer. "I understand Gretchen had a close friend who works in this diner."

She tries to give me a sympathetic smile, but she shows too many teeth, reminding me of a shark. My hair sticks to my neck. I dig through my pockets looking for a pencil even though I know there's one tucked behind my left ear. "Look, I've got other tables—"

"Sonia Feldman? That's your name, isn't it?"

I don't answer.

"I'm sorry for your tragic loss." Her eyes trace the red scratches peeking out of my sleeves. I pull my arms behind my back. "It's my understanding that you were attacked in the woods not far from where Gretchen died. I was wondering if you'd be willing to sit down and talk with us about what happened? You're very brave...."

My eyes burn. I open my mouth, but my throat catches. I want to tell her exactly what happened. I want to tell her bravery is shit and I should be dead. I *want* to tell her to get the hell out and never come back, but the air in my lungs is so thick.

"Oh, I didn't mean to upset you." She frowns and looks at her notes. "Never mind that, do you happen to know a boy named Marcus Perez?"

I pull away from the table. Because if there was one button left to push after Gretchen, Marcus was it. My mom and Dina are each so busy with their orders they don't see me lurch through the crowded dining room toward the kitchen. And then I'm out the back door, gulping spring air.

The scent of recent rain and exposed earth invades my senses and I gag, my vision flashing with darkness and branches and fear. I force my eyes open, drinking in the sunlight with all five senses, waiting for the world to stop spinning. But as long as Gretchen's gone, I'm afraid it never will.

I brace myself against the brick, stumbling down the alley and around the side of the building. I raise my head and find myself staring across the street into Hidden Falls Park.

My vision blurs. I press my hands to my chest, but the ache never subsides.

Gretchen's house is on the far side, on Park Drive. You can't see it from here even when all the trees don't have their leaves, but there are several trails through the park, and a little bridge over the creek. I knew every step of the route by heart until Friday night, when I thought I'd never find my way out—when I thought I was going to die. I close my eyes. If I cross the road right now and peer down the slope, I'd probably see the lines of yellow police tape spider-webbing through the trees. I look down at my hands, scratched and raw from branches that used to feel like a shelter. I never want to step into the park again.

I wish you were dead.

"Sonia!" My aunt Dina yanks me around the corner, back through the door into the kitchen. She pulls the security door shut and locks it while I sink to the floor, heart racing.

"What were you doing out there alone? Are you crazy?"

I look from Dina to the door and break a cold sweat. What was I doing?

"I—I just needed some air," I say, fighting back nausea.

"You're white as a sheet."

I let out a long breath. "There was this reporter asking questions . . ."

"What did they say? I'll throw them out." Her eyes are fierce, but when she looks at me her voice softens. "You know we all just want you safe. Did you remember any more about the person who chased you? Do you think it could've been the Perez kid?"

Out of my face, Gretchen—God, I wish you were dead.

The words are clear in my memory. I just can't believe Marcus actually said them.

I study my scraped hands until I realize they're shaking again. I don't understand much of what happened the other night.

Sometimes the only thing that's clear is that Gretchen ended up dead and I didn't.

Gretchen. My best friend. How is that even possible?

"I don't know," I whisper.

She sinks down beside me. Dina is usually the calm, levelheaded member of our family, but since Friday night we've all transformed into more paranoid, neurotic versions of ourselves. She scrutinizes me until a tear escapes down my cheek.

"Oh, sweetie, I know you're scared. I'm sorry."

I wipe my face and she wraps me in her arms.

"I'm fine. I'll be okay." I say it as much for myself as for her.

"Look, I get it, Sonia." She shakes her head. "It's busy down here, all you have to think about is french fries and sodas and whether someone wanted dressing on the side or extra cheese. But you need to give yourself room to let all of this process. Maybe if you do, you'll remem—"

"There's nothing wrong with my memory." I take a painful breath. "I just never saw a face."

She takes my hand and squeezes. My mom says I'm an exact copy of her little sister, which always used to make me blush. We do have the same facial expressions, dark curly hair, and bright green eyes, but she has a sprinkle of freckles across her nose that make her look even younger than she is, and she's taller and more athletic. When Dina took me and Gretchen out to a movie once, Gretchen told a group of cute high school guys that Dina and I were sisters. Dina started to correct her, but Gretchen kept embellishing until Dina went with it and even flirted with one of the guys. Dina laughed about it later, but it was clear Gretchen had made her day. The realization that Gretchen will never do anything like that again sits heavy in my chest. I cover my face with my hands.

I'm startled back into the moment when my uncle starts yelling.

"What do you mean you don't know where she is?"

"She's here, I *just* saw—"

"I can't believe you let her convince you this was okay, Marlene."

"What was I supposed to do, lock her upstairs?"

"Under the circumstances? Yes."

"Don't start in on the parenting bullshit, Noah, if I—oh—" My mother rushes to where Dina and I sit behind boxes of plastic straws and paper napkins. "Sonia, thank God. Are you okay?"

"Sonia's fine," Dina says, rising to face her older brother and sister. "She's just going upstairs for a bit."

I stand to protest, but blood rushes to my head and I have to steady myself against a shelf. Maybe I should lie down for a little while. Uncle Noah's face softens when he sees me. He looks a little like old, out-of-shape Elvis when he frowns.

"Those reporters get in your face?" he asks.

"You look exhausted." My mom feels my forehead. "Dina's right, you should go upstairs."

"Isn't the sheriff coming by?"

My mom and Uncle Noah exchange a glance.

"What?"

"He got tied up, but he'll be by later, sweetie."

I look from my mom, to my uncle, and finally to Dina, who seems just as clueless as me. "What's going on?"

"We'll talk about it when the sheriff gets here," my mom says.

"Something happened, didn't it?" My voice goes shrill; I knew this was coming. "What is it? Did they find something?"

"It's nothing like that," Mom says. "Now please, go upstairs."

"Just tell her, Marlene." Noah double-checks the lock on the security door.

My mom gives me this look like she wants to throw herself between me and her own words. "Marcus Perez claims to have an alibi. They had to let him go."

TWO

THE LAST OF THE DAYLIGHT fades from my little bedroom until I'm left in blackness. I tiptoe across the wood floor and turn my closet light on. To chase away the shadows, and whatever else might lurk in the dark.

The sheriff is still out looking for bad guys and all I can do is sit here thinking up my own.

If Marcus has an alibi, he couldn't have attacked me. He couldn't have killed Gretchen. He wouldn't go to jail. I can't decide if I should be relieved or scared.

A long-buried part of me never wanted it to be him, but it made so much sense.

And if not Marcus, who else could it have been?

I bend to touch a small carving inside my closet door that says *Zack & Ken.* The edges of the letters are so worn they look like they've become part of the floor rather than something slashed into it. I have no idea who Zack and Ken were, but when I was little I made up personalities for them and they became the boys in the closet who kept monsters away. I leave the door ajar and climb under the quilt with my clothes on. Some primitive part of my brain feels safer this way.

I close my eyes, focusing on neutral things like the weather getting warmer, Aunt Dina's recipe for rainbow cookies, and what I'll wear to commencement. But my eyes burn when I think Gretchen will never see another spring. Rainbow cookies were her favorite. And when I imagine her absence at graduation—an awful punctuation mark at the end of everyone's high school memories—tears spill down my cheeks. I curl into a ball, fighting waves of fear, guilt.

It didn't have to be her. It could have, *should* have been me.

I pick up my phone. All my feeds are clogged with memorials to Gretchen and people voicing shock and despair over her death and what happened to me. But there's nothing concrete about who did this. Nothing I didn't already hear at the diner. I like a few statuses and all the condolences, but I can't bring myself to post anything or comment. That would make it too real.

Serial Experiments—a comic book based on the UltaShock video game—lies on top of a couple textbooks by the bed. Right where I dropped it before we went to Brianne's party Friday night. I pick it up, in desperate need of a distraction, but when I find where I left off, Gretchen's voice dances through my head.

"Wait, tell me again why she wears pigtails?"

"I don't know, because she's badass."

"They're *pink* pigtails. I thought she was supposed to be a ninja or something."

"An assassin—and that's the whole point. She's smart, and deadly with a crossbow. No one expects it."

Gretchen dropped the comic into my lap, twisted my hair into thick pigtails, and laughed. "Bad. Ass."

It's well after dark and I'm half dozing when I'm startled by the clomp of shoes on the stairs. From the sound of it, more than one pair. My heart pounds with every creak of the floorboards as they tiptoe down the hall, stopping at the door of my room.

"She's asleep, finally. Can't you come back in the morning?" my mother asks.

"Why don't you wake her. This won't take long." I recognize the sheriff's voice in a whisper.

"You said they're just routine questions."

"They are, but I've got Carlton Meyer breathing down my neck, Marlene."

The hall goes quiet and I hold my breath. I'm ninety-nine percent sure they're hugging now. My mom and Sheriff Wood dated briefly when I was little, and though I was never sure why they broke up, it's clear they still care for each other, if just as close friends. Eventually, my mom peeks her head into my room and I look up at her in the dim closet light.

"Oh, you're awake."

She crosses the tiny space to perch on the edge of my bed. My mom had me young. She's only thirty-six, but right now she looks a lot older than that. Her thin brown hair is pulled away from her face and I can see every crease around her mouth and eyes in the light of my closet. She lifts my comic book off my chest, setting it carefully aside without losing the page.

"Roger's here, sweetie. I know it's late, but do you feel up to running through things with him again?" She doesn't usually refer to him as "Roger" with me. I think she's trying to make me more comfortable.

"No, of course it's fine." It takes effort to make this sound like I mean it. I barely remember what I said the first time he questioned me and I'm nervous about having to talk through it again. But Sheriff Wood's the one person in town who might be able to figure out what happened to me and Gretchen, and I'm counting on him to be straight with me. I need to know what's going on with the investigation or I'm going to lose it.

His uniform fills the room when he walks in, and my stomach churns, but I remind myself this is *Roger*, my mom's old boyfriend, who used to give me chocolate bars and let me run the emergency lights on his car. He's not even wearing his hat like usual. Like he was when he came rushing into the diner Friday night. I give my room a self-conscious once-over as he and my mom shuffle to make room for each other. There're no dirty dishes lying around or underwear left out, but I still pull the covers closer around me. It's probably impossible to feel entirely comfortable with a uniformed cop in your bedroom.

"Sonia, how are you feeling?"

I pull my knees up, but I'm not sure how to answer.

"I'm sorry, I know this is hard. It's been a tough couple of days." He nods at my desk chair. "Do you mind if I sit down?"

I shake my head. He perches on the edge of the purple chair and I think how Gretchen would spin lazily in it, pushing herself with one foot. I have to look away.

"I'm sorry it's so late. I kept meaning to stop by earlier to at least see how you were doing." He wrinkles his brow. "Your mom told you about Marcus Perez?"

I look at my mom leaning against the doorframe. She gives me an anxious nod. I swallow hard, wondering where this is going. "Yeah, she said you guys had to let him go. Does that mean he definitely didn't do it?" My heart quickens. "Do you have another suspect?"

"It just means we've got to be extra vigilant to try and figure out exactly what happened the other night." He clears his throat, but this is so vague, I want to yell. "Listen, I know we went over what happened to you Friday, but because we talked before we knew— before Gretchen was found—I wanted to go over the details again."

I knot my fingers under the covers. "Okay, I'll try."

"Thanks, Sonia. I know this isn't easy." He pulls a notebook from his pocket and looks at my mom. "We'll keep it as brief as possible."

She nods, but she doesn't leave.

"I have here that you drove Gretchen back to her house from a party at Brianne Prashad's around eleven o'clock Friday night," the sheriff says.

I nod.

"You were driving her car and you were the designated driver?"

I squirm, looking at my lap. It feels wrong to acknowledge my friends' drinking to his face, but the sheriff isn't stupid. "Yes. Our curfews weren't until midnight, but she and Kirsten had a fight and Gretchen wanted to go home."

"That's right . . . Kirsten said you all arrived together, but you and Gretchen left without her."

My face goes hot. "We shouldn't have. Kirsten was drunk."

"Was Gretchen?"

I shake my head. "She might've had a beer or two—that's why I drove—but Gretchen wasn't really a big drinker."

Sheriff Wood looks at me. "So, what was the fight about?"

I bite my lip. "I actually don't know." Gretchen almost never let her little sister tag along when we went out. I was surprised she let Kirsten come that night, but it wasn't a shock that they ended up fighting. Leaving Kirsten drunk at Brianne's seemed harsh though, even for Gretchen. "She barely spoke once we were in the car."

The sheriff raises his eyebrows. "Really? Not even to confide in her best friend?"

"She never liked to talk when she was mad." I stare at the floor. There's been chatter that Gretchen found Marcus and Kirsten hooking up, but it's so hard to believe, I can't bring myself to repeat it. "I—I heard a rumor the fight had something to do with Marcus."

He makes a few notes, but this doesn't seem to surprise him.

"Okay. Gretchen's phone records show she called her house at 11:04 p.m. and someone there answered. Do you know if she spoke to anyone?"

I furrow my brow. "No, she didn't call anyone from the car."

"Are you sure about that, Sonia?"

"Yes. Like I said, she was upset. She hardly said a word the whole drive. She must've made the call after she was home . . . but why would she do that?"

He jots a bunch of stuff down and ignores my question. "You said before that you parked Gretchen's car in front of her house and she went inside. What happened next?"

I look up, uncertain. We already went over this on Friday night. "Nothing right away. I ran into Haley Jacobs walking her dog. We talked a few minutes, then I started home through the park."

"Did you have Gretchen's keys with you then?"

"No, I gave them back to her."

"Are you sure, Sonia?"

20

"Positive. Her parents were at a benefit that evening. She couldn't have gotten into her house without them."

Sheriff Wood's face is stern. "Did you actually see Gretchen go inside her house?"

"Yes."

"Did you see her come back out?"

I frown. "No."

"Do you know if Gretchen was planning to go anywhere else after you dropped her off?"

I shake my head slowly. "No, she said something about taking a bath and going to bed."

He flips the page of his notebook and I wonder when this will be over. When it will be my turn to ask questions. "So you started walking home on the main path through the park, straight down from Gretchen's house, right?"

"Right. That's the route we've always taken."

"Did you stop anywhere along the way?"

"Not until I got to the bridge." My voice wavers.

He leans forward on the edge of my desk chair. "Okay, I want you to think for a second. This is important. Did you see anything suspicious before you entered the park? Any strange cars around, people you didn't recognize?"

I imagine someone sitting in a car, watching me walk down the trail, and shudder. There are so many important details I could have missed. "I wasn't really paying attention to cars."

"What about other people in the park?" His eyes are intense. "Think, Sonia. Was there anyone unusual you might've passed on the path? Anything out of the ordinary as you approached the bridge?"

21

"I—I don't know. There might've been. It was dark." The scratches in my skin burn, but his questions keep coming.

"There might've been, or there was?" His voice rises. "Because if you saw the—"

"Roger," my mom warns.

He looks at her, then back at me and runs a hand over his face. "I'm sorry."

I stare at my quaking hands. Then I imagine Gretchen being chased by the same shadowy figure as me—but not getting away. I take as deep a breath as my ribs will allow. I can do this. I'm doing this.

"No, it's okay." I pull a pillow into my lap and manage a nod. "I know this is important."

The sheriff clears his throat and glances through his notes again. When he looks up he's all protocol once more. "In your statement, you said you were grabbed from behind just before you reached the bridge. You struggled with your attacker, but you never saw a face."

"Yes." I fix my eyes on the space between us, where it feels safe.

"Could you tell if they were male or female?"

"Male." I hesitate. "I think."

The pen scratches across his notepad, sending a shiver up my spine. I do everything possible to avoid thinking about the next part. The moment hands clamped around my neck and dragged me toward the falls. When I felt the icy spray on my face and realized I was going to die. I close my eyes, fighting the sting of tears. But then the sheriff surprises me with a different question.

"Can you remember which way you ran? How long you were pursued after you got away?"

"I—I'm not sure." I look at my lap, racking my memory for any useful detail. "It felt like I ran forever, I got so turned around. At some point I made it back to the bridge, and then the diner." My voice quavers, but I force myself to go on. "I guess if I hadn't . . ."

A muffled sob issues from the doorway. I open my eyes to see my mother wiping her face and I wish I'd spared her that detail.

"This was very helpful, Sonia, thank you." The sheriff's face softens as he pockets his notes.

I exhale. "I feel like I'm no help at all."

"What you've been through, the fact that you're even *able* to talk about this is huge." He leans toward me. "I might send Amir over tomorrow. Maybe the two of you can work out a sketch of the person you saw."

"But I didn't see—"

"Sleep on it. You never know."

I give in, sinking back into my pillows. "Sheriff?"

"Yes?"

"Do you have a list of other suspects?"

His forehead creases. "You leave that part up to me. I don't want you worrying about it."

I frown, a heavy feeling building in my gut. "Do you really believe it wasn't Marcus?"

"Sonia, you know I can't speculate about stuff like that."

I tighten my fingers in my lap, but it's clear he's set on keeping me in the dark.

"Listen, I'm aware you and Marcus Perez don't exactly get along—"

"It's not that." I fold my arms, though he's right, partially. Marcus

23

does hate my guts. It would be easier if I felt the same way. "Can you just stop trying to protect me? I was attacked by this person too, don't I deserve to know who you think it was?"

He rests his elbows on his knees. "I'll be the first to admit I'm trying to protect you. It is likely that the same person attacked you and Gretchen. And they're still at large. I promise I'll do everything in my power to get them secured behind bars, but you're just going to have to trust me." He rises, squeezes my mom's shoulder. "Try to get some sleep, both of you."

My mom sees him downstairs. When she comes back she lingers in the door, hugging herself. "I'll ask the school to send your things over tomorrow."

I look up. "Why would you do that? We still have class."

"A few days off will do you good," she says.

"But it's almost finals." My mouth goes dry. "I can't afford to mess up my grades."

"I don't see how you can even think about grades right now."

I straighten, prepared to argue, but think better of it. My mother always says she's learned more from life than she could in any class-room; that college is a waste of time. But it's wrong to lace that tired dispute into a night like tonight. "I just can't lose my scholarship."

She sits on the edge of my bed. "I don't think the weight of all this has hit you yet."

I clench my jaw, because if I don't, I'll scream. It hit me two nights ago as soon as I set foot on the bridge. It hit me when my face was shoved into the ground and I couldn't breathe, when I ran for my life, imagining my mother finding me dead. But it hit me hard-est in the cold light of morning, when Gretchen was found instead.

She takes my hand in hers. "You know, I've been saving a little money. I thought we could pack up, get out of town for a week. You've always wanted to drive up the coast, and—"

"You want to go on a *vacation*?"

Her chin trembles. "I just hate the idea that whoever did this is still out there."

I swallow. "Does the sheriff think they might come after me again? Because if he does, he should've said so."

She exhales. "I just thought some time away would be nice . . ."

Under the quilt, my fingers find their way to the cool skin of my left wrist, fumbling for the bracelet Gretchen gave me for my birthday. I haven't seen it since that night, but I keep looking. I can't stand the feeling of it *not* being there.

"Look, maybe I do need some downtime." It takes effort, but I force myself to relax, lean into her. "But Gretchen's funeral is Friday and I have to be there."

My mother pulls the covers up, tucking them under my chin with tentative hands. "We don't have to go on a trip. Just promise you'll stay close to home. I don't want you at school. I don't want you out anywhere without telling me."

"Okay."

I take her hand, staring at the small scar on my knuckle from when I fell off Gretchen's swing set when we were five. It used to seem big and ugly, but now I realize how small it is, and I'm afraid it'll disappear, taking more of her away from me.

I fight the sting of tears, but then my mom leans in to kiss my cheek. Her touch is warm and comforting, and so *mom*-like. I curl into her, letting her stroke my hair, and for the briefest moment, I feel like I did when I was little. Like her kiss will magically make everything better.

"I just can't believe she's gone," she whispers. "If you hadn't gotten away—I don't know what I would've done if it was you."

I turn my head to one side, afraid to let her see that thought on my face. But when I close my eyes, my body feels cold and lifeless, like I'm floating in freezing water. I hug my mother tight, cling to her warmth, but no matter what I do I can't seem to shake the chill.

THREE

I DRESS IN THE DIM early-morning light and tiptoe downstairs holding my boots. My mom's shift doesn't start till ten, but she'll be awake by the time school starts. If I'm going to get an idea of who else was in the park Friday night—who I could put on my suspect list—I need to be in school. I just have to get there and let my mom know I'm safe before she realizes I'm gone.

Uncle Noah's alone behind the griddle. Usually my little cousin, Felicia, likes to hang out with her dad before school, but Aunt Elena has been keeping her close to home since Friday. Noah waves at me over a batch of hash browns that smell like salty gold. I ignore my grumbling stomach and pull on my boots. They're tall and black with thick soles and lots of laces, and, along with my blue Penn hoodie, make me feel like I stand a chance against the world.

Uncle Noah eyes my backpack. "Your mom letting you go to school today?"

"Oh, you know, she didn't want to . . ." I say, not looking at him. "Aisha's giving me a ride."

He frowns. "You still have that pepper spray I gave you?"

I pat the pocket of my backpack.

"Good. Stay aware of your surroundings. Use common sense. If your friends can't drive you home, call me, Dina, or Elena. She'll be home with Felicia this afternoon."

"I will, I promise."

His face screws up for a second and I'm shocked to see the slightest tremble in my big, burly uncle's chin. "Come here, kiddo."

I've never really been one for hugging, but I let him fold me into his arms.

"We all love you. *Nothing* that happened was your fault, I hope you know that."

My throat closes up, turning my chest into a crushing weight. I've lain awake, failing to convince myself of this, the last three nights, but I manage a nod squashed against his vast form. I pull away and glance at the blank screen of my phone. "Aisha's here. I'd better go."

I slip out the security door with my backpack over my shoulder and peer around the corner through the front window of the diner. Sheriff Wood is sitting with two of his deputies, Shelly Robson and Amir Rashid. He used to joke that breakfast was the only meal he could count on in the day, before people started waking up and getting into trouble. I wonder if that's true anymore. It's all I can do not to walk back in there and demand to hear his list of suspects, what the other witnesses have said. Find out what they think happened to me and my best friend.

But they won't tell me anything that isn't already in every news report, so I turn away and head to school.

It's only five blocks from the diner to Hurlburt High. I could easily walk, but I'm already taking enough chances. I peer around the corner. Aisha's Jeep is nowhere in sight. I look at my phone, keeping a nervous eye on the street. She was supposed to be here two minutes ago. When I texted her last night, she sounded happy to help. I told her I was desperate for the routine of being in school, which is true. My mom's crazy if she thinks I'm going to last another day at home. It also doesn't hurt that Aisha's house is next to Gretchen's. She might have some sense of what's going on there. I text her again:

Where are you?

The town of Hidden Falls is bisected by Black River Creek, which snakes lazily through the region before plunging sixty-five feet off the edge of a limestone gorge where it becomes the waterfall the place is named for. The town sprang up around the falls, and the land surrounding it turned into a park with nature trails, picnic areas, and a playground. My uncle's diner sits in the business district to the north, while most of the nicer homes in town run along Park Drive on the southern side, where Gretchen's house is. The park has always been a central place to hang out. When we were little Gretchen and I would spend all day as warrior princesses in the trees, and met for parties as we reached our teens. We never thought twice about being there, even at night.

People have died at the falls, but there's never been a murder.

Until three days ago.

The hairs on my neck rise. Something moves in the corner of my eye and my limbs go heavy . . . like something's coming for me. I look up, but all I see is the wind rustling the trees at the edge of the park. First Avenue is eerily quiet, almost deserted. It only takes five minutes to drive to the covered bridge, over the creek, and back down. What could be taking Aisha so long? I scan the border of the park again, pressing my back against the bricks. My battered ribs ache, but at least it's a reminder I'm still breathing. And then it dawns on me how stupid this is. Cowering alone in an alley where anything could happen and no one would see—I could've been safe at school by now. I straighten my shoulders, step out onto the sidewalk, and then a shadowy figure appears from nowhere and grabs me.

He holds me by my arms, breathing heavily. Fire shoots through the scratches on my skin, my scream gets caught in my throat, but just as I start to lash out, he steadies me and lets go.

"Sonia, sorry, I didn't see you. What are you even doing out here?"

It takes me a second to calm down and recognize Tyrone Wallace, Aisha's older brother.

"I'm on my way to school." I step back to study him more carefully, taking in his big frame, noting his sneakers and jogging pants, and the sheen of sweat on his dark skin. I thought he was away at college playing football. He has a reputation for being intimidating on the field, but he's never been anything but kind to me. My body relaxes, just a little.

"You startled me." His face shifts from surprise to disapproval. "You shouldn't be out by yourself."

"I . . . I guess I wasn't thinking."

He looks toward the park. "Let me walk you the rest of the way, it'll make me feel better."

I'm grateful for his company, but hesitate as I catch my breath. Why would he be home from school so soon? Tyrone and Gretchen had kind of a thing last year, but it didn't end well for him. Could he have come home to settle a grudge?

"When did you get back in town?" I ask.

"Friday." He frowns. "Kind of wish I'd stayed away now."

"Yeah." I take another step back. Tyrone is the last person I want to consider a suspect. "You know, Aisha's supposed to pick me up. She'll be here any minute."

As if on cue, two tinny little honks sound at us from down the street. Aisha pulls up to the curb and rolls down her window. "I'm sorry, are you okay? I got here as fast as I could." Some tightly coiled place inside me loosens at the sight of her, at the sound of her voice. She raises one eyebrow when she sees her brother. "I thought you went running on the track."

"Does Mom know you're not really holding a special meeting with the student council this morning?" Tyrone asks, raising his eyebrow right back.

She rolls her eyes. "I have missed having you in my life, looking over my shoulder."

I cough. Their sibling banter feels too weird. Too normal. "It was good to see you, Tyrone."

He follows me around to the passenger door and I can't get in the car fast enough.

"Sonia, I—I just wanted to say I'm so sorry."

The pain in his voice makes me lower my gaze, guilty for letting my mind get carried away. I'll put him on my list, but that doesn't have to mean anything yet. "Thanks."

When I look up again, he's disappearing down the sidewalk. I pull the door shut, lock it, and buckle my seat belt, but I can't seem to secure enough barriers between me and the rest of the world. Aisha pulls the Jeep out onto First Avenue and almost collides with Shelly Robson in her black-and-white patrol car.

"Oh God, sorry!" Aisha mouths through the windshield.

Shelly waves us on, looking flustered.

Aisha stops at one of the few traffic lights in town, chattering nervously about not getting a ticket. I look away, my attention drawn back to the edge of the park, to the gap in the trees where the trail leads toward the falls. The surrounding leaves are so green and alive—but there's a branch snapped, hanging limp and dead by the road. I close my eyes at the memory of scrambling up that trail, clothes torn, hands raw. And the moment I glimpsed the diner—I thought I'd never see it again.

When I open my eyes, I see a shadow moving among the trees. I lean against the glass for a closer look and there's a person in a hood standing at the head of the trail. He steps forward, raises his head to look at me, and my heart stops.

Marcus Perez.

FOUR

HURLBURT HIGH IS TUCKED INTO a picturesque green hillside just beyond the business district. Directly next door, the ground is torn open where the skeletal frame of a new community center rises from the earth. It's been the most exciting thing to happen in Hidden Falls for half a decade. The plans include an indoor pool and track, fitness area and senior center, along with an array of classes and activities available to the public. They just broke ground on it two months ago, and the construction site usually buzzes with activity by this hour, but today the bright yellow equipment sits as still as the air. The project is funded by Gretchen's parents, Carlton and Marcia Meyer.

Judging by the cluster of news vans and reporters gathered at the edge of campus, the school grounds have been deemed off-limits to the media. I guess this ought to be a relief, but even with our windows rolled tightly up, we pull into the parking lot through an onslaught of cameras and people shouting Gretchen's name.

"Ask you a few questions—"

"Take a minute of your time—"

"Did you know Gretchen Meyer—"

My stomach turns. Maybe this was a mistake. I could've waited to come back, made my mother happy, laid low for a couple of days. I notice the toothy reporter from the diner and my skin crawls at the idea of people exploiting Gretchen's death for a news story. If she'd wanted to be a headline, she would've found a more fantastic, glamorous way to do it—hosting a celebrity tennis tournament, or even skydiving for charity. I imagine her posing for cameras, stylish in a tennis skirt or a jumpsuit, and I can't help smiling. But as Aisha and I climb out of the Jeep and walk toward the low-slung building, I realize if I'd stayed home, the crowd of gossip-hungry reporters would be my only lines of information. If I want to figure out who could've attacked me and murdered Gretchen, there's no replacement for being inside the walls of the school—surrounded by potential killers.

"Hey." Aisha touches my arm. "You okay?"

I nod quickly, pull out my phone, and text my mom.

Went to school. Got here safe. Love you.

I turn the phone off.

Conversations fade to whispers as we approach the building, just as they did at the diner yesterday. Some kids stare, some offer condolences about Gretchen, but the unasked questions are in their eyes and the anxious hum of their voices.

"Do you think she saw him push—"

"—haven't slept since Friday."

"My dad bought a gun."

"Good idea, the killer could come after *you*!"

"Fuck off, that isn't funny."

My mouth is like sandpaper. If Gretchen were here, I'd know

exactly what I should be doing, thinking, saying. Like after the bus crash that hospitalized half the lacrosse team. She reached out immediately to the victims' families and friends and started a fundraiser, and I stepped in to help her get organized. She never told me *what* to say, but she set the tone and I adjusted accordingly. Without her, I feel adrift. I hover at Aisha's side, but she doesn't seem to know what to do or say either. I think we're both relieved when Haley spots us and swoops in.

"You look awful. Why are you even here?"

I give a nervous shrug. "Same as everyone else. I want to know what's going on."

"Nobody knows anything." She sighs, tightening her ponytail and brushing her spiky bangs out of her eyes. "I've heard everything from Marcus stalking Gretchen to her dad having a disgruntled employee to it actually being suicide to her *sister* killing her."

"Kirsten?" I shake my head immediately. Gretchen might have disliked her little sister, but it was completely one-sided.

"They had that fight at Brianne's party. . . ." Aisha frowns. "But yeah, deranged killer on the loose seems more likely."

I squeeze my eyes shut at the idea of the killer in the woods actually being a crazed lunatic. But it could have been someone random, no one Gretchen knew at all. . . .

"The cops still haven't found her Mercedes," Haley continues. "Oh, and they're questioning Kip Peterson."

"What?" This is a surprise. To my knowledge, Kip never even spoke to Gretchen that night. "Where did you hear that?"

"Reva Stone. She said she ran into him on his way to the sheriff's office."

I hesitate. Reva was no friend of Gretchen's, but when I think about it I guess I understand why Kip might be questioned. He'd been following her around with cartoon hearts in his eyes since at least the sixth grade. Gretchen was never interested in dating him, but he always seemed good-humored about it.

"What did they want to ask him about? The car?"

She shakes her head. "No, I guess he saw something that night."

I look at her, wide-eyed. "He said that? What did he see?"

Haley bites her lip. "He claims he saw Gretchen in the woods before she died."

I stop in my tracks. I hung out with Kip for at least an hour at Brianne's house Friday night. We played UltaShock in the basement, as we usually do at her parties, but if he left when we did, he might've actually seen what happened to Gretchen—if not what happened to me first. "But I thought he stayed at the party. *Was* he in the park?"

"Sonia." Aisha touches my elbow, looking worried. "Do you think Kip could be the person who chased you?"

I freeze up. I hadn't thought of it that way, but I guess I should. "Is he a suspect?"

"He was so creepy about her, he should be," Haley says. "The way he followed her around with that camera."

"You talking about that perv Peterson?" Derek comes up, wrapping his arm around Aisha. She gives him a look. "What? He carries that camera around all the time, but when he's not 'on assignment' for the yearbook, all he does is take pictures of tits. What about that isn't pervy?"

Aisha stops and raises her eyebrows. "You seem to know a lot about these pictures."

Derek grins. When he leans in to kiss her, Haley makes a face and pulls me aside. "Are you okay, Sonia? Like, really? Everyone's so freaked out about all this, but I can't even imagine how terrified you must've been . . . or how you must feel now."

"Thanks. It was scary—I just—" I pull my sleeves over the marks on my wrists, but my hands have started trembling again. "I miss her."

She presses her mouth into a line and gives my arm a reassuring squeeze.

I try to ignore the way my skin stings under her hand. Haley, Gretchen, Aisha, and I all used to be close. We've known one another since kindergarten, grew up at each other's houses, but at some point around middle school, Gretchen and I paired off. We hung out with each other exclusively more and more, and she started inviting just me to sleep over and even convinced her dad to bring me on the occasional family trip. It felt so intimate at the time, almost like having a sister. I didn't realize how much we had alienated Haley and Aisha until it was too late. We never fought or had a misunderstanding; we were still friendly with one another at school. It just sort of happened. But it's always felt weird.

There's a mandatory assembly after homeroom and the halls fill with low chatter as we file toward the cafetorium. I get stuck behind a couple of snickering guys and I'm about to ask what they could possibly find funny until I tune in to their conversation.

"Bullshit, man. Friday night?"

"That's what he's telling everyone."

"Why would Kirsten Meyer hook up with that little shit freshman?"

The guy shakes his head and laughs. "Kid claims he's *got moves.*"

The first guy snorts too and now I recognize Kevin Fowler, Gretchen's onetime indie rock boyfriend from last summer. "Oh man, if she's anything like her sis—"

"Excuse me." I push between them before I have to hear any more. Kevin was bent out of shape for months after Gretchen dumped him for Marcus. He was also at the party Friday night. I add him to my list.

Haley waves me over to where she's sitting against the far wall and I pull my backpack to my chest, scanning the room for Kirsten, even though I know she isn't here. I need to talk to her, ask if she's okay—only that immediately strikes me as stupid. Of course she's not. By the time she stumbled home after midnight Saturday, Gretchen was already missing. Kirsten looked up to her so much, following us around since we were little, trying to look and act like her big sister no matter how often Gretchen pushed her away. It was like she thought if she just kept trying, Gretchen would change how she felt about her.

Someone leans over from the row behind us. "Hey, anyone seen Perez?"

My neck goes hot.

"He wouldn't dare come to this."

"Heard someone tossed a brick through his window last night."

A couple of guys in front of us high-five.

"Assholes." We all turn to look at Yuji Himura, Gretchen's long-time tennis opponent and one of Marcus's few friends. "He didn't do this."

Haley gives him a cool look. "Does that mean you know who did?"

Yuji holds her gaze. He and Haley were a thing freshman and sophomore years, until Yuji started playing extra tennis games with Gretchen on the weekends. "Gretchen had a lot of exes. It could have been any one of them."

"I heard they had sex at the party before she died," Haley says.

"So what if they did?"

There's a tap on my shoulder and Brianne Prashad leans over from the next table to hug me. "Sonia, I can't believe this. I just keep thinking how we were all at my house Friday night." Her voice wavers and a lump forms in my throat. "Did someone really go after you too? Do they think—" She looks at my face. "Oh God, I'm sorry."

I know I should say something, tell her it's okay, but everyone's breath and bodies seem so close, it's like suddenly there isn't enough air. I cross my arms and look away, wondering if it would make a scene if I fled the room, but then Aisha lands in the seat next to me, practically squirming.

"You guys aren't going to believe what I just heard." She looks at her phone. "Right before Gretchen was reported missing, her parents came home and surprised an intruder in her room."

My mouth drops open. *"What?"*

"Get out," Haley says. "Did they see who it was?"

"I guess her dad caught a glimpse of him as he ran out. They think he took something with him."

"Where did you hear that?" I ask, my eyes darting around the room.

"My mom." Aisha lowers her voice, shifting in her chair. "She said the cops have been trying to keep it secret."

My breathing goes short. Aisha's mom is a high-profile lawyer and not generally a gossip, but if this is true, it changes how I've been thinking about the whole night. If someone was in Gretchen's bedroom, were they waiting for her to come back, or did they break in after the attack? And in either case, why? I bite my fingernail, wondering if they could be the same person who went after me. "God, it might've been anyone."

"Yeah, maybe even Derek." Haley snorts.

Derek looks up from his smartphone. "What did I do?"

Aisha sighs.

I can think of a handful of boys who have snuck in and out of Gretchen's room under more benign circumstances—Kevin Fowler, Marcus Perez, and Tyrone Wallace, to name a few. But I hesitate saying so since this might be news to Aisha. "Hey, didn't your brother come home Friday?"

Derek rolls his eyes, tucking his phone away. "Of course. Beautiful white girl gets herself killed, let's blame every black dude in town."

"*No.*" My face flushes. "I didn't mean it like that. I just thought . . . it's just that Tyrone and Gretchen did go out a few times. If it was him, maybe it was something innocent."

"It wasn't Tyrone." Aisha frowns and takes Derek's hand.

I reach for her, but she pulls away. "I'm sorry, I didn't mean—"

"Maybe it was Kip," she says brusquely.

"It was Marcus," Haley says. "The guy's family is bad news." When I don't say anything, she raises her eyebrows. "Please don't tell me you're going to defend him too."

"I'm just not sure what to think," I mumble.

"I thought you guys couldn't stand each other."

My skin flushes hot.

Maybe if I understood why Marcus hated me I could genuinely share the feeling. At least it's easy to mimic. It seemed just as well Gretchen set her sights on him before I could make a fool of myself thinking he might be interested in me.

Principal Bova taps the microphone at the front of the room, instructing everyone to please take their seats. Sheriff Wood stands beside her and I sink in my chair, curious and a little nervous about what the police are going to add.

"As most of you probably know by now, your friend and classmate Gretchen Meyer passed away over the weekend." The principal's normally calm, authoritative voice wavers over the sound system into the pin-drop-silent room. My vision clouds. Haley grasps my hand. "Gretchen was a bright light in these halls. Her absence is already keenly felt throughout our community. This is a difficult time for all of us, and we want you to know the staff and administrators of Hurlburt High are here to listen as we come together in this time of mourning. Grief counselors will also be available this week through the guidance office." Her voice breaks and she takes an extra moment to collect herself. "If you'll please remain seated, Sheriff Wood would like to say a few words on personal safety in the days and weeks ahead."

I blink at the stage, as if I'm in some kind of bizarre dream. Any second I'll wake up to find myself sleeping over in Gretchen's big white canopy bed. She'll laugh at me about the whole thing. We'll creep downstairs, heat up Pop-Tarts for breakfast, and joke about how shocked everyone was over her death. She always had a morbid sense of humor. When Kirsten was eleven, she almost choked to death eating Skittles. Her dad walked into the room just in time, but Gretchen gave Kirsten a big bag of Skittles for her birthday every year after that.

Sheriff Wood approaches the microphone with his hat in his hands. I've always gotten the sense he loves his job, but even from across the room I can see that his usual affable smile is gone. My mom used to tease that he'd make a better movie sheriff than a real one; that he looks too much like a young Robert Redford to be taken seriously. Today he appears every inch the person in charge, though it's clear in this moment he'd rather be doing just about any other job.

"I'll just say briefly that I knew Gretchen Meyer, and I think I speak for us all in saying her death marks a tragic loss to our community." He clears his throat. "I'm here today in part because we need your help. Gretchen attended a party the night she died, and some of you may have seen or heard something that could help our investigation." My friends and I look at one another. "A few of you have already spoken to us, but even the most trivial details may prove helpful, and I encourage you to come forward."

Deputy Robson appears from the wings and hands the sheriff a piece of paper. He looks at it and gives her a small nod.

"In light of recent events, the mayor's office has agreed to issue a temporary curfew of nine p.m. for those under the age of eighteen." A low grumble erupts through the crowd, but there's still enough fear in their eyes that no one actually protests. "We don't feel there's

42

any reason to panic, but we ask that you exercise good common sense. Be aware of other people and your surroundings at all times. Don't go out alone at night. If you see something suspicious, call the sheriff's office to report it."

A hand shoots up somewhere in the front row. "Is it true there's a big reward for whoever catches the guy?"

Sheriff Wood's face tightens. "Gretchen's father, Carlton Meyer, is offering a generous reward—fifty thousand dollars—for any information leading to the arrest of the person responsible, but I want to emphasize that this is a police matter. Please do not put yourselves in a dangerous situation by trying to get involved."

Another murmur passes through the audience and I clasp my hands. Fifty thousand dollars. Surely if anyone out there knows something, they'll have to come forward now.

Principal Bova returns to make some closing remarks and the bell rings. Everyone floods out the doors for their classes. A couple of girls embrace just in front of me, wiping away tears.

"This is so scary," one of them says.

"I just want to graduate and get away to college."

I close my eyes and wait for them to go, missing Gretchen between the slow beats of my heart. We'd only found out where we were each going to college last month. I'd been awarded a scholarship to the University of Pennsylvania and Gretchen was headed to Stanford, on the opposite side of the country. She was upset we'd be apart and I was hurt she couldn't just be happy for me. We'd ended up fighting about it.

"Just wait, I'll find a way to keep us together," she said.

"What are you going to do?" I snapped. "Bring Pennsylvania

closer to California? Even you can't do that."

My eyes sting at the memory of her face. How her expression went blank, then closed before she turned away. In truth, I was looking forward to some time apart. Gretchen and I were so close, but she wasn't always the easiest person to be around. We listened to music she liked, went places she wanted to go. But I couldn't remember a time without her, what it was like to exist by myself. I only wanted a little distance. I never asked for . . . this.

I wish I'd said something, anything different. Let her know I'd truly miss her.

Now I'll never have the chance.

FIVE

BY FOURTH PERIOD, AT LEAST one person in every class has burst into tears and had to leave, but I've managed to hold myself together. I don't know how. I head for psychology on autopilot, but stop as soon as I'm through the door. Gretchen and I shared this class. Her empty desk greets me like a ghost in the front row. I take a breath, try to move my feet forward, but someone bumps me from behind and my vision goes black. I freeze, afraid I'm about to pass out, but then *cold hands close around my throat. My heart races, my ears fill with the sound of rushing water, my own ragged gasps.* I scratch and pry at the fingers on my neck until I finally manage to scream.

"Sonia?"

I blink.

Ms. Arehart crosses the room, brows knit with concern. Beyond her, all eyes rest on me.

My own hand grips my throat.

"It's okay," my teacher says. "Do you want someone to walk you to the nurse's office?"

I open my mouth, turn, and run out the door.

The second-floor girls' bathroom is just down the hall. I close myself in a stall and crouch over a toilet, shudder and gag, but all that comes up is grief. And guilt. Because once I'm brave enough to face myself alone in the scratched mirror, I have to admit I'm relieved it wasn't me.

I hate myself for it.

As the pain in my ribs subsides, I wonder things I never used to think about . . . if events in the universe are predetermined . . . if I would be standing here today, alone, no matter what. Or if Friday could have gone differently.

Did it have to be one of us?

When the bell rings, I assume a sluggish pace all the way to my sunshine-yellow locker. Gretchen's was in the purple row across the hall—I'm afraid if I look over there, I might not make it through the rest of the day. I spin my combination mechanically, adding it to the long list of things that feel lonely to do after your best friend is dead. When I look down the row to my right, I notice Reva Stone. She's kneeling in front of her locker, shuffling notebooks, long earrings swaying under her short blue hair. She doesn't seem to be paying any attention to me, but I keep looking at her and after a few moments she peers around the door and our eyes meet.

"Sorry for your loss," she says.

I lift the latch of my locker, but don't pull it open yet. "Thanks."

"You know, Gretchen's death bumps you up to salutatorian." She stands. "I guess you'd better prepare a speech."

I stare at her. Reva and Gretchen have hated each other since middle school, but this seems callous, even for her. "That would make you valedictorian. Guess you must be pretty pleased."

"I will not rejoice in the death of one, not even an enemy." Her eyes and voice are flat.

I shake my head. "You weren't paying attention in Chamberlain's class. Martin Luther King never actually said that."

"Just offering my condolences." She picks up her bag and heads down the hall.

My shoulders tense as she saunters away, but my mind immediately locks onto the possibility that Reva might've wanted Gretchen dead. She might've gladly attacked me too. I add her name to my growing list and turn back to my open locker, the tension in my heart shifting to a dismal ache. Gretchen decorated the inside last September. If it had been up to me, I might have just hung the mirror and dry-erase board, and been done with it, but she spent a ridiculous amount of time lining the door in pink and green construction paper, cutting out frames for pictures she printed of us, and spelling out my name in an acrostic:

Serious
Observant
Noble
Intelligent
Adorable

There are pictures of us on the ski trip to Vail her dad took us on, a couple shots from last Halloween—I was a black cat, she was a witch—and of course Gretchen's favorite, a selfie she took on an ill-fated hiking trip last summer. In it, our faces are crushed so close together, if it weren't for my dark eyebrows and her freckles, you'd barely be able to tell where she ended and I began. I made the worst face when she took the picture, so of course she stuck it prominently in the middle of my locker.

"You can't use that one," I'd said when she'd finished decorating and showed it to me.

"I can't *not* use it. That was the best day ever."

"We were lost for twelve hours in the wilderness. Did the dehydration affect your brain?"

She rolled her eyes. "Your memory is so selective."

I tried to remember anything good about what was supposed to be a two-hour day hike up to some cave in the middle of nowhere. We forgot bug spray, ran out of trail mix after an hour, and managed to completely lose the trail. We never did find the cave. After five hours we gave up and hunkered down, waiting for someone to come looking for us. We built a shelter as the sun went down and tried to start a campfire. When that failed, I started to panic, but Gretchen stayed cool. It was her idea to tell spooky stories as a distraction. We scared the crap out of each other for hours. A ranger finally found us because we were laughing so hard he could hear us from Gretchen's car. Apparently we were only half a mile from the parking lot.

I pull the photo down, staring at Gretchen grinning in full color, and my eyes brim over. I need her here, to reassure me *now*. As fresh tears spill down my cheeks a gentle hand touches my back and I open my eyes to find Aisha pulling down the rest of the pictures.

She pauses, waiting to make sure it's okay. I reach out and pull another picture down, then another, and together we make a pile of my face sandwiched with Gretchen's. When we're done, I place them on the top shelf. Nearby, but out of sight.

"Thanks," I say.

Aisha gives me a sympathetic nod. "You need to go home? Or can I walk you to class?"

I wipe my face in the now naked mirror. I really *don't* feel up to the whispers and the gossip and the stares, but if I go home I'll just be proving to my mother I can't handle normal routine.

"I'll be okay."

Aisha fiddles with her hair as we walk down the hall. I can't remember when she stopped wearing it braided, but now it falls around her shoulders, relaxed into soft waves. Haley would've already found a way to fill the air with chatter, but Aisha remains silent at my side.

"I really didn't mean to suggest anything before, about Tyrone being in Gretchen's room."

She keeps her gaze straight ahead. "I know it wasn't Tyrone. And I don't think it was Kip. But Derek had a point, so let's just be clear—my brother doesn't need an accusation like that being spread around."

"You're right, I'm sorry." I bite my lip. Neither of us wants it to be Tyrone. "Your parents must be thrilled to have him home."

"Yeah, he finished the semester early." She says this so quickly, I almost don't catch it. Then she stops in the middle of the hall and ducks her head close to mine. "Look, Tyrone was holed up in his room all night, but I saw Marcus leaving the park after Gretchen disappeared."

"Leaving the park?" My eyes widen. "When? Did you tell Sheriff Wood?"

She nods. "It was a little before midnight. I heard something outside and when I looked out, I saw him coming up the path out of the trees." She straightens, her eyes clear and confident. "Whatever alibi he came up with will have to be good to explain that."

My skin prickles. She's right. "You're sure it was him?"

"Yes." She glances over her shoulder at something going on down the hall. "It must've been right when Mr. Meyer reported the intruder. All the cops showed up a few minutes later."

I nod, remembering the muffled call coming in, and every officer but Shelly abruptly clearing out of the diner.

The warning bell rings and I hurry down the hall toward Government, clenching my jaw, trying to imagine Gretchen's moody artist boyfriend chasing after me in the dark. He was already at the top of my list, but it's easier than I expect. I slow as I pass a large group clustered around a bank of lockers. Once I'm close enough, I realize it's just one locker people are looking at. A janitor is there, brushing a fresh coat of purple paint over Marcus's yellow locker door, covering large black letters that spell out *KILLER*.

SIX

BY THE TIME AISHA DROPS me at home, my throat is so tight, I only manage a whispered thank-you for the ride. I look across the street to the place I saw Marcus this morning, but all that's there are the trees. I rub my hands over my arms. Several versions of the intruder story floated around school after lunch, including one where it was a serial killer leaving a calling card and another where Marcus was trying to convince Gretchen to elope. The only thing people seem to agree on is that there was, in fact, some guy in her room, but this is the part that disturbs me most. Who was he? What was he doing there? And why wouldn't Sheriff Wood tell me about that?

I volunteered at the sheriff's office my sophomore year to fulfill a school requirement, but ended up spending so much time with the deputies that I know them all by name. If I can catch one of them— Shelly or Amir—they might answer my questions more freely than the sheriff.

I move out of view of the diner, walking quickly down the sidewalk, gripping the pepper spray inside my pocket. I'm halfway up the stone steps of the sheriff's office when a tall, beautiful dead girl steps outside.

Gretchen?

My heart leaps, a cold flash of relief rushing through my veins. I trip over my boot and crash to the stairs, pain radiating through my knee. It's a moment before I realize what I'm actually seeing and begin to breathe again. Kirsten Meyer, Gretchen's younger sister, walks down the steps toward me. She's a natural blonde, but I'd forgotten she experimented with dyeing her hair a couple of weeks ago. At the time, Gretchen was annoyed, remarking that she'd never match her own vibrant natural red, but it's startling—no, *disturbing* how much Kirsten looks like her now.

I wish she would dye it back.

Kirsten's mouth presses into a quivering line as I get to my feet, and I instantly feel guilty. She seems so lost. For as long as I can remember, Gretchen had rejected her, treating *me* more like a sister despite Kirsten's attempts to win her affection. She never seemed discouraged—if anything, she just tried harder. But it makes my heart sick wondering what she's left with now.

Kirsten had begged to go with us to the party Friday night, like she always did, and it was one of the rare times Gretchen actually gave in. But of course they ended up fighting. I try not to think of *that* as the event that set the rest of the night in motion, but I wonder if she's considered it too—what might've happened if she just hadn't come along.

There's so much I wish I'd done differently that night. I should've at least said something to her. I have no idea what to say now.

"Kirsten, I'm sorry." I move toward her, intending to offer a hug, but when she folds her arms in front of her and scowls, I draw back.

"We came to collect her things." She stares across the street into the park. The rush of the waterfall is just audible from where we stand.

"Oh." My mouth goes dry. "What did they—"

"One black ballet flat, two five-dollar bills, a hair clip, some earrings, one bracelet, and one very water-logged smartphone—if you have to know. Thought I'd get some fresh air while my mom finishes crying."

I manage to swallow the lump in my throat. "I . . . I can't believe she's gone."

She turns to me, her teeth bared like a wild animal. "Save it, Sonia. You don't know what it's like to have a sister and you'll never understand what it's like to lose one."

My hand goes to my face like I've been slapped. Kirsten is usually so quiet and awkward. She's clearly hurting, but I don't know what to do. Before I can find any words, Gretchen's parents come out the door; him, slightly balding in a three-piece suit, and her, trailing behind, balanced on stilettos, her normally perfect blond hair coming out of its restrictive bun. Mr. Mcyer turns and barks over his shoulder.

"Tell the sheriff I want an update immediately."

He continues down the steps, practically carrying his wife to the car. Kirsten walks around to the back of the Range Rover and climbs in. I lower my head and start to walk away, but Gretchen's mom sees me and calls my name.

I approach the SUV, unable to look directly into her red-rimmed eyes. "Mrs. Meyer, I . . ."

She gestures me closer, taking a long, deep breath. I don't think she can bear to look at me either. "Sonia, I'm so relieved you're all right."

It's all I can do to stand here, wishing I didn't exist. If I could make it me instead of Gretchen, in this moment, I would. But then Mrs. Meyer surprises me. I've never known her to be particularly affectionate, but she rises from her seat and wraps me in her arms until I'm enveloped in the scents of cashmere and perfume.

"You meant so much to her," she whispers.

I gasp as she squeezes my aching ribs. Kirsten glares at me from the back of the car.

Mrs. Meyer sinks down into her seat. Gretchen's dad turns and looks at me like he's surprised to find me standing here. "Sonia, you should get inside." His face is so stricken. I just nod, stepping back toward the sheriff's office. "We'll see you at the service Friday."

"Of course," I whisper. And then they're gone.

I turn back to the old stone building, unsure what I'm doing there anymore. Before I can move I'm stopped by a flash of red light and the blip of a siren. An unmarked Explorer pulls up to the curb and Sheriff Wood climbs out with a strict law-enforcement expression. All I want to do is bolt, but I force myself to stay put. He pulls his phone out of his pocket and dials, but doesn't take his eyes off me as he approaches.

"I found her. We'll be there shortly."

"Who was that?" I ask, trying to maintain my cool.

"Your mother. Sonia, do you have *any* idea—" He stops himself, looks me over, and rubs his hand across his face. "God, I'm glad you're okay."

"I don't underst—"

"Your uncle went by the school to pick you up since you weren't answering your phone. When he realized you'd already left, he called the diner and your mom panicked." He stares at me, frowning.

I lower my head and look at my feet.

He exhales, his voice softening. "Just don't disappear like that again. I barely managed to convince her you'd be safe when you ran off to school this morning. When you didn't come straight home . . ."

I avoid his eyes, focusing instead on the six gold points of his badge. "I'm sorry."

"Hey. She's just worried about you." His tone is gentle and when I'm brave enough to steal another glance at his face, his eyes are warm again. "Come on, let me walk you home."

I look back at the sheriff's office once and fall into step beside him, trying to figure out how to ask about the intruder without him shutting me out. "Has anything new happened? Anything you want to tell me about the leads you're following?"

He looks away, listening to a call over the radio, but shakes his head. "Nothing you need to worry about. I'm going to send Amir over this evening to work with you on that sketch."

I dig my nails into my palms. Maybe the sheriff thinks he's keeping it confidential, but even if the whole school hadn't been talking about it, I deserve to be told what's going on.

"Sheriff, I need to know—"

He opens the diner door and I look up to find my mother waiting for us behind the counter. She doesn't smoke anymore, but I notice she's gripping a cup of coffee, which has become her go-to replacement for nicotine.

"Thanks, Roger." She barely looks at the sheriff as he tips his hat to head back out, no doubt to deal with Mr. Meyer. I shrink under her gaze, trying not to notice the traces of fear still on her face. There are a couple of truckers and an elderly couple seated in the booths on the far wall, and I really wish the diner was busy just so I could avoid this moment. "I'm not even going to bother telling you what a stupid move that was this morning, because I think you know."

I stow my backpack behind the counter, find an apron, and tie it around my waist. "Aisha took me to school. It was fine."

"You lied to Noah. Do you know how much that hurt him?"

I stare at the floor, guilt stabbing me in the chest. "Mom, I know you guys want what's best for me, but—"

"You need to tell me when you're going to leave and who you're going to be with." She lifts my chin so I have to look at her.

I push her hand away. She might've agonized over my safety all day, but I'm the one who can't shake the feeling that someone is at my back.

I gesture to the door. "Don't you think the sheriff's got more important things to do than follow me around like a babysitter?"

Her mouth tightens. "There was no reason for you to sneak off like that."

"You would never have let me go."

"You agreed you wouldn't."

"My best friend is *dead*." I smack my order pad down on the counter. "She died Friday night instead of me. Excuse me for trying to deal with that."

"Sonia—"

"Just forget it, okay?" I jam a pencil over my ear and clock in for the evening, ignoring stares from the few customers as I wipe fresh tears from my face.

"I'm just trying to help!" Her voice gets small. "What can I do?"

My lip trembles. "I told you, I just need to focus on my grades. I can't risk them right now."

This is true, even if it wasn't my whole reason for going to school this morning. Other than a small amount of money I've scraped together working for my uncle the last few years, I've never had anything resembling what my classmates would call a "college fund." That changed a couple of months ago when Gretchen and I were both accepted to Stanford and her parents gave me the shock of my life, offering to send us both to school together. There was no point in even pausing to think it over, but I didn't know how to process an offer like that. I was just about to accept when the University of Pennsylvania offered me a full four-year scholarship. I felt guilty turning the Meyers down, and Gretchen too, but part of me was relieved. It feels awful to be thinking about my grades of all things in this moment, but I can't afford not to. Now more than ever.

"Honey, if that school of yours holds something like this against you—"

"Then I guess I'll end up working *here* for the rest of my life."

As soon as the words are out, I regret them. She turns, silently organizing rolls of receipt paper in a drawer by the register, but not before I see the hurt flash through her eyes. This whole topic is something I try to avoid—why the diner is enough for her, why I've always wanted more. My whole life she's been afraid something awful would happen if I left home. It turns out I didn't even need to leave town for that.

The bells above the door jingle and she grabs a couple of menus from under the counter. "Roger said the school is safe. Just make sure you tell me everywhere else you're going to be."

The evening gets steadily busier and eventually my mom retreats upstairs with a migraine. Some of the major news crews are starting to leave town since no arrests have been made and the sheriff hasn't been any more forthcoming with them than he has with me, but the local reporters are holding out. I guess they have nothing better to cover than a town preparing for a young girl's funeral.

Deputy Rashid comes by to work on the composite drawing just before seven, and I do the best I can to give a coherent description of a face I never saw. He guides me through it, asking basic questions, and eventually I'm able to provide a few specific details. We end up with a sketch of a shadowy, androgynous person who looks a little like every guy in the world.

"Well, you never know, *someone* might recognize him," Amir says, putting his pencil down.

My mouth goes dry staring at the picture. It's a *person*, even if I'm not sure where some of the details came from. I imagine some deranged psychopath with this face coming after me, then Gretchen. I want to will it to come to life just so the sheriff can make an arrest.

Amir finishes his coffee and picks up his sketchpad, but I stop him before he slides out of the booth.

"Amir . . . did Kip really see it happen?" This isn't quite what I was told at school, but it gets his attention.

He glances uncomfortably at the door. "Look, Sonia, I'm not

supposed to talk about the investigation."

"Please." A lump rises in my throat, but I force myself to talk around it. "I just keep thinking—what if he could've stopped it?"

"He couldn't have." He sets his things back down, training sad dark eyes on me. "The kid must've passed through the woods right after you escaped and right before they attacked Gretchen. He saw her sitting alone at the top of the falls about the time we were here at the diner, trying to figure out what happened to you."

I lower my head, letting out a long breath.

"I wish it could've been different, Sonia. I'm truly sorry."

"Does that make Kip a suspect, then?" I look up and it's clear I've caught him off guard, but it seems like an obvious question.

He rises quickly, avoiding my eyes. "I can't discuss that with you, kiddo." He holds up the composite drawing and thanks me for my time. "The sheriff will give you an update once we know a little more."

The dinner rush is still going strong when he leaves, and I hustle to help Uncle Noah catch up while trying to wrap my head around everything Amir said. And didn't say.

Around nine o'clock I'm coming out of the kitchen with a couple of slices of peach pie when I notice a figure slumped in the booth at the far corner of my section. I'm not sure how the guy ended up there. Dina just got in from her business class at the community college, but she knows I'm about to clock out for the evening. I retie my apron and dutifully shuffle over. He has a dark hoodie pulled over his head, despite the warm night. I pull out my order pad, trying to catch Dina's eye, but she's busy with the book club that meets here every month.

"Hi, can I get you something to drink?"

"Think I'll go with coffee."

I almost drop my pencil at the familiar, gravelly voice.

Marcus looks up from under his hood. "Better make it black."

SEVEN

MARCUS'S EYES ARE A DARK, impenetrable brown. It's been so long since they were trained on me, I'd almost forgotten the intensity of his gaze. His hood falls back, revealing black hair mussed like he's been running his hands through it for hours. His brows are straight, his full mouth pressed thin. He's unshaven, which gives him an appealing rugged look, but enhances the exhaustion in the sharp lines of his face. He rests his arms on the table in front of him, tapping his right index finger to a rapid beat only he can hear. For a moment it looks like his hands are bruised, but then I realize it's just traces of green and purple paint.

I swallow, trying to keep my voice steady. "What do you want?"

"Coffee?" he says again.

For six months Marcus has gone out of his way to avoid me like I was something he didn't want to step in, and now he wants me to bring him coffee? I look over his shoulder to Dina hovering over the book club. She hasn't noticed him yet.

"I think you'd better leave."

He leans forward. "Can't I just talk to you for a second?"

I grip my order pad in one hand and my pencil in the other, but

I can't seem to keep them still. If he'd asked me to talk two years ago, I would've stumbled over my own sentences and then called Gretchen, giggling. But he didn't talk to me then. We'd shared a look here, a smile there, and every time butterflies would freak out inside my stomach. But after he registered on Gretchen's radar that was the end of that. I kept my distance, hid my crush. Gretchen got bored with boys easily, so I thought I'd wait it out. Everything seemed normal—I ceased to exist to either of them for a little while. But for whatever reason, as Gretchen's infatuation started to wane, Marcus began acting like he *wished* I didn't exist. At first I tried to fix it, or at least figure out why, but after a few encounters where he complained openly about my presence, it hurt less to steer clear of him altogether.

I was thrilled when they broke up last month.

He looks at me with hooded eyes, and I flash back to this morning. To him staring at me from the woods like I had something he wanted. My skin buzzes with warning, but there's a familiar ache in my chest. Alarmed, I step back. I start to turn away, but his hand lashes out, his fingers encircling my wrist. Pain ignites the scratches on my arm. My pencil hits the floor with a clatter, but when I try to pull free, his grip tightens.

"Sonia, wait." His eyes connect with mine. For a careless moment my body thrills with electricity and I'm sure something stirs in the space between us. But then he looks away. "I need your help."

A couple of people turn to see what's going on. My heart thunders in my ears. I stare at his hand on my arm, then raise my gaze to his face.

"What are you doing in here?" Dina's voice cuts between us,

startling me. She's across the room and by my side before I take my next breath.

Marcus stiffens, but doesn't look away from me. "Just trying to get a cup of coffee."

"Get out before I call the sheriff."

His eyes widen, but his jaw goes tight. "Has ordering coffee become some crime I'm unaware of?"

"If you don't let go of my niece, I'll have you arrested for assault."

He looks at his hand on my wrist. His face reddens and he lets go. "I didn't mean to—"

"Out. *Now.*"

I cradle my tender arm against my chest, the heat of his touch cooling as I step away.

Dina looks like she might physically pick him up and throw him out, even though he's twice her size. Marcus slides out of the booth, slouching when he gets to his feet like he's trying to disappear inside his own skin. He glances at me one last time before pulling his hood up, and I want to say something, but Dina's glare keeps my lips sealed.

"Thanks for the hospitality," Marcus mutters.

Everyone in the diner watches as he slips out the door.

"Good on you, Dina."

"Can you believe the sheriff let that monster run free?"

My thoughts get lost amid the rise of voices and I don't realize one of them is speaking to me until Dina puts her hands on my shoulders and looks straight into my eyes.

"Sonia? Do you want me to call the sheriff?"

"What?" I blink. "No."

She frowns. "What did he want? What did he say?"

"He . . . tried to order a coffee."

Through the window, I watch Marcus cross the street and disappear into the shadows of the park, his head bent low. My memory automatically flashes back to the woods, running, unable to breathe. Somehow it's harder to imagine his face behind me . . . but maybe it's just that I don't want it to be him. A chill runs up my spine.

"Hey, listen to me." Dina grips my shoulders. "If he comes here again, I don't want you anywhere near him, okay? You come get me or Noah and we'll take care of it."

I hesitate. An hour ago, I wouldn't have argued. But my heart is unsettled and there's nothing I'm sure of anymore. "He didn't do anything. . . ."

"With parents like his—" She stops herself. "I don't trust that kid. And he's not good for business."

I look at the remaining customers, who still seem restless. Marcus has lived with his grandmother for the past four years. It's no secret both his parents are in jail on drug charges, but he's never done anything to indicate he'd be following in their footsteps. He isn't what I'd call popular, but he wasn't disliked either before this week. He doesn't do drugs, doesn't even drink. He has a few friends, but mostly keeps to himself and his painting. Until he started dating Gretchen, I doubt many people thought twice about his past. He just seemed like someone trying to do better for himself—a lot like me.

"Why don't you head up to bed," Dina says.

I nod. My head is spinning and it feels like ages since I left for school this morning. When I reach the top of the stairs, I peek in on my mom, who's lying in the dark with her head under a pillow.

Never a good sign. She hasn't had a migraine this bad for months. She only gets them when she's stressed. I close the door carefully and cross the hall to my own room.

I dump my backpack out on my bed, staring at the array of texts and notebooks, but I don't open any of them. I go straight to my closet and sink to my knees, digging through the sneakers and winter boots beyond *Zack & Ken* until I unearth a small tin box. I've had it as long as we've lived here. It's decorated with snowmen and I think it originally held some kind of holiday candy. Inside, I mostly keep mementos. A gaudy old pin that belonged to my grandmother; a ticket stub to the first concert Gretchen and I ever saw; my first driver's permit. I sift carefully through the contents until I spot what I'm looking for—a mini SD card tucked in the corner. A pang of guilt shoots through me. It's something the sheriff would love to see.

I retrieve my phone from my backpack, stick the small plastic rectangle into its slot, and search until I find the right video. Gretchen showed it to me a month ago, the day after she and Marcus broke up. But so much has happened since then, I might be remembering it wrong.

Because the way he looked at me just now . . . for a second it was like the past six months had never happened. It doesn't make sense.

Marcus is desperate. I just need a reminder. Something to help me be smart about this.

I hit Play, and after a second, the video starts. They're in the little shed Marcus uses as an art studio behind his house. I skip forward until I reach the place where the camera starts bouncing around.

"You bitch." Marcus's voice is venom. He spits the word at the phone.

The shot stays on his furious face—barely recognizable compared to how he looked tonight—until something flies at the camera. A shriek sounds behind the lens. I flinch.

"Out of my face, Gretchen—God, I wish you were dead."

"Wouldn't that be convenient?" Gretchen's voice is steady. My heart aches at the sound. "You could declare your love for Sonia and live happily ever after."

The camera jerks toward the ceiling, the walls, then a paint-streaked hand closes over the lens.

The sound cuts out and the picture goes black.

I close my eyes. I'd never let on that I was crushing on Marcus, so when Gretchen showed me the footage, I didn't know what to say. They were her words, not his. Her accusation felt like a huge misunderstanding, and it probably was. But his words are what ring true to me now.

I wish you were dead.

I watch the whole thing through two more times and sit motionless on the floor of my closet, fighting my own regrets. I think of Marcus coming into the diner, sitting there asking for my help. Each time I run through it in my head, the luster fades, and I'm more convinced. His feelings toward me haven't changed; he's just looking for an out. A wave of nausea passes through me, but once it's gone, my whole head seems to clear.

This is exactly what I needed to see.

I'm not sure what kind of "help" Marcus is looking for—but once I find out, maybe I can get close enough to prove he *did* kill Gretchen.

EIGHT

DINA DROPS ME AT SCHOOL on Tuesday, and from the time I step out of the car, the whispers are practically a roar. I think it's worse than yesterday. I catch Marcus's name here and there, but people's voices drop when I approach and what I do hear is closer to gossip than information.

The SD card is tucked safely back inside the box at the bottom of my closet, but the recording sits in my heart like a shard. On the one hand, it undeniably incriminates Marcus. I just wish Gretchen hadn't decided to bring my name up. The thought of the sheriff asking me to explain a nonexistent romance with a suspect in her murder makes me sick to my stomach. That's why I decided not to deliver it to him this morning with his pancakes and eggs.

That, and Gretchen wouldn't want him to see what else was on the card.

A lot of people wouldn't.

I pass the guidance office as a girl from the tennis team walks in, sobbing. The grief counselors beckon to me with compassionate faces, making me all too aware of the absence sucking up the air around me everywhere Gretchen ought to be. But talking about my feelings is not going to make me feel better. Ever.

Aisha appears at my side halfway down the main hall. "Hey, heard you had a run-in with Marcus. Did he really threaten you?"

"Threaten me?"

She frowns. "Sasha Fadley said he came to the diner and said all kinds of crazy things."

I hesitate. "He did come to the diner, but he just ordered a coffee."

"Oh." Her face flushes and she adjusts her books. "Maybe Sasha heard wrong."

As we round a corner the air goes still. I look up to see a lone figure standing in front of a row of yellow lockers. It would be obvious which one was Marcus's even if he wasn't standing in front of it, ignoring everyone like it's his job. The purple door stands out from the surrounding yellow lockers, but someone's also drawn a big *X* over it in black. A few people near me whisper *Killer.* And *Can you believe he had the nerve to come back?* One girl giggles. Students move around him down the hall, but everyone maintains a wide berth.

Including me.

I feel him watching as we pass. Marcus has never been much of a talker, but there's always something going on behind his eyes and I've spent too many hours wondering about it. I focus on my locker, just past his along the same wall. I'm not sure when I'll get the chance to speak to him, but it's not going to happen in front of the whole school. Aisha glues herself to my side, taking a position in front of me like a sentry.

Someone behind us whispers: "So, could he get lethal injection?"

"Nah, he'll just rot in jail for life."

"Fuck off, all of you."

Yuji walks by with a scowl, pushing past everyone. He goes right up to Marcus, clapping him on the shoulder as if they're talking tennis or football.

"Douche," someone mutters.

You might never think to pair Yuji, the tennis player, with Marcus, the brooding artist. But Yuji's dad got into financial trouble with his company right about the time Marcus's parents went to jail. The Himuras lost their house, their car, and just about everything else you can lose and still maintain a shred of dignity. Marcus lost his family. I think he and Yuji found something in common in their respective aftermaths. Something besides a depressing amount of pity.

"Sonia!" Haley rushes down the hall and catches up to us, out of breath. "Oh my God, I just heard—are you okay?"

"I'm fine, why? What's going on?"

Haley stops short, scanning my arms and face. "Jill Barkman said Marcus came into the diner last night and pulled a knife on you."

Aisha and I exchange a glance. I hold up my hands. "I'm okay. See?"

"But—" Haley stares at me like stab wounds might appear on my body at any moment. "She said there was an ambulance, and the place was crawling with cops."

I look over my shoulder toward Marcus, who's openly watching us now. I shake my head. "Didn't happen. He just came in for coffee."

Haley's eyes widen when she sees him. She leans closer. "You're joking. What did he say?"

I need your help.

69

"Not a whole lot before Dina kicked him out," I say quickly.

The first bell rings. Haley glares openly as Yuji and Marcus move past us, and then she startles me with a quick hug before leaving for class. "I'm glad you're okay."

People start heading in the direction of their homerooms and I'm trying to focus on my locker combination and the books I need this morning when a shadow passes over me and lingers at my shoulder.

"Just hear me out," Marcus says.

My heart races. I stare at my closed locker, thinking of all the ways I planned to approach him, but I'm not prepared for it to happen now. "The bell's about to ring."

"Fuck the bell, Sonia, just listen to me."

There's a failing fluorescent light fixture blinking like a bad dream over our heads. I look up into his face, expecting bared teeth or an angry snarl—something murderous. But the desperation in his eyes makes my hands shake. "I need to go."

He steps in front of me. "I slept with her that night, okay." His voice is low. He wipes his hand over his face. "It was consensual. But I think the cops are trying to spin it like it wasn't."

I hesitate. Gretchen disappeared at the party—I'm not sure for how long. I was in the basement playing the first level of UltaShock with Kip and a couple of junior guys, and I was winning. When she came back, she was in a hurry to leave, but before I could ask what happened, she and Kirsten got into it. I'd heard the rumor about Marcus and Gretchen hooking up, and I guess I'd been hoping it wasn't true.

I open my mouth, but before I can speak, a voice growls behind me. "She doesn't look comfortable talking to you, Perez."

Marcus looks up wild-eyed from under the brim of his ball cap as Kip Peterson places a hand on my shoulder. I freeze, the weight of his touch noxious against my skin. People are closing in now, forgetting the bell, positioning themselves to get a good look if anything happens. I slide out from under Kip's heavy palm, backing away to where I can safely blend with the other students. When I stare across the semicircle I notice Reva Stone among the vultures.

"You know, I thought you were nuts, or maybe just an asshole, when you showed up here today," Kip says, moving closer. "But I'm starting to think all you are is stupid."

"This is none of your business," Marcus mutters.

"It's everyone's business if *you're* walking the halls."

Marcus is silent.

Kip steps closer. "No one wants you here, killer."

Marcus raises his head and stares him straight in the face. "It must've hurt, Gretchen rejecting you over and over like bad meat. But trust me, you were better off for it."

Kip has never been a very big guy. He might be five foot five, 150 pounds with his shaggy hair soaking wet. If he were bigger, the look in his eye right now might be terrifying, but I don't think Marcus even sees it. He pulls his cap down and tries to brush past him, and just as I realize what's about to happen, Kip's fist flies into Marcus's face.

There's a crunch.

The bell rings.

I step forward, one hand over my mouth. Marcus is on his hands and knees, blood dripping out of his nose. Kip lunges toward him again just as Marcus tries to get off the floor. I can't watch this

71

happen—I throw myself in his path. He slams into me hard, knocking the wind out of me, setting my healing ribs on fire. I have to grab on to him to avoid landing on top of Marcus. Kip yanks at my arms, eyes blazing until I barely recognize him and I'm afraid of what I've done. But I don't let go. The hall spins with his movement and I don't have to see straight to register everyone gaping around us.

Principal Bova appears with Deputy Brennan, the school resource officer, and pulls us apart.

"Oh my God, Sonia," someone says.

"He had it coming!" Kip cries.

I stand wide-eyed and paralyzed, trying to catch my breath. What did I just do?

"Why don't we go talk about this in my office?" Ms. Bova says, calmly squeezing my arm.

Mr. Kendrick, the senior English teacher, helps collect Marcus off the floor.

Kip yanks out of the deputy's grip. "I can't believe you're letting a murderer roam the halls with us."

"We can discuss this now, Kip, or after school with your parents," our principal says.

He glares at me one last time, then spits on the floor in front of Marcus. Deputy Brennan escorts him down the hall.

I follow, passing in front of Marcus. He stares at me, surprised, falling in beside me without a word. He cups his hands to his face, his fingers stained with blood.

NINE

I MAKE IT BACK TO my locker about fifteen minutes into second period. After a stern lecture from the principal and Deputy Brennan, Marcus and Kip were both sent home; I was given a warning for getting involved. I'm slightly more at ease knowing neither of them is in the building. Kip is clearly more upset about Gretchen than I realized. And though I'm not sorry I ended up shielding Marcus, after the way he cornered me I have no reason to think his opinion of me has improved. Now I just need to figure out how to approach him. If I can get him to think I *want* to help, maybe I can catch him in a lie, or look for a flaw in his alibi. Some reason the sheriff might reconsider him as a suspect so I won't have to hand over Gretchen's SD card.

Someone put up prom posters last week and there's one right next to my locker. The student council voted on a masquerade theme months ago and the poster is decorated with a mask of purple and gold feathers. When I see it, my throat closes up. Gretchen was going to wear the most exquisite flowing purple gown—it never felt right just calling it a prom dress. Once she slipped into it, everything about it was *her*. She'd custom-ordered a mask to go with it and made appointments for both of us to get our hair and nails done, something I normally hated. But the poster becomes a bright purple-and-gold blur now when I think about the ridiculous primping and fussing we'll never do. I wonder stupidly if someone canceled those appointments, or if I ought to call. I'm so distracted by this thought that at first I'm not surprised to see her face grinning at me from the inside of my locker.

I blink, skimming over my otherwise-bare locker door, but there she is, stuck over my mirror in the very middle, her auburn hair piled up, messy tendrils framing her startling smile. It's not a photo I recognize, but at the same time, something about it seems familiar. Gretchen looks vivacious, her head tipped back, frozen in one of her great peals of laughter. She's sitting on a couch, her arms wrapped around another girl, whose face has been disturbingly scratched out of the picture. I narrow my eyes, my muddled brain trying to puzzle out why someone would have scratched this girl out. But then I notice the big black boots crossed in front of her, the bracelet clasped on her wrist, and I recognize the rest of the outfit I wore to Brianne's party that night.

My stomach clenches.

I'm the girl with her face scratched out of existence.

TEN

MY BREATHING GOES RAGGED. I look up and down the hallway, trying to figure out if this is some kind of sick joke, but there's no one left to see it besides a teacher working on a bulletin board and a couple of freshmen whose names I don't know. I grip the cold steel of the locker door and try to collect myself, stay calm. I don't even remember the picture being taken. There were so many people at that party, one of them had to have done this.

It could've been anyone. It could've been—

Marcus.

My hands curl into fists. I think of him lurking in the woods, sneaking into the diner. And this morning, right here by my locker.

I trace my finger over the rough part of the photo where my face used to be and my chest tightens.

Does he want my help . . . or is he threatening me?

"Hey, thanks for the ride," I say, stepping onto the curb in front of Aisha's house.

"No problem," she says. "Let me know if you need a lift home. They'll be glad to see you."

She heads up the stairs to her own house and I walk along the iron fence toward the front gate of Gretchen's. My knees threaten mutiny with each step I take. I can still see Gretchen disappearing through her front door after I dropped her off that night, letting her hair down as she walked inside as if she was ready to sink into a hot bath, not plummet down a freezing waterfall. My heart thuds, heavy with sorrow, regret. Maybe if I'd just stayed with her, none of this would've happened.

My footsteps drag until I reach the iron gate. I look back to make sure Aisha is safely inside, then I take a deep breath and walk briskly down the street past the Meyers' house. Across the road, the branches of the trees arch over the pavement, reaching for me like I'm something that shouldn't have gotten away. I used to feel safe in the park. Gretchen and I spent so much time there growing up, I'd memorized every plant and rock by the time I was six years old.

I wrap my hoodie more tightly around me and give a nervous glance over my shoulder, thinking of Marcus watching me yesterday morning. A part of me wishes the photo was some misguided plea. I want to feel bad for him, do what I can to help. But if it's really a threat, I'm not messing around—I'll prove he killed Gretchen. Somehow.

The homes at the very end of Park Drive are a little smaller and not quite as opulent as Gretchen's and Aisha's houses, but Marcus's grandmother's family is one of the oldest in town. A few of the surrounding houses have started to look a little run-down, their trim in need of paint and gardens desperate for weeding, but they're still some of the nicest homes I have ever seen. I've been to Marcus's house exactly twice. The first time was with Gretchen right after they started dating. We were supposed to go to the movies, but she decided to drop in on him as a surprise. Those were the early days, before Marcus's all-out aversion to me, and it took everything I could muster to wait for her on his front porch, trying not to envision the two of them making out upstairs. The second time, just before they broke up, she sent me over to get her lip gloss while they were fighting. Gretchen had a hundred lip glosses, but she still wanted me to go. Marcus met me at the door with it and never said a word, even after I managed an awkward smile and thanked him. I walked back to Gretchen's feeling stupid for having tried to be nice at all. I stare up at the pale gray Victorian now and it looks much as it did before. Aside from one recently boarded-up front window, it's tidy and well cared for.

The picture from my locker burns a hole in my back pocket.

I climb the steps to the big wraparound front porch. The doorbell has been painted over, so I knock. I attempt to peer through the curtains, but I don't sense any movement inside. I rap again, more forcefully, unsure what my next move is, when I remember the little shed Marcus uses as a studio out back. Gretchen called it his "sensitive artist clubhouse."

I wish you were dead.

I hesitate a long time before walking around the side of the house. Maybe I should just take the photo to the sheriff, let him handle it. But then I think of Marcus taking a punch in the face today just to ask me to hear him out, and it doesn't make sense. I'll just show him the photo, find out what he's after, and go home. I'll be fine. Every nerve in my body thrums by the time I head down the gravel path to the backyard. I palm Uncle Noah's pepper spray.

The shed stands in one corner and actually looks like it might once have been a fancy kids' playhouse, built to match the main house. It has a window with a frilly curtain and a flower box with nothing planted in it. The door stands ajar and there's angry music pulsing through the air. I try to peer in the windowpane, but all I can see through the curtain is light and shadow. A huge dark spider crawls from the glass over the back of my hand and I shriek, flinging it to the ground. The door swings the rest of the way open and I find myself standing red-faced under Marcus's gaze.

His jaw drops at first, but he closes it, wiping his hands on an old cloth hanging out of his pocket. He's wearing a ripped pair of jeans and a fitted dark blue T-shirt, and he looks more comfortable than I think I've ever seen him. I used to think Marcus seemed so much more my type than Gretchen's. She was manicured and high maintenance. He's rumpled and reserved—the way I always felt when I wasn't with her. There's green paint in his hair above his right ear and a large purple bruise blooming under his left eye. I wince when I see it, but when I meet his gaze, something surges in my chest. I grit my teeth and remind myself why I'm here.

He pulls the door shut behind him, digs a key out of his pocket, and locks it.

I cross my arms in front of me, hoping I look confident. "Let's talk."

He hesitates, his eyes darting around the yard as if searching for someone else. I touch the little can of pepper spray through my pocket. His fists tighten and he starts toward the house, but I hang back by the shed. I wonder what he's working on, and why he would lock it.

Halfway to the door of his house Marcus looks back. "You coming inside or what?"

The aging Victorian was cluttered and dark the one time I went in. There's no way I'm stepping foot inside it now.

"I'll stay out here."

The corner of his mouth pulls into a frown, or maybe a grimace. "Fine. I'll be right back."

When he's gone, I look up at the house, then back to the shed, feeling exposed. There's an empty fountain in the center of the yard and an ivy-covered arbor with a small table and chairs at the far end of the garden. I pace up and down the gravel path between the two, trying to decide if I should just throw the photo at him, or give him a chance to own up to it first.

The back door slams and Marcus lopes over to where I stand under the arbor. He's changed into a white shirt and managed to wash most of the paint off his face and hands. He looks different in the sunlight. His face is more relaxed and his skin has a healthy glow, or maybe it's just that we're in his own backyard, out from under the stares of a suspicious town. He gestures me to a chair at the little table and I shift my feet, unsure what to do. Before I can decide, he loses patience and slumps into the seat instead.

"So, I guess this is where I throw myself at your feet for holding off Kip this morning." His lip curls. "I didn't think you cared."

"Trust me, I don't." I clench my jaw because I almost mean it. I'm angry about the photo, but also that he can't even be civil in the wake of Gretchen's death.

"Then why are you here?"

"Honestly? Until this morning, I was considering helping you."

He straightens. "What?"

I take a deep breath, cross my fingers, and then pull the photo out of my back pocket and drop it on the table in front of him. "But I don't respond well to threats."

He leans forward and picks it up, turning it over like he's never seen it before, even going so far as to run his thumb across the place where my face ought to be. My jaw grows tighter the longer he takes. When I thought I wanted his attention, this wasn't what I had in mind. He looks up, his expression blank.

"I don't get it, is this a joke?" he asks.

"Don't try to bullshit me."

"I'm not!"

I roll my eyes. "If I'd seen this before Kip came along this morning, I would've told him exactly where to punch you."

He drops the photo to the table, his face white. "Wait. You think *I* did this?"

I falter at the panic in his voice. "Who else?"

"I don't know—it could've been anyone at school."

"Marcus, why would anyone else do this?"

"To fuck with you? To be a douchebag? I don't know." He stops and looks at me, his expression shifting to alarm. "To scare you."

I pause. "Why would anyone want to do that?"

"Because *you're* still here."

"What's that supposed to mean?" Even as I ask, a spike of fear shoots up my neck. The pepper spray in my pocket doesn't seem so reassuring.

"Sonia, someone's sending you a message."

I struggle to keep my voice steady. "Someone like you?"

He runs his hand over his face. "You know it wasn't me—"

"The only thing I know is ever since Gretchen died, you refuse to leave me alone."

His eyes darken. "Then why didn't you just go straight to the sheriff? If you think it was me, why risk coming here by yourself?"

I hesitate.

He fixes his gaze carefully on me as he speaks. "Between that and not letting Kip come at me again this morning, I think you know it wasn't me. Or at least you're not sure."

My stomach drops. I look away so he won't see the doubt in my eyes. "Maybe you didn't chase me. But you still could've killed Gretchen."

"I *didn't* kill her." He spins the photo around on the table and pushes it toward me. "Think about it. Why would someone put this in your locker?"

"Because you're a desperate asshole who thought it'd get me to help you."

His eyes widen. "You think I'd try to threaten you into helping me? Like that would get me anywhere."

I throw up my hands. "Fine. If you didn't leave it there, then who did?"

Marcus sits back in his chair, his face solemn. "Whoever killed Gretchen."

I look up at the sky through the leaves above our heads. "Clearly."

"Come on, Sonia. Even if you weren't the intended target, what if you saw something that night and you don't even realize it?"

"Now you're trying to tell me what I saw?"

"I'm trying to tell you you're not safe." His voice goes quiet.

"What if the person who sent this is the same person who attacked you?"

I sink into one of the garden chairs, my legs refusing to support me anymore. Gretchen grins up at me from the picture, hugging my faceless form. I look more closely at the scratches—jagged, violent, almost slicing through the paper. Like someone really, really didn't want me there.

All I want to do is run home and scream as hard as I can into my pillow, but I stay put, fighting to keep my voice steady. "Okay, but that doesn't mean it wasn't you."

He looks away. "No. I guess it doesn't."

Marcus has always had this slightly haunted look. I figured it was just part of the whole misunderstood-artist thing, but now I notice dark circles under his eyes and the way he clenches his jaw so tightly I can see the tension in his neck muscles. I bite the inside of my cheek, wondering what it would feel like to be blamed for a crime. Especially one you didn't commit.

"Look," he says. "Whatever you believe, you should take the photo to the sheriff."

I blink, surprised. "What does that get you?"

"Probably more scrutiny." His face seems oddly conflicted. "But let's be real, it would look worse for me if something happened to you."

I raise one eyebrow, staring uneasily at the picture. If he's telling the truth and he didn't do this, I wouldn't know where to start guessing who did. Or actually, that's not true. I wouldn't know which suspect to focus on from Gretchen's SD card.

"Supposing you didn't attack me, or kill Gretchen, or put this in my locker . . . what were you hoping for when you asked for my help?"

"I need to clear my name." He pauses, takes a breath. "I was hoping whatever you saw that night . . . you could at least say it wasn't me."

I close my eyes, but as soon as I do I'm back in the woods, running terrified through darkness. I open them fast, gripping the arms of my chair like I'm clinging to the daylight.

"You want to know what I saw."

"What you can remember, yeah."

I weave my fingers together. I'm not ready for this. When I think about telling Marcus everything I told the sheriff, I feel sick. "I—I just can't right now."

"Come on, Sonia," he says, like he's losing patience. "This is important."

"Really? For who?" My voice comes out sharp, but my jaw trembles.

Marcus studies me a long time, but then his eyes soften. "Maybe you'd feel better if you talk about it."

I grasp the edge of the table, surprised. "Talk? To you?"

He shrugs.

"Thanks, but no thanks." Even if I was ready to buy half the stuff he's saying, he's the one who should be explaining things to me. "If I need to, I'll find myself a shrink."

He lifts his chin, but doesn't take his eyes off me. "Sonia, I know you're scared. It's okay. I know what it's like to—"

"Has anyone ever tried to *kill* you?" I wipe my cheek and glare at him. "You're just thinking about college plans and what there is to eat in the fridge, and the next instant you're wondering if this is the moment you're going to die. It's so fast—you're just crossing a bridge, and then you're on the ground, and the sky gets mixed up with the earth and the trees and you can't breathe." I gasp. "Instinct makes you fight, adrenaline makes you scream, but there's a second when everything goes dark and you think, *This is it*. And you just hope it's over fast."

Marcus's eyes are black.

"It feels like shit to talk about," I say.

His jaw hardens. "If I'd been there—" He stops. "I *wasn't* there, I promise."

I take a long, deep breath, trying to erase hot tears with my sleeve. "Well if you weren't there, where were you? How come even the sheriff thinks you killed her?" I know I'm pushing it with that last part, and it has the desired effect.

He balls his hands into fists. "Did he tell you that?"

"He hasn't exactly been singing your praises."

"I left the party to check in on my grandmother—she's been sick. I was home with her until eleven thirty." He pauses. "Then I went for a walk."

"A walk? Where?"

"In the park." He sighs. "But the sheriff said you were attacked closer to eleven. It wasn't me."

Something flits through the back of my mind, and when it finally settles, I draw in a breath. "Aisha saw you."

"Yeah, I know." He sounds irritated. "Trust me, the sheriff has already been all over that."

My right eye begins to twitch. "Guess they must believe you if they haven't arrested you yet."

Marcus's face clouds. "Look, Sonia, I'll admit I've been a total ass to you. If I were you, I wouldn't want anything to do with me, either. But is there any way we can put that behind us for now? I . . . I really need you."

My mouth falls open. Until he and Gretchen broke up, Marcus had been a grand champion at loathing me. If I walked into a room, he'd leave. If he came over when I was with Gretchen, he'd flat out ask her to get rid of me. Nothing could have prepared me to hear him say this. My heart pounds.

He glances at his house. "Listen, I'm going to tell you something—basically, what I'm about to say could really fuck things up for me. But I'm telling you because I want you to trust me."

I shift in my seat. Trust is not something I have in abundance anymore, but I guess I'm afraid enough to hear him out.

"My grandmother lied to the sheriff about seeing me that night." He exhales. "She's scared to death about what's happening, but she believes me. I *was* here until eleven thirty, but she was already asleep when I got home. Basically, I have no alibi."

I cover my mouth, letting the weight of his words sink in.

"You can go notify the sheriff if you want, but I wouldn't be telling you this if I was guilty."

"So, it could have been you. . . ." I speak slowly, not sure if I'm more shocked that he really has no alibi or that he actually just told me as much.

"But it wasn't." He leans forward, resting his hands on the table. "I might not be able to prove I didn't kill Gretchen, but if I can figure out who did—"

"I don't think Sheriff Wood will appreciate you trying to do his job for him, not to mention being lied to."

"This whole town wants to see me go to jail just so they can feel better faster." His eyes are fierce. "She was your best friend, Sonia. Don't you want to know the truth?"

I shove my hands inside my hoodie pockets, but they feel cold no matter what I do. The truth won't change anything, fix anything. I don't want the truth, I want a do-over. I want Gretchen alive and the last week to be nothing but a bad dream. I wish for the thousandth time that night had happened differently. That Gretchen hadn't fought with Kirsten. That we'd just stayed at the party and gone home later, like we always did. But every time I start speculating about what-ifs, the whole nightmare just replays itself in my head.

He pushes his chair out from the table, but lingers over the photograph. "Whatever you do, I meant what I said about showing this to the sheriff."

I peek at the photo, flip it facedown. Somehow looking at it felt safer when I was sure Marcus was behind it. Now I can't tell where amid the scratches my own features ought to go.

"Sonia?" Marcus says.

Our eyes meet. Something inside me stirs.

He seems to struggle, but finally manages to speak. "Look out for yourself."

My mind swims with memory, grief, regret—*can* I be the person who decides Marcus's fate? He stands and turns toward the house, his shoulders already hunched, like he's accepted defeat. I think of Gretchen slipping in the door of her house, then turning around, heading back out into the woods. I think of the video, of all the times Marcus and Gretchen fought, when he treated me like I wasn't worth the dirt on his shoe. But then there were the moments I couldn't help admiring him. When I ran into him walking his grandmother through the grocery store, or the few times I saw him holding his own with Gretchen—something I'd seen only a few guys do. He'd still made her feel like the only girl in the world. I can't help wondering where all of us might be if they'd never dated at all.

I close my eyes, and when I open them again, I'm staring at the back of the photograph. If Marcus is the one behind it, he's going to an awful lot of trouble to deny it. But if he didn't leave it, I need to figure out who did . . . and why.

"You know, this could just be a stupid prank," I say, trying not to sound like I'm more scared than when I got here. "One of the assholes who graffitied your locker might've done it after I stopped Kip."

"Maybe." He turns, his mouth uncertain. "You should still be careful."

I rise, tucking the photo back in my pocket without looking at it. He regards me with a subtle, hopeful look. It reminds me of the times I used to catch him watching Gretchen when she wasn't paying attention. Sometimes his face surprised me. I would wonder what was really going through his head, just the way I'm wondering now.

"Maybe we could help each other," I say before I lose my nerve. "I mean, because if it's not you, then . . ."

He straightens, steps toward me, the look in his eyes unmistakably relieved. "We could come up with a list of possible suspects first."

"Okay. Let's start there and compare notes," I say, wondering if I've just made a huge mistake. "But Marcus, let's get one thing straight. After everything is said and done, if all the evidence still points to you . . ."

The hopeful look fades and he nods. "Sometimes innocent people rot in jail."

I look away. "And sometimes they get killed."

ELEVEN

AT THE END OF THE day Wednesday, Principal Bova announces there will be early dismissal Friday so students and staff can attend Gretchen's funeral service. The hallways immediately fill with chatter. Who's going, who isn't, who else will be there. I've never seen a funeral turn into a social event before.

Monday couldn't come any faster.

"I've never even been to a memorial service," Aisha says. "What should we wear? Is it a long skirt thing? Do you just go all black?"

Aisha would look good at a funeral in blue jeans, but I get it. Gretchen inherited her mother's innate sense of style and they were often featured together in the society page of the local paper. I never had to think about what to wear if we had somewhere to be— Gretchen supplied the wardrobe and I followed her lead. She always knew exactly the look to go for, even for a grim event like this. In a twisted way, she might've had fun dressing me for her own funeral.

"Black, I guess? Or gray." My face reddens. This is the last thing I want to think about.

My phone vibrates in my pocket and I'm happy for the distraction. It's been miserably silent this week, apart from arranging rides with Aisha and a few nagging messages from my mother. Not having a best friend is a hard thing to get used to. I slow my pace, ready to type out *just fine, on my way home, love you too*, until I look at the screen.

Meet up before your shift? Need to talk.

I freeze. The number isn't one I recognize, but I can guess who it's from. I scan the crowd around me, though I know he isn't here. Principal Bova took the precaution of suspending Marcus until after Gretchen's service.

Don't text me.

I shut my phone off before he can answer. I'm working on my suspect list, but so far the only people other than Marcus with a clear motive to kill Gretchen are Tyrone, Kevin, Reva, and maybe Kip. I'm not even sure how to narrow down who might've left the photo in my locker. Whatever it is can wait. I don't need my friends looking over my shoulder while I text a murder suspect.

When Aisha drops me at home, my mom and Uncle Noah are up front, arguing over how to change the receipt paper in the cash register we've had for ten years. They straighten, plastering on concerned expressions when I walk in, but I can't help noticing my mom's knotted fingers or that her bottom lip is chewed raw.

"How did it go today?" she asks.

"About the same as yesterday."

"You could take the night off. Wednesdays are slow."

"Who would cover my shift?"

"I will!" My little cousin, Felicia, pipes up from behind a milk shake in a booth. "Dad's been showing me how to bus tables."

I raise an eyebrow at Uncle Noah. "Ever hear of child labor laws?"

He chuckles. "She thought it was fun."

"Nice try." I kiss him on the cheek. "I need the tips."

I run upstairs to change my clothes. There's still enough time to finish my calculus homework if I'm quick. I swap my jeans for a denim skirt and pull a cardigan over my cami, but when I look in the mirror something seems off. I tie my hair back, add a little lip gloss. My cheeks still look hollow and no amount of makeup will hide the shadows under my eyes.

But that's not it.

I trace the buttons of the black cardigan and let out a slow breath. It's a hand-me-down from Gretchen and a little dressy for waiting tables. I think the last time I wore it was to my Penn interview. I pull the tag up behind my neck and squint at it in the mirror: Kate Spade. Gretchen culled her closet four times a year, with the seasons, and since we were almost the same size, she'd give her old things to me instead of taking them to Goodwill. She liked to joke that I was her own personal charity case. I never knew how to respond to that, so I would just say that I was probably the best-dressed waitress for miles.

But now the sweater feels wrong against my skin. I slip it off and pull on my Penn hoodie. Something in my body eases. I find a pair of cutoffs I bought at a secondhand store a couple of years back and swap them out for the skirt, which was also Gretchen's, and then frown at my overflowing closet. The few clothes I've bought for myself might not be flattering or well made, but I can't deny that I feel better in them.

My right hand goes to my wrist out of habit and anxiety creeps back into my chest. It seems silly to be upset about a tiny bracelet after everything else that happened Friday night, but I can't help it. Gretchen bought one for each of us last September for our seventeenth birthdays. She wanted to make a statement about our friendship, but with something more grown-up than those cheesy broken-heart friendship necklaces. She found a style she liked—a black leather strap held together with a silver infinity symbol—and we'd been wearing them ever since.

It's out in the park somewhere, I know it. I haven't had the chance to go back and look—if I'm honest, I've been afraid to. Especially after finding the photo in my locker. But the sun is bright this afternoon, the birds are singing, and there's still almost an hour till my shift starts. I know it's a slim chance I'll ever find it. But every time I look at my bare wrist my stomach turns.

I need it back.

I shove my pepper spray in my pocket and creep down the stairs, reminding myself there are always people in the woods during the day. Mom's and Noah's voices drift back from the diner, but their conversation seems to have returned to day-to-day business. I turn the latch on the security door and push it open.

"Where are you going?"

I turn. Felicia comes around the corner wielding a tub of dirty dishes.

"I just need a little air that doesn't smell like french fries."

She wrinkles her brow. "My mom said we can't go outside because of Gretchen."

I peer through the metal mesh of the door, my heart heavy. "Your mom is right, you should stay inside. I'm just running next door—to the flower shop. I'll be right back."

"Oh." Felicia relaxes. "It does smell good in there."

I hesitate as the door creaks open. Lying to an eight-year-old is easy, but somehow makes me feel worse. "Hey, Fe, don't tell my mom. . . . I want to pick something for Gretchen myself."

I hold my breath dashing across First Avenue—in part because I don't want to be seen, but also because this is the first time I've crossed this pavement since Friday night, and it's upsetting and surreal, retracing my footsteps in the sunlight.

The rush of water is just audible at the edge of the park. The path leading to Hidden Falls branches in two halfway down, and if you follow it to the right, you reach the playground and picnic area just upstream along Black River Creek. This was the place Gretchen and I always met until about seventh grade when it started to feel silly sitting by the toddlers on the swings. I can see the old equipment as I pass through the trees. Its peeling painted structures stand abandoned, awaiting the passage of time, and fear, for play to resume.

The sun transforms the woods, replacing dark shadows with a flood of light and color. Death seems like an impossibility as I listen to the squirrels and woodpeckers chatter amid the bright green leaves. I follow the hard-packed trail down the slope, increasingly alert as the water's rumble drowns out little sounds. I jump at a flutter of movement to my left, but it's only a couple of crows winging their way between trees. My heartbeat accelerates with my pace.

And then I'm at the top of the falls.

The air takes on a chill as I grow close, but I tell myself it's from the freezing snowmelt. Black River Creek swells deep and cold, spring runoff gushing along the stream bed and over the rocky ledge in a single powerful jet. By August the water slows to a lazy trickle, and the shallow pool below lures everyone in town to escape the stifling late-summer heat. But for now it's flowing high, and you wouldn't want to be under it, let alone fall over the edge.

My skin prickles. I turn my back on the falls, scanning the stones and fallen trees dotting the clearing. It's one of those natural places that just begs to become a hangout. Close enough to walk to, but secluded from watchful eyes. I smile, recognizing the spot back in the trees where we had our first drinks—Gretchen traded a kiss in ninth grade for two sips from a senior's flask. More recently, she preferred a hollowed-out seat in a giant rock. It was almost like a throne. There was enough room on it for both of us to sit, but I usually let Gretchen have it to herself. Some sort of music was always playing, and if no one brought drinks, we'd just sit around talking, watching the guys leap back and forth over the creek. It was the place to be. My smile fades as I realize that's over. Forever.

There's a pile of flowers, stuffed animals, and notes people have left at the base of one of the rocks. I scan the small items left in tribute to Gretchen, half hoping my bracelet has found its way there. If it has, I might even leave it, let it remain as my own memento, but it isn't among them. I can't bring myself to read the cards or look at the pictures, so I step away.

A branch cracks behind me. I turn, lose my breath—but no one's there. I count to ten before daring to move. Coming here seemed like a better idea in the security of my bedroom. The day doesn't seem as bright or safe under the canopy of leaves. I scan the trees for movement, my heart racing, then hurry up and begin my search.

The dirt at my feet is tracked with hundreds of footprints, but not from any party. Big sheriff and deputy boots alongside smaller medical shoes. I wish they had scuffed the whole night from the earth, but their presence makes it even harder to forget. I inspect the nearby underbrush, keeping one eye trained on the edges of the trees. It's hard to remember exactly *where* I was and when, now that it's light. I take a closer look everywhere I see trampled plants, but the longer I search the more I understand the whole needle-in-a-haystack thing. A small silver charm on a black bracelet wouldn't exactly stand out among the shale and soil.

I look again toward the falls, my stomach tying in knots. Even in the dark, I knew how frighteningly close I came to the edge. There's a flat rock near the top that juts out over the pool. Gretchen and some of the more daring kids used to hang out on it, dangling their legs. I could never bring myself to join them—the height freaked me out. I creep toward it now, crouching low on the ground, sifting my fingers through moss and leaves, holding on to my last hopes.

The water thunders over the rocks beside me, sending up an icy mist. When I get to the ledge, I pause. Maybe it's guilt, or morbid curiosity, or maybe I'm just looking for closure. I take a deep breath and lie flat, looking down into the churning pool. My stomach lurches immediately, the last moments I was here crashing back into my head. Kicking and scratching, blind in the dark, scrambling to escape, my screams drowned by the falls. But then something shifts and suddenly I see Gretchen—fighting for her life as hard as I fought for mine.

My whole body shakes.

Why would I make it out when she didn't?

What made the difference?

I close my burning eyes, but I can't escape the horrors of her final moments manufactured inside my head. Falling, suffocating, pinned under the icy spray. Or maybe it didn't happen that way. If she was lucky, she would've blacked out when she hit the water.

There's a hard pull on my leg and I shriek, nearly rolling off the ledge, but something holds me fast. I whip my head around to find Marcus crouched over me, his hand clamped firmly around my ankle. His eyes are wide, alarmed.

"What are you doing?" he yells.

I scoot back on my knees and he lets go, allowing me to work my way from the edge to the clearing, set away from the water's roar. I rest my hands on my knees, my pulse hammering so hard, it's difficult to breathe.

"Are you crazy?" he asks. "Do you have any idea how stupid that was?"

I brace myself against a tree and look away. "I know."

"Then what were you doing?"

I look up into his face. "I just needed to see it."

He looks toward the falls and exhales, his posture easing. I let go of the tree, my legs still shaky beneath me.

"It's not pretty to think about," he says.

I grimace, my body cold from the spray. "Why are you here?"

His eyes narrow. "Apparently I'm not allowed to text you. I had to talk to you somehow."

"So you decided to follow me like a creeper?"

His expression turns stony and I wish I'd said something else.

"I wasn't following you. I was on my way to the diner and saw someone was at the falls—I didn't expect to find you, *alone*, dangling over the edge."

I shift my feet, feeling stupid all over again. "I wasn't dangling."

"Have you never heard criminals tend to return to the scene of their crimes? If the wrong person came along, you could have shared a funeral with Gretchen."

I shudder. He's right, but how can I know who the wrong person might be?

"Sneaking up on people in the woods doesn't make a great case for *your* innocence."

"Hanging out here alone doesn't do much for your life expectancy," he snaps.

I draw back, but there's nothing I can say to that. Coming here was stupid. I know that, but I had to do it. I don't want to admit that if I had to run into anyone, I'm relieved it was him.

"I was looking for my bracelet," I mutter.

"Seriously?" He scowls. "A piece of jewelry?"

"I need to find it," I say, trying to hide the urgency in my voice. "Gretchen gave it to me, and I lost it that night."

He looks around the clearing, and then back at me. When he does, the tension in his face has eased. "Where were you attacked? Was Gretchen with you then?"

I glance at the bridge arching over the creek and a cold flash of memory shoots through me. My feet on the planks, heading home—

"I can't—I don't want to talk about it."

Marcus walks over to the little footbridge and places one boot on the boards. "It was here?"

"That's where it started." I press my palms against my eyelids, attempting to keep a headache from coming on. "I was alone; Gretchen—she was at home."

"Okay. So they grabbed you how? Did you see them coming?"

I force my legs stiffly toward him. "No. I was halfway across, and then—" *Cold hands on my throat, hot breath in my hair.* I cringe. "They came from behind."

"What happened after that?"

"Look, I really don't want to—"

"The more I can understand how it went down, the more I can help, Sonia." His voice is calm, compassionate. Almost enough to put me at ease.

"I thought I was the one helping you," I say under my breath.

"Please. Trust me." He looks me straight in the eyes, catching me off guard. My chest surges with heat. "What happened next? Is that when you ran?"

"No." I take a breath, forcing myself back to Friday night. "They dragged me into the brush."

He furrows his brow, pacing out a line into the trees. "Like here?"

I shake my head, pointing. "No, over there."

Marcus frowns, clearly not following. "Will you show me?"

I wait for him to say he's kidding. The edges of my vision blur and I'm starting to feel light-headed. I look up the path toward home. But maybe if I just do it, he'll finally let this go.

I retrace my steps the best I can from memory, shuffling backward from the bridge until I reach the edge of the clearing. I keep my eyes wide, filled with light the whole time, but my heart still pounds loud enough that it almost drowns out the falls.

"This is about where we fell down."

"You both fell?"

I nod. "They—he was on top of me." My voice is barely a whisper.

"So it was definitely a guy. . . ."

I stare down at the moss and dirt, thinking of Amir's composite sketch. "I . . . the more I think, it had to be. . . ."

"Did you get a look at him then? Did he say anything?"

"It was so dark." I shake my head and then pause. "He was wearing a hood, I remember that."

"That's good." Marcus's voice is encouraging. "What happened next?"

"I was so caught off guard . . . at first I didn't resist." My mind tumbles over the self-defense classes Gretchen and I both took and I look down, ashamed. My hands close into fists. "Once we were on the ground, it became a fight."

Marcus's jaw hardens. "Good for you."

"It gets fuzzy after that." I close my eyes, holding back tears to summon my memories out of the dark. I trace my fingers along my scratched arms, my ribs lightly throbbing. "There were a lot of branches and rocks, and I wasn't sure where I was until we were on top of the falls."

I turn that way, intending to show him this too, but Marcus stops me with a light hand on my elbow. When I look at him, his eyes are gentle. "It's okay, I get the idea."

My skin tingles where we touch. I cross my arms and nod, grateful not to relive the moment. "It was dumb luck I got away and managed to run in the right direction. I felt him behind me every second until I was through the door of the diner." This memory stands out in vivid color and I can no longer hold back tears, thinking of my mom's face when she saw me.

Like every mother's worst nightmare had burst through the door.

A flutter of wings behind Marcus grabs my attention. I peer up the narrow path and spot a lone shadowy figure making its way toward us. Marcus's expression shifts to alarm when he sees my face and he turns to follow my gaze. It could be a person leaving a token at the memorial, or just someone taking the path as a shortcut. Or maybe whoever scratched out my photo is coming to get the rest of their message across. I scan the rocks and plants, but there's really nowhere to go. Marcus shifts between the approaching person and me just as the heavy footsteps reach my ears.

"Marcus Perez, I wasn't expecting to see—" Amir's words cut off when he notices me. He takes in my tear-streaked face and stiffens. "Sonia. Is everything all right?"

"I—I'm fine," I say quickly, wiping my cheeks with the back of my hand. I'm not sure if I'm relieved to see the deputy, or more scared.

Marcus gestures to the makeshift memorial. "We were leaving flowers for Gretchen."

"Both of you . . . together?" I don't know how familiar Amir is with Marcus's and my relationship, but he looks unconvinced.

"Not together. We just ran into each other," I say, but the truth never sounded so lame. "Anyway, I should go. They're waiting for me at the diner."

I turn toward home, but Marcus clears his throat. "Yeah, I better head out too."

He joins me on the path and my face burns. I can't bring myself to look back at Amir.

"Sonia?" the deputy calls after me. When I turn, he's holding out the pepper spray canister Noah gave me. "Did you drop this?"

My hand flies to my empty pocket. I jog back to where he stands, but he doesn't hand it to me right away. "Are you *sure* you're okay?" he says in a low voice.

I force an appreciative smile. "I'm fine, Amir, really." I take the pepper spray and tuck it back into my pocket. "Thanks. Don't want to lose this for sure."

Marcus waits for me on the path, but I hurry past him without a word. He follows me up the slope. I try not to think what Amir might be radioing to the sheriff right now. I stop just shy of the road and scan the woods behind us, but there's no sign of him, or anyone else following. The deputies have been making periodic foot patrols through the park. He's probably most of the way to Gretchen's by now. I swear under my breath.

Marcus shifts beside me. "That seemed to go okay—"

"If that gets back to Sheriff Wood, it won't be."

He touches my shoulder. "Look, I'm sorry, I just . . ."

"Was whatever you wanted worth being found like *that*?" I ask.

He pulls back. "You're right. What could possibly be worse than being seen with me?"

"Everyone thinks you murdered—" I start, but break off when I see the hurt in his eyes.

"Do *you* think I killed her?"

My heart skips. I press my lips together.

Marcus steps close. Closer than my own shadow, his breath warm on my cheek. "Then you better get home. It isn't safe here."

I falter, rushing away from him across the empty pavement, a cool breeze cutting through my hoodie. I grip the pepper spray canister, but my pace slows when I reach the opposite curb. Guilt pools in my stomach and I wish for just a second that I'd said . . . something.

I glance over my shoulder, but he's already headed back down the path, slipping into the trees until he merges with the shadows.

TWELVE

I ALMOST CHOKE WHEN I see the reporters lined up shame-lessly outside Grace Community Church, ready to sink their teeth into people coming to terms with the loss of Gretchen. Dina drives past them, ignoring their thoughtless calls. I slip on a pair of cheap sunglasses, though the day is suitably cloudy. The snap of their cameras follows us to the doors. Gretchen would have loved the attention, which gives me some comfort. She could have made it as royalty—always put together with the right smile, the right words. But there's no way for her to bask in this now.

Once we walk through the doors it's standing room only. People fill every pew and line the walls. Uncle Noah closed the diner for the afternoon out of respect for Gretchen's family, but he correctly predicted the whole town would be at the service anyway. Dina loaned me a plain gray knit dress, which I decided is okay since I'm not keeping it and the label is nothing to speak of. My arms no longer sting, but since the scratches still stand out red on my skin, I'm grateful for the long sleeves. I recognize teachers, students, friends, families, even a couple of minor celebrities—a tech sector pundit and a talk radio figurehead. All of them look as shell-shocked to be here as I feel. I take an extra moment to study faces, wondering who among them might have been in the park Friday night. But the harder I focus the more people's features blend together until I give up trying to see anything through this thick haze of grief. An usher leads Uncle Noah; his wife, Elena; and my cousin toward a row of reserved seats near the front of the room. My mother grips my hand and follows. Dina positions herself on the other side of me. My body flashes hot, then cold at the sight of a closed white casket laden with pink roses near the altar. My mom and Dina squeeze my hands, get me into a seat, but I have never wanted so much to crawl out of my skin.

There's a white screen above the casket and I'm startled by an enormous projection of Gretchen. It's a black-and-white picture from her senior photo shoot, and though she's gorgeous, of course, something about it seems off. I think it's the color—Gretchen's hair was vibrant red. I could never decide exactly what shade—it looked brighter or darker on different days, in different lights. She called it "mood hair," and she had such varied moods, I could never argue with that. But in black-and-white she almost looks blond, and so much more like Kirsten. I swallow hard as it occurs to me they had to use this one because all the color shots of her were taken near the waterfall.

The church is decorated with candles, flowers, and wreaths. A solemn woman plays a grand piano at one end of the room. After a few minutes Gretchen's family is escorted to a group of seats in the front row. I hold my breath when I see their faces. Her mother wears a blank, medicated expression and leans heavily on Gretchen's father, who looks just the way he always does, like one of those men who never cries. Kirsten's hair is blond again, thank God. She hides her face behind a tissue, but not being able to read her expression just makes me feel worse about seeing her the other day. Like if I'd somehow said the right thing I could have made her hurt less.

A minister begins speaking. Gretchen's family has never been religious. I'm not sure how they decided on this church for her service except that I think it's one of the largest in town. The woman's words float over the speakers into the air, slipping away before I really tune in and hear them. She didn't know Gretchen, but she says things about her. About mortality. And life. I sit there feeling like a live moth speared with a pin, desperate to flee and unable to move. Every time she says Gretchen's name, I blink in stupid surprise, like she must be talking about someone else.

Gretchen and I had plans. We might've been going to different schools this fall, but that was a whole summer away. We still had lazy days to spend in the park and drives into Ithaca to the movie theater. We were supposed to go to Cape Cod one last time with her family before packing up for college. We were going to say good-bye. Last Saturday, she had tickets to some indic film premiere in New York—something about a dog that never dies. She'd begged her dad until he agreed to put us up in a hotel and we were supposed to sneak into the after-party and stay out all night. Instead, Saturday morning, her body was found under Hidden Falls.

"Wind Beneath My Wings" comes on over the sound system. Gretchen would be horrified. She used to joke that the only time this song should ever be played was at funerals for middle-aged ladies.

By the time the music ends Mrs. Meyer is sobbing audibly. I join her more quietly, along with most of the room. Dina passes me a tissue and I peer across the aisle at Kirsten, whose arms are around her mom. I take my own mother's hand and squeeze, grateful she doesn't have to be the Mother of the Dead Girl, then hate myself for the thought.

Kirsten trudges to the front and reads an Emily Dickinson poem. Her voice wavers at first, but as she continues her words grow more confident, as if she's challenging grief to trip her up again. So very like her sister. Some of Gretchen's relatives and friends of her parents get up to speak about how beautiful and giving and talented she was. And then there's an open invitation for anyone who loved Gretchen to come forward and say something about her. Everyone in my family turns to look at me.

Panic closes tight around my throat. "I—I can't."

"It would mean a lot to Gretchen's parents," my mother whispers.

"I think you should, Sonia." Uncle Noah's voice is grim. "You might regret it if you don't."

My hands shake, but Dina touches me gently. "You don't have to. Stay here if you're uncomfortable."

I raise my gaze to the front of the room where a small queue of students has formed. Yuji is at the podium, talking about the first time Gretchen handed his ass to him on the tennis court. A slide-show of Gretchen advances in the background. I look at her family. Her mom and Kirsten are facing straight ahead, but her dad has turned to look at me. He puts his arm around Gretchen's mother. Mr. Meyer is so often businesslike and unemotional, but now I plainly see a gloss of tears on his cheeks.

I rise and tread carefully up the aisle. I can't hear what Yuji is saying over the thundering in my head.

The line dwindles too quickly and then it's my turn. I climb behind the podium, wiping my palms on my dress. When I look out at the room, my stomach drops to the floor, and for a split second I wonder again how my own service might have compared. I clear my throat and say the first thing that comes to mind.

"Gretchen and I couldn't have been less alike." I glance up through my curls at a picture of us on the screen, and our contrasting figures trigger a memory. "When we were eight, she was obsessed with *The Parent Trap* and insisted we pretend to be identical twins. She convinced our parents to go along with the charade, pretending to get us mixed up, acting like they couldn't tell us apart." I look at Mrs. Meyer, whose eyes hold a ghost of a smile. A lump rises in my throat and I struggle to find my voice. "I've never been lucky enough to have a sister, but Gretchen was as close as I think I'll ever come—" My voice breaks. I look at Kirsten, but her face is flat, emotionless. Sweat trickles along my hairline.

The room tilts.

My dress is too warm.

I look down at the casket, and now it's open, full of water, and the gray-skinned girl floating inside has a mass of dark curly hair. I open my mouth to scream, but when I blink again, the rose-adorned box is closed.

"I—I'm sorry," I gasp, and a hush falls over the congregation.

Someone has opened the doors at the back of the church, but it's like the fresh air won't reach me. I know I should step away from the podium, move out of sight, but I grip the wood instead, digging my fingers into the sides. I'm afraid I'll fall if I let go.

Fall like Gretchen.

The minister appears at my side and takes over the microphone, thanking everyone for coming to honor Gretchen, and making announcements about the reception to follow the burial. People start shifting in their seats, looking at me, unsure if it's okay to leave. My mother comes up the steps, trying to pry me away from the podium. I want to tell her I just need a minute, but my voice won't work. I stare desperately at the open doors, to the air outside, but it's so far away. And then I notice a figure standing there, looking in to the congregation. My mouth drops open.

Marcus's gaze connects with mine.

A couple of people follow my stare and a low murmur moves through the crowd. Marcus steps out of the shadows and enters the building once he realizes he's been spotted. Kip Peterson rises from a seat not far from him at the back, and I catch a few hostile words shot into the air. Other people get up from their seats, including Sheriff Wood, who I hadn't noticed, and the group around Marcus moves not-so-quietly outside. Mrs. Meyer breaks down, collapsing into her husband's arms. As he attempts to soothe her, his shoulders quiver, and a tear cuts down my cheek. I look up to see Kirsten slipping out the doors. She closes them behind her, but not before I see the reporters swoop in for their reward.

THIRTEEN

"IF YOU'RE NOT FEELING UP to this, we only need to stay a few minutes."

The weight of the week is evident in Dina's voice, but all I can focus on are the huge planters lining the front steps of Gretchen's house. They overflow with pink petunias, and when I close my eyes, I see the two of us darting along the terrace when we were eight, hiding from Kirsten amid the flowers. I draw in a ragged breath. The sun sinks slowly toward the horizon, but every light in the Meyers' house burns bright and warm when we ring the bell. We're greeted by Gretchen's uncle, who directs us inside. A waiter approaches us in the main hall with a tray of hors d'oeuvres and there's an arrangement of delicate-looking entrees and desserts in the dining room. Even in the worst of circumstances, Gretchen's mom knows how to host an event.

I spot Aisha and Haley in a corner, sipping what looks suspiciously like white wine. I pretend not to see them, scanning the room for Kip Peterson while my mother greets Haley's mom and dad. Kip wasn't at the burial after the service, but I'm hoping he shows up here. Whatever happened with Marcus was over by the time I got outside, but I need to talk to Kip, regardless. His infatuation with Gretchen and his account of that night make him suspicious, but I need to ask more questions before deciding for sure if he belongs on my list.

I recognize most of the people in the great room from the service, except I don't see the sheriff or a single deputy. I wonder if that's a conscious effort not to disturb Gretchen's family with their presence, or if something else is keeping them busy. Principal Bova is in the middle of the room talking with the mayor. Gretchen's father is surrounded by businessy-looking men. I already heard the new community center is going to be named in Gretchen's honor. I notice Kevin Fowler standing in a corner with a group of football players, and when I see him, I almost smile. He looks so uncomfortable. If Gretchen were here, she'd laugh out loud.

"Thank you all so much for coming," a cool, familiar voice says over my shoulder.

I turn to see Kirsten in a plain black dress, blond hair spilling down around her shoulders. Her mother is at her side in a dark suit, her fading yellow hair pulled back. A more mature version of her younger daughter.

"Oh. Marcia, I'm so sorry," my mother says, leaning in for a brief, awkward hug. My mom and Gretchen's parents have always gotten along, but they aren't exactly friends. I doubt their worlds would ever have overlapped if it hadn't been for me and Gretchen.

Mrs. Meyer glances at me over my mother's shoulder, her eyes flashing with regret, then guilt. I look down. I didn't think it was possible for my heart to sink lower, but I guess I can't blame her. I spent the week thinking how it could've been me instead of

Gretchen too. She embraces me next, squeezing a little too hard for a little too long, perhaps to make up for the thought.

"Thank you for coming, Sonia, and for what you said today. I know it must've been difficult."

My throat closes up. Even if I knew how to respond, I couldn't speak. I wipe my eyes, careful not to let my burning tears fall on her tailored shoulder.

"The service was beautiful," I manage.

"The music, the flowers, everything was just perfect," adds Dina.

"Kirsten picked out the flowers," Mrs. Meyer says with a tight smile.

Our words sound generic and insincere, but I think it's all any of us can handle. I look at Kirsten, expecting to be met with an icy glare, but she's channeling Gretchen again. Her face is placid, her body language calm and composed.

Several people have gathered around us, waiting to express condolences. My mother and I start to excuse ourselves, but Mrs. Meyer touches my shoulder, looking straight into my face.

"Sonia, she came to me in a dream the other night. I don't think she's really gone."

My eyes widen. Gretchen's mom has always been pragmatic, businesslike. If we skinned our knees when we were little, she would give us a bandage and send us on our way. When Gretchen's cat was hit by a car in fifth grade, she simply said they'd get another. The funeral and reception have been planned to the last detail, like she had some kind of contingency plan for losing one of her daughters. But there's a hint of something strange and desperate in her eyes and I'm not sure it's simply a haze of sedatives.

Kirsten takes her arm. "Mom, the mayor is waiting."

Something snaps back into place in Mrs. Meyer's face and she turns away. Dina calls my mom over to speak with Principal Bova, but I hang back, watching the procession of people offering sympathy and words of comfort. After a minute or two Gretchen's mom has regained her poise and the whole thing seems like a nonincident. Kirsten stands by her side, thanking people for coming in a way that strikes me as so self-possessed, it sends a tingle up my spine. Gretchen always knew the right questions to ask and the right answers to give, while Kirsten mostly improvised . . . badly. It drove Gretchen crazy.

If she could see her sister now.

"I can't look at you here without expecting her to come bounding into the room." Mr. Meyer joins me. His voice is sad, but lacks any hint of bitterness.

I've hardly ever spoken to Gretchen's dad alone. For someone so powerful, he's not a big man, but I find myself tongue-tied whenever he speaks warmly to me.

"It's hard to be here without her," I say to the floor.

"I hope you won't change your plans, Sonia. She wouldn't want you to. She was so proud when you got that scholarship."

I weave my fingers together and nod. Gretchen and her dad were close—closer than she was to her mother. But I've often wondered if either of them truly knew her at all.

An older man approaches with a well-preserved blonde in Chanel. "Carlton, if there's anything Mindy and I can do . . ."

Mr. Meyer gives my arm a reassuring squeeze, and as he walks away I watch, confused, wondering exactly who should have been comforting whom.

A familiar figure catches my eye across the room. Aisha's brother lurks just outside the main group of football players. I dart over, glad for the chance to talk with him alone.

"Hey, Tyrone."

"Sonia." He's wearing a dark suit that looks like it's probably his dad's. The expression on his face makes me think he can't wait to take it off.

"It's good to see you again." I'm still unclear why he's home from college, and though Aisha swore he was holed up in his room all Friday night, there's no way she could be sure. She was still at Brianne's party when I left. "So, how was freshman year?"

He lowers his voice. "Aisha probably told you what happened."

"She . . . didn't," I say, a little afraid to ask.

Tyrone shoves his hands in his pockets, glancing at his parents standing by the dessert table. "It didn't really work out with Notre Dame."

"Oh. No." I open my mouth, not sure if I should ask why or just say I'm sorry. But then Aisha comes up beside me, wrapping me in a quick hug.

"Hey. It was really nice, what you said at the church."

"Thanks." I flush, unable to recall anything but the parts I'd like to forget.

"Can you believe Marcus showed?" Haley whispers. "If he *is* guilty, that took major balls."

Tyrone clears his throat. "I'm heading home. Aisha, you ready to go?"

She shakes her head. "I'll stay for a bit. Derek can walk me back."

Tyrone gives a wary look over his shoulder at Derek, who's

loading up a huge plate of food in the next room. "Text me if you need me to come get you."

She nods. Tyrone looks at me once more, lingers over a framed photograph of Gretchen on the piano, and disappears without another word.

Aisha frowns.

"Is he okay?" I ask.

"Yeah, he's . . . just taking all of this really hard."

The expression on her face is so conflicted, I'm not sure if she means Notre Dame or Gretchen.

Tyrone is one of those guys who wouldn't have gotten over Gretchen even if she hadn't died. They started hooking up last year when he was a senior, but never progressed to actual dating. Gretchen liked her boys a little dangerous—guys her parents wouldn't approve of. Tyrone didn't exactly fit the bill. Instead, they snuck in and out of each other's bedroom windows, or occasionally the back of her car, until right after he graduated, when she called the whole thing off. She cited his impending departure for college, but Tyrone was crushed when she immediately hooked up with Kevin.

That was almost a year ago, and I still can't picture Tyrone ever hurting Gretchen, let alone sending me threats . . . but he does seem unsettled. I start to ask Aisha to clarify, but a waiter approaches us with a tray of small vegetable pastries, and as soon as he leaves, we're joined by some kids from school who all want to talk about Marcus.

"Did you hear he carved Gretchen's name into his arm?"

"Do you think he showed up out of guilt?"

"I bet he got off on it."

"Shut up, he didn't do it." Once again, Yuji is the lone voice of dissent. Or maybe just the only one brave enough to speak up.

Haley glares at him. "You sound pretty sure of that. How do we know it wasn't *you?*"

Yuji just gives her one of his usual wounded expressions, though I hesitate at her words. Haley wasn't happy with Gretchen after their breakup, but she was furious with Yuji. I think it took him a while to piece together that rescheduling their dates and letting Gretchen fill up his weekends with tennis practice was the problem, but it's clear he's never gotten over it. I suppose either one of them could've held a grudge against Gretchen, but anything more than that seems doubtful. I can't come up with a great reason it *couldn't* have been Yuji in the woods that night, but I know for sure Haley was home, grounded.

The longer I look at the people around me, the more everyone seems like a potential suspect. My mind returns to the photo in my locker, the jagged lines where my face should have been. I clench my jaw. If I can figure out who's after *me*, maybe I can tie them back to Gretchen. But I can't do anything until I narrow the pool. I hide my trembling hands behind my back and raise my voice enough for the whole group to hear.

"Hey guys, did any of you happen to leave a picture of Gretchen and me in my locker? I found one the other day and wanted to say thanks."

I watch every face to see how, or if, they react. I don't expect a confession, or even overt guilt, but I'm hoping for *some* clue one of them knows about it.

Aisha looks thoughtful. "I didn't, but I have one of you guys on the class trip if you want it."

No one else even blinks.

"Thanks," I mumble. "That'd be great."

I excuse myself to the restroom, but head for the staircase instead. I've attended more of Mrs. Meyer's fancy parties than I can count. Enough to be sure no one will notice if I slip away for a few minutes to clear my head. If this was another fund-raiser or political dinner, Gretchen and I would have already retreated to her room, where she'd recount salacious facts about each of the VIPs while I laughed. I hold my breath on the polished steps, feeling a little like I'm trespassing without her, but as I reach the landing my feet regain purpose. There might be something useful in Gretchen's room. Some clue the sheriff's office missed that I could connect to the intruder—maybe even the person threatening me. All I need is a few minutes to look.

The second-floor walls are lined with family portraits; the kind where everyone sits on the beach wearing khakis and a plain white shirt. Mr. Meyer always insisted they take a picture on Cape Cod at the end of summer. I'm even in the last one—the Honorary Meyer.

Downstairs, the conversation carries on in a dour murmur, but up here the air is still. I could almost breathe normally if my heart weren't pounding so hard. When I reach Gretchen's bedroom door, it's closed. I hesitate with my hand over the knob, trying to convince myself she's in there, lounging on her bed reading fashion blogs. I'll walk in and sprawl next to her, complaining about what a downer the whole day has been and that it's all her fault.

The door swings open.

Kirsten stands in the doorway looking like a girl from a

Hitchcock film. She's changed into a stylish gray skirt suit I recognize as Gretchen's and she's swept her blond hair up away from her face. Both of us step back, but she's the first to recover.

"Sonia—" She blocks the door. "The reception's downstairs."

I look past her into Gretchen's bedroom, wondering what exactly she was up to. She used to be forbidden from even going in. The pink rug and white canopy bed look just as they always have. There are a couple of socks on the floor by the desk. The door to the balcony is open, as if Gretchen might step back in any minute. I think of what Mrs. Meyer said and I get a chill.

"I . . . I'm sorry . . ." I say, realizing I have no legitimate excuse to be here anymore.

A line forms between her eyebrows and I brace myself for another bitter tirade, but she leans against the doorframe. "I'm the one who should apologize. The other day was . . . rough. That was the first time my mom really lost it, and the first time I guess I realized Gretchen wasn't coming back." She pauses. "It was no excuse, though. I shouldn't have said . . . what I said."

I open my mouth, unsure how to respond.

She steps into the hall, pulling Gretchen's door firmly closed behind her. "I can't imagine how *you* must be feeling."

The air is thick. For a split second, I imagine her scratching out my face, slipping the photo into my locker. But that's ridiculous. She hasn't even been in school. I step back, guessing we both just want out of here, but then she reaches out and touches the fabric of my dress.

"I don't think I've seen this before."

My cheeks flush. I wonder if I should have worn something of

Gretchen's after all, but when I tried a few things earlier, they still seemed wrong. "I borrowed it from Dina."

I study her more closely, the gray suit a little too loose in the hips, a tiny bit too flat in the chest. The way she swept her hair back is really pretty, but a bunch of pins are showing. She looks like a sad little girl playing dress-up in her dead sister's clothes.

"Are you doing okay, Kirsten?"

She gives me a small smile, then surprises me by slipping her arm through mine, guiding me down the hall, away from Gretchen's room. "We should probably get back downstairs."

I turn to face her on the landing. "I mean it. I'm sorry we left you at the party. I was the DD, I never should've let that happen."

"You were just doing what you were told." She shrugs. "Like always."

I wince at the accusation, wishing it wasn't true. "It was wrong—anything could've happened to you."

Her blue eyes darken. "Maybe it should have."

"No." My face goes hot. I grab her hand, clutching it as if she *was* Gretchen. "I just keep thinking that if things had been different, the whole night might've gone another way."

Kirsten parts her lips, her voice barely a whisper. "But then it might've been you instead."

FOURTEEN

I'M IN THE TREES, SURROUNDED *by a darkness so thick it blankets the air like wool. The only sound is my breath being carried in, then out of my lungs.*

And the rush of water.

I pick up my pace, walking faster, though I don't seem to actually be moving. Everything just gets blacker. Footsteps come up behind me, crunching into the earth. I break into a run, but I'm no longer touching the ground. The trees close in like predators, first brushing me with their leaves, then tearing into my flesh and clothes with branches of blades.

I crash suddenly to the earth, and now I'm pinned by the weight of my body, paralyzed beneath the brush. I can't close my eyes, let alone blink. All I can do is listen for something.

Coming for me.

I bolt upright in my bed.

By the time I'm calm enough to lie back down, I've scrawled six names on a notepad: Marcus, Kevin, Tyrone, Reva, Kip, and Kirsten.

FIFTEEN

". . . AND IN LOCAL NEWS, a service for seventeen-year-old Gretchen Meyer, daughter of TechCorp mogul Carlton Meyer, was interrupted Friday in Hidden Falls when the girl's ex-boyfriend, eighteen-year-old Marcus Perez, appeared unexpectedly at Grace Community Church."

The camera cuts away from the sober-looking anchor to a shot of Marcus struggling with deputies outside the service until Kirsten approaches the sheriff, shaking her head. I watch, confused. The next shot shows Marcus walking to his own car. Maybe there was something to the rumor of Marcus and Kirsten hooking up. I can't think why else she would get involved.

"Members of the congregation, including sheriff's deputies, assisted in removing Perez without incident. The teen was briefly considered a person of interest in Gretchen Meyer's death, but official charges were never filed. It is unclear what his intent was in disrupting the service."

The screen goes blue and the number for Crime Stoppers appears beside Gretchen's picture.

"There is a reward of up to fifty thousand dollars for any information leading to an arrest in the case."

I switch the channel to a morning show doing a spot on viral pet videos. Conversations slowly resume around the diner, but the tension never completely dissipates. If I don't leave for school soon, I'm not going to make homeroom, but Dina's having car trouble and asked me to cover till she gets in. All I want is to start this week with some sense of normalcy.

My mom comes downstairs, tying her apron, as I hurry back to the kitchen.

"Dina called. Sounds like she'll be stuck at Wilson's Garage all morning."

I stop in my tracks. "But she was going to let me take her car to school when she got in."

"Aunt Elena will give you a lift as soon as she drops Felicia off."

I nearly crumple my order. "But the elementary school doesn't even start till nine."

"When I was in school I would've been glad to miss a class."

I'm in no mood to discuss her life as a teenager versus mine. I take off my apron. "I'll walk."

"You will not."

I grit my teeth. "It's five blocks, Mom. The streets are crawling with cops."

"It isn't safe. I'll write you a note." She grabs some clean coffee mugs and heads for the door. "Missing one class might even be good for you."

I storm after her, but when I round the corner, Deputies Rashid and Robson are climbing out of their booth, adjusting their gear.

"You guys taking off? Food's almost ready."

Shelly sighs, turning down the chatter on her radio. "It's going to be one of those mornings. Can you box it up and set it aside for us?"

"Sure, I'll tell my mom," I say, even though she's right behind me. "I'm leaving for school."

Shelly raises one eyebrow and looks over my shoulder. "You need a lift, Sonia? Amir and I are heading past the school anyway."

I open my mouth, appalled by the idea, but my mother's fingers rest heavily on my shoulder.

"That would be wonderful; Dina's car is in the shop. Are you sure it's not an urgent call?"

Amir leaves some cash on the table and digs out his keys. "Just another tip someone called in. We've had a bunch of duds, but the sheriff wants us to follow up."

I look back and forth between them, but they're not giving anything else up, so I decide to dig. "Is it about the guy who broke into Gretchen's room?"

My mother gasps.

Amir's face goes serious. "Where'd you hear about that?"

I hesitate. "The entire school was talking about it. Is it supposed to be a secret?"

He and Shelly exchange a look. Amir grunts and heads out to the parking lot.

"It isn't a secret," Shelly says. "We're just trying to protect the Meyers as much as possible."

My mom wrings her hands. "When did this happen? Are we not safe in our own homes?"

"It's okay, Marlene." Shelly and Dina went to high school together and she used to babysit me before she went to the police academy. But right now she switches to full-on deputy mode. "The break-in occurred the night of Gretchen's death, after Sonia was attacked, but before Gretchen was officially reported missing. We have reason to suspect it was somehow connected, at the very least to Gretchen's missing car, but there are no other reports of intruders in the area."

My mom looks at me with wide frightened-animal eyes.

"I know it's upsetting, but I promise Sonia will be safe and sound at school," Shelly says.

I grab my bag from under the counter. At this point I'm willing to endure the discomfort of showing up in a cop car just to have space away from my mother.

Shelly calls over her shoulder. "Tell Dina I know a garage in Jamesville if Wilson's tries to rip her off."

There are few places I can think of as claustrophobic as the backseat of a patrol car. Once you're inside, someone else has to physically let you out, and they actually call the divider between the front and back seats a "cage." I've ridden in the back of Sheriff Wood's unmarked Explorer a few times, but when Shelly sets me free in front of the school, my palms are dotted with marks where what's left of my fingernails dug into my skin.

"Hey, Shelly," I ask before she can climb back in behind the wheel. "Tell me what's really going on?"

"It's nothing you should worry about," she says.

I roll my eyes. "Does the sheriff make you guys practice saying that?"

She cracks a small smile, but it quickly fades.

"There's something else, isn't there?" I ask, nervous that she won't meet my eyes. This could be my only chance to get a real hint at what's going on. "Come on, I feel helpless when you guys won't

123

just say what's happening."

She exhales, glancing nervously to where Amir waits in the car. "You'll probably hear about it at school anyway. Someone trashed the memorial last night in the woods."

My throat closes till I can barely breathe. "Gretchen's memorial?"

"It was probably just some asshole kids. They threw all the flowers and stuff into the falls." She looks away like there's something she doesn't want to say.

"What else, Shelly? I promise I won't breathe a word . . . I just need to know."

She turns back to me, her face grim. "Look, I don't agree with the sheriff keeping you in the dark, that's the only reason I'm telling you. There was some graffiti left behind on the rocks."

My voice barely comes out a whisper. "What did it say?"

"It said . . . *One bitch down.*"

SIXTEEN

VKIP USUALLY SPENDS HIS LUNCH in the library. I ran into him there once when I was doing a project for extra credit. I think he prefers reading comics alone in a study carrel over the pizza-scented crowd. I'm anxious to feel him out about the photo in my locker, but I tiptoe into the blue-carpeted space holding my breath. Shelly assured me there was nothing to be afraid of in the school, but the tremors I thought I'd left at the funeral are back. Ms. Jensen, the school librarian, isn't at her post behind the desk. I wander around the edge of the stacks by the windows, but even the couch and chairs in the corner are vacant. Guess no one wanted to miss the post-funeral lunch gossip. I shift my backpack on my shoulder and take a shortcut through nonfiction, hoping I can join my friends before I've missed any information about the memorial . . . or who might've been sick enough to destroy it.

I'm halfway down the row when a guy clears his throat on the other side of the shelf. I startle, peering around a copy of *The Poisoner's Handbook*.

"So, did I miss anything at the reception?" Marcus asks.

After his stunt at the funeral he's lucky there are a few hundred books and a metal shelf between us. If he was reachable, I might seriously do some damage.

"Just everyone in town deciding you look guiltier than ever," I say.

His jaw tightens. "It seemed like a nice service, too bad I had to leave."

"And I have to get to lunch."

I head for the end of the row, but he beats me there, blocking my way in paint-splattered jeans and a dark T-shirt. I can't help wincing at the fading bruise under his eye, casting a purple shadow across his otherwise-handsome face.

"Why did you come to the church?" I hiss.

"I was paying my respects." He looks at the floor. "Put yourself in my shoes—could you have stayed away?"

Something inside me weakens. I think of his expression at the service, how intense, how solemn he looked the moment before I gave him away. But then I remember Gretchen's mother collapsing, her powerful father at a total loss, and my anger resurges.

"Gretchen's family deserved to say good-bye in peace."

"And I deserve not to go to jail." He speaks through his teeth, voice so low I can barely hear. "Now, are you going to fill me in on what I missed?"

He leans closer, resting one hand on a nearby shelf. His gaze burns so hot I have to step back to clear my head. The door to the hall is open and it's tempting to just scream—bring every administrator in the building running. But I can't make myself do it.

"Why on earth would I want to help you again?"

He hesitates. "I thought we agreed to put the past behind us."

"Because why all of a sudden?" My body quivers, upset by how natural hating him feels in this moment. "What exactly has changed that would make me set all of your bullshit aside?"

He studies me carefully. "Because you cared about Gretchen."

"*You* seem to care more about getting blamed for her murder than the fact that she's dead."

"Come on, Sonia—"

"I guess sharing air with me is more tolerable than a prison cell, there's that."

He straightens. And if I didn't know better, I'd swear I saw hurt flash over his face. "Look, none of that— It wasn't about you," he says.

"Oh, really?"

He rakes a hand through his hair. "Please, Sonia, that isn't how I really feel."

I stop, caught off guard by his tone. "What?"

"Just what I said." He stares at his feet. "That had more to do with Gretchen than it did with you, and . . . I'm sorry, okay?"

I blink, trying to decide if I heard him correctly. Because if I did, does that mean he's been *pretending* to hate me for the past six months? And if so, why? He raises his head and the look in his eyes sets my skin on fire. "I don't understand."

He opens his mouth like he's searching for the right words and I try not to think about the blood rushing to my face because I'm scared of what he might or might not say. I step back, grazing a shelf with my elbow, and a book falls to the floor with a sound like a gunshot.

We both jump.

Marcus steps away and exhales. "Look, what happened at the reception?" he says hastily. "Can we just talk about that?"

I cross my arms over my chest, confused and disappointed. "Nothing happened. Everyone in town was there. There were people I didn't recognize, but no one who screamed *killer* more than you, as disappointing as that was."

His eyes are flat.

"I didn't get any leads on the photo," I say. "I was *hoping* to talk to Kip, but he didn't show, thanks to you."

Marcus scowls. "I don't know what that guy's problem is."

"He cared about her." I look away. "And apparently he saw her before she died that night."

"I wouldn't be surprised if he killed her himself."

"Easy for you to say."

"Who else was there?"

"Haley, Aisha, Kevin, Yuji . . . Tyrone, who came home from Notre Dame the day Gretchen died." I decide to leave it at that. "And Kirsten, of course. She was acting kind of strange."

Marcus raises his eyebrows. "How so?"

"She dressed up in Gretchen's clothes. It seemed odd at first, but Kirsten was always trying to be like her . . ." My voice trails off as I recall her coming out of Gretchen's room. Had she been holding something in her hand?

Marcus shifts uncomfortably and I file the thought away for later. She might have taken anything. She had on a whole outfit that wasn't hers.

"What did she say to you after the service?" I ask.

"What?"

"I saw it on the news. She came out of the church and said some-thing. Then you left."

"Oh . . . she just said something about peace and respecting Gretchen's memory."

"That's it?"

"Yeah," he says quickly. "And then I left."

I tilt my head because he refuses to look at me, but before I can open my mouth a door slams and Ms. Jensen shatters the silence, whistling tunelessly.

Marcus turns away so fast I have to grab his arm to keep him from dashing into the open. He's stronger, more toned than I expected, but he stops.

"Thought you didn't want to be seen with me." He looks point-edly at my hand.

I let go. He's right. I don't want to be caught alone with him again.

"I want to see your list," I whisper. "Who could have done it, what motive they had . . ."

He gives a tight nod. "Can you come to Evil Bean tomorrow? I want to see yours too."

The whistling moves closer and my pulse jumps. I step back. "Okay."

"I'll wait a minute before I leave." He gestures to the door, but steps toward me like he doesn't want to be left behind. "Just—just watch your back, okay?"

I hesitate, still doubtful I should trust him, but what he said about Gretchen and his feelings lingers and I can't help wondering what else he was going to say.

I want to believe him, despite myself.

I grab a book off a shelf and shuffle as noisily as I can toward the desk. The librarian's auburn head snaps up. A sad look crosses her face when she sees me, but she's polite and doesn't say much as she helps me check out. I exit the library, looking over my shoulder once. Marcus watches patiently from the stacks.

SEVENTEEN

YOU CAN FIND ALMOST ANYTHING online. A used couch.
Lost pets. The love of your life.

Potential murderers are a little harder to come by.

Tricky, but not impossible—Gretchen loved to say that. But she
was used to getting what she wanted.

I was supposed to be downstairs five minutes ago, but I scroll
through my social media feeds with a pencil between my teeth.
Since Kirsten headed me off before I could get inside Gretchen's
room at the reception, I've been looking for clues everywhere else I
can think of. Most of my classmates' posts have given way to gossip
and general weirdness. "One bitch down" seems to be the current
trending topic, complete with pictures of the vandalized memorial.
I study them briefly, but the scrawled words and mess of ruined
flowers make my stomach sick.

Sasha Fadley recorded herself singing a song dedicated to
Gretchen, which was strange because the song didn't seem to have
anything to do with Gretchen at all. Reva Stone shared a link about
waterfalls drying up with climate change. Kevin Fowler changed
his profile picture to one of himself with Gretchen in a bikini last

spring, which led to a heated debate with Tyrone over when exactly they dated.

Gretchen had immortalized almost all of them in one way or another on her SD card. It contains photos of Sasha with a handful of other classmates smoking bongs or saluting the camera with their beers. There's a short video of Kevin keying Principal Bova's car—a senior prank that still remains "unsolved." There's even footage of Brianne sneaking answers on a test. Some people clearly didn't know they were being recorded, but I pay attention to the names of those who did, making notes about who was at the party and who might've been in the woods.

Kirsten posted a picture of her and Gretchen from the family photo shoot on the beach. They had been posed in a hug, which wasn't a natural position for the two of them, but my eyes sting when I see it. I scroll past quickly.

Marcus doesn't have a profile that I can find, which disappoints me more than I expect. He's in a few of Yuji's photos, broad-shouldered and tan on a fishing trip, or looking oddly mysterious peering out from under his hoodie in the woods. It's strange seeing him out of the context of school or Gretchen. His mouth twists in a cute way when he smiles. His eyes have a playful gleam I'm not sure I've ever seen in person.

There must be two hundred photos from the party scattered on people's timelines. Most contain at least glimpses of Gretchen, like a ghost in the feeds, but when I look at them as a group it becomes more of a complete scene. Kirsten isn't in any shots, but she disappeared soon after we got there. There are a few people I don't recognize, but no one who stands out.

I sit back in my chair, rubbing the bridge of my nose. Anyone could have taken that picture. Whoever put it in my locker might not have even been *at* the party. They could have easily pulled it off someone else's page.

I click halfheartedly through another couple of albums—then stop.

I've never felt dread reach all the way to my fingertips, but there's no mistake.

It's the photo.

I pull the scratched-out copy from between the pages of my chemistry book for comparison, but I know without even looking that it's the exact same shot. Gretchen laughing, her arms around my neck. My hand is on her arm, bracelet dangling on my wrist. With my face intact, it's clear I'm not half as amused as she is, which I think was the point. Gretchen loved to push my buttons and knew better than anyone I wasn't into hugs. My gaze is trained on the ceiling, frozen in something like annoyance or maybe just impatience while she subjects me to her embrace. I hold my breath, staring at this moment, one of the last Gretchen and I ever shared. We look so . . . typical. A sad smile brushes over my lips.

One bitch down.

My eyes go to the name of the person who posted the picture and my face falls.

Kip Peterson's profile picture is one of the characters from Ulta-Shock. A rugged guy wielding a shotgun with a busty redhead pulled close to his chest. Brianne has a sweet gaming setup in her basement and I found him there the other night once Gretchen got bored and went off to look for Kirsten. He was still there when she stormed downstairs and said we were leaving.

I look at the photo on the screen again. There are eighty-nine likes and eleven comments. Anyone could have found this and printed it. But when I examine the paper version more closely, I notice it's glossy and thick—clearly not home-printer quality. It was either printed in a store or done on professional equipment. I pause. Kip may sometimes abuse his role as yearbook photographer to take boob shots, but he takes the hobby seriously enough that he's had photos in the local paper and won several awards. This picture of Gretchen and me is nothing special, though. It's dark, grainy, and unimaginative, like a snapshot taken on someone's phone.

I pick up the defaced photo again and frown. Marcus is probably right; I should take it to Sheriff Wood.

There's a knock at my door and I quickly shove the snapshot back inside my chemistry book. My mother leans against the frame, looking like she's been on her feet at least two hours longer than she should've been. "Are you feeling okay, sweetie? Do you need me to cover your shift?"

"No, sorry—I was just finishing some homework." I close the lid of my laptop. "You okay?"

"Just tired. Shelly told Dina about a garage that'll give her a better deal than Wilson's. I started early to cover her shift."

"Mom, you should've told me, I could've done this later."

She holds up her hand. "If going away to college is really what you want, then you definitely need that scholarship now."

I grimace. She might be blunt, but she has a point. Even if I'd accepted the Meyers' offer to send me to Stanford, I could never ask them to follow through on it now. I just can't help wondering if I *had* accepted, if Gretchen would somehow still be alive.

"I saw the flowers you sent to Gretchen's family." My mother's tone lightens. "It was sweet of you to send them from all of us."

I look away, toeing the edge of my rug. "It wasn't a big deal."

She steps back like maybe she's headed for bed, but then she lingers in the door. "If you're having trouble sleeping, Sonia, we could get you some meds."

I raise my head, surprised. "How did you know that?"

"You didn't used to cry out at night," she says quietly. "And I've heard you moving around at odd hours. Dr. White came in for lunch today and assured me losing sleep, feeling guilty . . . it's normal under the circumstances."

I close my eyes and bite my tongue. I was hoping she hadn't noticed.

"It just sort of came up," she continues. "He asked about you, and . . . well, I guess he probably should've charged *me* for the meal." She clears her throat. "But he assured me it's all part of the grieving process."

"Thanks, Mom. I guess I can't help feeling guilty . . ." My voice fades to a whisper, but when she touches my shoulder, I stand abruptly and start to change clothes. "Listen, if you're getting another headache, you should go lie down. I'll be out in just a sec."

She nods, hesitating like she wants to say something more, but I pretend not to notice. I don't want to know what else she's been discussing with the local shrink.

After I hear her door close, I reopen my notebook and underline *Kip Peterson* at the bottom of the page. The initial list of suspects I came up with looked more like a roster of our entire student body, though I've managed to cross a bunch of names off after doing a little research into where people were and when. But as soon as I saw Kip's name next to that picture, a chill settled under my skin. Pulling on my Penn hoodie didn't make it go away.

I'm halfway down the hall when I hesitate and turn back. I reopen my chemistry book and carry the photo to the back of my closet. I'm an extra minute late after digging around for my tin box. I know hiding it is irrational and will do nothing to keep me safe, but my chill fades to an endurable shiver knowing it's tucked out of sight.

EIGHTEEN

WHEN MY BOOTS HIT THE kitchen floor, we're already busy, and I don't stop for breath for at least an hour. Sometime after seven, the bells above the door jingle and I look over my shoulder to see Kip Peterson seating himself in my section. My stomach knots. Here's my chance to talk to him, but after seeing the photo on his feed, I'm not sure I want the answers anymore. I look at Dina across the room. I didn't mention the fistfight at school last week or she'd probably hustle him right back out the door. The soreness in my ribs was just becoming tolerable before he slammed into me.

I work my way over to him, refilling glasses and dropping off checks while I picture him scratching my face out. Before I know it, my thoughts put us both in the woods—him chasing me in the darkness before moving on to Gretchen. Or maybe not—maybe he just came along too late to save anyone. I stop, close my eyes, and lean against the counter. Kip and I struck up a sort of friendship back in sixth grade, the one year Gretchen and I ended up in different classes. He was awkward back then—well, more awkward. He's always been smaller than other guys and back then he had a hefty set of braces, but we share an affinity for comics and video games that Gretchen never cared for. He could have tried to use me to get close to her, but he never did, despite her refusal to acknowledge his existence.

How could it be him?

"Sonia." He waves me over.

I grip my stubby pencil. "Kip, how's your hand?"

He makes a show of shaking it out like it hurts, then gives me a bashful smile. "Guess I kind of lost it the other day. That was embarrassing."

"You were upset—everyone's upset."

"I came by to say sorry. I didn't mean for you to get dragged into that."

I shrug. "I'm not the one you punched."

He stiffens. "I'm not apologizing to him."

I look around the slowing diner. "Well, luckily, he's not here."

His expression shifts and for a second he looks the way he did in Brianne's basement. Like the only thing that matters is who's going to be Player 1 and Player 2. But then a shadow passes over his face, reminding me this isn't a game.

"Why *did* you get in my way?" he asks.

I hesitate, studying his stiff posture, the angry set of his jaw. "Do you really think he did it? How can you be sure?"

Kip picks at a chip in the white tabletop. "He's an artist, right? You ever see his work?"

This makes me pause. Everyone's seen Marcus's paintings. The art teacher, Ms. Pilar, displays them every chance she gets. He sells them in a local gallery. I think Principal Bova even has one in her office. Each of them is beautiful, but none have come close to the first one I saw. I was getting some watercolors from the supply room in art class sophomore year and while I was in there I noticed an easel in the corner, positioned to face the wall. I still remember the way my breath caught when I peered around the edge. I can't even really describe what I saw—it's more the feeling I remember. Like I'd just seen something I didn't even know I was looking for. There was a figure, but it was abstract, the colors bright and bold. The brushstrokes were visible, but so light they looked like they might've been breathed onto the canvas. I guess I'd already had a little crush on him before that, but Marcus's name at the bottom surprised me almost as much as the work itself. I didn't understand how anyone so sullen could create something so moving.

"Once," I say hastily. "I mean, yeah, of course."

"Yeah, well, I saw him doodling in a notebook in trig a few months back. He was drawing Gretchen—it was clearly her—but the way she looked in the picture . . ." He clenches his jaw. "He turned her into this thing, with teeth and claws. There were wounds dripping blood and her expression . . . the whole thing was just violent. Like he wanted her to die."

My skin goes cold. I've never seen anything of Marcus's that looked like that. But it disturbs me that I have no trouble picturing what Kip's describing.

The bells jingle again and Haley walks in with Yuji. They're not holding hands or even standing that close, but I raise my eyebrows because the two of them together is something I never thought I'd see again. They were inseparable freshman and sophomore years. Like, so much no one else could stand to be around them. I'm ninety-nine percent sure Gretchen and Yuji were never interested in each other except as decent opponents on the tennis court, but the time they spent together drove Haley nuts and Gretchen knew it. When Haley finally told him she was ready to try out being single, it hit him pretty hard. The poor guy wandered around looking wounded long after tennis season ended.

Haley meets my gaze and gives me a nervous wave. Dina peeks her head out of the kitchen, covered in flour. When she sees Haley, she smiles at me, looking relieved, and disappears again.

"Hold that thought, Kip, I'll be right back." I grab a couple of menus and lead Haley and Yuji to a table by the windows. "Hey, guys . . . what's new?"

Haley flushes, sweeping her hair to one side, but Yuji glances behind me with a frown. "Didn't you mix it up with Kip and Marcus the other day?"

"I did." I search for my pencil, pretending not to notice the hostile glare he directs at Kip. "You guys going to split a chocolate milk shake?"

Yuji leans forward with a solemn expression. "Good for you."

I tilt my head, unsure what to say. Haley presses her lips together.

"Look, what happened to Gretchen . . . it was horrible," he says. "But Marcus is a good guy. He would never have hurt her."

Haley's eyes widen. She opens her mouth and I prepare for the diatribe regarding Marcus's guilt to launch off her tongue, but instead she folds her hands in front of her. Marcus is the closest friend Yuji has in Hidden Falls.

"For someone who's supposed to be innocent, he's sure been acting weird," I say.

Yuji shakes his head. "I'd be freaking out too if I were him."

"Then I guess it's good he has a solid alibi," I mutter.

He frowns. "That doesn't even matter. Gretchen had—"

"I thought we weren't going to talk about her," Haley says.

Yuji's gaze snaps back to her, the tips of his ears going red.

Haley picks up her purse. "But if you want to continue, I can go—"

"We're not." He grabs her hand, freezes like he's gone too far, but she puts her purse down and he relaxes.

Haley looks at me with a thin smile. "One chocolate milk shake, two straws."

I nod, relieved to step out of their crosshairs, though I wonder briefly just how much Haley blamed Gretchen for their breakup. She's one of the few people not featured on the SD card.

I look at Kip, but he's busy, hunched over something in front of him. I make my way back to the kitchen, stopping to bus an empty table and take an order from a trucker. I bring Yuji and Haley their milk shake—with whipped cream and two cherries—and run back to the kitchen for the BLT Kip will undoubtedly order. His arms rest on the table when I come out, and I notice he's holding my little nub of pencil in one hand and a small pocketknife in the other.

"What's that for?" I ask.

He turns the knife over, examining it like he really hadn't thought about it. "Sometimes I use it for photography, but today it's a pencil sharpener." He hands my newly sharp pencil back to me and sweeps the shavings onto a napkin. "You dropped that; it was looking pretty dull."

I peer closely as he wipes the blade, imagining it scratching out a face in a photograph. I draw back, goose bumps rising on my arms.

But the picture of Gretchen and me was grainy and amateurish, clearly not taken by someone who knew what they were doing.

Unless it was supposed to look that way.

I set the BLT on the table before my arm can give way and drop it.

"Hey, thanks, how'd you know what I wanted?" Kip asks.

I force a smile, hoping he doesn't notice I've clasped my hands so tightly, I snapped my pencil. "Psychic, I guess."

He picks up a french fry and gives me a wistful grin. "You should use those powers to find the killer."

I fold my arms and stare at the floor. "Did the cops really question you the other day?"

He hesitates. "Who told you that?"

"I heard a rumor at school."

He pushes the food aside and gnaws on his lip. "I talked with Sheriff Wood. But he just wanted to know what I saw."

What if you saw something that night and you don't even realize it?

I tilt my head. "After the party?"

He nods. "I was walking my bike home with a flat through the woods. I saw Gretchen sitting on the rocks by the top of the falls."

My heart picks up as I try to envision this as he saw it. "She was alone?"

"Yeah. She was just kind of sitting there, looking sad." The corners of his mouth pull down. "I wanted to say something but, I don't know, I didn't want to bother her."

I shake my head, my jaw trembling.

Glasses and plates clink at a nearby table. A news report drones softly from the TV mounted in the corner. There's a group of old ladies a few tables away arguing about politics. And suddenly the diner lights are so bright, they wash everything out in a fluorescent haze. I struggle to focus on Kip's face.

"Sonia?"

"Yeah?" I wipe my cheek.

He screws up his mouth. "Do you think she would've given me a chance . . . eventually?"

I exhale. I always used to think Kip deserved a chance. He's a guy who would rather play video games than drink beer at a party. He never cuts class, always gets As, and wouldn't think of crossing the street without a walk signal. Not exactly Gretchen's type. I couldn't bring myself to tell Kip she'd never date him while she was alive, and I'm not going to say it now.

"What—exactly what time did you see her?" I ask.

"Huh?"

"I'm just trying to understand what happened, or how . . ."

Kip lowers his head, but when he looks up, his eyes are clear, confident. "It was right around eleven thirty."

I tense, my brain calculating when I left Gretchen, when her parents discovered the intruder, and when Marcus was supposedly "walking" in the woods.

"Are you sure?"

"I was already half an hour past my curfew—I remember that," he says, looking shamefaced. "I wish I'd said something to her. Maybe if I had . . ."

Haley catches my attention, waving good-bye as she and Yuji exit the booth across the aisle.

I force myself to swallow. Kip's story sounds reasonable, but it also places him in the woods with Gretchen without an alibi right before they think she died. I wonder what the sheriff makes of that. "Thanks, Kip."

"Does it even matter?" he continues. "I told you, Marcus Perez wanted her dead."

This makes me pause. "You really think? Because of one drawing?"

"Did you see the graffiti?" Kip balls his hands into fists. "It was done with a paintbrush."

I open my mouth, but there's an argument over my shoulder, and before I can turn to see what's going on, Yuji's at my side. "Hey, man, just back off Marcus. Let the cops do their jobs."

Haley comes over and rests one hand on his shoulder. "Um, we were just taking off. Don't want to be out after curfew."

Kip looks up, eyes flat. "I wouldn't be too worried . . . just watch out for artists in the woods."

Yuji doesn't even blink. "Look, dude, for all anyone knows, *you* might've killed Gretchen. So why don't you back the fuck off."

Kip starts clambering out of the booth and Yuji steps forward. I flash back to the hall at school and though my ribs protest, I grab a cold pot of coffee off the next table and thrust it between them. "Take it outside, guys."

"C'mon, this isn't worth it." Haley hurries to take Yuji's arm and steers him toward the door. I shoot her a grateful look and she mouths *talk tomorrow.*

Kip sinks back into the booth, picks up his knife, and tucks it away in his pocket.

"Like I said, everyone's upset." I set the coffeepot down so it won't be obvious how much I'm shaking. "Look, Kip, there's this photo you posted of Gretchen and me at the party . . ."

He scratches his head. "Oh, that . . . wish I'd taken one myself."

"You mean it wasn't yours?" I say a little too eagerly.

"Give me a little credit." His nostrils flare. "Someone must've grabbed my camera. It was loaded with terrible shots the next day. But after I heard what happened, I saved that one."

"Did you print a copy?" My voice quavers.

"No, but I can if you'd like me to."

I shake my head.

"I've barely slept a night since." He sighs. "I just keep wondering if I could've done something. If there's something I missed."

I turn away and whisper, "Me too."

NINETEEN

"IT'S NOT THAT GRETCHEN DYING suddenly fixed everything." Haley turns red and tugs at her hair. She's abandoned her usual ponytail to let her brown hair hang straight today, but she keeps fiddling with it like she's desperate to get it out of her face. "God, that sounded awful. I just mean we've both been thinking about getting back together for a while."

"No, I think it's great," I say.

"Totally, you guys should never have broken up," adds Aisha.

Haley's shoulders relax, her face returning to its normal color. She waves to Yuji in the pizza line across the cafeteria. "I was a little worried about what people would say, under the circumstances."

Aisha and I exchange a look, but then my phone vibrates in my pocket. I hesitate, turning to one side before looking at the screen.

Still on for after school?

I lift my head and scan the room.

Marcus sits with his hood up in a corner by himself. He looks down when I glance over and doesn't raise his head again. I narrow my eyes. Derek and Yuji just sat down and Haley and Aisha are busy talking about prom, of all things.

My fingers hover over the screen, trying to figure out how, or *if,* I should answer.

"Hey. Is anyone sitting here?"

I almost drop my phone. Kirsten stands next to me, holding a brown paper lunch bag. Her voice sounds so much like Gretchen's, it's a minute before I'm breathing normally again. The conversation stalls as the rest of the table notices her, but I reach for my backpack, which is sitting in an empty chair. I slide it to the floor and pull the seat out for her.

"Not at all. Come sit with us."

"Thanks." She looks over her shoulder and sinks into the seat. "I just need a change of scenery. You don't mind, do you?"

I follow her gaze and recognize a couple of her friends at a table of juniors.

"Of course not. Is everything okay?"

She sighs. "It's fine. I'm just kind of tired of it, you know? No one will have a normal conversation with me. They're too busy asking how I'm doing or they're worried about saying the wrong thing."

Aisha looks at her lap when Kirsten says this. Haley leans into Yuji. After our last couple of meetings I'm not sure why Kirsten would choose my company, but she's acting more like the timid girl I'm familiar with. There's a clear tremor in her voice and she hardly looks up.

I touch her arm. "I've been getting that too. Especially at home."

"Oh, my parents are the worst." Kirsten tips her head toward the ceiling. "They won't stop hovering and asking if I want to go to therapy."

"Don't worry, I've had years of therapy and it hasn't helped me."

Haley slides a bag of chips toward Kirsten. "You want these? I'm not going to eat them."

Kirsten smiles tentatively. "Thanks."

I roll an unpeeled orange around in front of me while Kirsten crunches through the bag of chips and Haley manages to make sharing peanut butter and jelly with Yuji look romantic.

"So, what about you, Sonia? What are you going to wear?" Aisha's voice is light, like all of this—me sitting here with Gretchen's little sister, Haley and Yuji at the same table, holding hands—is totally what we all expected to happen two weeks ago.

"Wear?"

"To prom."

"Oh." I look at Kirsten, the blood rushing to my face. It seems wrong to discuss this in front of her, until I realize that's exactly what she was just complaining about. "I'm not sure I'm even going to go."

"What?" Haley pulls herself away from Yuji. "You have to. The student council voted to put it on in memory of Gretchen. That's the only reason we're even still having prom."

"I don't have a date," I say, hoping she'll drop it. "I'll probably just work that night."

The bell rings and I get up quickly, avoiding everyone's eyes. I turn away to organize my backpack, but then I notice Kirsten lingering at my side. I pull my sleeves down over my fingers.

"What class do you have next?" I ask.

She wrinkles her nose. "Trig."

"I've got chemistry. I'll walk you there."

She falls into step beside me and we move in silence. Growing up,

Kirsten was the kind of kid who was terrified of spiders, but never wanted anyone to kill them. Gretchen would roll her eyes every time she said *shoot* instead of *shit*. Disregarding a few understandable moments this past week, she's probably the most benign person in Hidden Falls, but halfway down the hall I get this urge to run away, as far as I can get from her. I immediately feel awful. Kirsten lost Gretchen every bit as much as I did—more. They were sisters. If she's reaching out, I should be there for her. It just feels . . . weird.

"The school asked us for approval about the prom thing," she says.

"Oh, I wondered. I guess if your family is comfortable with it . . ."

"Principal Bova didn't want to do it without the okay from my parents, and my dad was ready to say no, but then my mom got stuck on how excited Gretchen was for prom. She had that dress hanging on her closet door for weeks. She didn't have a date anymore, but she didn't care. My mom swore she'd never forgive herself if Gretchen's ghost couldn't *glide around the dance floor the way she'd planned.*"

I trip over my own foot. "Your mom said that?"

Kirsten coughs. "She's been going a little heavy on the painkillers."

I don't know how to respond to that.

She stops in front of the door to trig. "You know, we've been packing up some of Gretchen's things. Mostly clothes and stuff. You should come over and take a look. See if there's anything you want."

I raise one eyebrow. Hanging out with Kirsten at lunch and between classes is one thing, but raiding Gretchen's closet? It doesn't take a lot of imagination to guess what Gretchen would have to say about this. There were few things she got truly livid about, but Kirsten even setting foot in her room was one of them. She went so far as to lay a piece of masking tape across the threshold that her little sister couldn't cross without winding up grounded. Agreeing to this would be like a huge betrayal. But I never did get inside her room during the reception, and the intruder could have left anything behind that the sheriff might have missed if he didn't know how things should be. I study Kirsten out of the corner of my eye, wondering if this is really about clothes, or if it's something else.

"It'll just end up at Goodwill if you don't. I'm sure there are things she would've wanted you to have." She slides her bag off her shoulder and looks at her feet. "Okay, I'll admit my mom asked me to ask—she said it'd be nice to see you. But I mean it, you really should come."

"Your mom said that?" Guilt twists through my gut. I could've actually stopped by their house on the way to Marcus's the other day. At the same time, walking through Gretchen's front door after the funeral was one of the hardest things I've ever done. I was hoping I'd never have to do it again.

"You don't have to," she says. "It was just an idea."

"No." I exhale. "I—I'd like that."

Her face lights up in a warm smile. "Great."

I falter at her enthusiasm. This is so different from our conversation outside of Gretchen's room. I wish I could figure out what's changed. My stomach twists with guilt when I think of her name on my suspect list, but until now it was easy to imagine Kirsten scratching up my picture. Maybe I can simply rule her out.

"Can I ask you something, though?"

She raises her eyebrows and I struggle to find the words I'm looking for.

"Do you remember taking a picture of me and Gretchen at the party?"

I study her face carefully, but she just blinks like I asked her to name the capital of Europe.

"I don't remember much of anything from that night. Is it important?"

"Probably not," I say quickly. "I just found a photo of us in my locker last week."

"I've had a bunch of people send me pictures of her or tag me online."

"Me too. I guess it just seemed odd, the way it was done . . ."

"How do you mean?"

I pause, not sure I should mention the scratches. If she put it there, wouldn't she have said so by now? I don't want to scare her if she didn't. "I don't know . . . it just felt like someone was trying to get my attention. I wish I knew why."

Her eyebrows draw together, uneasy. "Maybe you should take it to the sheriff. He keeps saying even small details are important."

"Oh—I don't think it's that big a deal," I say quickly. She gives me a doubtful look, but I shrug and clear my throat. "Anyway, when did you want me to come over?"

She smiles so sweetly, I feel bad for wanting to turn her down. "How about tomorrow? I'll give you a lift after school."

I manage to return her smile. "Great. I'll look forward to it."

She's gone before I even realize the bell rang, and though we ended on a slightly less awkward note, the invitation still piques my guilt. The masquerade posters lining the walls remind me of the dress hanging in Gretchen's closet, the one that will never be worn. I push down the hall toward chemistry, avoiding the masks staring at me from the flyers, but by the time I get to class, I'm picturing myself at prom, dancing without a face.

TWENTY

THERE ISN'T A BELL ABOVE the door at the Evil Bean, but it wouldn't matter if there was. The punk rock music is always turned up so loud you have to yell your order at the baristas. If you don't mind that, or the staff acting like you ruined their day when you walked in, their lattes are pretty amazing. Marcus has worked here since before he and Gretchen started dating. She used to drag me along to "study" just so she could flirt with him while she ordered and I pretended not to care. A guy with a ring through his nose and a tattoo of a dragon wrapping around his neck shouts my name and places a large purple mug on the bar. An intricate butterfly glides through the foam on a swirling coffee-colored breeze. I say thank you and the guy spits into the sink.

Sometimes I wish I could get away with that at the diner. I drop some change into the tip jar.

This time of day, the mismatched tables and chairs are packed with students from the community college, or people carrying out shady business meetings they don't want overheard. Small groups cram in front of laptops tethered to overcrowded outlets. I watch a couple guys in business suits pass an envelope under a table. There's a gas fireplace in the corner that's never turned on no matter how cold it gets and a couple of lopsided sofas huddled on either side of it like they haven't abandoned hope. The place is always decorated with artwork for sale and today the whole back wall has been turned into a gallery of bright, colorful abstracts. I recognize them instantly as Marcus's.

My list of suspects is in my backpack, and I'm anxious to see the names he's come up with—if there's any overlap. I also sort of hope he'll give me more reasons *he* shouldn't be included, but I'm trying to stay objective. After I connected Kip to the photo and he told me he'd seen Gretchen in the woods, he became my strongest candidate. But I still hesitate. Maybe I'm too trusting, but threats don't seem like Kip's style . . . let alone murder. He just isn't that calculating. I worry there's something I'm missing.

I don't see Marcus when I scan the room, so I pick up my mug and wander awkwardly between the tables, trying not to imagine I'm being watched by each person I pass. Finally, my gaze lands on a familiar hunched form.

The thronelike purple chairs in the corner are nestled so close together, my knee rams into his when I sit down. I overcorrect, trying to sit as far back as possible, but when I do I end up sinking into the cushion until my feet lift off the floor. I pull myself forward to balance on the edge of the seat, which apparently has at least one spring left because it's poking me in the ass.

"Nice meeting place," I say.

"Guess you're serious about the text thing. I wasn't sure you'd show." Marcus lifts his head. The swelling under his eye is almost gone and I spend a second too long studying the smooth planes of his face. "Anyway, I figured no one you know would ever come here."

I set my mug on a side table with a frown, but I have to admit this place wasn't a bad idea. There's little to no chance anyone from school is going to walk in—there's a gentler, cheaper coffee shop much closer—and even if someone did, we're unlikely to be spotted in this corner. Dina does come here to study, and to get away from the diner, but I'm picking her up from school in Uncle Noah's Passat since her car is in the shop.

"Yeah, well, let's not linger," I say, trying to stay on task. "Show me what you've got."

"Okay." Marcus pushes his hair out of his eyes and leafs through a sketchbook. "I think, in addition to compiling a list of suspects, we should probably come up with some kind of timeline. If we can figure out where people were and when, we can determine who had opportunity, then work our way back toward motive."

"How much of a timeline do we need? The picture wasn't in my locker at the end of the day Monday. The building was locked overnight. Unless someone had access—"

"I'm talking about Gretchen's murder, Sonia." He raises his eyebrows.

Heat floods my face, warming up the whole room. "Right. Well, *I'm* talking about the creepy photo with my face scratched out like I'm next on someone's list."

His eyes darken. "So, you're actually worried about that now?"

I pull at a rip in my jeans. "Until I know who left it and why, I'm being cautious, yeah."

"So cautious you go walking in the woods by yourself."

My head snaps up. "Remind me why you suddenly care?"

A line forms between his eyebrows. "I've always cared."

My lips part, but I can't make a sound. He couldn't mean that the way I want him to.

He stares down into a black cup of coffee and exhales. "Look, Gretchen could bring out the worst in people, and I was no exception. She *wanted* me to dislike you . . . so I did my best."

A sharp pain opens at the center of my chest. Because what he said about Gretchen is true, but the way he treated me the last six months felt too awful not to be real.

"It was wrong, Sonia. I know that doesn't fix anything. I just want you to know so maybe—" He stops, meets my eyes. "Maybe you'll stop being angry with me."

I search his face for some hint this is a lie, that he's only saying this to win me over. There's nothing but apology in his eyes. I sip my coffee just to look away. It was amazing the things Gretchen could get perfectly nice people to do. And as terrible as this makes me feel, I'm guilty of following suit. No one wanted to be on Gretchen's bad side.

"Why don't we focus on the photo and work backward." I pull out my notebook, ignoring his frustrated frown. He's clearly eager to forgive and forget, but this is too much at once. I'm going to need more time. "If we're assuming whoever killed Gretchen is the same person who left the photo in my locker, why don't we start by seeing where our lists overlap."

Reluctantly, he hands over his pad of paper, and I give him mine.

Kip Peterson	Marcus Perez
Kirsten Meyer	Reva Stone
Tyrone Wallace	Kirsten Meyer
Aisha Wallace	Tyrone Wallace
Haley Jacobs	Yuji Himura
Reva Stone	Kevin Fowler
	<u>Kip Peterson</u>
	Person Unknown

"Haley and Aisha? I don't think so." I almost laugh.

"Why not?"

"For one thing, Haley wasn't even at the party. She was grounded."

"Reva wasn't at the party either," he says. "That didn't stop you from adding her."

My temples throb. "Right, but Reva leaving the photo makes sense. Haley and Aisha wouldn't—"

"Do yourself a favor, Sonia. Stop looking at these people as your friends and start seeing them as suspects. Haley hated Gretchen's guts. Aisha lived next door to her."

"Haley didn't *hate* Gretchen." I say it, but I'm not sure. "And since when does living next door to someone make you a murder suspect?"

"What you should be asking yourself is, do either of them have a problem with *you*?"

I open my mouth. He waits.

"Of course they don't."

"Not that you know of."

I fold my arms tighter. Haley and Aisha had their issues with

Gretchen—quite a few people did—but I know my friends. I've never given them reason to fall out with me.

"I don't see Yuji on your list."

"He stayed at Brianne's till after midnight. She and a bunch of other people verified that."

"So, in your world, everyone's guilty till proven innocent."

"I know how it feels." A shadow passes over his face. "Anyone as gorgeous, charming, and intelligent as Gretchen is bound to have her share of enemies. That being said, I'm sure you do too."

I blink, trying to decide if he meant that as a compliment or an insult.

"I don't have enemies. Or if I do . . . it's neither Haley nor Aisha."

He hands back my notebook. "Okay, fine. Why is Kip Peterson underlined on your list?"

I hesitate, flipping through empty pages so I won't have to look at him. "Because he says he was in the woods with Gretchen right before she died . . . and because he posted that photo online."

Marcus pounds his fist on his knee. "That fucking idiot. I knew—"

"But he wasn't the one who took it."

"Did *he* tell you that? It makes perfect sense to me."

I shake my head. "Not when you think about it. The composition is bad. It's grainy and dark. Kip's a good photographer. I don't think he could take a picture like that if he tried."

"Then why would he post it? Why would he even have it?"

"He said someone took his camera at the party."

Marcus rolls his eyes. "Let me see it. I want to look at those scratches again."

"I don't have it with me."

He straightens. "I hope that's because you took it to the sheriff."

"No . . . but it's in a safe place." I reach for my latte and find what's left of it cold. "I don't want to show him unless I have to."

"You're serious? Two minutes ago, you think you might be next on the murderer's list, but now you're telling me you don't want Sheriff Wood to know?"

I flinch. There's no way I can explain this so it will make sense to him. But if I show the photo to Sheriff Wood, I lose what little control I have. He'll take it from me and tell me nothing about the investigation, just like he's doing now. I might have to turn in Gretchen's SD card on top of that, which I'm not ready to do. I'm guessing Marcus and everyone else featured on it aren't ready either.

"It's complicated—he and my mom are close. But yeah, that's what I'm saying."

He sits back in his chair. "What's complicated about telling people you're being threatened?"

"I don't even know if it *is* a threat, or a prank, or . . . something else." I steel myself as I say this, maybe because I need to believe it. "If someone wanted to scare me, don't you think they would've been more explicit? Written on it in blood or something?"

"Is that what it would take to scare some sense into you?" His voice rises.

"What would it take to make you consider you're overreacting?"

His jaw is hard, but he doesn't say anything.

I cross my arms over my chest, trying not to let on how scared I really am. "I'll show it to the sheriff if I get worried, but so far nothing else has happened."

"I see you've kept my name on your list." His eyes are flat.

I shift uncomfortably. "Guilty until proven innocent." I study the rest of the names without looking up. "The only other people who overlap are Reva, Tyrone, and Kirsten."

Marcus fiddles with the spoon in his mug. "I only included Kirsten because they fought. I'm not sure she could've done it."

"I heard she stayed to hook up with some freshman at the party." I feel guilty bringing this up, but there've been too many rumors.

He presses his lips together. "A couple people thought she left, but yeah, I heard mostly the same thing."

"You don't sound very sure of that."

He shrugs. "The kid she was with was pretty convincing."

I curl my lip, making a note to ask Kirsten about it myself.

"So that leaves Reva, Tyrone, and your 'person unknown,' " Marcus says.

"Reva hated Gretchen more than any—"

"But she was working that night."

I hesitate. "Are you sure?"

"She says she was cleaning First Union Bank with her mom. I haven't verified it yet."

I exhale, getting frustrated. I'd been counting on Reva as a possibility to contend with Kip. "Well, it would've been hard for Tyrone to get inside my locker."

Marcus frowns. "But not so hard to attack you and murder Gretchen."

"I thought you were sure the killer was behind the photo."

"It would make sense." He steeples his fingers, touching them to his lips. "But I can't really be sure, no."

I flip the page of his sketchbook, trying not to feel over-whelmed, but as soon as I do, my thoughts derail completely. There's a girl I recognize on the next page. Or rather, a character. She wears a cropped hoodie, cargo pants, and black boots. Her pink hair is in pigtails, there's a crossbow over her shoulder and a smirk on her lips.

"You play UltaShock?"

He hesitates, scratches his head, and takes the sketchbook out of my hands. "Not so much lately, but I like it. I'm just not very good."

I raise my eyebrows. "Summer Wentworth is my favorite character . . . you captured her perfectly."

Gretchen loved to make fun of Summer's hair or outfit, saying she lacked sex appeal. I'd never really paid attention to it. You can't win the game without this girl. Everyone underestimates her and she knows it. She never goes in guns blazing, but her crossbow take-downs are works of art.

Marcus closes the cover and I watch her coy expression disappear between the pages. "Thanks. I'm better at drawing her than playing her, I guess."

"Badass drawing either way," I say.

When he looks up, his face is a deep shade of red.

Silence hangs awkwardly between us and I reopen my own note-book to get back on task. "How about we work on your timeline. Maybe it'll help to write out where people were the night Gretchen died and when."

I spend a few minutes jotting down the events I've collected and gone over in my head a million times:

~10:00 p.m. Sonia, Gretchen, and Kirsten arrived at Brianne's party. Kirsten got drunk. Marcus and Gretchen hooked up.

~10:50 p.m. Gretchen and Kirsten fought. Gretchen left the party with Sonia, telling Kirsten to get her own ride. (Kirsten likely stayed behind at the party.)

~11:00 p.m. Sonia and Gretchen arrived at Gretchen's house. Gretchen went inside and Sonia briefly spoke with Haley Jacobs, out walking her dog. From there, Sonia walked home through Hidden Falls Park.

~11:04 p.m. Gretchen called her own house from her cell phone.

~11:05 p.m. Sonia was attacked in the woods.

~11:30 p.m. The sheriff was called to the diner after Sonia's attack.
   -Mr. and Mrs. Meyer arrived home, but Gretchen wasn't there.
   -Kip Peterson saw Gretchen sitting by herself near the top of the falls (the last person to see her alive).
   -Marcus went for a walk in the park.

~11:45 p.m. Gretchen's father discovered a male intruder in Gretchen's bedroom. The intruder escaped over the balcony. Gretchen's parents called the sheriff.

~11:50 p.m. Aisha Wallace heard a commotion outside her house, looked outside, and saw Marcus leaving Hidden Falls Park.

~11:55 p.m. Police arrived at the Meyer home in response to the break-in.

~12:30 a.m. Kirsten came home, very drunk.

~6:15 a.m. Gretchen's body was spotted floating in the pool at the base of Hidden Falls. Her Mercedes is still unaccounted for.

Marcus studies the page a long time after I finish. I expect him to amend it somehow, maybe fill in a few blanks, but he just nods and hands it back to me.

"That's it?" I say. "You have nothing to add?"

He shrugs. "I didn't know about the phone call. Everything else looks about right."

"Really." I fold my hands in my lap. "Well, there's something I've been wondering. You hooked up with Gretchen at the party, then she and Kirsten got into that huge fight. What exactly was that about?"

"She didn't tell you?"

I just look at him. He dated her long enough that he should know better than to ask. If Gretchen was mad about something, there was no talking to her. If you tried, she deflected your words back at you like shrapnel.

He runs his hand through his hair. "Kirsten tried to come on to me. Gretchen found us."

"Wait. Did you say Kirsten?" I was sure the two of them hooking up was just a rumor.

"She was pretty drunk. She just started kissing me. I would never have let it go anywhere, but Gretchen found us in a room together right when Kirsten decided to take her shirt off. Gretchen made her put it back on and threw her out."

I try to imagine this. Shy, awkward Kirsten, who Gretchen teased on her sixteenth birthday for never being kissed, trying to seduce Gretchen's loner ex-boyfriend. Neither she nor Gretchen had been acting like themselves the night of the party. I can't remember ever seeing Kirsten drunk before. But it still strikes me as nuts.

I raise my eyebrows. "I thought you had sex with Gretchen."

"Yeah . . ." He looks at his shoes.

I force my mouth closed, but it's actually starting to make sense. Gretchen's exes always seemed to have trouble moving on after she was done with them—and she was always the one to end it. I can't think of a single time she was dumped. If Kirsten was drunk and trying to prove something to her sister, poor rejected Marcus would've been an easy target, and Gretchen wouldn't have reacted well to finding them together.

"So, help me out with something here," I say.

He raises his head.

"You and Gretchen had breakup sex—sort of. After her sister came on to you. Kirsten got pissed, they fought, Gretchen and I went home. You supposedly went home too, to check on your grandmother." He nods slowly. I wet my lips, knowing this is a long shot. "At some point, Gretchen went back out into the woods . . . and so did you. Is that just a coincidence?"

Marcus stares at me, his face reddening. I stare back. I've had a feeling he wasn't telling me everything, but I wait for him to speak. He exhales, closing his eyes.

"I missed her . . . I wanted to get back together."

I press my mouth into a line. I'm not exactly shocked to hear this—I swear Gretchen left a permanent mark on guys' hearts. I just had this idea Marcus wasn't like the rest of them.

I look away, annoyed with myself for being disappointed.

He grabs his mug and rises to his feet. "I need more coffee."

I open my mouth, but he's gone before I can speak. Behind him on the chair, he left his sketchbook open to a blank page. I look in the direction he disappeared and lean over, lifting just the top couple of pages, hoping for another glimpse of Summer Wentworth. An intricate flowering vine grows wild and twisting all over the first page I turn to, like it was planted there instead of sketched. It's strange and beautiful, like nothing I've ever seen. But then I look more closely and notice the flowers have faces and each of them is frozen in a scream.

I think of what Kip said about the sketch of Gretchen and I let the page drop, the tremor in my fingers telling me it's past time to leave. I reach for my bag, pull myself out of the awkward seat, but then Marcus appears and shoves me back, landing in the chair with me.

"Sheriff Wood and Deputy Rashid just came in and ordered coffee."

His voice is low, but surprisingly calm in my ear—a sharp contrast to my heart, which is attempting to hammer its way free. I twist sideways, trying to peek around the edge of the upholstery, but Marcus's hands are on my shoulders, holding me in place.

"They won't stay long—at least they don't usually." His grip is warm through my sleeves and there's the slightest hint of hazelnut on his breath. "If we stay still, there's a good chance they won't come over and see you with me."

I shift my hips, but there isn't enough chair to keep us from touching and I'm very aware of the places we meet. I turn my head and our noses brush. His eyes are locked on mine, our lips a breath apart. The more I try not to think about my body pressed against his, the hotter my face gets. He tilts his head—

I panic.

"What if they do come over?" In my head this sounds like: *What would Gretchen think?*

He takes his hands off my shoulders and I wish I hadn't asked. He holds one finger to his lips. "Shhh."

The guy behind the counter calls out something unintelligible, and I panic for a moment, wondering if this is some kind of raid and the sheriff will question everyone here. But a moment later, Marcus gets to his feet. I peel myself out of the chair and peer out the front window in time to see Sheriff Wood and Amir crossing the parking lot with cups of coffee before climbing into the Explorer.

Marcus scratches his head and gives me a funny look. I swear his cheeks are pink.

"I'm going to go." I gather my things, trying to think of something coherent to say over my pounding heart. "Ma—maybe we should look more closely at Kirsten, Tyrone, and Kip."

"Okay." He sinks back into his own chair, a tiny smirk at the edge of his mouth. "And you're welcome."

I pull the elastic out of my hair and let my curls loose to hide my face, which has decided to light up neon. The music shifts from electric guitars and piano to electric guitars and drums.

I meet his eyes at last, and I swear there's something—maybe just something I want to see.

"Thanks."

I stride across the room, misdialing Dina's number three times while I try to process what just happened. Because it felt like something more than Marcus simply hiding me from the cops. I push out the door with my phone to my ear, glancing back inside Evil Bean one last time.

By the front window, in the corner, a familiar blue catches my eye. Reva Stone stares at me from behind a paperback.

TWENTY-ONE

KIRSTEN TURNS THE KEY IN her yellow Volkswagen Beetle and the whole car throbs with an R&B ballad that makes my chest vibrate. She swats at the beads hanging from the mirror and fumbles to turn down the volume. I open the passenger door and she hastily clears the seat, tossing a water bottle, some random school papers, and an empty bag from Super Donut behind her.

"Sorry, haven't had a lot of passengers since Gretchen died."

I sink into the leather, the smell of Fritos wafting up at me. Gretchen's Mercedes was spotless and smelled like new car even after she'd driven it for two years. She refused to play anything but classical music in it, either to be eccentric, or just to annoy me since I prefer music with a beat. I doubt she ever wanted to let me drive it, but she was too smart to risk a DUI.

I take several deep breaths as Kirsten pulls out of the school parking lot. I *am* anxious to poke around in Gretchen's room, but since I've gotten used to the idea, I'm also curious to spend a little time with Kirsten. Now that I know what went down between her and Gretchen at the party, I want to figure out how she spent the rest of that night.

"Thanks for the ride—and for inviting me."

"I'm the one who should say thanks." She purses her lips. "My mom's been seeing this therapist every day, but he's totally making things worse. I kinda don't want to deal with this by myself."

"She really wants to give Gretchen's stuff away? Already?"

"The dude says it's part of the grief process, but seriously, he's got her carrying around crystals and lighting special candles." She puts her signal on to turn onto the covered bridge.

"I wouldn't have thought—"

My head jerks back against the seat. The car accelerates and I look up in time to see the left-turn arrow ahead of us cycle red just before Kirsten blows into the intersection. For a split second all I see is the huge grille of a gravel truck closing toward me—*it goes dark, I'm in the dirt screaming for Gretchen, for anyone*—and then the Beetle speeds through the bridge. The truck driver leans on his horn behind us and I grip the door with one hand, the other clamped over my mouth. I saw my whole life flash before me just a week and a half ago. I guess it makes sense that's all there is left to replay. Once I've gotten hold of myself enough to turn my head, Kirsten's face is neutral.

"Sorry, I just went for it. That light is so slow." She looks at me, the corner of her mouth rising, just barely.

As she says this, I'm reminded so much of Gretchen, it hurts. But Gretchen never acted on impulse. Everything she did was carefully planned.

Kirsten pulls up to the curb in front of her house and I manage to get both legs working beneath me, but I keep my eyes locked on the sidewalk, the gate, the steps. It's hard enough coming back here without letting my emotions get dragged away into the park. The front hall smells strongly of lavender and vanilla when I follow her in the door, but otherwise the place appears like it always does.

"Sonia, I'm so pleased you could come."

Mrs. Meyer comes gliding out of the kitchen in a T-shirt and yoga pants, her fading yellow hair loose around her shoulders. For a second, I can't think of a thing to say. I'm so used to her business suits and tightly sculpted bun.

"Kirsten said it was a little overwhelming trying to sort through everything." I barely get my voice above a whisper. "I'm happy to help however I can."

Mrs. Meyer gives me an overly mild smile and I wonder briefly if Kirsten was right about the painkillers. "The house has been so quiet . . . it's nice to see you here again." She smooths her hair like she can't quite get it to sit the way she'd like. "Why don't you girls go grab yourselves a snack and I'll meet you upstairs."

I swallow hard. That's exactly the kind of thing she used to say when I'd come home with Gretchen after school. But back then she only had time to crunch a few carrot sticks and ask about our day before leaving for her next event.

Kirsten leads the way into the enormous gourmet kitchen, which has always been my favorite room in the Meyers' house. The smooth granite countertops and stainless steel appliances seem so elegant compared to the restaurant's commercial sink, deep freeze, and grill. Kirsten dumps a huge bag of Fritos into a bowl and offers it to me, but I hesitate.

"Oh wait," she says. "I forgot. Would you rather have popcorn?"

She holds up a bag of Smartfood and my stomach turns. We

did always have cheddar popcorn when Kirsten was around. She's extremely lactose intolerant and Gretchen kept a big bag of it on hand specifically so her sister would have no reason to share with us. I actually can't stand cheddar popcorn, but I never bothered to tell Gretchen that.

"No, Fritos are great," I say. Normally I might even wolf the whole bag down. But right now I can't even bring myself to touch them. We grab a couple of Diet Cokes and carry the food upstairs.

When we reach Gretchen's room, Kirsten walks through the door without hesitation, but my breath catches and I linger on the threshold, trying to hold myself together. The white canopy bed has been disassembled and rests in pieces against the wall, the impressions where it once stood pressed deep into the pink rug. There are stacks of books piled on the desk, a laundry basket full of random items—a music box, a telescope, old horseback-riding ribbons. The tall white bookshelves are empty; the walls are bare. Nothing looks the way it should. Like it would have the last time she left . . . or when the intruder entered. I let out a slow breath to mask my disappointment. I'll never find anything useful here.

Mrs. Meyer startles me, emerging from the closet. "I was just getting ready to tackle in here. Kirsten went through and took what she wanted already. Why don't you have a look, Sonia, and pick the things you'd like."

I know I need to answer, but I can barely speak around the lump in my throat. Everything about this is wrong. I should've turned Kirsten down when she asked me to come. "Are you sure that's what you want, Mrs. M?"

"I'd much rather you have them than some other person shopping at Goodwill." She bustles across the room, organizing and labeling boxes like this is just another auction or charity event. I bite back the sting, reminding myself that's exactly the way Gretchen saw it. When she notices I still haven't moved, she crosses her arms in front of her and looks at me with watery eyes. "Please, Sonia. I can't have her spirit trapped here because of things she left behind."

I look at Kirsten, who raises one eyebrow and shakes her head, then stuffs her mouth with Fritos and resumes organizing stacks of Gretchen's paperbacks.

I place one foot on the carpet and wait for something to happen. Another foot and I'm in the room. I look around for—something, I don't know. The space is familiar, and yet it isn't. I give Mrs. Meyer a wary look, half convinced she's right and Gretchen's ghost is going to swoop down and haunt me. When it doesn't happen, I take another step. By the time I reach the closet, I can almost breathe without gasping.

"I know Gretchen would want you to have this." Mrs. Meyer stands at the dresser, a small object clutched in her outstretched hand.

She opens her fingers when I approach, and a familiar bracelet drops into my palm. The strap is black leather held together by a silver infinity symbol on one side and a delicate clasp on the other. My hand shakes as soon as I touch it. The metal burns cold into my skin as if it's permanently chilled from the freezing waterfall. I was with Gretchen when she picked them out, when she laughed and declared our friendship infinite.

Kirsten knocks over a stack of books and curses behind the desk.

I shake my head, handing the bracelet back to Mrs. Meyer. "I shouldn't—"

"Your friendship was everything to her." She wipes a tear from her cheek and closes my fingers around the strap. "Please take it, Sonia."

I think of my own bracelet, somewhere out there, and fight hard to swallow. I don't know how else to say no, so I just say, "Thank you."

She turns away and I look down, unsure what to do with it. It wouldn't feel right inside my pocket, but I could never wear it on the same arm where mine goes. I fumble to slide it on my left wrist, but my hands quake so badly, I can't get the clasp open. Kirsten comes over and clips it together with calm, steady fingers.

"There, that's better, isn't it?" she says.

"It was worse before, leaving everything the way it was." Mrs. Meyer drops a pair of earrings back inside Gretchen's jewelry box, her whole body trembling. She clutches her arms to her chest. "Every time I walked by, I expected to see her on the bed, at her computer, hear her talking—"

Her words dissolve and Kirsten goes to comfort her. I squeeze my eyes shut, preserving the memory of what this room used to be for me—the place we had our first slumber party with Aisha and Haley, where I first confided to Gretchen I had never met my dad, where Gretchen whispered to me what it was like to have sex.

When I open my eyes, the air seems different. I'm overwhelmed by a strange sense of relief and all I can think is Mrs. Meyer must be right. When I stood outside her door the night of the funeral, Gretchen's ghost *was* lingering. Now, looking around the room, it's like she's packed up and gone.

Kirsten takes her mom into the hall, whispering something about a glass of water. I step into the closet, unsure where else to go. In sixth grade Gretchen had the adjoining bedroom converted into one massive wardrobe. It's about the size of my bedroom, and so organized I used to tease Gretchen that even if she got dressed in the dark she'd still come out perfectly matched. I swing the door until it's almost shut behind me, shivering when my skin brushes the purple velvet prom dress. It hangs on the back of the door in all its splendor, right where she placed it the day she brought it home. Even after a long day trying on dozens of dresses, when she slipped into this one, there was no question. She was stunning. The bodice is covered with swirling purple feathers that plunged low over her chest and even lower down her back. These gave way to the flowing velvet skirt, which dropped to the floor, interrupted by a side slit that teased up her thigh. The thing seems dark and shapeless draped over a hanger without her. I step away from the dress and turn a slow circle in the center of the room. There's nothing I want here. Nothing I could take with me and ever actually wear.

Kirsten steps in. "Find anything you like?"

I look away, wondering what she wants me to say. Why I'm really here. I study the shoes, the one thing Gretchen and I couldn't share. She wore a six and I'm an eight and a half. "Is your mom okay?"

"She's gone to lie down and read up on essential oils." Kirsten runs the hem of the purple dress between her fingers. "She feels guilty—I overheard her talking to the therapist. This whole 'spirit' thing is about trying to forgive herself."

I rub my hands over my arms. Despite all the vacations and sleepovers, I've never been especially close with Mrs. Meyer. Although, if I'm honest, Gretchen never really was either. Her mom was never negligent, always kind—just preoccupied. Gretchen's dad, on the other hand, would plan getaways from his job, looking for fun. He was the one who seemed happy to invite me along. But none of that makes Mrs. Meyer's pain any less real. Imagining my own mother going through this, trying to deal with the unthinkable, makes the beat of my heart feel more and more like an ache.

"How can she even think that? It wasn't her fault," I say.

"Lying in bed every night, the same way I do, I guess."

I stare at my hands. "I guess it's hard not to rehash the details. Every time I go over it, I think of something I could've done different."

Kirsten sinks to the floor and shakes her head. "At least you're not the one who got drunk and kissed Gretchen's boyfriend. I'm the reason she left the party in the first place."

The pain in her voice catches me off guard. I drop to my knees, but everything I think to say seems stupid.

We sit in silence. I let my eyes wander over the four quadrants arranged by season, and then again by color. Whites and pinks, purples and greens, blacks and blues. Gretchen blamed her freckled complexion as the reason she refused to wear red or yellow.

"What happened that night, Kirsten? I mean, after you guys fought?"

Her lip quivers like she can't decide whether to curl it up or down. "There's a rumor going around that I hooked up with some freshman."

"I heard that . . . is it true?"

"I woke up in the dark alone." She shrugs. Her gaze is unfocused, staring somewhere into the air in front of her. "I guess it could have happened."

My blood goes cold. "Kirsten, were you—"

"I was fully clothed. I don't have reason to think anything

actually went down . . . but I really don't know. Someone at the party offered me a ride home, but I was afraid to face my parents and thought the walk would sober me up." She closes her eyes. "When I saw the police cars I remember thinking I'd be grounded for life. I don't remember much else."

A tear rolls down her cheek. I wipe my own face with my sleeve.

"It doesn't really matter what happened to me. I just keep thinking I could have helped her if I'd been there. If I hadn't been so stupid."

I touch her shoulder. "It sounds like you blacked out."

"I walked home through the park. I was so drunk. Why didn't they go after me? *I* wouldn't have struggled."

"Kirsten—" My voice cracks.

She eyes my arm with its fading crosshatched scratches. "At least you fought for your life—I was too wasted to even die."

I shake my head, but my throat closes before I can speak.

"It would've been better." She looks at the door with a familiar downcast expression. "My parents lost their perfect daughter. Now all they're left with is me."

"Gretchen wasn't perfect." I find my voice, though the words are bitter on my tongue. "You don't need me to tell you that."

She looks at me and sighs. "You know what the worst part is? People assume that since we were sisters, we were close. They make this big deal like I've lost my best friend. And I *want* them to think that."

I draw my knees to my chest and think of Kirsten as a little girl, desperate for a sister Gretchen refused to be.

Kirsten tilts her head back till it thuds softly against the wall. "I didn't even really *like* Marcus. I just wanted to see if I could do it."

I wait for her to say something more. The kind of stuff people usually add, like calling him a murderer or saying he got a bad rap, something to make it clear she thinks he did it or not. When she doesn't say anything else, I just ask.

"Kirsten, do you think Marcus killed her?"

She stares at her hands, at dark polish that looks black in the dim light. "I'm not sure."

I bite my fingernail.

"I might've picked Kevin or Tyrone first. They seemed a little more . . . bitter about being dumped. Marcus doesn't really strike me as the murdery type. But after what Gretchen said to him at the party—"

"What did she say?"

"It was something about their breakup." Her face burns bright red. "And him getting it up for the right girl."

I raise my eyebrows. "Like she was accusing him of cheating?"

"Maybe." She clears her throat. "I don't know, I guess he could've killed her."

I stare into the winter section of the closet. If Marcus was cheating, that would explain why Gretchen dumped him so suddenly. She would've been pissed; I don't think she'd ever been cheated on in her life. And if she found out who he'd been seeing, she would have gone out of her way to make that person miserable.

Maybe I'm going about this the wrong way. Maybe I should be looking for whoever came between Marcus and Gretchen.

I look doubtfully at Kirsten. "Was that the first time you kissed him, at Brianne's party?"

"It was my first kiss ever." Kirsten's blush deepens.

I shake my head. Gretchen broke up with Marcus more than a month ago. She would have told me in no uncertain terms if it was over Kirsten. She brought up my name on the video with Marcus, but it was clearly meant just to get under his skin. She knew it wasn't me. So who else could it have been? And does this mean Marcus was lying about wanting to get back together with Gretchen?

Kirsten gets up and starts looking through Gretchen's shoes. Behind her, I notice the light pink top Gretchen wore that night. The one she had on in the photo. It's hung haphazardly, out of place with a bunch of black shirts and dresses, which means at the very least she stopped to change before heading back out. It seems like a little thing, but Gretchen never would have left it there unless she was distracted, in a rush.

Or maybe someone else misplaced it after she was gone.

"Hey, did you ever figure out who left that picture in your locker?" Kirsten asks.

I look over and she's standing in front of the full-length mirror, wearing a pair of her sister's heels.

My throat goes dry. "No. I haven't given it much more thought," I lie.

"But you seemed worried about it."

"I was . . . I guess I still am," I admit. "But it's been a week and nothing's come of it."

She kicks off the shoes. "Hmm. Well, I guess that's good."

I pull myself to my feet. "Are you sure you're okay, Kirsten? I mean, of course you're not, but . . . I shouldn't have let her leave you at Brianne's. Anything that happened—"

"It's okay." She takes my hand, admiring the friendship bracelet. "I'm sure I would've had a hard time saying no to her too."

I close my eyes, the air in the closet suddenly too thin.

"Well, I guess all of this is going to Goodwill tomorrow." She drops my wrist and turns with a wistful sigh. "Thanks so much for coming today. I don't think I could have come in here alone."

"Of course." I think of her dressed up in Gretchen's clothes after the funeral and an uneasy feeling settles over me. I grab the pink shirt from the row of black clothes and put it back where it belongs.

TWENTY-TWO

FROM THE SIDEWALK ALONG THE edge of the park I can just make out the cascade of Hidden Falls gushing beyond the new spring leaves. From here, the rush of water is a pleasant murmur, not a deafening, drowning roar. A breeze runs up my arms, weaves through my hair, and I shiver, wondering if Mrs. Meyer's crystals are actually working. I felt less haunted in Gretchen's bedroom than I do standing out here. My fingers go to my wrist, tucking the bracelet safely inside my sleeve.

Someone clears their throat behind me.

"You know, you're not supposed to be out walking without a buddy." Reva Stone strolls toward me with a look of mild disinterest.

"Technically, I'm not out walking. Kirsten just dropped me off."

She peers down through the trees toward the waterfall below. "She probably broke her neck, if that's what you were wondering. Fall like that, I doubt she drowned. It was probably real quick."

I stare at her, a bitter taste in my mouth. If Reva did want Gretchen dead, she's making zero effort to hide it. "That's not what I was thinking about."

She shrugs. "My bad. Maybe you were angsting over who killed her. Everyone thinks Marcus Perez did it, though that does seem . . . obvious."

I give her my full attention, but she's focused somewhere out among the trees.

"Privileged kid with troubled upbringing murders overprivileged girlfriend after she dumps him." She pretends to stifle a yawn. "Sounds like the plot to a boring crime novel."

"Where exactly are you going with this?" I glance over her shoulder toward the diner. I'm not late yet, but my mom will be looking for me soon.

"What do you think Marcus had to gain from Gretchen's death?"

I narrow my eyes. "Why do you even care?"

She tucks her ice-blue hair behind one ear. "I'm just interested in the truth, same as you."

Somehow I doubt that. But I'm surprised she's not hailing Marcus as a hero if she thinks he's guilty.

"The sheriff said he has an alibi."

"So you think he's innocent."

"I didn't say that." I look away, tugging at the strap of my backpack. "Why do *you* think Marcus might've wanted Gretchen dead?"

"Lots of reasons." She smirks. "But primarily? Money."

It's all I can do not to laugh in her face. "Marcus doesn't need money. He lives on Park Drive."

Reva shakes her head like she's being patient with a child. "The guy's hard up. Can't you tell?"

I picture the large gray Victorian on the far end of the park and it just doesn't make sense. Marcus's parents might have gotten into trouble, but his grandmother is from a wealthy, respected family. They're not the Rockefellers or anything, but when I think of the cramped apartment my mom and I share, it's hard to imagine them struggling. Marcus does drive his grandmother's old Cadillac instead of having his own car like most kids in his neighborhood, but I always figured his grandmother was just strict. Reva's mom runs a busy cleaning service, though, and she's one of the more reliable sources of town gossip.

"Even if he does need money, how would Gretchen dying have helped him?"

"Maybe someone paid him to do it." She looks right at me for the first time and smiles.

I don't smile back.

"C'mon, Sonia. It makes more sense than him killing her in the heat of passion. Don't even try to convince me he actually loved her."

I hesitate when she says this, noting the tremor in her voice. "What are you getting at? Why do you care?"

She bares her teeth. "I just want people to know she wasn't some beautiful saint. Maybe she finally got what was coming to her."

I shake my head. "Fuck off, Reva."

She smiles again, but it's more like a grimace. "I'm only trying to offer a little advice, especially after bumping into you at Evil Bean. You might want to be careful who you hang out with."

"Kind of like right now?"

Reva laughs, but there's an edge to it that makes me uncomfortable. A few years back I would've described her as shy, but pleasant. She hung out with us occasionally, but she was more the kind of girl you could work with on a project for class without it feeling awkward than an actual friend. That changed toward the end of freshman year when she and Gretchen had their infamous fight. Neither of them would ever say what it was about, but I knew.

Reva tried to kiss Gretchen. It didn't go well.

"Is it that easy to keep hating someone, even after they're dead?" I ask.

She stops laughing, her mouth reverting to a scowl.

"What's *your* alibi for that night?" I ask, trying to keep my cool. "Unless you're saying you hired Marcus to push her off the top of the falls, I don't see how this is relevant."

"If it had been me, I would've done it myself." She yanks all the flower petals off a low crab apple branch. "But you're not the only one Marcus meets with in secret."

My neck prickles.

She looks at her phone and shakes her head. "I'm going to be late to work and so are you."

She turns away, but I grab her sleeve. "Who else?"

"I don't exactly follow him arou—"

"Who else, Reva?"

"You two seem close." She pulls out of my grip and backs away. "Figure it out for yourself."

"Wait." I think of the SD card in my closet and bite the inside of my cheek. "She—she had video of you and her."

She stops and stares. "Is that a threat? How very Gretchen of you."

My face floods with heat. "I didn't mean it like that."

"Right. You just spent all your time with her because you were nothing alike."

"We *weren't*." I nearly choke. Because I loved Gretchen, I miss her, but I don't want anyone to think I was on board with some of the things she did.

Her eyes flash.

"Look, I'm sorry," I say. "I just don't know who to trust."

"I know how you feel."

"Reva, I would never—"

"Maybe you should get inside." She tosses her short hair. "There's only *one* bitch down. It'd be a shame if someone came back to finish off the second."

Before I can open my mouth, she's halfway down the block. She walks boldly, head high, like someone not at all worried for her life. I peer through the trees toward the vandalized memorial and wonder if that was her way of taking credit for her work. Maybe she likes scratching faces out of photos too. I hurry back to the other side of the road.

The diner door swings open as I approach, and Tyrone steps out, shoving his wallet in his pocket. He smiles when he sees me, though it doesn't reach his eyes.

"Sonia. How you doing?"

"Surviving. How about you?"

He exhales. "The same."

His posture is stooped, his eyes duller than I've ever seen them. We're alone on the sidewalk, and if this wasn't such a perfect moment to pin him down with some questions, I might offer him a hug. Tyrone and I have never had much in common, but until recently, he had Notre Dame, I had Penn, and we both had Gretchen.

"You want to come back in for a milk shake? On the house if you don't tell Dina."

He manages a smile, but shakes his head. "Thanks, I just ate." He looks at me and hesitates. "Why do you ask?"

I step closer, keeping my voice low. "How are you really doing? Forget all this polite bullshit. I know that you and Gretchen—I mean, she told me a lot."

He clenches his teeth, looking up at the sky. "I guess I didn't realize how I actually felt till I left town. It was just a fling for her. But when I got back, I thought—" He exhales. "I didn't even get a chance to see her."

He stares at the ground, clutching one arm. Tyrone's a pretty massive guy, but right now he seems like he just wants to disappear. I touch his elbow, trying to keep him talking. "Were you supposed to see her? That night, I mean?"

He tenses, pulling away from me. "I texted her. She was vague about meeting up."

I look down the street, thinking over everything Reva said. She was clearly trying to ruffle my feathers, but she's not the kind of person to blatantly make stuff up.

"You didn't happen to meet Marcus instead?"

His eyebrows draw together. "Look, I don't have a problem with Marcus, but we're not exactly friends."

The diner door opens and Mr. and Mrs. Abramson say hello as they leave. I wave at them automatically, glancing at the clock through the window. I'm officially late, of course.

"I've got to go help my dad with some stuff," Tyrone says.

"Yeah, I should go too." I reach for the door handle, more relieved than I should probably feel, but he calls out before I can open it.

"Sonia."

I look back and he lifts his chin, staring me straight in the eyes.

"That wasn't me who climbed in her window. Just so we're clear."

My stomach drops. I guess I can't be mad at Aisha for telling him what I said. I just wish I'd never said it out loud. He could be lying, of course, but if it wasn't Tyrone in Gretchen's room that night, who was it? Why was he there?

I bite my lip and nod. "Okay. That's good to know."

Dina pulls the string, shutting off the neon Open sign in the front window. She double-checks the lock while I turn out most of the lights and the television above the counter. This is my favorite time at the diner, when everything is still and the only sounds are rubber soles on linoleum and the clink of coins being counted out in the cash drawer.

"You crashing on our couch again, or is Uncle Noah driving you home?"

Dina sighs. "Couch. I've got a paper due and I don't want to wear Noah thin when I need a ride to class tomorrow. If they can't fix the stupid car at this new place, I don't know what I'll do."

I wipe a damp cloth over the counter next to the register while she counts the money into piles. "Shelly said they have a way better reputation than Wilson's. Cheaper too."

"Let's hope." She rubs her back. "After I graduate, I'm buying your mom a new couch."

"Only a few more weeks."

She nudges me and cracks a smile. "Yeah, for you too."

I set the cloth down. I get unsettled every time I think of graduation, the end of high school. It feels abstract, like it might not really happen. Or it's going to happen, but I might not be there to see it. Sometimes I think if I just manage to get there, I'll be okay. But that seems harder every day.

Dina opens a roll of pennies and looks hard at me. "Is everything all right?"

"Yeah, I'm fine. Just . . . thinking about Gretchen."

She stops counting the drawer. "You'll have a fresh start in the fall. New city, new school. You can put all of this behind you."

I shake my head. Maybe because I don't believe her, or because I just can't imagine a future without Gretchen, even though she's gone. "Mom would probably move into my dorm room if I don't come home once in a while."

"She'll be fine. You'll see."

I grab the Windex and wipe down the display case full of pies. "What are *you* doing after you graduate? You going to wave your business degree in Noah's face and tell him what to do?"

She laughs, then looks back toward the empty kitchen. "Trust me, I've thought about it, but . . . I actually want to start my own restaurant. Not here; maybe a couple towns over. There was a nice space in Fayetteville I looked at last week."

My eyes widen. "You're serious? You'd leave? What about Mom and Noah?"

She shrugs. "They've hired people before. They'll have to get someone when you go to school."

"Yeah, but they're family. How can you—" I stop when I realize I sound just like my mother.

Dina smiles and squeezes my shoulder. "When we were growing up, this place was always going to be Noah's. Marlene was okay with that, but . . ."

"It's not enough for you."

She nods. "I knew you'd get it."

I've never understood why my mom doesn't want more. How she can stay on her feet day in, day out, working a meaningless job for someone else.

"Your mom is happy," Dina says, reading my mind. "She got everything she didn't even know she wanted when she had you."

I straighten the salt and pepper shakers along the counter. "What about money? Are you going to have to get another loan?"

Dina's lip curls. "I'll be digging myself out of debt till the end of my days. But it'll be *my* debt. Hopefully I'll have something to show for it."

I smile, but it fades as I think about what she said. Dina has made big things seem possible my whole life, even when everyone else around me was saying no. Our conversations have always been about hard work and making something from nothing. But I'm not sure how to focus on long-term goals when I don't know what will happen tomorrow.

TWENTY-THREE

I HEAD STRAIGHT FOR THE guidance office early Friday morning. I got a message from my guidance counselor asking me to come in first thing to discuss "concerns" about my scholarship, and whatever they are, I want them sorted out right away.

Ms. Dixon ushers me in and asks me to have a seat.

"First, I want to ask how you're doing personally, Sonia. I was concerned when I didn't see you in here last week."

I stare at the mug of pens on her desk. "I'm holding up, thanks . . . I guess I'm just processing things my own way."

She studies me with warm brown eyes, her lipstick bright pink against her dark skin. "You know my door is always open, not just for academics, if you ever want to talk."

"Thanks, Ms. D." I tug at a loose curl.

"All right then, well . . ." She shuffles a few piles of papers until she comes up with an orange folder, but when she looks at me again, her face has shifted from compassion to unease. "I'm sorry to have to bring this up now, but I got a phone call from the dean of admissions at Penn yesterday. There's some confusion there over a website that has your name on it."

I shake my head, waiting for her to continue. "A website?"

She looks at me over her glasses. "They seem to think you've been selling essays online for cash."

I blink. Twice. There's no way I heard that right.

"Sonia?" Her face grows serious. "If you know anything about this—"

"I'm sorry, did you say *selling* essays? Like, for money?"

"Apparently it was set up three or four weeks ago. Yours is the only name traceable on the site." She types on her keyboard, swiveling her computer screen toward me.

"They have to be mistaken. I would never do anything like—"

The browser loads and I find myself staring at a familiar green and white screen. My breath hitches. A cold, slithering feeling seeps into my veins.

"Sonia." Ms. Dixon fixes me with her Do Not Attempt to Bullshit Me face.

My heart races. This was never supposed to be real. "It—it was a project, for her ethics class."

"Whose ethics class?"

"Gretchen's." I close my eyes, but my nostrils flare. "It was her idea of a joke."

Ms. Dixon lets out a fatigued sigh. "Are you telling me you knew about this, but it isn't your website?"

"Yes, sort of." I scramble to collect myself, try to make sense without completely losing it. "I didn't know it was live—it shouldn't have been. You can ask Mr. Hanover."

Ms. Dixon removes her glasses and rubs the bridge of her nose. "I will. But first *you* need to explain this to me, from the beginning."

"Okay." The edges of my vision go black. "She got the assignment a couple of months ago. The idea was to present a fictional example of an unethical business practice. Gretchen's was supposed to look like one of those sites that sells essays and term papers. She asked if she could use some stuff I'd written for content. She thought it'd be funny since that was *so* not me. . . ." I curl my fists in my lap. "She swore they'd never be posted online."

The room is silent apart from the hum of the computer and the roar in my ears. Ms. Dixon has always been laid-back, open, someone I could easily confide in, but the way she avoids looking at me now . . .

"I *saw* the assignment, or I never would've—" I stop, grit my teeth. I'm mad at Gretchen, but this is my own fault. *I* let it happen. I was so careful until I got into Penn, and then I got lazy and let my guard down. "How bad is this? Could I—could they take away my scholarship?"

She puts her pen down. "I'll get on the phone with the university and try to explain . . . but this is serious. It looks like the site was actually set up to accept payments." She shakes her head and frowns. "Did you ever make a profit from it?"

"*No*. Of course not. I didn't even know she'd made it functional."

She exhales. "I'll set up a meeting with the ethics teacher later this morning, though this is especially difficult with Gretchen—without her here to clear this up." She picks up her phone, drumming purple nails on the edge of her desk. "I'm sure the people at Penn heard what happened . . . in the news."

Minutes drag by. Ms. Dixon places calls, waits on hold, and I sit flashing hot and cold between rage and fear . . . until guilt takes over and the cycle starts again. Finally, Ms. Dixon gets through to the Penn admissions office, but she ends up getting voicemail and has to leave a message.

"Is there anything else we can do?" I ask.

"We'll have to wait for a call back." She reaches for a pad of paper to write me a pass. "I'll get everything straight with Mr. Hanover and have you paged as soon as I know something."

I bite my lip. "What if I go talk to them, in person? Would that help?"

She raises her eyebrows. "It might."

It's probably a dumb idea, but if it makes any difference pleading to the dean with my own eyes, I'll do it.

I've got everything to lose.

I dig my nails into my legs, trying to remember Dina's schedule. It's almost four hours between here and Philadelphia. My mom would never let me go alone, but if I pick a day the diner is slow . . .

"How about Monday? Do you think someone would see me then?"

She purses her lips. "It's short notice. And I'd have to excuse you from your classes . . . but I'll find out."

I look at the clock and stand abruptly, but hesitate in front of her desk.

Ms. Dixon waves me on. "There's no sense waiting here, Sonia. Get to class. I'll catch up with you once I know what's going to happen."

What's going to happen. I pick up my backpack and head for the door, but my vision clouds in a rush of panic, betrayal—anger. Gretchen pushed and pried until I gave her those essays. And now she's not even here to admit this is her fault. I swallow hard, shame rising in my throat, because it's not like I can stay mad at her now. But *it was set up three or four weeks ago*—right after I chose Penn over Stanford. After she declared she'd keep us together.

"Sonia?" Ms. Dixon calls over my shoulder.

I look back.

"I'll be damned if they take that scholarship from you. I don't know anyone who deserves it more."

My mind is completely preoccupied by the time I make it to my locker. I only notice Aisha and Derek making out in a doorway down the hall because Kip snaps their picture and they protest. Haley walks by and waves, but hurries past me into a classroom. Reva is kneeling in front of her locker, not looking at me. I'm vaguely aware that Kirsten's not here—she's been waiting in front of my locker the past two mornings—but all I can really think about is Penn. I've envisioned myself there so often, the future seems like a big blank hole without it. I barely notice the rectangular card that flutters to the floor when I open my locker until some well-intentioned guy from my gym class picks it up and hands it to me.

"You dropped this."

I'm searching my bag for a calculator, pencil in my mouth, but I grab the card with my free hand. "Thanks."

I look at it, but I don't get it. It's a postcard of Hidden Falls. A classic photo of the less-lethal autumn waterfall sprinkling over the ledge, framed by yellows and reds and golds. The shot is angled in such a way that you can see water rippling toward the surrounding rocks in the pool below. Postcards just like this are sold all over town. We might even have this one by the register at the diner. I'm not sure why it was stuck in my locker until I turn it over.

A
LONG
WAY
DOWN

The words are dark, almost blood red, scrawled down the back in block letters. My first inclination is to drop the card again, throw it out, set it somewhere I don't have to look at it, but I can't seem to unclench my fingers. An anxious feeling comes over me—like maybe someone's watching. I swallow, my mouth dry, and raise my head. The first person I see is Marcus. He's a few lockers down, staring at the postcard in my hand. Our eyes connect and his face mirrors everything I'm feeling. His skin is pale, his eyes wide and scared. I press the card flat against my chest, as if hiding the words might somehow make them cease to exist.

The fire alarm starts ringing. I jump, confused why everyone is flooding into classrooms when clearly we all need to exit the building.

Now.

But there isn't a fire, it was just the bell.

A dark voice whispers in my ear. "Girls' room, end of the hall."

My feet move on autopilot purely because they've been given directions. When I push through the door, there are a few people at the counter, chattering something about updos and dresses, but then they see me, and the bell rings a final time, and they filter out quietly, one by one. I listen to my breath for half a minute, half a lifetime, and then the door pushes in and I realize I'm still holding the postcard to my chest.

"Let me see that," Marcus says.

He studies it. I study him. And just for a second, I almost feel safer with him in this dimly lit space. But then I look at the card again and close my hand around the pepper spray in my backpack. Marcus's focus is critical at first, examining both sides as if he's looking solely for answers. His face changes and he turns it over again. This time more slowly, with a careful artist's eye.

"Did you just get this now?"

"It wasn't there yesterday." My heart is pounding so hard, my vision swims with stars.

Marcus reaches toward me and I stumble back.

"Hey. Just take some deep breaths, okay?" His hand is open, his face smooth and calm. I focus on this, on the edges of his mouth. How they turn up a tiny bit when he's nervous. I move toward him, eager for comfort. But when I look at the dark red words on the card I stop cold.

"I said the photo should've had writing in blood." I slide along the counter, trying to move for the door. "Is this your idea of a joke, or . . ."

He takes a step toward me and I jerk away, ramming my elbow into the paper towel dispenser. Marcus hesitates, a line forming between his eyebrows. "It wasn't me," he says through his teeth. "Sonia, I'm just trying to help you."

I hesitate. Something in my chest pulls toward him. I want to believe it wasn't him. But I've already let my heart get the better of me. I have to remind myself he's still a potential suspect.

"I'll be the judge of that."

He steps back. "You haven't turned me in yet."

"Maybe I've been saving it for the right time."

His jaw tightens, but he doesn't speak.

I take a breath. "I just want to know who did this—who's *doing* this."

"Kip was there," he says. "And Reva. Aisha wasn't too far away . . ."

"It wasn't any of them."

"How do you know?" His lip curls. "'Cause they're your friends?"

"Reva is *not* my friend," I say. "How do I know it wasn't you?"

He hands the postcard back with a humorless smirk. "Because I wouldn't be stupid enough to leave a fingerprint in red ink."

I turn the picture over and over—and there it is. Only a partial print, but it's there in the corner, obscured in a patch of autumn leaves. He holds up his hands and I scan his fingers. They're surprisingly clean. The only time I've ever seen them without a trace of paint.

"Maybe you washed them. Maybe I should ask the sheriff."

"I think you should anyway."

I look up, surprised. I didn't expect him to say that.

"Did you ever show him the other photo?" His eyes are warm, wide with concern. A pang of guilt shoots through me before I have the chance to rationalize it away.

I set down my bag.

"That's what I thought," he says.

I place the postcard on the counter, anxious to step away from it. "I don't understand, why are they doing this? What do they want?"

"It seems pretty clear. They're trying to scare you."

"But *why*?"

"I told you before, I think someone's unhappy you're still alive." Marcus's face twists. "Did you hear what they did to the memorial?"

It'd be a shame if someone came back to finish off the second.

I shudder, looking at the card . . . maybe it could have been Reva. "You think it was the same person?"

"That, or there are two sick assholes in this town. Maybe they like baiting you before they pounce. Maybe they did the same thing to Gretchen."

I close my eyes.

"Sonia, has anything come back to you? It would help if you could remem—"

"I didn't see anything." I struggle to keep the panic out of my voice. "If they think I did, they're wasting their time."

He looks at me pointedly. "Is there anything else you have that someone might want?"

Bile rises in my throat. The SD card. All the videos and pictures on it. Gretchen was a collector of people's worst moments. I guess anybody might kill for that. I lean heavily on the counter. How could anyone know I have it?

Marcus watches me closely. "Sonia, if you do—"

"No. There's nothing else."

He frowns. "We need to be honest with each other . . ."

He's one to talk. I glare at him, but his dark hair falls into his eyes and his expression softens. I think of Marcus before he hooked up with Gretchen. The cute guy with the shy smile who always held the door for me walking into homeroom. My traitorous heart skips.

This was so much easier when he would just glare back.

But maybe that's tactical on his part.

"Speaking of honesty, have you been meeting with someone else?"

His eyebrows draw together. "Huh?"

I study the soap dispensers, trying to play his bluff. "Reva had some interesting things to say about you meeting with people in secret."

His voice cools. "I thought you weren't friends with her."

"I'm not."

He clears his throat. "Okay, yeah. Sometimes I meet with people in secret, if that's what you want to call it. It's kind of a business arrangement."

I stare at him. "A *business* arrangement?"

He frowns, looking down at his clean-scrubbed hands. "Occasionally, I get art commissions. It's not really my thing, but it brings in extra cash. Usually it's a portrait of someone's pet or a person they love. Sometimes it's more personal. I had a fifty-year-old woman commission a nude of herself to give to her husband. . . . I don't ask questions."

I blink, imagining Marcus infusing some nervous Chihuahua or middle-aged woman with a burst of color and beauty. Of course they would want that. He could probably make anything seem beautiful.

"Have you done this for anyone I know?"

Marcus exhales, leaning against the puke-yellow tile. "Tyrone Wallace asked me to do a painting of Gretchen."

I raise my eyebrows.

"It was right after she dumped him. He knew it was over, but he wanted something . . . to remember her, I guess. We'd been in an art class together and he'd seen my work. That's the whole of it. I did the painting, he paid me, we haven't really spoken since."

I think back, trying to place this transaction in last year's timeline. "So he must've approached you in the spring, and you gave him the painting when . . . ?"

"Right before he left for college."

"Right before *you* started dating Gretchen."

He straightens. "She showed up at my house. Said she'd seen the portrait and she liked it."

I bet she did. Gretchen could be vain like that, but I guess I can't really blame her. To my knowledge none of the other guys she dumped responded by immortalizing her in art. And I can only imagine what Marcus could do with a subject like her—with her flawless skin, high cheekbones, and sparkling eyes, she was the definition of a muse.

"I don't need the details of how you hooked up," I say, trying to force the thought out of my mind. I turn the postcard over between my fingers. "I just want to know if Tyrone's involved."

"You think he had something to do with that?"

"It seems unlikely, but that doesn't mean it isn't a possibility." I clear my throat and meet his eyes. "Tyrone used to climb in Gretchen's window all the time."

A sharp tone pings through the air, followed by a secretary's voice crackling over a speaker in the ceiling: *"Sonia Feldman, please report to the office, Sonia Feldman."*

My body goes rigid. I didn't think Ms. Dixon would have an answer from Penn this soon. I pick up the postcard with a shaking hand, wondering how every part of my future could crumble so fast.

Marcus pushes off from the wall and picks up his bag.

"Wait. One more thing," I say. I haven't forgotten my conversation with Kirsten about Marcus cheating on Gretchen. I shove the postcard and its menacing script deep between the pages of my history book. "Were you seeing someone else when you and Gretchen broke up?"

He looks away from me, shifting toward the door. "No. Why?"

"You're sure of that?" I don't know if I believe him or just wish I did.

"That isn't really something you can be sure or unsure about. I was only seeing Gretchen. She broke up with me. I'm not seeing anyone now."

I hesitate, my breath bottled up in my chest.

The tone pings again and the announcement is repeated.

Marcus curls his hands at his sides. "You might want to get to the office before they come looking for you."

I exhale, pushing past him, but then he touches my arm. A surge of anticipation—*hope*—shoots through the veins leading straight to my heart.

"Please, Sonia . . . I know you still don't trust me, but be careful. Stay out of the woods."

I look up, and when I meet his eyes, they're so intense I have to step back. His hand falls away and I reach for the door handle, more confused than ever.

The air is too quiet, too still once I'm in the hall, and an ominous feeling settles in my stomach. I make my way around the corner, down the main corridor, toward the office. My sturdy black boots squeak tiny shouts of protest along the tile. I look over my shoulder once to see Marcus following at a distance. He's far down the hall, but trailing me nonetheless. I straighten a little. My steps come quicker knowing he's there, despite the postcard sitting like a weight inside my backpack.

Kip was there, and Reva, he'd said . . . and so were *you*, Marcus. But would he go to all this trouble? I'm less sure about Kip leaving a postcard than a photo, and Reva's style seems more direct. Kirsten wasn't around, and neither were Kevin or Tyrone, but I guess that doesn't mean anything. The fingerprint could answer a lot.

As I reach the windows looking into the main office, there's no sign of Ms. Dixon. Principal Bova is there with Sheriff Wood, Amir, and Shelly. The sheriff uniforms are so out of context with the school, they look more like characters than officers of the law, but my heart skips a beat nonetheless. I consider just walking by, exiting the building, running home to my bed, and hiding from whatever they're here to say. It can't be anything good. But the sheriff spots me through the glass and the look on his face steels me enough to enter the office.

"Sonia, why weren't you in class?" the secretary, Ms. Maynard, chastises when I walk in.

"I—I was in the bathroom, I didn't feel—"

Sheriff Wood steps toward me, and that's when I notice Kirsten sitting behind him against the wall, her eyes wide and scared.

"What's going on?"

The sheriff greets me with a brief hug. "Some things have happened this morning. We've already spoken to your parents, but they wanted to make sure you and Kirsten heard it from us first. Why don't you sit down."

Kirsten tenses as I sink into the chair beside her, but the next thing I know she's squeezing my hand. I stare at her long, slender fingers laced with mine. Her nails are bare, but rounded. Not carefully painted like Gretchen's, not chewed and raw like my own. I don't see the slightest trace of red ink, not that I expected to. But I can't help studying everyone's hands.

The adults in the office are facing us, but as Sheriff Wood clears his throat, something catches my eye in the window behind Principal Bova. I look over in time to see Marcus sink down behind the cracked-open door.

"Sonia, we got a call from your aunt Dina early this morning," the sheriff says. "She was picking up her car at a garage over in Jamesville when she thought she spotted Gretchen's Mercedes."

My jaw drops.

I look from the sheriff to each of the deputies until I realize I have a death grip on Kirsten's hand.

"The plates were removed, but we confirmed it's hers. After some initial questions, we took one of the technicians, Alex Burke, into custody. Does that name ring a bell for either of you?"

Kirsten and I exchange a look, but I can tell by her face she's as confused as I am.

The sheriff takes a folder from Shelly and holds a mug shot up in front of us. The guy has close-cropped hair, a deep tan like someone who works outside, and there's something about his eyes that makes it hard to look away. But I've never seen him before.

Kirsten shakes her head and I follow suit. If Sheriff Wood is disappointed, he does an excellent job hiding it.

"This is going to be in the news real fast," he continues. "I've spoken with both your parents, and they want you to be prepared."

My chest feels like it might explode. "Does this mean you think *he* murdered Gretchen?"

The sheriff gives Kirsten a wary glance, but she's sitting forward, as eager as I am to hear what he says. "Okay, listen, you girls are not to repeat what I'm going to tell you, understand?"

We both nod.

"This Burke kid claims he knew Gretchen . . . that they had some kind of relationship. He could be our guy. There's likely going to be some gossip around all of this, but I need the two of you to stay strong. Finding this guy with Gretchen's car is a major break in the case. We're a lot closer to figuring out exactly what happened to her. I just need you to sit tight while this information develops."

I nod again, but that's all I can manage through the sudden buzzing in my head. I want to get up and shout, cry—run around the room—but all I can do is sit and listen, trying desperately to wrap my mind around everything I'm hearing. That Gretchen had a relationship with some car mechanic she never mentioned and now the cops think he might've been her killer.

I'm afraid to hope it's that simple.

"Of course, Sheriff," Kirsten says, solemn and attentive. "Anything we can do to help."

I look up in time to see Principal Bova escorting the sheriff and deputies out the door. There's no sign of Marcus in the hall, and I wonder if he heard all of that.

"Do you want me to drive you home, Sonia?" Kirsten hovers in front of me, her face clouded with concern. "I'm sure you could be excused for the day."

"No—" I rise from my chair too quickly, letting my bag slide out of my lap and hit the floor. "Thanks, no, I need to stay. I have an exam this afternoon. My mom will just worry more if I go home."

Kirsten stoops to pick up my backpack, but when I remember the postcard, I yank the strap out of her hands.

"Sorry—I'm sorry," I say, forcing myself to exhale.

"It's okay," she says, leading the way toward the door. "That was all . . . really unexpected."

"That's a good word for it," I mutter, and then I notice the troubled look on her face and I feel awful. Catching a killer won't make her situation easier. "Are you okay? I mean, with—"

"My sister's secret life?" She shrugs just as the bell rings. "Gretchen never talked to me about the life she *didn't* keep secret. I guess this is just more of the same for me."

I shake my head. It's new for me, and I'm not sure how to feel about it. I don't remember a time Gretchen passed a hot guy on the street without gushing to me afterward. I can't imagine her carrying on an entire relationship without telling me. But she didn't mention she'd made the ethics website real either.

I touch Kirsten's arm. "I never understood why she closed you out like that."

"It wasn't your fault." The hall is getting crowded and I can tell she wants to get away, get to class, as much as I do. "Let me know if you want a ride home later or if you're going with Aisha. Good luck on your exam."

She disappears into the surge of students. I make my way alone toward history, and while my step feels lighter than it has in weeks, one detail sticks like an unsettling sliver in my head. Why would a car mechanic from the next town bother putting pictures and postcards in my locker?

TWENTY-FOUR

"YOU SURE YOU DON'T WANT me to come with you?" Aisha leans over the seat, gazing past me toward the sheriff's office.

"You'd miss your date with Derek. Go, have a good time. I just want to find out if the rumors are true. I'll sleep easier tonight if there's really been an arrest."

"Text me if you do find out. I'm dying to know." She shifts the Jeep into drive and I start to close the door, but she calls after me. "Hey, I meant to ask you earlier. Can you come over tomorrow?" She cringes. "I'm sorry, I hate to ask, but since I'm up for prom queen now, I could use all the help I can get choosing a dress."

I blink. Aisha filled Gretchen's place on the prom ballot alongside Brianne and Jill Barkman. I know this shouldn't bother me, but it does. I force a smile.

"Yeah, sure. I'm off tomorrow afternoon."

I head up the flight of wide stone steps as she pulls away, trying to recenter my thoughts. Ms. Dixon called me back to her office this afternoon. The Penn dean of admissions will be reviewing the "incident" over the weekend, but wants to meet with me Monday before making a decision. I'm as much terrified as I am relieved. A meeting isn't a no . . . yet. I spent my free period with Mr. Hanover going over the guidelines for Gretchen's assignment and forwarding copies to Ms. Dixon. I *have* to straighten things out once I see the dean.

Before I can do that, I need to tell the sheriff about the postcard. Marcus is right. I'm still trying to process the idea that Gretchen was seeing someone I never knew about, though it was easier to imagine once I saw the guy's mug shot. Gritty-good-looking was 100 percent her type. And there might be a hundred reasons he could have killed her. . . . Gretchen tended to leave a trail of unhappy guys in her wake. It's possible she miscalculated and pissed off the wrong one. But I can't figure out how to connect him to the postcard or the photo. Or even how he could've gotten them into my locker. The fingerprint could clear up a lot of things, but I'm not exactly sure how to ask the sheriff about it without drawing a lot of attention and causing my mom to freak out.

I text her before I get to the door.

Hanging with Shelly for a few. Be there before my shift starts.

The sheriff's office has always smelled of ink and linoleum. It doesn't look like anything fancy when you first walk in. The building might be historic, but the inside still suffers from a decades-old renovation that left it with lots of ugly tan cabinetry and countertops. I head straight for Martina Blake, the desk sergeant, approaching her with a concerned but hopeful smile. She's on the phone, but puts the call on hold as soon as she sees me.

"Sonia, it's been ages." She comes out from behind the desk and squashes me in a hug. "How are you doing?"

I set my backpack at my feet. "I'm holding up."

The phone starts ringing again and she exhales sharply. "It has been a total circus in here since they brought that kid in."

"He's here?" I stiffen. I'm not sure where I thought they might've brought a murder suspect besides the jail, but now that I know the guy is in the building I want out of here even faster.

"Downstairs, under lock and key, thank God. We can all get some sleep. He won't be going anywhere for a while." She holds up a finger and reaches for the phone, which hasn't stopped ringing. "Hang on one sec— Black River County Sheriff, is this an emergency? Yes. No. The sheriff will be holding a press conference later this evening. He'll answer questions then." She hangs up again, smiling apologetically. "Sonia, is there something I can do for you?"

"I don't know, maybe I should come back later. I just kind of had a question for Sheriff Wood."

"He's currently in a meeting . . ." She checks her computer screen, pursing her lips. "Is it something I can answer? Or I could see if one of the deputies is free."

"Don't worry about it. It's not a big deal if he doesn't have time." I pick up my backpack, ready to leave.

"Have time for what?" Sheriff Wood pokes his head out of the conference room behind Martina. His face is more relaxed than it's been in weeks. "Everything okay, Sonia?"

I take a deep breath. Here goes nothing. "Do you have a minute?"

"I happen to have several. We can't do anything else in here until Amir gets back with more doughn— I mean bagels." He grins at Martina.

"I just had a question. . . . It's kind of about Gretchen."

A wrinkle cuts across his forehead. His smile fades. "Why don't we talk in my office."

I follow him down the familiar narrow hall, past the wanted posters and missing persons bulletins, including the composite sketch I did with Amir. It looks nothing like Alex Burke. The sheriff closes the door once we're inside his office, gesturing for me to sit in one of the visitor chairs. He shuffles papers on his desk, unearthing a new legal pad and setting aside a mug that reads DAMN FINE COFFEE.

"What is this about, Sonia? Did you remember something new?"

"No, it's not that." I hesitate, staring at the little plaque engraved with his name. "Someone left this thing in my locker. . . . I feel kind of stupid even asking you about it. It's probably just some kind of mean prank."

He frowns. "Do you have it with you? Can I see?"

I nod, pausing as I pull the zipper of my backpack. Once I hand over the postcard, I could lose control of this very fast. He's more likely to tell my mother what's going on than me, and I need exactly the opposite. "The thing is . . . I don't want my mom to know about this."

"Sonia, if it turns out to be—"

I rise from my chair. "If you don't think you can keep it confidential, I'd rather not discuss it at all."

"Wait, wait, wait—hang on." He holds his hands up. "Just sit down and let's talk about this."

I sink slowly back into my seat.

"Look," he continues in a more controlled tone. "I know how your mom feels about you going away to school. I know everything that's happened has made her concerns more intense and made you want to get out more than ever—I get all of that." He folds his hands on his desk and I falter. I didn't realize he was so tuned in to our push and pull. "If this turns out to be something she doesn't *need* to know about, we'll keep it between us. But I care about both of you, so until I see what it is . . ."

I close my eyes and exhale. If I don't show him the postcard now, he might dig around on his own, which will just get more complicated and upset my mom even more. Gretchen always said I needed to work on my delivery.

My hand trembles as I dig through my backpack until I've found my history book. I'm careful not to touch the corner of the postcard as I slide it out and hand it over. My eyes stay glued to the red fingerprint.

Sheriff Wood studies it for a minute, taking in every detail of the written words and the picture. "You say you found this in your locker? Today?"

"Yes."

"Is this the only time you've received something of this nature?"

I curl my toes inside my boots, trying to keep my face neutral, but I guess I hesitate a little too long.

He sits forward. "Sonia, if something else has happened, I need to know."

I clasp my hands in my lap, but it feels like my grip on the situation is slipping anyway. I take a long, slow breath, trying to keep as calm as possible. "Someone left a picture of me and Gretchen in my locker last week. I thought it was just a prank—it might still be."

"A photograph? Why do you think it was a prank?"

I bite my lip. "Someone had kind of scratched it up. But seriously, it's probably just some stupid kid at school."

His brow furrows. "Do you still have it?"

"Yeah . . . it's at home."

"I'm going to need to see that, too."

I study his face. There are lines I don't remember seeing a few weeks ago, but just this afternoon an easiness has returned to his eyes. "How sure are you that this Alex Burke guy killed Gretchen?"

"You know I can't—"

"Speculate, yeah. But everyone seems pretty relieved he's been arrested."

He sighs. "Sonia, what does this have to do with showing me that photo?"

I stare at the space between my feet. "I just want to know what's going to happen if I do."

He sits back in his chair. "I see. This is about your mom too."

I press my lips together.

"Let's just back up a moment. You sound pretty convinced these are both just tasteless pranks. Do you have any guesses as to who might be responsible?"

"That's kind of why I'm here." I raise my head. "There's a fingerprint on the postcard."

He holds it up to the light and squints, even though I know he saw it the first time he touched it. "Yes, there is."

"Would it be possible to identify whose it is?"

"More likely whose it isn't." He digs through his desk drawers. "But I can run it if I submit it into evidence."

"Can you do that without telling my mom?"

He crosses his arms. "Sonia, I've known your mom since before you were born. She can be a little anxious, but she's only trying to protect you."

I close my eyes. "I know. But she's already been through so much these past couple of weeks. She's having migraines again and just— I don't want to put one more thing on her mind. Is there any way . . . ?"

He sits back in his chair, his jaw moving like he's chewing on my words. After what seems like a small eternity, he looks at me with a stern expression. "Okay. I'll run the fingerprint. If it doesn't come up as Alex Burke's and you don't experience any other 'pranks' in the next few days—which you will tell me about, if they happen—I won't mention it to your mother *yet*. But I'm going to have a conversation with your principal to see if there have been any similar reports, and I'm including this as part of my official investigation until I'm satisfied there's no real connection to Gretchen's death."

I swallow. "Okay."

"Don't get me wrong, Sonia." He examines the postcard again. "If I didn't have a guy sitting downstairs all but ready to be charged with Gretchen's murder, I would be approaching this very differently."

I think of Reva's suggestion that someone might've hired Marcus to kill Gretchen. Surely this puts her argument to rest and sets him in the clear.

"I understand." I let my shoulders drop, though I don't feel at all relaxed. "Thank you, Sheriff."

He gets up to walk me to the door. "Now, why don't you get me that picture, then go home and get some rest. I think we've all earned it after today."

I hesitate and look up at him once I'm in the hall. "Do you think he was working by himself—the guy you arrested?"

A line appears between the sheriff's eyebrows. "I've got no reason to believe he wasn't."

I nod. "I'm glad you caught him."

His jaw is firm, but there's a hint of uncertainty in his eyes. "I promised your mother I'd keep you safe, and that's what I intend to do."

TWENTY-FIVE

MY MOM AIMS THE REMOTE at the TV above the register, clicking it over to baseball, as soon as the sheriff is finished speaking.

"Let's hope that's the end of it."

"Not likely," someone mutters. "They haven't even charged the guy yet."

"I'm keeping my doors locked. He and the Perez kid could've been in on it together."

"Shameful what they did to that memorial."

"To think of that sweet girl—leading a double life."

Uncle Noah changes the subject with a comment about the Mets and I throw all my energy into busing tables. I think I'm more relieved than anyone about Alex Burke's arrest, but every time I think about the postcard, I still look over my shoulder. Hopefully the sheriff will get back to me about the fingerprint soon.

I haven't approached my mom about the last-minute Penn visit yet, but I'm counting on the news easing her mind enough to let me go without a fuss. Dina already said she'd go with me and I know she'll back me up.

"There she is, let's hear it for Dina!" Mr. Tardiff shouts over his pot roast. There's a smattering of applause as my aunt comes out of the kitchen.

Dina shakes her head, crossing the room to warm up his coffee.

"How did you know he was the killer?" his wife asks.

Mr. Tardiff grunts. "I've always said you can't trust a stray dog in Jamesville."

"I never even saw the guy," Dina says. "I noticed the Mercedes at the back of the lot when I picked up my car. I thought it looked like Gretchen's, so I mentioned it to Shelly—she deserves all the credit. I never dreamed it would lead to something like this."

"You going to collect that reward money? If anyone in this town deserves to, it's—"

"I don't want the Meyers' money."

I look up, surprised. Fifty thousand dollars would put a huge dent in Dina's student loans. She could even use it to get her restaurant started.

"You look like you could use a cup of coffee," my mom says, taking a loaded dish bin out of my hands.

This is the truest thing anyone's said to me all evening. I sit back down, not bothering to point out that her shift should've ended an hour ago.

"I've got this, Sonia." Uncle Noah picks up where I left off busing. He's been running back and forth between here and the kitchen all night. Now he lumbers from table to table a bit more slowly than usual, and I worry he needs a break more than I do. Aunt Elena's always saying he pushes himself too hard.

When my mom comes back with a fresh pot of coffee and two

mugs, I scoot to the end of the booth. "This place is a mess, I should—"

"Sit with me and talk." She slides into the opposite side of the booth and hands me two creamers. "How's school?"

This feels odd. My mom stopped asking about anything to do with academics after my first day of kindergarten. But the mention of school brings all my anxieties about Gretchen's website and my scholarship back to the surface, and this is as good an opening as I'm ever going to get.

"Actually, I need to talk to you about that. . . ."

"Oh, great." She smiles. "I want to know how you feel about finals. Are you prepared? Graduation is just a few weeks away."

I wrinkle my brow, suspicious. "Why do you ask?"

She waves to the Tardiffs on their way out the door and takes a long sip of coffee. "I'm just trying to help, sweetie. You were really worried about losing your scholarship. I want to make sure you're still on track."

I don't know how else to approach this. "Well, I'm not, exactly."

"What's going on?" She cocks her head, setting her mug down, and I'm disconcerted by the sudden fear that I'm going to disappoint her.

"I need to make a quick trip to Philadelphia on Monday," I say, like it's a run to get milk.

Her eyebrows shoot up. "A 'quick' trip?"

I sigh, staring down at a chip in the table. "A problem came up with my scholarship. I need to go have a meeting about it."

She purses her lips. "And it has to be Monday?"

I nod.

"It's so last minute. . . ." She looks at Noah wiping down the counter. "Do you know how long this meeting will take? I'll have to make sure Elena can cover. If I can get us bus tickets tonight—"

I shake my head. "I already asked Dina to drive me."

"Oh." She hesitates, taking the spoon out of her coffee. "Well, I'm taking you. There's no need to disrupt her schedule. She's got finals too, you know."

I sit back in my seat. It was all I could do to drag my mom there last time to show her the campus during my interview, but now she's suddenly interested in coming? "Alex Burke is in jail, Mom. I'll be perfectly safe."

"I wish that was more reassuring." She bunches a napkin on the table in front of her and I wonder if she senses my own lingering unease. "But I want to come to support you. You've made sacrifices for that scholarship other kids would never make. Did they say what the problem was?"

"There's some confusion about my eligibility," I mumble, not wanting to explain the whole thing about Gretchen where other people might overhear. "Anyway, it's faster to drive than take the bus. Dina said it wouldn't be a problem."

"Sonia, I want to go with you." My mom reaches across the table and touches my hand. "Look, I'll admit, I've never really understood you and Dina. When you set your sights on a goal, you don't look back until it's yours. I guess I just never found anything I needed that badly." She shrugs. "It might not be what I would choose, but you've worked so hard for this, I want to see you succeed."

I'm not sure what to say. I look at our reflection in the big pane windows. My mom always says I'm a picture of Dina, but my nose and mouth are hers. Still, there's always been something very different about us. I think it's because she *fits* here, at the diner. She's as much a part of it as the vinyl booths, checkered floor, and shining chrome—things that make me claustrophobic in a way I can't explain.

Still, she's never made an effort to understand or support me like this. My chest feels tight. I wish I knew where this was coming from.

I clear my throat. "Thanks, Mom. Maybe Dina will let us borrow her car so we don't have to take the bus."

She gives a slow nod. "How are you feeling? About this arrest?"

"Okay," I say, trying not to think about the picture or the postcard. "He had Gretchen's Mercedes—that says a lot."

"It does." Her voice is strained, but she manages an encouraging smile. "I want you to get this school stuff sorted out. You can't feel guilty forever. You'll still go on with your life when this is over."

I sink in my seat. I wish hearing her say it out loud made it easier to believe.

She studies me with kind of a far-off look. "I never thought I'd say this, but after the past few weeks, I guess you leaving town isn't the worst thing that could happen."

My breath hitches, but when I meet her eyes, they're clear. "No, I guess it's not."

TWENTY-SIX

FINGERS CLOSE AROUND MY THROAT, *long and frozen, winter choking spring. I don't gasp, I can't struggle. I'm already dead. My neck snapped so long ago, I only thought I was still breathing. Water rushes over my face, covering me like a shroud, but then I surface, I see a face—and I'm under the waterfall, under the crush of nature. The hands holding me under aren't hands, it's water, seventy-five cubic feet per second, and I was wrong about the breathing, and now I gasp, but the air crushes out of my chest. I can't move. My lungs fill with ice. All I can do is stare.*

I bolt out of bed and across the room, clinging to my dresser. My hands shake, I lift my chin and stare into the mirror, and that's when I notice my hair, shirt, and pajama pants are all drenched in sweat. I move toward the door to tiptoe down the hall, wash this all away with a hot shower. But I gag at the thought of standing under the water spray, letting it run over my body. I change my clothes, climb back into bed, and shiver beneath my sheets.

A picture . . . a postcard . . . if I don't figure out who sent them I'm afraid to find out what's next.

TWENTY-SEVEN

IF I COULD PICK EVERYTHING I wanted in a bedroom, it might look something like Aisha's. It sprawls over the front half of the Wallaces' attic with wood floors and dark green walls and an actual turret with a window seat. Bookshelves line the walls like ladders to someplace magical. There are plenty more traditional bedrooms downstairs, but I can see why she chose this one. Her closet, however, is about the size of the one I have at home—a relic from another era. While Gretchen had a spare room converted to a closet, Aisha compensates by treating the rest of her space like an extension for her wardrobe. There are hoodies draped over bedposts, jeans piled over the big comfy chair, and dresses hanging from a floor lamp. This inventory does not include the random mix of socks, T-shirts, and underwear strewn over the floor. Gretchen could never stand sleeping over at Aisha's. She always said she preferred her own bed since it was only thirty feet away, but I think she was convinced Aisha's room would give her hives or something. Every time we came over here, I'd notice her sorting colors or compulsively pairing socks.

It turns out I'm not the only one Aisha asked for prom dress advice. When I show up, Haley is already lounging on the bed. Ten minutes later there are footsteps on the stairs and Kirsten peeks her head into the room like she thinks she's intruding.

"Sorry I'm a little late."

"No, I'm glad you came!" Aisha sets aside a pile of empty hangers. "I don't even know how I got on the prom court ballot. I figure if I take three opinions and average them, I won't make a total fool of myself. Plus I think Derek will lose his mind if I ask him to look at one more dress."

"Yeah, mathematics won't save you." Haley scoots over and pats a spot next to her on the bed. "Kirsten, I hope you don't have any other plans this afternoon."

Aisha tosses a shoe across the room, missing Haley's head by a few inches. Kirsten looks uncomfortable until Haley laughs and throws it back.

My throat tightens. If Kirsten were Gretchen, it would almost be like old times. All of us together as a group again—me, curled on the chair watching Aisha and Haley at each other's throats, Gretchen on the bed staring at her phone, telling them they're both morons. But it's not Gretchen on the bed. It's Kirsten. And this isn't anything like it used to be.

I spent all morning rehearsing what to say to the Penn dean on Monday, but suddenly I'm not sure I can give useful feedback on a prom dress. My thoughts are thick and blunted, my heart too heavy to care. I sit up, trying to think of an excuse to go home, but then Aisha laughs at something Haley says and it brings me back into the moment. I bite back a sting of tears. I need to be able to do this, for myself as much as for my friends.

I pull my hair into a braid while I get my breathing under control. Kirsten gives me a tentative smile and I manage to smile back.

"What are *you* wearing, Haley?" Aisha calls out, her head halfway buried in the closet.

"A few weeks ago I was all set to show up in a black unitard or something. Go totally anti-prom. But since Yuji asked me, I'm kind of rethinking it."

Aisha resurfaces with a long yellow gown in a plastic garment bag. "This should fit you. My mom picked it out. It's pretty, but I can't do strapless bras."

Haley hesitates. I shift in the chair. Her family lives a block and a half south of the diner. It's a normal enough neighborhood and a normal enough house, not a rent-free apartment above a relative's business, but I know for a fact she's going to state school this fall on a well-earned soccer scholarship. The dress is beautiful. I don't even have to see it out of the plastic or read the label to know that. She'll look stunning in it. But I want to tell her to turn it down, that it might look nice on, but it will never feel earned.

She takes the dress.

I exhale. "That color will look great on you."

"Okay, I'm going to the stairs to change because I love you all, but not that much." Aisha drapes three or four gowns over her arm and points next to the bed. "There are sodas in the mini-fridge, make yourselves comfy."

Kirsten hops off the bed once she's gone and wanders over to the dresser. She lifts up her blond hair, twisting it into a couple different updos in the mirror, then lets it fall loose around her shoulders.

"I guess I have a whole year to figure out what to wear to my prom."

"You should come this year, with us," Haley says.

Kirsten shakes her head. "Thanks, that's really nice. But I'll probably enjoy it more next year."

I nod, maybe a little too quickly, but I can't help feeling relieved. If anything seems less appropriate than *going* to prom, it would be going with Kirsten in Gretchen's place.

"Kirsten." Haley clears her throat. "How are you doing after Alex Burke's arrest? I mean . . . sorry, do you mind if I ask?"

"No, of course not, it's actually kind of a relief. My mom's been so weird about it." She leans back against the dresser and looks at me. "It was a shock. None of us had ever heard of the guy before."

"That's what freaks me out!" Haley says. "Marcus still seems . . . I don't know, so much more obvious."

Kirsten nods, her gaze far away. "I know. But my dad identified this Alex Burke guy as the one who snuck into her room, and he admitted it."

I sit forward. "Seriously? He said he did it?"

If he'd been looking for something, say the SD card, in her room, maybe he *would* go to the trouble to track me down and threaten me.

She frowns. "Well, at first he said he just came to pick up her car, as like a favor. I guess she'd dinged up the fender and wanted to hide it from our dad. He claimed she left him a set of keys on her desk, and that's all he took. But then he changed his story. Now he's saying Gretchen was supposed to meet him—at least, that's the last I heard from the sheriff."

"She was going to meet him in her bedroom?" Haley asks. "What, for like a hookup?"

I glare daggers at Haley, but she just sits there looking eager.

Kirsten's face reddens. She turns toward the mirror. "I guess."

Haley's phone goes off, thank God, and she's immediately engrossed with texts from Yuji.

I get up, joining Kirsten at the dresser. She doesn't seem upset, but it's hard to tell sometimes. She's studying the pictures jammed around the edges of Aisha's mirror. I recognize one of me, Aisha, Gretchen, and Haley all grinning with our arms around one another. I pluck it carefully from the glass.

Kirsten peers over my shoulder. "Wasn't that the trip you broke your arm?"

I frown. I guess I wanted to forget that part. The photo was taken just before we set off on the ninth-grade camping trip up the Black River. It was a weeklong expedition of hiking, mosquitoes, and misery, crowned by a final day of trail riding through the woods. That was how it happened. "It was a stupid accident."

Kirsten lingers over the picture. "Tornado, right?"

I tilt my head. "Yeah, how did you know?"

I had been assigned a sweet mare named Peaches, but Gretchen asked if I would switch with her at the last second. She'd been given a gray stallion by the name of Tornado. I said no at first. Gretchen had taken riding lessons and I hadn't. Peaches seemed like a safer bet. But as usual, she ended up getting her way. As it turned out, Tornado was very tame. We even joked about him being unfairly labeled. But just as we were packing up after lunch, Gretchen shook out a plastic grocery bag to gather trash and Tornado spooked. My arm happened to be tangled in the reins at that moment and he dragged me a terrifying quarter mile before someone caught up to us and calmed him.

"Gretchen told me," Kirsten says. "He used to be mine, you know—until she decided to ride him once and he threw her. It was her own fault, but Dad donated him to the trail-riding program. She felt so bad you got hurt. I remember she must've brought you ice cream for like a week."

My stomach turns to stone. I wait for her to shake her head or blink—make some indication that she's messing with me. That it wasn't actually a horse Gretchen knew. But she just places the picture carefully back on the mirror while I fight the lump rising in my throat.

"They euthanized him afterward. Gretchen insisted." Her eyes are steady, but sad when she looks at me. "You did know about that, right?"

I cover my mouth and whisper, "I'm so sorry," but the words might've been too soft for her to hear. The door opens and I'm vaguely aware of Kirsten and Haley turning their heads, of Aisha standing there. But all I can think about is that strong, beautiful horse running away scared. And that it wasn't an accident like I've always tried to tell myself. Gretchen *knew* what would happen when she shook that bag.

"*No,*" Haley says.

Kirsten murmurs, "Maybe not . . ."

"Seriously? That bad?" Aisha asks. "Sonia?"

I wipe the corners of my eyes, trying to pull myself out of the past. I look at Aisha's bright pink and purple polka-dot gown, but my brain is going in too many different directions for honest opinions. "Let's see some of the others before we decide."

An hour or so, and some half-dozen fuchsia, black, and champagne gowns later, the four of us finally settle on a classic cocktail dress in red satin. It hugs Aisha's graceful curves, sets off the dark tone of her skin, and makes her look "completely bangable," as Haley so delicately put it. Aisha just seems relieved we're all in agreement.

Kirsten's phone chimes on the bed and she jumps up, looking flustered. "Oh. I forgot I need to help my mom with something tonight. The dress is beautiful, Aisha."

"Yeah, tell your boyfriend he's welcome," Haley says, joining Kirsten as she heads for the door. "You want a ride home, Sonia? I need to run too—meeting Yuji."

Aisha frowns. "I was hoping everybody could stay. There's a *Slyvana Hart* marathon . . . we could order pizza?"

I glance at Kirsten lingering halfway out the door. I feel like there's something more I should've said to her, but I'm not sure what. I feel awful about her horse, and even more conflicted about Gretchen. But I don't understand why she would bring that up now.

"Can I catch a ride home later?" I've never been excited about Aisha's foreign-exchange-student-super-spy-detective show, but I could use a good distraction. If I go home now, I'll climb the walls thinking about Alex Burke, Gretchen, and Penn.

Aisha grins. "Of course."

It's still early, but we order pizza and wander down to the kitchen to wait for the delivery. Tyrone is watching basketball in the den with the sound cranked so high I can feel the game through the floor. Otherwise the house seems deserted.

"That was nice of you to invite Kirsten," I say as Aisha fills a couple of glasses with ice.

"I feel bad for her . . . I kind of always have. She seems like someone who could use friends."

Tyrone hollers over his shoulder. "Isha? Can you throw me a Red Bull?"

She rolls her eyes, but pulls a can out of the fridge. "I didn't realize you'd gone deaf," she yells over a commercial, handing him the can as she climbs over the back of the couch.

Tyrone looks up, doing a double take when he sees me. "Mom and Dad are 'conversing' about me in the study again."

"Ooh . . ." Aisha glances down the hall toward the door and cringes. "Then by all means, turn it up."

I perch on the edge of the sofa, but I'm not at all focused on the screen. Tyrone looks up at me and raises his eyebrows. "Told you that wasn't me next door."

"What?" Aisha tilts her head closer.

Tyrone leans over and shouts. "I was telling Sonia that's what happens when you get kicked out of Notre Dame."

My stomach tightens. I'd been hoping *it didn't really work out* meant he'd dropped out, not this.

Aisha stares at him, then shifts her startled gaze to me. I guess this isn't news everyone wanted to share.

The doorbell rings. Aisha digs around in her pockets. "Shit, I left my cash in my other jeans."

"How much is it? I'll get it."

"You're *not* paying."

I roll my eyes. "It's pizza."

"And Tyrone will probably eat half of it. You can't pay for it."

"Okay, then at least let me run up and get the cash for you." I head for the stairs before she can stop me. "I left my phone up there anyway."

"Fine. There should be a couple twenties in the denim capris by the desk. Left side, back pocket," she says, making for the door.

"Got it, be right down!"

Once I'm on the second floor, I head straight down the hall toward the attic stairs, but I stop in front of Tyrone's room. At first glance, it isn't the neatest place on earth, but it's a far cry from Aisha's spectacular disarray. I look once over my shoulder to make sure no one's coming before poking my head in. If there was ever a shrine to football, this could be the template. There are trophies and awards all over, posters from movies about football, even an actual football inside a plastic display case. Pennants from every major Division 1 school decorate the walls, including one from Notre Dame placed prominently over the bed. I look at the walls and shelves, but I don't see any hint of a portrait of Gretchen. I leave the room.

I take the attic steps two at a time, coming to a halt at the sight of the heaps of laundry. There must be ten different pairs of jeans strewn around. I dig through my own pockets, but what I thought was a twenty and some ones turns out to be just a ten-dollar bill. I fall to my knees and search every pair I find with no luck. I'm about to give up and holler down for Aisha when I notice a patch of denim sticking up on the floor of the closet. It seems like a slim chance, but I kneel down and tug. The jeans pull free easier than I expect, setting me off balance, but when I see what else came with them, I gasp.

A white purse lies on top of the clothes. Out of it spills a pile of cash.

I freeze. It's not loads of money like they show in TV bank robberies, but it's more cash than I've ever held in my hands. I look toward the door, trying to decide what to do. There are several stacks of tens and twenties wrapped in bands like you might see at a bank—five thousand dollars after I've counted it all twice. I look more closely at the purse—a familiar white Michael Kors tote with a gold clasp—and that's when everything inside me goes numb.

TWENTY-EIGHT

AISHA CALLS UP THE STAIRS, asking if I'm okay. Her feet follow on the steps and my heart races into action. Even if I had time to put everything back, I'm not sure I could pretend I didn't find this—Gretchen's purse filled with cash, hidden in Aisha's closet.

"Sonia, I can only entertain the delivery guy so lo—"

I hold the money in one hand, the purse in the other, and blink up at her.

Her eyes are huge. "Where did— What are you *doing*?" She comes across the room, grabbing the purse and cash out of my hands, stuffing the bills back inside.

"What is this about?"

"It's nothing—it's not even mine."

I swallow. "Yeah, I know."

"Look, I don't know what you're thinking, but whatever it is, you're wrong."

"Aisha . . ."

She wraps her arms tight over her chest, her nostrils flared. "I mean, this is *my* closet. What were you even doing snooping through my stuff?"

I step back at her tone. She hardly sounds like herself . . . or not like she has in a long time. When we were in middle school, Aisha went through this phase where she would take things at the mall. It was stupid stuff, a headband, a pair of socks, sometimes just a tube of lip gloss. Always little things she insisted no one would ever miss. Any time Haley or I tried to say something about it, this is how she sounded. She finally got caught one day, shopping with Gretchen. For whatever reason, that was the day Aisha decided to aim bigger. She took a sapphire ring from a jewelry store and was stopped the second she walked out the door. The police were called; Gretchen's and Aisha's parents had to come get them. It took a bit of smooth talking from Mr. Meyer, but the store finally agreed not to press charges. I only heard about it later, from Gretchen. Aisha never brought it up and I didn't know how to ask her about it.

"How did you get this?"

"It's mine, okay?"

"You just said it wasn't."

"I'm hanging on to it for a friend."

"Aisha, c'mon—" My voice breaks. "We both know it's Gretchen's."

She nearly backs into her floor lamp. "Maybe you should go home."

I stand my ground. "Not until I know—"

Heavy footsteps clomp up the stairs. Aisha's eyes widen. She shakes her head at me, panicked, gripping the purse like it's some kind of bomb. I snatch it out of her hands and shove it to the back of the closet just as Tyrone steps through the door carrying a pizza box.

"Yo, I paid for this thing—gave the guy a twenty-dollar tip for waiting around on your ass. You can pay me back now."

The air fills with the scent of cheese and pepperoni. I try not to gag. Aisha stoops, pulling a crumpled wad of cash from a pair of jeans I somehow missed. She smooths out several twenties, handing them over to her brother.

Tyrone takes them, his gaze shifting back and forth between us.

I wait for Aisha to say something, but she just stands there looking sick.

"Thanks, Tyrone, I'm starving." I grab the box and usher him out the door. The scent of pepperoni wafts up at me. I open my mouth to breathe.

Aisha sinks onto the bed and stares at the closet. "Thanks."

"He cared a lot about Gretchen." I close my eyes.

"So did I."

I don't say anything.

"I was on my way home from the party . . ." Aisha exhales. "Derek had just gotten into Cornell—we'll be there together in the fall. We were planning a big date Saturday to celebrate. I was thinking about what I wanted to wear, and when I walked by Gretchen's car, the purse was just sitting there. I was going to ask if I could borrow it, I swear. I waited outside her house for a while, but she never came out . . . so I took it."

I lean against the doorframe. "I'm just going to assume the sheriff doesn't know about this."

She shakes her head. "I didn't realize it was full of cash until I got home. I couldn't figure out how to bring it back, and when I heard what happened to Gretchen . . . I got scared."

I tap my fingers against my lips, the glaring issue finally dawning on me. "Why would Gretchen have five thousand dollars in her purse?"

"I don't know. The car was unlocked. If I hadn't taken it, it could've been stolen."

"It *was* stolen." I swallow. Because I know Gretchen hadn't left her purse in the car when she went inside the house. She must've left it there for some reason on her way out, before she went into the woods. Before she could get it to . . . whomever. "What time was this? Do you remember?"

"Maybe like eleven fifteen? We didn't stay long at the party after you left."

Every time I think back on that night, the details seem more scrambled. At the very least, what she's saying makes sense based on when I left Gretchen and when her parents came home. "And you didn't hear or see anything while you were stealing Gretchen's purse?"

"I didn't steal—" She sighs. "I might've heard some yelling, I don't know. It just sounded like the typical stuff you hear in the park at night."

I go to the closet, pull the purse out, and dump the contents on the bed. In addition to five thousand dollars, there are some cosmetics, a receipt for gas, a set of keys, and a couple of tampons.

"You have to take this to the sheriff."

"I can't."

"You *have* to, Aisha."

"They caught the guy who did it—this has nothing to do with anything."

"They still have to prove he did it." I hold up the cash. "What if this is tied to him somehow?"

"What if it isn't?"

I grip her shoulders, speaking through my teeth. "Did you kill Gretchen?"

Her eyes get huge. "Of course not!"

I let go. "Then there's no reason you shouldn't turn it in."

Her lip trembles. "I can't get caught with this, Sonia." She wipes at her face, choking on her words. "If my parents find out—and Cornell—"

I nod. "Your parents are going to be pissed. But Cornell might not have to know."

She stares at me, sniffling.

"Look, I can't promise anything, but I know Sheriff Wood. He's going to be way more interested in solving Gretchen's murder than prosecuting you for 'borrowing' her purse."

"You'll back me up? You won't tell him I stole it?"

I pinch the bridge of my nose. "Doesn't he already know about your previous record?"

"If I'm going to tell him what I did, I want to know whose side you're on."

I drop my hands into my lap. Aisha has done nothing but try to support me the last two weeks. I'm pissed that she took it, that she hid important evidence, but I can't turn my back on her either. "Fine. You saw the purse in Gretchen's car and you were just borrowing it. I would never doubt for a second you were going to give it back."

"Okay." Her shoulders seem to loosen. She looks down at the purse between us, running her thumb around the edge of the gold emblem. "What do you think the money was actually for?"

My lungs are so full I have to think to breathe. "I have no idea."

TWENTY-NINE

SHERIFF WOOD SETS DOWN HIS phone and picks up the paper evidence bag that now contains Gretchen's five thousand dollars. "All right, I have some questions for you girls, and I need you to be completely honest with your answers."

Aisha shifts in her chair. "What kind of questions?"

"First, I want you to understand we're talking about Gretchen here. Whatever you say to me about your own activities in relation to hers will not leave this room." He sets the money down and looks right at me. "Was Gretchen ever involved with any kind of drugs?"

I clutch my hands in my lap. It was my first thought too, after I found the money. Gretchen had her own credit card and checking account. When she went shopping, that's all she used. I can't think of any reason she might've wanted that much cash unless it was for something illegal.

"It doesn't make any sense," I say. "I mean, she smoked a joint here and there at a party, but I wouldn't call that a drug problem. She barely even drank."

Aisha shakes her head in agreement. "She just wasn't the type."

"Right." The sheriff nods. "She was valedictorian, captain of the tennis team, up for prom queen . . . not under any kind of pressure."

"It would've gotten in her way," Aisha says, missing his sarcasm. "Gretchen liked to win."

"But it makes sense to both of you that she had a secret boyfriend no one else knew about?"

I press my lips together. Because it makes sense that she would keep it from everyone but me.

"Sonia, you were closest with Gretchen." His face is stern. "But you've suggested there were things she didn't always tell you."

Obviously. She hid a whole relationship from me. But he's right; there were things she kept to herself. Gretchen would never let me touch her phone, making sure it was locked every time she set it down. And the night of the party I drove home in silence while she seethed next to me, never saying a word about what happened.

"I know there were."

"How do you know? Did she exhibit odd or uncharacteristic behavior? Sneak out at strange hours? Did you find things that made you suspicious of her activities?"

Aisha and I exchange a look. It's hard to explain all the things Gretchen said or did that made her who she was. Or who she wanted people to think she was.

I clear my throat. "Well, she did sneak—"

"She had, like, a file she kept on people," Aisha says. She looks nervously at me, but I just sit there, openmouthed. "It was kind of like a black book. I only saw her looking at it once, on her phone."

The sheriff glances at me and my pulse picks up. I didn't realize Aisha knew about the files. I think of the video of Marcus, of Gretchen suggesting he cared about me, and him wishing her dead.

I nod slowly. "It was just a thing she liked to do. She kept track of things people said and did. She wanted to know what they were up to."

"Kept track? Like to use it against them?"

"Not exactly. . . ." It seems unfair to drag this side of Gretchen through the mud when she can't explain it herself. "Sometimes she'd show things to people, to make them uncomfortable, but it was like a game to her."

"I think it was more of a control thing," Aisha says, a hint of bitterness in her voice. "Gretchen was a huge control freak. She liked to have power over people."

I think of the essay-selling website and shift in my chair.

"I wish someone had mentioned this earlier," the sheriff mutters, jotting on a pad in front of him. "You say she kept it on her phone?"

"She liked to keep it with her," Aisha confirms.

I clear my throat. "Do you think she might have had something on this mechanic guy? Is he connected in some way?" There is nothing on the SD card related to Alex Burke, but Gretchen might not have had the chance to record anything about him before she died.

The sheriff eyes the bag of money, but doesn't say anything.

I bring my hand to my chest. "You don't really think she—"

"I'm not going to speculate with you about how the two of them were involved," the sheriff says. "But Alex Burke is a known low-level drug dealer—someone who wouldn't have wanted to get in trouble."

Aisha bites her lip.

"Thank you, girls, this has been extremely helpful." He flips his notepad to a clean page and looks at us. "I do want to ask you one favor. Could you please keep this to yourselves, about finding the money?"

Aisha's relief is palpable. She nods quickly. "You don't want people to know about the purse or the money?"

"We'll have to say something about it eventually," he says, rising behind the desk. "But I'd like to keep it quiet as long as possible. Someone is probably looking for that cash. I'm hoping to find them before they learn we have it." He ushers us toward the door, but pauses with his hand on the knob. "Sonia, could I speak with you alone for just a moment?"

"Yeah . . . sure." I look at Aisha.

"I'll wait for you," she says.

Once she's gone and the door is closed, Sheriff Wood pulls the Hidden Falls postcard and defaced photograph from a drawer in his desk. They're sealed in plastic bags now, which somehow makes me feel safer.

"I ran this print, like you asked me to. Nothing came up in the database."

I stare at the huge red letters scorching toward me through the plastic. The computer system can only identify fingerprints of people who've been arrested or have their prints on file for some other reason. Which means it couldn't have been Marcus or Alex Burke . . . but now leaves me wondering who else it could've been.

"Thanks." I shift from my right foot to my left. "I guess I don't know what to think."

He sits on the edge of his desk. "Your principal supplied me with a couple of other reports of defaced photos in people's lockers.

There's no clear pattern, but each of them were recent photos taken with Gretchen."

"I wasn't the only one?" My eyes widen. "Who else?"

"I'd like to keep that confidential for the time being."

I grind my teeth. "Come on, Sheriff, is it really that huge a secret?"

His eyes drift back to the bag of cash. "You *were* the only one to receive a postcard after the initial photo. At least, you're the only one to report it. We've been following up on that."

My lip trembles as I let that sink in. "Do—do you think there's some connection between the postcard and the money?"

He frowns. "Is there any reason someone might think you were holding on to the cash?"

"Why would they? I didn't know about it. I don't even know what it's for."

He pauses a long time, then stands, setting the money down next to a second paper bag, which holds Gretchen's purse. "Look, Sonia, we're building a strong case against Alex Burke, and I think this purse of Gretchen's is going to help tremendously. But I want you to keep your eyes and ears open. There's still a good chance the vandalism of the memorial and your picture and postcard were just pranks, especially since no overt threats were made, but you need to tell me if *anything* strikes you as odd or makes you feel uncomfortable as we move forward." His eyes soften. "And try not to worry too much."

I nod, rising from my chair. "So you still haven't mentioned it to my mom?"

His brow furrows. "Not for the time being."

When I meet Aisha in the lobby, I notice Marcus sitting slumped in a chair off in a corner by the windows. He straightens when he sees me, and I struggle not to rush over to him immediately. I'm almost certain he isn't behind the photo and postcard, and if they link Gretchen to Alex Burke, Marcus might be cleared of her murder too. I pause, surprised at how much I want this to happen now. Our eyes meet and I take a step toward him, but then Kirsten and her parents come through the main doors. Kirsten gives me a relieved smile, but her father looks nervous and upset.

"The sheriff asked us to come down to discuss new evidence." His voice booms at Martina, cowering behind her desk.

She picks up her phone. "Of course, Mr. Meyer, I'll let him know you're here."

His brow wrinkles when he spots me. "Do you know something about this, Sonia?"

Aisha gives my arm an anxious squeeze.

"They're here to see Gretchen," Mrs. Meyer says. We all stare at her, and I can't help noticing the fuzzy pink slippers on her feet. Gretchen's mom never used to leave the house without at least three-inch heels. She covers her mouth and laughs, leaning on Kirsten's shoulder. "Oops, I always get you and your sister mixed up."

Kirsten looks like she wants the floor to swallow her.

"Thanks for coming on such short notice, sir." Sheriff Wood comes around the corner behind us and shakes hands with Gretchen's dad. "If you'll step into my office . . ."

Mr. Meyer hustles his family around the corner. Mrs. Meyer waves like she's bidding us bon voyage. Martina slumps back in her chair.

I glance one last time at Marcus, who looks just as anxious as Gretchen's dad, but Martina calls him over just as Aisha grabs my arm and pulls me out the door.

"Oh my God, I can't believe the sheriff didn't call my parents."

"He's still going to tell them," I say, trying to collect my thoughts.

"I know, but not right now." She lets go of my arm, leaving my skin hot and sweaty. I follow her down the block toward the diner, where she parked her Jeep. "I just can't disappoint them too, not now."

She hasn't said a word about this to me yet, so I just ask. "What do you mean?"

She looks up and down the street as if someone might be watching, and I wonder if this is how I look all the time now. She leads me closer to the windows in front of the post office.

"Tyrone told you he got thrown out of Notre Dame—which I can't believe he actually shared. Our parents are mortified."

"Yeah," I whisper. "What happened? He didn't really explain."

She closes her eyes and inhales. "He got caught using steroids. They nailed him with a random drug test and kicked him to the curb."

I cover my mouth, but this is exactly what I was afraid she'd say. Tyrone worked himself half to death to play at Notre Dame. His father was an alumnus, and after Tyrone made the team, Mr. Wallace could hardly stop talking about it.

"I just don't want them to find out I screwed up too. They sent me to therapy and everything last time. They think I'm cured."

"You're going to have to tell them if the sheriff doesn't. . . ."

"I know—I mean I will." She sighs. "I just need to wait for the right time. Maybe after this investigation stuff blows over."

My stomach twists into a knot. "I didn't realize you knew about Gretchen's files."

Her lip curls. "From what I saw, she had dirt on just about everyone."

"How much did you see?"

"Enough."

I raise my eyebrows.

"She knew Tyrone was doping." Aisha frowns. "She made sure I saw video of that, even before he got caught."

"What would be the point of that? Did she want you to stop him?"

"I begged him to stop. I'm sure she knew how that would go." She shakes her head, focused down the street. "You know, we were in the dollar store before I took that stupid ring. I was about to slip a tube of toothpaste in my pocket, but she stopped me. I thought she was going to try and talk me out of it like Haley." Her eyes flash. "Instead, she dared me to go for something bigger."

A familiar heaviness creeps into my stomach.

"After everything went down—the cops, my parents, Mr. Meyer calling in favors to get the charges dropped—I got this weird feeling. Like she somehow set it all up. Like she knew what would happen and was just sitting back to watch."

I look into the empty window of the post office, afraid to admit she might be right. "Aisha, that sounds a little—"

"I tried to distance myself from her, thinking that would help, but I felt the same way after what happened with Tyrone."

I hesitate, wondering if it was Aisha who pulled away back then, or Gretchen who isolated me. I turn back and her face is so serious. I can't bring myself to confess I know how she feels, so I shut my mouth and just nod.

"Look, I don't think Gretchen had any particular beef with me and my brother. I know we weren't the only ones she messed with." She looks hard at me. "All I'm saying is, there were a lot of people she could've pissed off. Maybe she finally did it to the wrong person."

THIRTY

AFTER AISHA DRIVES AWAY, I text Marcus. I have so many unanswered questions, and a lot of them still center on him, but a strange charge works its way through my limbs, down into my fingers and toes. It's a while before I recognize it as hope.

Meet me later. Need to talk.

As soon as I hit Send, my phone starts ringing with a call from my mother. I frown. When I phoned to tell her I was spending the evening with Aisha, she couldn't have sounded more thrilled. I'm not sure why she'd be calling now. I walk over and open the restaurant door.

My mom looks up from behind the counter, confused. "I thought you were having pizza at Aisha's."

"I was, but . . ." My voice trails off. I take in her knotted fingers, the purse over her arm. "Is something wrong?"

Her forehead creases. "Do you think you could stay with Felicia while Aunt Elena takes Noah to the hospital?"

"What?" My eyes widen. I look around for my uncle, but don't see him anywhere. "Where is he? Of course I will. Is he okay?"

She picks up the phone behind the register again. Dina hurries out of the kitchen balancing two trays, too busy to notice my anxious gaze. Most of the tables are full, typical for a Saturday night. Uncle Noah would normally be here making sure everything runs smoothly. My phone vibrates in my pocket.

"Sonia just walked in." My mom pauses, setting her purse on the counter. "He is? Okay, don't worry about Felicia, she'll be right over."

She hands me a set of keys as soon as she hangs up.

"I could run there faster."

"Just take Dina's car, okay?"

"What's going on?"

She frowns. "He's been feeling dizzy, having pain in his chest. He keeps telling Elena it's nothing, but you know . . ."

I nod, clutching the keys and heading for the door. Noah isn't exactly in tip-top shape, and my grandfather died young of a massive heart attack. She isn't saying it, but I know it's weighing on her mind.

"Sonia," she calls after me. "Text when you get there—and when you're on your way back."

I don't pause to argue. "I will."

It's after six by the time Elena gets Noah into the car and drives away. When I got to the house he looked pale and afraid, not at all like my strong, burly uncle, barking orders from behind the diner counter. Felicia and I play checkers until she's ready for bed. I offer to read her a story, but she asks me to just sit with her until she falls asleep.

"Do you think Gretchen's still around, like, watching things?" she asks.

"Like a ghost?" I think of Mrs. Meyer's anxiety about Gretchen's spirit being trapped here and a chill moves through me. I dig my hands into my pockets. "I don't know . . . I guess she could be."

"My dad said if anything happens to him or Mom, they'll still watch over us."

I pull the covers up closer around her. "Your dad's at the hospital. He's not going anywhere else tonight."

"But do you think it's possible?"

"What do you mean?"

"If someone dies, could they keep hanging around to see what happens?"

I don't feel equipped to have this conversation, especially right now. "I guess a lot of people might want to . . ."

She turns her head, studying my face. "Would Gretchen have wanted to?"

I think a long time before answering. "Yes. Absolutely."

Once Felicia's breathing shifts to an even rhythm, I head into the kitchen to find my phone lighting up with texts on the counter. They go back hours.

Marcus 6:01 p.m. **Thought you said no texting.**

Marcus 6:02 p.m. **Am I allowed to ask where we're meeting?**

Mom 6:32 p.m. **Elena says you got there ok. I love you.**

Aunt Elena 8:13 p.m. **Noah ok, docs not sure what's wrong . . . More tests.**

Mom 8:20 p.m. **Hanging in there?**

Marcus 8:27 p.m. **Hello?**

Marcus 8:28 p.m. **What did the sheriff tell you?**

I dash off quick replies to my mom and Aunt Elena, letting them know everything's fine, Felicia's asleep, and I'm settling in to watch a movie. I do turn on the TV, but more out of a need to fill the silence than an actual desire to watch anything.

I text Marcus.

Change of plans. Meet tomorrow. Evil Bean.

My phone buzzes a few seconds later.

Not tomorrow. Tonight.

Can't tonight. Family emergency.

Should I ring your uncle's doorbell, or do you want to step outside?

The back of my neck flares hot. I tiptoe to the front window, peek between the curtains, and gasp. The old Cadillac is across the street, right behind where I parked Dina's hatchback. The dome light comes on and Marcus climbs out, loping toward the house. I look over my shoulder at the empty stairs and hurry to the front door, barely opening it a crack.

"I could report you for stalking."

"We need to talk."

"What are you even doing here?"

Marcus gazes up at the sky. "Do you want to have this conversation here, or are you going to let me in?"

I listen for sounds from the second floor. Part of me badly wants to let him in, but something in my gut makes me hold back. Maybe I've been too careless with my feelings. His fingerprint might not have been on the postcard, but it's still unclear what role he played the night Gretchen died. And I can't forget Reva's accusations that he might be working with someone else.

A car drives by slowly. My fingers dig into the doorframe.

"The patio. Around back."

I stumble through the darkened house, somehow making my way to the kitchen without knocking over anything that could break into a million loud and messy pieces. When I open the patio door, Marcus is leaning against the barbecue grill. His baseball cap is pulled low over his eyes; his jaw is unshaven.

I close the door firmly behind me. "How did you know where I was?"

"I saw you take off when I was leaving the sheriff's office. I'd just read your text and thought you might be going somewhere to meet me."

I shake my head. "Babysitting my cousin. My uncle's in the hospital. So you've just been sitting out there for the last two hours?"

"I hope your uncle's okay." He ignores my question, but the gentle tone of his voice makes it sound like he does care. "Why were you at the sheriff's office?"

"Why were you there?"

"Sergeant Blake had me come in. She asked all kinds of questions about my history with drugs."

I wrap my arms around my waist, not sure I want to hear this. "What did you tell her?"

"That after the time my mother got busted hiding her cocaine in my lunchbox, I pretty much decided to avoid the stuff."

"That's a good answer."

"It's the truth." His voice is flat.

I avoid his eyes, thinking of the money in Gretchen's purse. "Even if you don't use, people pay a lot to move that stuff around, don't they?"

Marcus looks at me like I've slapped him. "Are you going to tell me what you and Aisha were chatting about with the cops?"

I stare at my hands. The sheriff said not to tell anyone about the money, and that probably goes double for Marcus, but I'm not sure how else to go about this. Gretchen was supposed to meet Marcus in the woods. She had a large amount of cash. According to Reva, Marcus needs money. I just wish it didn't make so much sense. "Look, some new evidence has been . . . brought to light."

"Brought to light?" He pushes up his cap and glares at me. "Sonia, what the fuck is this about?"

I step back, bumping into the wall of the house. His eyes are wild, uncertain.

Afraid.

"I found the purse Gretchen was carrying that night. Aisha and I turned it in."

He doesn't move or say anything. The only light on the patio shines through the kitchen door, but even in the dim glow, it's clear his face has paled.

"Was there anything in it?" he finally mutters.

"Would you know something about that?"

"What was inside?" he snaps.

I start, crossing my arms over my chest. "It sounds to me like you know exactly what it was."

He looks away.

"Okay, here's how this is going to work," I say, trying to sound calm. "If you still want my help with this, you need to tell me exactly what you were up to the night Gretchen died and what that money was for. If you can't be straight with me at this point . . . you're on your own."

His eyes come back to mine, bright and focused. "I never wanted to get back together with Gretchen."

I hold my breath.

A bold look flashes across his face. His gaze moves along the arch of my brow, over my jaw, down my neck and collarbone. My skin warms as if he'd actually touched me in each of those places.

"I was meeting her to pick up the cash . . . five thousand dollars. It's *not* what it sounds like."

There's a drumming in my ears. He did know about the money. And if he lied about his feelings for Gretchen, he could be lying about everything else. "Then where does Alex Burke come in?"

"Who?"

I frown. "The guy who's sitting in jail instead of you?"

"I'd never even heard of him before this week."

"The sheriff says he's a drug dealer."

His face darkens. "Oh, then I *must* know him. Since my parents are addicts and that's how that works."

I pause. "That's not what I—"

"Look, you don't need me to tell you Gretchen wasn't into drugs. I don't have the first clue what she was doing with that guy, except that he seems to fit her type." He glares at me, but there's hurt in his eyes. "Apparently she assumed I was a *bad boy* too, or right now my life would be a lot less fucked up."

I pull my hoodie tight. It's colder out here than I expected. "Then I don't understand . . . what was the cash for?"

He turns his head, staring into the shadows of my uncle's yard.

"I told you, my grandmother's been sick. She ran her finances into the ground fighting my parents for custody, and then her medical bills reached the point where she was going to have to sell her house to pay her debts. It wasn't even a huge amount of money, but it was more than she had." He shakes his head. "After everything she did for me, I couldn't let that happen."

"Okay . . . so you asked Gretchen for money and she decided to give you five thousand dollars out of the goodness of her heart?"

Marcus sits on the edge of a large wooden planter. "Why don't we cut the bullshit, Sonia."

The air thickens in my chest. His gaze is black.

"You know the things Gretchen was capable of, probably better than I did. Goodness wasn't one of them."

My face goes hot, even though I wasn't the one to say it.

"We slept together right away, even though I barely knew her. I have to admire how tactical she was—there's power in vulnerability." He looks at the ground and pauses.

I shift my weight, trying not to imagine these details in my head.

"It didn't take her long to figure out my grandmother's situation and offer to 'help.' I was selling paintings here and there and working at Evil Bean, but it wasn't enough. She had access to cash, her dad's a philanthropist . . . at the time it seemed to make sense. Five thousand dollars was more money than I'd ever seen in my life, but she made it seem manageable, something I could pay back." He takes off his cap, raking his hands through his hair. "Unfortunately, my grandmother deteriorated. Five thousand dollars became ten thousand, then another five . . . if she'd given me what was in her purse that night, I would've owed her twenty grand."

My pulse races. Everything inside me wants to reach for him, but I clench my fists in my lap. I need to be careful about this. "Twenty thousand dollars . . . that's a lot of reasons to want someone dead."

"You know I didn't kill her."

"I didn't say you did."

He looks at me and frowns. "It's funny, for a while I figured you had to be in on it—what she did to people. But once I really paid attention, I changed my mind." His eyes soften. "It was worse for you than anyone, wasn't it?"

My cheeks flash hot. I look away into the shadows. "I don't know what you mean."

He rises from the planter and steps toward me. "How long did it take her to get you right where she wanted you?"

I step back. "Look, Marcus, I'm sorry you and Gretchen had such a screwed-up relationship, but—"

"What would she have done if you said no to her? When was the last time you tried?"

I swallow, but my mouth is dry.

"Did you know Reva Stone would've been valedictorian *before* Gretchen died, but Gretchen made her fuck up her grades just enough so she could be on top?"

"Wh—why would Gretchen do that?" I ask, not even convincing myself.

"Because a long time ago, Reva made the mistake of coming on to Gretchen."

I look at my feet. I'm not ready to talk about this. I never will be.

"Reva's parents don't know she's gay—maybe they won't even care. But Reva isn't ready to come out and she didn't want Gretchen to do it for her." His face is stony. "Did you know Tyrone Wallace started using steroids at Gretchen's suggestion? His parents put all that pressure on him, but he couldn't quite find his edge—so Gretchen 'helped' him kinda like she helped me."

A gust of wind sweeps across the yard, making the trees dance in the shadows. My hair blows across my face, forcing me to blink. I was cold a second ago, but now I'm burning up. "How do you know all this?"

His lip curls. "That's just the kind of Girl Scout she was. She got me so far under her thumb, she just had to gloat about what she'd done to everyone else." He steps closer to me, his scent like paint and cedar. "You already knew, didn't you?"

I look away, at a crack in the siding on my uncle's house, unsure if I'm more relieved or afraid. Marcus shouldn't know any of this. The whole reason Gretchen had so much power was because she could keep secrets and not tell anyone. But maybe it was different between her and Marcus. It was certainly different between Gretchen and me.

My voice comes out shaky. "What did she say about me?"

He pauses a long time. Long enough that I wonder if he heard me, but when I look at him, his gaze is steady.

"Not a single thing."

I shut my eyes. I want to keep them closed forever. I open my mouth instead.

"She made a video of you saying you wanted her dead."

"I know." He exhales. "If I knew where that was right now . . ."

My cheek twitches, but the SD card is safe where it is. He doesn't need to know I have it. Yet.

"Look, Sonia, she thought she had me with the money. She almost did. But she was patient and she knew my weakness was in who I cared about." His eyes are gentle, focused. "Maybe she knew my feelings better than I did. I hardly saw it coming." He brushes my hair away from my cheek and my skin comes alive. He's looking at me the way he did before, almost like he's painting a mental picture. *You could declare your love for Sonia and live happily ever after.*

My eyes widen. I pull away. This can't be real.

He wipes his hand over his face. "Sonia . . ."

I stare at him, forcing my feet to stay put. "Y—you're not serious."

"If you think I'm an ass, I deserve it. Being a dick to you seemed like a good way to protect you . . . but maybe it wasn't the best idea."

I open my mouth, but no words come out. When Gretchen showed me the video, I had laughed. Despite all the feelings I couldn't get over, Marcus clearly hated my guts. I figured she'd only said that to work him up for the footage.

Every nerve in my body burns. It isn't fair to be hearing this now.

"Look, once I knew I was in deep with Gretchen, I spent a lot of time observing, trying to figure my way out." He pauses, like he's searching for the right words. "That's when I started to notice how strong you were. She ruined everyone else around her, but you seemed—untouchable." His voice hitches. "I admired you for that."

Untouchable. I almost choke. If he thinks I'm someone to admire, he couldn't have been looking very closely. He'd have been better off despising me. He watches me now, his eyes burning into me like a need. I can't let him see this on my face, so I stare down at my hands.

"But I was *in* on it," I say through my tears.

THIRTY-ONE

"WHENEVER SHE WAS UP TO something, she made sure I played a part." I close my eyes. Take a breath. "She knew Reva had a crush on her. She led her on, let her think she was interested, then made me hide and take video when Reva tried to kiss her." My hands are shaking, but now that I've started, I can't stop. "She had me pick up the steroids for Tyrone. I don't know how she got them; all I did was drive. She told him he could just use them until he got ahead, but when they worked, he was afraid to stop . . . just like she knew would happen." I swallow. "I was afraid of her, afraid what she might do to *me*. I didn't want any part of it, but I went along with everything she did. I'm no one to admire."

I raise my head, but I can barely bring myself to look into Marcus's eyes. I don't think I can take the judgment, the disappointment. Not after everything he's said. When I finally gather the courage to steal a glance, his face is solemn. But his gaze is soft.

"I figured it was something like that," he says quietly. "At first I thought she didn't have anything to hold over you, that you were just like her. But that wasn't the way Gretchen worked. She was clearly in control—but she wasn't *destroying* you. She was so pissed when you got your scholarship, I almost confessed everything to you right then. I wanted to know how you did it. I wanted to see you win."

I shake my head, haunted by Gretchen's website, what will come of the meeting on Monday. If she were here, I'd probably be begging to go with her to Stanford. And, of course, that's what she wanted. A tear slips down my cheek.

"I was never going to win. She let me live this whole other side of life, let me see just enough to know what I wanted . . . or what I didn't want." I lower my eyes, thinking of my mom. "When I got into Penn, it seemed like I might actually have a chance, three thousand miles away from her, but even then—" My voice catches.

Marcus reaches out, hesitates, and I let him take my hand. My fingers disappear in his and a shot of warmth, comfort, travels up my arm, spreading through my chest to every terrified, anxious point of my body. It's everything I've wanted and don't deserve and I struggle not to pull away. He moves closer and the low tingling inside me passes through my skin until my whole body vibrates. He isn't wearing a jacket and I need somewhere to focus that isn't his eyes because my heart is already beating so fast, I'm dizzy. I look at his shirt, watching the steady rise and fall of his chest.

"It even crossed my mind she might've planned her death—this whole thing." I wipe my cheek with my other sleeve. "Like she was willing to go that far just to mess with me."

"I never even thought of that." His voice is grim. "I wouldn't have put it past her."

I let out a long breath. "You might think this sounds messed up, but Gretchen wasn't always awful. Sometimes we just had sleepovers and watched movies or went to the beach. I could talk to her about things . . ." I think of her distracting me with ghost stories in the woods. Of the time I came down with the flu at her house and she insisted I stay a full week until I felt better. One time she'd even offered to track my dad down so I could meet him. "I—I really miss her."

"You deserved better. . . ." Marcus traces his fingers through my curls, leaning close. I tip my head back, hesitate, afraid to fall into him.

A light comes on inside the house and the back door opens. I pull away, let go of his hand, but not before Dina steps onto the patio. She stands there with her mouth open.

Marcus backs away. "I'd . . . better get home."

"Okay," is all I manage to say before he disappears into the shadows. It takes a full thirty seconds to get my heart enough under control to raise my head and look at my aunt.

"Sonia. Why don't you come inside."

"They decided to send Noah home, but Elena has no idea when the paperwork will be done." Dina leans against the kitchen counter, her voice flat. "I'll be covering his shift in the morning and thought I'd crash here so you could head home."

"So, he's okay?" I'm light-headed with relief, only now realizing how terrified I was to think I might've been lying to my cousin all evening. "It wasn't serious?"

"He's going to follow up with his cardiologist." She folds her arms and nods toward the back door. "So, you want to tell me about that?"

I stare at the white linoleum. I want to climb into my own bed, close my eyes for about twenty-four hours, and process *that* myself. The last thing I want to do is stand here trying to explain it to Dina, but she doesn't ask rhetorical questions.

"The sheriff has someone else in jail for Gretchen's murder."

"Yes. I'm aware of that," she says.

I falter. Of course she's aware; she's the whole reason Alex Burke was even arrested. I take a deep breath, trying to pull myself together.

"Look, Marcus and I . . . we've both been really mixed up about all this. We were just talking, trying to figure things out."

"*Talking.* Here. Tonight." She raises her eyebrows.

"I . . . didn't really plan for it to happen this way."

She steps across the floor and looks down at me. She isn't that much taller, but I can't help feeling like a little girl. "Sonia, I'm not your mother. Even if I were, I would never tell you who you can and can't see. I just want you to be careful."

"Marcus hasn't done anything." I'm a little surprised by the intensity of my voice, but after the moment we just shared, I'm surer of the words than ever.

"That might be true." She sighs. "But there are still a lot of unanswered questions."

My phone buzzes in my hand, but I don't look at the screen. "Please don't mention this to my mom?"

Her face goes slack. "Noah and Elena think you're here, snuggled safe on their couch, looking after their kid. I found you outside in the dark with a boy I don't trust, unaware that anyone had come in the unlocked front door. I'm not mentioning this to your aunt and uncle—they have way too much on their plates right now. But I'm sure as hell going to tell your mother."

I close my eyes.

"Why don't you go home and get some sleep." She hands me her car keys. "We're short-staffed. It's going to be a busy morning."

THIRTY-TWO

Are you in trouble?

I look around the diner, half expecting to see Marcus watching me from some corner, but he isn't among the Sunday brunchers and post-church crowd, and if he was, it would be obvious. I look up from the coffeemaker at my mom, running back and forth between the kitchen and the register with a smile even though she barely slept and we're not exactly speaking. She knew everything by the time I walked in the door last night. I could tell because she didn't say a word about it. She asked a couple questions about Felicia, told me the latest on Uncle Noah, and said she was going to bed. But I heard the television come on around two a.m. and she was up with a cup of coffee at six when I finally gave up trying to sleep and got dressed.

Wouldn't come in here if I were you.

Need to see you.

Tuesday, library? I have fifth period free.

Why not tomorrow?

I hesitate. I've been afraid to ask my mom about the Penn trip, but there's no way I can miss that appointment. If I have to drive there by myself, I will.

Going to be in Philadelphia.

It's a long minute before he replies. **Text as soon as you're back.**

"That coffee done, Sonia?" Dina passes by, looking pointedly at my phone. "They could use refills at tables six and two . . . whenever you're free."

I rush back into action, refilling every low coffee mug I can find and busing a few extra tables for good measure. I know overcompensating won't really help me, but it keeps Mom and Dina off my back and my mind busy. The bell above the door rings and Kip walks in by himself. I hesitate, the bold red letters on the postcard flashing bright in my memory. I wet my lips, reminding myself that Kip leaving the photo never really made sense even before Alex Burke was arrested. I pick up a menu and cross the room, grateful to see anyone smiling at me.

"Hey, Kip," I say. "Table for one, or is there someone you're meeting?"

He shrugs. "No, it's just me."

I lead him to a booth and tap my pencil against my forehead, trying to think. "Okay, you'll have a coffee with cream and the steak and eggs over easy with a side of green chili?"

His brows draw together. "Uh, actually, I was thinking pancakes and bacon . . . but the coffee sounds good."

My face heats up. I realize a minute too late it's Marcus who always orders steak and eggs. "Yeah, no problem, I'll go put that in."

"Sonia?"

I turn back, holding my order pad between us.

"I was wondering if . . . you might go with me to prom?"

My mouth falls open. I blink at him and notice how rigidly straight he's sitting. His hands are clasped in front of him. It looks like he even tried to style his hair.

"Thanks, Kip, but I . . ."

"It doesn't have to be like a date. We could just go as friends."

I didn't think my face could get any hotter. *Why* would he ask this? "You know, I'm not even sure I want to go. Gretchen and I had planned to go together . . ."

He contorts his mouth, his own color deepening, and I worry for a second he's really upset. "Okay—I just, you know, thought I'd ask."

"No, I—I'm glad you did." I feel like there's more I need to say, but I just tear a sheet off my order pad and crumple it in my hand. "I'll go get you that coffee."

I spend as long as possible in the bathroom, trying to decide if Kip is really that desperate for a date, or if there was another reason behind his request. The possibilities make me uneasy. He did say he was in the woods before Gretchen died. But does that mean Alex Burke was in Gretchen's room just by coincidence? When I come back out, I nearly trip over my own feet. Kirsten is sitting with Kip, smiling pleasantly. She leans toward him and he smiles back. It looks as though they're having some sort of in-depth discussion, but both of them stop talking as soon as I approach.

"Sonia, hey." Kirsten gives me a gentle smile. "Deputy Robson told me about your uncle. How's he doing?"

"They think he's going to be okay." I fumble with my apron. "Thanks."

Kip barely acknowledges my presence when I pour his coffee. I'm happy to pretend the last ten minutes never happened too.

"Let me get you a—"

"I'll do the granola bowl," Kirsten says quickly. "Extra fruit, hold the yogurt."

I pause, my skin prickling. The granola bowl was always Gretchen's order. It strikes me as weird her little sister would ask for that, but I push the thought away. Kirsten hardly comes to the diner; I doubt she even knew. "Coming right up."

When I come back from the kitchen, I spot Haley through the window and wave to her. She looks over her shoulder and comes inside wearing shorts and a track jacket, looking like she just finished a run.

"Hey, where's Yuji? Is he meeting you?"

"No, Aisha." Her eyes dart over the nearby faces. She spots Shelly and Amir in the corner and lowers her voice. "Is it true, about Gretchen's drug money?"

I drop the menus I'm holding. I steal a glance at Kirsten as we both stoop to pick them up, but I don't think she could have heard.

"Aisha was supposed to keep that quiet," I whisper.

"It's okay, I won't tell."

I narrow my eyes. Haley has never been the greatest at filtering her thoughts before they reach her mouth. I lead her over to a table on the far side of the room. "You and Aisha doing breakfast today, or grilled cheese?"

"Grilled cheese!" Aisha slides into the chair across from Haley. "Sorry I'm late. Drama at the Wallace house this morning."

Haley makes a face. "Tyrone?"

"More like my mom and dad." Aisha rolls her eyes. "Tyrone is handling this whole thing like an adult."

I clear my throat. "So, you told Haley about that too?"

Aisha hesitates, then lifts her chin. "Telling Haley is like telling myself. She's trustworthy."

"Did you find something to wear to prom, Sonia?" Haley smiles, making a calculated change of subject. "I can't believe it's this Saturday."

My neck is stiff. This seems to be on everyone's mind except mine. I guess it might be a welcome distraction if it didn't make me so sick to think about Gretchen not being there in her purple gown. "Um . . . I'm still kind of working on it."

This isn't quite true. Gretchen gave me a dress. Actually, she wanted to buy one for me, but I wouldn't let her, so she selected a beautiful pink chiffon gown out of her closet, swearing she hadn't worn it in at least two years. We'd just returned from a marathon shopping trip in the city, where I'm pretty sure she tried on every dress in creation, aside from two because she didn't like the colors. I accepted the gift, complaining all the while that it was pointless since I didn't have a date, but that's when she said she didn't either, and told me about breaking up with Marcus.

"You're welcome to try anything in my closet," Aisha says. "Want to come over later?"

I wince, but manage to make it look like a smile. Serving as Gretchen's charity case was one thing. I think I'd rather find a dress in a discount bin than let the rest of my classmates take up the cause. Today I'm sporting a concert T-shirt and the same pair of worn cutoffs I've been wearing all week. I bagged up most of Gretchen's clothes the other day, and so far I haven't been tempted to dig back into them. It hasn't been easy, trying to dress like me, but I haven't changed my mind about it.

"Are you girls talking about prom?" My mom appears next to me with an empty tray. "I thought you had a dress, Sonia."

I guess prom is one of the few subjects worth speaking to me about. I'll take that over hearing what a disappointment I am. "I . . . don't."

She frowns, and I'm afraid she's going to remember the one Gretchen gave me and insist it's a perfectly good gown, but she just sticks her pencil behind her ear and says, "It's so late in the season, there are probably some great sales. You should go shopping this afternoon."

Haley raises her eyebrows as my mom walks away. "Want company?"

THIRTY-THREE

I CAN'T WORK MYSELF UP to enter the mall or any of Gretchen's usual favorite boutiques, but I end up finding a dress at Decades, a vintage store in Ithaca that Gretchen hated. The fabric is teal chiffon layered over bright yellow taffeta, which had me skeptical on the hanger, but once I tried it on, the colors worked. The zipper is a little tricky and the lining has a tear, but it has a shawl collar that drapes in a pretty way over the neckline and there are no stains on the skirt. It'll never be the dress Gretchen gave me, but that's kind of the point. I end up paying fifty dollars, which is about twenty-five dollars more than I'd like, but Haley tells me I'm crazy, that it's a steal since it's authentic, and she won't stop talking about how good it'll look with my hair up.

She drops me at the diner on her way home, and judging by the number of occupied tables in the restaurant, we're already in for a busy evening. This is fine with me. My mom and I leave for Philadelphia at eight in the morning. I've done everything I can think of to ready myself for the meeting—gathered documents, transcripts, rehearsed—and now I just wish I could work all night since I know I'm not going to sleep. I hurry up the back stairs, ready to throw the dress in my mostly empty closet before heading down. My mom calls something up the steps after me, but I don't put the words "Kirsten" and "upstairs" together until I walk into my room and find her perched on my bed.

"Sonia, hey."

She stands, tucking her hair behind her ears as soon as I walk in, but it takes my brain about fifteen seconds to catch up. Kirsten—in my room. Gretchen always seemed at odds with my bedroom, but in a different way, like she was too big for it or something. Not literal big, but presence big. Sort of how when there's a full moon the stars in the sky don't seem as bright. Seeing Kirsten here . . . she's too blond, too quiet, and she was sitting too straight when I walked in. I take a careful step into the room, looking around for something to indicate why she's here, but nothing strikes me as out of order.

"I didn't realize you were here," I say once I manage to find my voice.

"Your mom invited me up—I hope you don't mind." There's something odd about the way she's standing, how she's looking at me.

I set the plastic bag containing my dress on the purple chair. "Have you been waiting long?"

"Not really." She smiles, but the way she holds herself is more crooked than relaxed, her movements so repetitive, it's like she's doing everything she can to appear at ease.

A heavy feeling twists through my gut. "Kirsten, is something wrong?"

She shakes her head with a nervous laugh, looking everywhere around the room but at me. "I stopped in downstairs for a milk shake and just thought I'd say hello."

I narrow my eyes. I've spent enough time at the Meyers' house to know Kirsten can't drink milk. But why would she lie about something like that? The clamor of banging pots and Dina singing some old U2 song drifts up from the kitchen. I reach behind me, gently closing the door.

"What's going on?"

She clutches her hands tightly in front of her, looking past me at the door. Then she takes a deep breath and reaches into her purse, pulling out a Hidden Falls postcard exactly like the one I got. She flips it over with a trembling hand and holds it out, but I don't need to touch it to read the dark red words.

My breath hitches. "How did you get that?"

She doesn't say anything, her face a mix of unreadable emotions.

I snatch it out of her hands, turning it over, but there's no fingerprint anywhere. I hesitate, relieved at first, but then my heart starts pounding again. "You got one too?"

Kirsten opens her mouth.

"I got one just like it. Where did you find this?" I ask again.

"It came in the mail yesterday, in an envelope, but I thought—" She stops, a flash of accusation in her eyes.

"You thought *I* sent it?"

"Not exactly . . ."

I close my eyes. "Why would I ever do something like that?"

"It—it actually seemed like something Gretchen might've done." Kirsten's tone is short, her eyes downcast.

"So you immediately thought of me?" Fury mixes with the hurt already filling my chest. Does everyone believe we were this much alike? "Gretchen would never have done something like this. She didn't do anonymous."

Kirsten's face reddens. She wraps her arms around herself. "I just . . . I thought you might be mad at me. If I hadn't fought with Gretchen that night—"

"Kirsten, whoever sent these is sick. What happened to Gretchen was *not* your fault." I hand the postcard back to her, anxious to get away from it. "I just wish I understood what this was about."

"Maybe we should ask the sheriff."

"I already showed him the one I got."

She raises her eyebrows. "What did he say?"

"He thought it could be a prank, but he's going to feel differently when he sees this."

"I'll take it to him. I'm going there next."

Something in her voice makes me pause. "What for? Did something else happen?"

She looks at her hands. "Yeah . . . Alex Burke is out of jail."

I can feel the blood drain from my face. I don't even realize I've sat down until Kirsten sinks next to me on the bed.

"I overheard my parents talking," she says. "Apparently he came up with an alibi."

"But your dad *saw* him."

"Yeah, he's not denying that part, but he found some friend to say they dropped him off at our house and met him in Jamesville ten minutes later." Her lip curls. "Guess there just wasn't enough time for him to properly kill Gretchen."

My limbs go numb. Maybe a solid arrest is too much to hope for . . . but how often can this happen? I think of Marcus's grandmother covering for him and my stomach feels like it's leading a revolt. "His friend could be lying."

"I know, that's why I wanted to talk to the sheriff." Her voice quavers and when I look up she's wiping her eyes. "I guess I didn't realize how relieved I was. I thought the right person was in jail. Now, with this, I feel like I don't know anything."

I know the feeling. My head spins at the thought of starting over with my list of suspects.

I reach out slowly and touch her hand. Gretchen was never very sensitive, but Kirsten is nothing like Gretchen.

"What can I do to help?"

She shrugs. "We all just have to wait and hope the sheriff can do his job." She sets her postcard on the bed between us. "Maybe this will lead to something."

I give the writing a wary look. "It gives me the creeps. Who do you think might have sent them?"

Her eyes flash, but I notice her cheeks are dry. "Sometimes I think Gretchen had more enemies than friends."

I swallow, thinking of last night with Marcus. "I know she did."

She sits up straighter, staring at me with a frown.

"The thing with Tornado—it wasn't an accident." I stand and turn to face her, my right arm throbbing at the wrist. "I didn't know for sure until you said he was your horse. She was annoyed that I didn't trade horses when she asked. She had me hold his reins. She even showed me just how to wrap them tight around my arm."

"You didn't know he was mine?"

I sink into the desk chair, crushing my dress, but I don't care. "She only said he reminded her of a horse she once had."

Kirsten shakes her head, her jaw trembling. "She made sure to tell me it wasn't personal. She wanted our dad to have him euthanized after he threw her, but he donated him instead. There was nothing wrong with Tornado except he spooked easily. It was just bad luck their paths ever crossed again."

"I'm sorry." A lump rises in my throat. "I didn't even know he'd been put down."

"Why didn't you say anything then?" Her tone is sharp. "If you'd just—"

"People tended to have accidents around Gretchen." I look at her without raising my head. "I guess after a while you want to believe stuff that isn't true."

She doesn't say anything. The hum from the diner drifts up through the floorboards until I work up the nerve to look at her again.

"Did she—did she ever do anything directly to you?"

"She would've had to speak to me a little more often for that."

The bitterness in her tone catches me off guard. "I don't understand."

She looks down. "I don't know, maybe she just didn't care enough to bother."

I think of Reva, Tyrone, Aisha, Marcus . . . everyone Gretchen paid "special" attention to. "Maybe she was showing she cared by *not* screwing with you."

Kirsten's eyes widen.

We both jump at a knock on my door. I didn't hear anyone on the stairs with it closed. Kirsten tucks the postcard back in her purse.

"Come in."

My mother's face is strained when she enters the room.

I look at the clock. "I'm sorry, Mom, we lost track of time."

"Sonia, the sheriff is downstairs to see you." Her voice is controlled and I know instantly he already told her Alex Burke is free.

Kirsten rises right away. "I'll walk down with you."

Sheriff Wood stands awkwardly in the diner kitchen. He looks like he's aged since the last time I saw him. He holds his hat in one hand, the fingers of his other hand tracing absently over the items on his duty belt. Shelly once told me how much all that gear weighs. The gun, the nightstick, the handcuffs. I don't remember what the exact number was, but the sheriff's posture is so slumped, it might as well be a thousand pounds.

"Kirsten, I'm glad you're here too," the sheriff says. "I already spoke to your parents—"

"We were just talking about it. You had to let him go," she says.

"For the time being, unfortunately."

I step forward. "How can you be sure he's telling the truth if it's just his friend vouching for him?"

The sheriff gives me his stony media face. "Don't worry, we're sure."

I ball up my fists. "Sure like you have actual evidence, or sure like you're guessing?"

My mom opens her mouth, but Sheriff Wood holds up one hand.

"It's all right, Marlene." His face is calm, but serious. "There's time-stamped security camera footage of him driving into the shop with Gretchen's car. We have that and the time Mr. Meyer found him in her bedroom. It takes about fifteen minutes to drive to Jamesville under the speed limit. Mr. Burke made it in eleven."

I swallow. Marcus doesn't have time-stamped anything.

"Look, this isn't to say he couldn't have been involved. The guy's only twenty-one, but he has quite a history. We're still looking into his whereabouts the rest of the evening. We'll be watching him closely."

My mother's hand rests on my shoulder. "What about Marcus Perez?"

Sheriff Wood glances at Kirsten. "I think I'd like to speak to each of you girls alone."

Kirsten and I exchange a look, but she nods, then surprises me by leaning in for a hug and whispering in my ear. "I'll show him my postcard. He'll figure out who did it."

She disappears around the corner, but my mother doesn't move. Aunt Elena is helping out tonight behind the grill, melting cheese on a couple of burgers, but she's so focused on what she's doing, I doubt she's listening.

"Sonia, your mom tells me Dina found you and Marcus sneaking around together."

I sigh. My mom would call it sneaking around.

I lower my voice. "He stopped by Noah's last night to see if I was okay."

"I wasn't aware you two were friendly."

"Look, we were just talking. Marcus didn't do anything wrong." I'm aware how defensive I sound, but I just can't stop digging myself a deeper hole. I should just shut my mouth, let the sheriff track down a suspect without interfering, but after last night I can't help it.

I don't *want* it to be Marcus.

"Did he tell you something about that night?" the sheriff asks. "Is there some reason you're having this change of heart?"

"I just think it's worth focusing more on the guy with the actual criminal history." I look down. "Besides, I never said I thought he was guilty."

"No, but you were never so sure of his innocence either."

I raise my head, staring him in the eyes. "All I'm saying is, you have two guys with alibis. Maybe neither of them did it."

"Or maybe somebody's lying," he says.

I cross my arms and look away.

My mom and the sheriff have one of their wordless eye-contact conversations. He puts on his hat like he's about to leave, but then he turns to face me.

"With no strong suspect in custody for Gretchen's murder, we'll be refocusing the investigation on the money found inside her purse, as well as the photos and postcard left inside your locker, Sonia."

My mother looks back and forth between us, confused, while my stomach drops.

"Sonia's locker? What are you talking about?"

I lower my head, clutching my arms around my waist.

"This might be overly cautious," he continues, "but I'll have a deputy assigned to keep an eye on you here during the day, and we'll be doing regular patrols after hours. Deputy Brennan will be monitoring you at school. I still think you're perfectly safe there, but since that's where the alleged threats have come in, I want to be extra cautious."

"Threats?" My mother's face is pale, her voice growing shriller by the second. "Someone tell me now. What is this about?"

I can't look at her. I stare at the ground. "But you said they weren't overt threats."

"They're not, which is why I'm not taking more drastic measures." Sheriff Wood turns up his radio to hear an incoming call and frowns. He moves for the door, tipping his hat apologetically at my mom. "Sonia, I think it's time you brought your mother up to speed."

THIRTY-FOUR

THE CLOCK IN THE ADMISSIONS office at Penn hesitates every time the second hand comes around to one. I've witnessed it almost twenty times now, but it must have gone through at least ten cycles before I focused on it. Before I had to see it happen to know another minute had passed.

Tick, tick, tick, *tick-tick*, ONE.

A door opens. The clock stops.

"You may step back in, Sonia," Dean Gunter says.

I rise, dropping my phone and hastily retrieving it from the carpet. The office of the dean of admissions looks a lot like you might expect a dean of anything's office to look. Dark wood, shelves of books, diplomas and certificates all over one wall. The woman returning to her seat behind the desk is dressed in a trim skirt and blouse, her short hair a no-nonsense academic gray. A pair of glasses rests on the blotter and she regards me coolly. When I first arrived, all I did was supply documents and facts. This is my second time through her door. I can't help wondering if it will be my last.

"I've reviewed the items you've shown me and had a chance to speak at length with my colleagues regarding the letter from your high school's ethics teacher," she says.

I stand mute in front of the desk. I can't form words. It feels like all I can do just to watch everything come apart around me.

She narrows her eyes. "Please, sit down, Sonia."

I sit.

"As I said earlier, I was extremely concerned once this website was called to my attention." The dean leans toward me with a stern expression. "I'm sure you're aware what a rare privilege a scholarship like this is. We don't tolerate any type of infractions."

"Yes, ma'am." I tug at the black pencil skirt I borrowed from Dina. "That's why I wanted to come in and talk with you personally. Since Gretchen—" My voice breaks. I still can't believe this is happening. That she's done this to me.

Dean Gunter shuffles the papers in front of her into a neat stack and looks straight at me. "Tell me, Sonia, why would you have set up a money-scheming website like this?"

"I *wouldn't* have." I sit forward, my voice rising at her choice of words. "I have a good, steady job in my uncle's diner. The website wasn't even set up till after I was awarded the scholarship. Why would I risk everything just to make a few bucks on some old essays?"

She shows no trace of emotion as she removes her glasses. "And why do you think your friend, Gretchen Meyer, might have done something like this?"

I press my back into the chair. I'm not sure where she's going with this now. I'm so used to keeping Gretchen's secrets, but now I hesitate, weighing how badly I need to tell the truth.

"It was a project for her ethics class . . ." I falter, staring at the hard line of her mouth. "But I think Gretchen put it online intention- ally."

"Is there a reason you believe that?"

I pause. "Will this be going on record?"

The dean sets down her pencil, but doesn't say anything.

I take a long, deep breath, and close my eyes. "Gretchen wanted me to go with her to Stanford. We were both accepted there, but I chose Penn after I was offered the scholarship." I open my eyes, looking at the closed office door. "It's hard to explain, but she was used to getting what she wanted. . . . She could make people change their minds about things. I think, in a backward way, that's what she was trying to do."

Dean Gunter raises her eyebrows. "That must have hurt your friendship quite a bit."

I look away. I'm beginning to understand the layers of our rela- tionship a little better now than I did three weeks ago, though if Gretchen had lived, I can't help thinking we would've been headed to California together in the fall. I try to imagine that, following her to the West Coast like a loyal spaniel—or maybe just one that's well trained. But my throat tightens with guilt when I think I'm only *here* because she's gone.

"Gretchen wasn't perfect. But she *was* my best friend. What hap- pened to her—" I close my eyes. "I just don't want people lingering on her bad choices. What she did with this site caused a huge mess for me, but I'm willing to take responsibility for it. I don't want her family, or her memory, to end up hurting more."

The dean sits back to ponder this and I do everything I can to pre- pare myself for what's coming. Dina has done well with community college. If Penn and Stanford are out, I could live at home and still take classes. After the last few weeks, I'll feel lucky if I get to college at all.

"This is a unique situation," the dean says, leafing through the folder in front of her. "After speaking with you and reading the letter from Mr. Hanover, I feel relatively satisfied you had no intention of profiting financially when you provided the content for the website."

I blink, too scared to venture breathing.

She looks up at me with a grave expression. "I will advise you to be more careful with your intellectual property in the future. Academic dishonesty is something this and *any* institution is going to take very seriously."

She stands abruptly. I hesitate, rising unsteadily to my feet. "I'm not sure I understand . . ."

Her mouth pulls into a tight smile, but she extends her hand. "We will be reviewing your file quarterly, at least for the short term. But you're a very bright student, Sonia. You show potential to build excellent character and that's something we're interested in on this campus."

I take her hand. "You mean I—"

"I believe you'll thrive at the University of Pennsylvania. We look forward to seeing you this fall."

Air floods into my lungs for what feels like the first time. "Thank you, ma'am, thank you so much." She gives my hand a firm shake before pointing me toward the door.

"Oh, and Sonia?" she calls just as I touch the handle. "I am so very sorry, about what happened to Ms. Meyer, and for everything you've been through."

The sun is just peeking out from the clouds when I exit College Hall, heading across Spruce Street toward the Quad where I told my mother I'd meet her. The temperature is mild and there's an air of spring fever exuding from everyone I pass. Or maybe it's radiating off me. When we arrived I was so nervous I couldn't do much more than locate the correct building for my meeting. Now I see the open spaces covered with students lounging and studying on the lawns, and my heart fills with a new sort of resolve. I *am* going to graduate; I'll be here in the fall. Not in spite of Gretchen, but maybe somehow . . . in memory of her.

A Frisbee sails toward me, tumbling in the grass and coming to rest at my feet. I pick it up, tossing it back to a couple of shirtless guys who wave at me, grinning. A group of girls pass by me discussing finals and I imagine myself joining them in the fall, walking back to my residence hall with a stack of books and assignments. I'll chat with my roommate about what to have for dinner, maybe even venture out at night to a real college party. I stop to inhale the scents of the campus, letting the blossoming trees and flowers overpower my senses. I gaze up at the historic Tudor Gothic buildings and I feel lighter, safer here than I have at home for the past month.

I twinge with guilt when I finally spot my mother resting on a bench outside the Quad. The fall semester is only a few months away, but I wish I could start now. I've never felt so close to this place. I don't want to leave it to go back home.

When she sees me, my mom sits up, looking anxious. "How did it go?"

"Good, actually. . . . I guess I'm back on track."

Her shoulders relax. "I knew you'd get it straightened out." She picks up her purse and phone and my daydream fades.

"I'm sorry again, Mom."

We didn't talk much this morning on the drive down in Noah's car. I tried to focus on driving while she shuffled through every radio station she could find. But the worst part about the last twenty-four hours was listening to her pacing up and down the hall all night, and the effort it clearly took her to smile at customers this morning before we left.

"You know, I thought I'd hate the idea of leaving you in this place. Now I'm not sure I want to bring you home again."

I look up, surprised. "I had the same thought."

She gives me a strained smile. "I don't know how you can act so calm when someone's out there just . . ."

Her voice trails off and I curl my fingers so she won't notice the chewed nubs of my nails. "Any news on things at home?"

"Dina only had a second to talk when I checked in, but I guess it was Shelly's day off so she came in to give them a hand. They're not very busy."

I relax a little. Shelly did a stint of waitressing at the diner in high school and she was good. She and Dina always competed to see who could make more tips.

"What about Noah?"

She sighs. "Elena had him in the doctor's office first thing this morning, but so far they're just telling him to take it easy."

"Well, let's hurry up and get home." I start in the direction of the car, but she hangs back.

When I turn, she inclines her head toward the intricate brick buildings. "We're already here, don't you want to look around?"

I blink, not sure I heard right. "I . . . but what about the diner?"

"We're not going to make it back in traffic before the evening rush. And Shelly's there. Dina and I agreed you should have a chance to get familiar. You'll be living here before you know it."

I manage a nod. I want to say something, but her words are so unexpected, when I start thinking about it, my throat feels like it's closing up.

"This place is huge. I don't know how you're going to find your way around." She takes my hand and squeezes as we start walking. "Actually, I know you'll figure it out."

THIRTY-FIVE

THE BELL RINGS AT THE end of sixth period and I'm out of my desk so fast, I make it halfway down the hall before it gets crowded enough I have to slow down. I wave to Deputy Brennan on my way toward the library. This is something I've always done when I've seen him, something I've continued to do all day. But ever since Marcus texted me last night, it's just felt like drawing the deputy's attention. My phone buzzes in my pocket as I reach the top of the stairs.

In the far lot. Parked by the art room.

I type a quick reply. **Two minutes.**

The deputy is supposed to check in with me between every class, but I missed him completely after calculus and we barely waved at each other just now. Maybe he's more concerned about following Kirsten—her dad has every cop in town on edge. I pause above the stairs outside the library. There's no sign of the deputy now, but my heart pounds as I make for the exit. I cross my fingers he's not taking a break in the parking lot.

I look at the clock on my phone before pushing through the doors. The only thing I have after study hall is phys ed. I told my mom Aisha would give me a ride home, though I didn't mention it to Aisha. Marcus and I should make it to Jamesville and back in plenty of time.

I step outside and force myself not to run.

The door of the Cadillac screeches like a wounded animal when I open it. The interior smells like air freshener and an old woman's cigarettes. Marcus smiles at me from the other end of the red leather bench seat, which would make my heart flutter if he didn't look just as nervous as I feel. I shut the door, trying to sink out of view as the car shifts into motion.

"Doing okay?" he asks.

"Fine . . . it's just been a while since I cut class." I sit up and look back at the windows of the school, as if they're going to turn red and start flashing to announce my departure. "I only used to do this with Gretchen."

"And she never got caught doing anything," he mutters.

The car is warm, but all the windows are down. I don't bother to ask if the AC is functional. We pass the sign that says Now Leaving Hidden Falls—Come Back Soon! And the space between us fills with the roar of the engine and hefty amounts of apprehension.

I fidget in my seat. "Are you sure this is a good idea?"

We stop at a light and he looks at me, surprised. "You were on board last night."

"I know. I just wish there was another way to do this." I stare at my lap. "I don't want to meet the guy."

"I told you, he might let his guard down talking to us in a way he wouldn't with the cops. We might get him to slip up."

"But what if he doesn't have anything to hide?"

"He already hid Gretchen's car. And he *was* the guy in her room."

I pause. This is all true. But if Gretchen had dirt on him before she died, she wasn't keeping it on the SD card. We have to come up with something—maybe nothing as incriminating as a recording of him wishing her dead, but everyone seems to agree Alex Burke was bad news. His true interest in her likely wasn't hearts and flowers.

"Maybe the cops have the timing off," Marcus says. "They've only got footage of him coming back to the auto shop, right? So, what if he attacked you first, then killed her, *then* went back to her room to cover it up?"

"I guess . . ." When he puts it that way, I'm even more uneasy about meeting the guy face-to-face.

Marcus grips the wheel until his knuckles go white. "He could be threatening you because he's scared you'll identify him as your attacker."

This could actually make sense. "But why would he do it like that? Why would he even have the picture from the party, and how could he get it into my locker?"

He goes quiet. "I don't know. Unless he's involved with someone else."

I sink in my seat, suddenly relieved to be away from the school. I'm afraid this trip might come to nothing, but I don't know what else to do.

I steal a glance at Marcus, in jeans and a black T-shirt. His face is mild, but he keeps his eyes glued to the road, like a gamer whose sole focus is making it to the next level. I think of everything Gretchen did to him—to us—and I just want to prove it *was* Alex Burke and *not* Marcus . . . somehow.

There isn't much to Jamesville aside from a few roadside antique

286

shops, a small historic district, and the auto garage. Marcus parks the Cadillac on the side of the road rather than pull into the lot. Then he gets out his phone, taps on the screen, and puts it in his front pocket.

"Testing . . . testing . . ." he says aloud.

"What are you doing?"

"I found an app that's voice activated. It'll record whatever he says." He takes the phone back out of his pocket and replays our conversation. I raise one eyebrow and he scratches his head. "Um, I read a lot of detective stories."

This actually gets me to smile. "Stealthy."

He reaches for the door, and I glance at the mechanic's shop. With its dirty windows and junky parking lot it just *looks* like a place where bad things might happen and no one would notice or care. Where a murdered girl's car could go unnoticed for weeks. A rough-looking guy with a shaved head peers out the door at us, and suddenly this all feels too real . . . too dangerous. My pulse picks up. I touch Marcus's hand.

He looks back at me, gripping his keys, his face a reflection of my own. "On second thought, maybe you should stay in the car."

"No way. I'm going with you."

He flinches, brushing a lock of hair out of my eyes. "What if he tries something?"

I touch my right pocket. "I brought pepper spray."

He swallows. "I just . . . I don't want you to get hurt."

"I'll be okay." I weave my fingers between his. "What are you even going to say?"

"I thought I might walk in and ask which one of them killed my ex-girlfriend." When I stare at him, he cracks a smile, but it's not quite convincing. "Or maybe something more subtle."

I slide across the seat. "Yeah, I'm going with you."

"Sonia . . ."

I gesture to the guy still staring at us from the door. "Pretty sure I'm no safer here, by myself, than out there with you."

He nods and squeezes my hand, the sensation traveling up my arm and deep into my chest. We climb out of the car together.

There are at least five vehicles in the lot that look like they haven't been mobile in years. A Rottweiler chained to one of them issues a low growl as we approach, but doesn't lift its head. The man we saw has disappeared into the small building. When we push through the door into the office, the walls are plastered with pictures of hunting expeditions. Men and boys posing with guns and animal carcasses. I shudder at the deadness of it all. There's a pinup calendar in the corner. Classical music drifts inharmoniously through the air.

"Can I help you?" The guy with the shaved head eyes us from behind the counter. He's a lot older than I'd guessed from across the lot.

"I wanted to ask someone about my car," Marcus says.

"The Caddy out there?" The man creaks out of his chair and gestures with interest through the window. "That there's a classic. Had one when I was about your age."

"Yeah . . . a friend of mine said to come here and ask for Alex?"

The man's face falls. He looks at me, then retreats behind the desk and cracks open a door. "Alex! Customer of yours!" He settles back onto his stool and frowns. "He don't handle any of his 'business' in here. He'll meet you outside."

Marcus and I exchange a glance. But maybe it's best if they think we're looking to score drugs. Back on the lot, the air is thinner, cleaner. I step toward the Rottie lying in the sun and she rolls over for a belly rub. I opt to scratch behind her ears and her nubby tail wags until we're joined by a glowering guy in coveralls. I recognize him immediately from his mug shot, though his tan has faded to a pasty white and his hair is longer than I remember. His sleeves are rolled up, revealing a tattoo of a devil on one forearm and an angel on the other. His eyes are intense. Gretchen probably fell for him at first sight.

"Something wrong with your car?" he asks.

Marcus straightens and clears his throat. "Actually, I was hoping we could just ask you some questions."

The guy stops. "Shit. Seriously?" His voice is gruff, eyes shifting from Marcus over to me. "Look, my uncle told the press—"

"We're not reporters," I say quickly.

"Then what the fuck do you want?"

Marcus steps closer to me. "We're friends of Gretchen Meyer's—"

"I've got nothing to say." He sneers, kicking an old hubcap on his way back toward the shop.

Marcus starts after him, but I call out. "Wait, Alex!"

He turns and glares at me.

"Gretchen was my best friend . . . but she never told me about you."

He snorts.

"She never could resist a guy she was attracted to." I force myself to smile. "She must've had it bad to want to sneak around like that."

Alex's shoulders relax a little. He looks back at the shop.

"Bet she came on pretty strong," I say. "And if *I* never heard about it, it must've been fast."

He scratches his head. "Look, we only hooked up a few times before—" He catches himself, narrowing his eyes at me. "Who did you say you were?"

"What, you don't recognize her when she's not running away in the dark?"

"Marcus."

Alex's eyes widen and I know we've screwed up. "You're that kid they think killed her."

Marcus's face darkens. "Pretty sure that honor goes to you."

"You come here to pin your shit on me?"

I jump in, trying to salvage what I can from this. "What were you doing in her room that night?"

"None of your damn business." He turns back to the shop and I call out.

"Alex, was she threatening you?"

He stops.

I take a deep breath, trying to stay calm. "I'm just saying, I know Gretchen wasn't always as sweet as she looked. If she had something on you—"

"I thought you said she never mentioned me." He comes close, looks me up and down. His breath smells like chew. "You know something about it?"

"I . . . I might." I hold his gaze, trying to maintain my bluff.

He spits at my feet. "Then maybe someone should push *your* sweet little ass in those falls."

I gasp.

Marcus shoves him. "Get away from her!"

They both go stumbling toward a car missing wheels and a hood. The Rottie gets up and starts barking. Marcus's hands are on Alex's arm, but the mechanic yanks out of his grip. He swings at Marcus and misses. I fumble for my pepper spray, but before I can get it out of my pocket, Alex lands a punch squarely in Marcus's gut. The old man sticks his head out of the auto shop door.

"I'll call the cops on all of you," he hollers.

"Good," Alex says. "Tell them I'm being harassed."

Marcus groans, but manages to stay on his feet. I grab his arm.

"Come on, we have to go."

He growls. "He threatened you."

"And you recorded it," I whisper. "Now let's get out of here."

THIRTY-SIX

"YOU SURE YOU'RE OKAY?"

Marcus shuts off the engine in front of his house, touches his side, and winces. "Aside from that being the second time I've been punched in front of you, yeah."

I search the planes of his face, but the bruise Kip gave him has completely healed. "You're getting better at it," I say, trying to lighten his mood.

He hits the steering wheel and I jump. "I'm sorry. I fucked up. He pissed me off . . . and when he threatened you, I just freaked."

"It's okay." I bite my lip. "He wouldn't have told us anything either way."

His shoulders droop. "He made it pretty clear what he'd like to see happen to you."

I pull my hoodie closer. I can't deny that.

Marcus turns, leaning toward me on the seat. "Sonia, there's something I've wanted to—I mean—" He hesitates, tripping over his words. "Can I show you something?"

I search his eyes, wondering what he has in mind, and nod.

Marcus makes a beeline around his grandmother's house and I

follow, straight toward the studio out back. He hesitates, looking at me with his key in the door. He takes a single deep breath, then opens it wide and invites me inside.

I have never seen so much color.

There are paintings all along the walls, some in frames, some just sheets of paper held up with tacks. Thin ropes crisscross the air above our heads, dangling landscapes and portraits, and bright, beautiful abstracts. There's an easel in one corner by the window and a table next to it covered in an array of tubes and jars and trays of different paints. The air has that clean smell that comes incongruously with an artist's mess.

"I like to work fast, so I mostly use acrylics . . . but sometimes oils." He mumbles, hesitant, like he's talking just to fill the air.

I'm drawn immediately to a pair of framed portraits—or at least that's what I think they are. Each of them is of a girl striking the same pose. Her head is thrown back, her hand splayed over her stomach, her wild orange hair floating around her head in a way that makes me think of laughter, though she has no actual facial features to complete the suggestion. The portraits are identical, but the colors are what make a distinctive contrast. One of them is done in bright tones—yellows, greens, purples, and reds. The other is all browns and blacks and grays. Except for the hair. That's the same in both of them, bright orange-red. Individually, they're smart, thought provoking. Side by side, they're jarring, like you're expecting to see a photograph and realize you're looking at a negative.

"I just sold those. It's a diptych—they go together."

I nod. They would have to. They're not at all what I imagined Marcus would do with Gretchen in paint—they're better. She almost seems alive. I find Marcus's signature at the bottom of each frame, but nothing else. "What are they called?"

"It's untitled. They're kind of a mash-up. . . ." He moves between the canvases and me and there's a distance in his eyes, like he can't wait to get them out of his sight. "For a while I was calling them *Good & Evil*, but that didn't seem right."

"They're beautiful."

"If you like that sort of thing." When I glance up, his back is to the paintings. He's looking right at me.

My skin heats up. I turn in circles, unsure where to look next, overwhelmed by the idea that I'm seeing everything Marcus sees and feels. There are faces and rivers and trees, and abstract explosions of color that seem like an expression of what thought might look like if you had to put it on paper. Finally, curiosity draws me toward the easel.

He clears his throat. "That one's not finished . . ."

I stop.

He runs his hand through his hair and now I notice traces of paint dried on his skin. "I don't mean you can't look . . . it just isn't very good."

I raise my eyebrows. "If you don't want me to—"

"You can." He frowns. "It's just not like the original."

I come around the side of the canvas.

This girl has a face, but only just. There's an arch of an eyebrow, a line of a nose, and just a hint of one side of her mouth. Her eyes are closed, and *she* seems closed. At first it looks like she's simply sleeping, so deeply perhaps she wouldn't hear if you yelled. But the look on her face is so remote, it makes me wonder. For a split second

I think I must be looking at a dead girl—until I notice the colors. They're streaming from her body in tones I could only describe as fear, hope, despair, beauty ... wrapping around her, emanating *from* her. And that's when I'm sure she couldn't be more alive.

I notice the shape of her face now, a little like Dina's, but without the freckles. Her hair is curly and dark. I gasp. Heat radiates off me just the way it seems to on the canvas, but what I'm looking at is so intimate, I feel like I should close my eyes. I never compared myself to Gretchen when it came to appearance. In some ways it's easier having a best friend who looked the way she did. There's no competition. You get used to not being seen. So I don't know how to explain this. If *this* is how Marcus sees me.

"I don't know what to say."

He comes up behind me, so close if he wrapped his arms around my waist his body would shape to mine. He runs his hand down my arm and my skin ignites. I close my fingers over his, hold them in place, and forget anything else exists.

He sighs into my hair. "I guess I didn't either."

I turn to look at him and a flash of panic crosses his face, like he's been caught with something he shouldn't have. I hold his hand fast and he closes his eyes, his chest rises, and finally, his shoulders relax.

"I thought I could re-create it," he murmurs. "It's not the greatest copy."

"Re-create what?" I stare at the portrait. "It's stunning."

"Gretchen destroyed the first one. It was one of the best things I've ever painted." He opens his eyes, looking sidelong at the canvas. "This one's okay."

I turn back from the easel to look at his face. "What do you mean, she destroyed it?"

His eyes darken. "You're the first person I've let in here since then—it seems kind of appropriate, since this is what set her off in the first place."

"This painting?"

"The first one. I don't know, I thought I was so careful, but I didn't used to lock the door. I guess she saw something in it when she found it."

I slide my hand out of his, stepping closer to the painting. If Gretchen saw this before they broke up . . . she'd have been upset to say the least.

But could she have thought I had any idea?

Marcus fidgets, collecting tubes of paint on the table, arranging them by color. "That video she made shows me flying into a rage, ready to kill her—and believe me, I wanted to—but what it doesn't show is the rest of the room. She was sitting back, admiring the diptych when I found her. It was the only one she didn't slash or throw paint on. I lost months of work."

Something deep within me starts to quiver. Marcus seems too far away. Or maybe the tiny shed feels too big. I move to the table, take the paints out of his hands, and set them aside. He watches me, eyes dark and warm, but he barely moves. My body flashes hot. I open my mouth, but I don't know how to say this, to allow myself this.

He casts his eyes down. "Sonia, what I said the other night, if you don't feel—"

"No—*yes*. I do."

I take his hand, and for one fleeting moment, I'm not sure what's happening. Our fingers lace together. A mass of energy builds inside me, or maybe inside both of us. It spreads through our limbs, connecting us in a way I've never imagined possible. Not outside my head. I look into his eyes, my heart pounding, and then our lips crush together. His hands are in my hair, my hips press into his. We knock brushes and paints to the floor, almost upsetting the table, but neither of us lets go. My body trembles, my head is spinning. I have no idea what I'm doing, but here, now—*this* feels right.

Time seems to slow, and when we finally part, my mouth vibrates along with every cell in my chest. Marcus traces a finger along the arch of my brow, down my cheek.

"I don't know what I would do if—" His voice hitches. He turns his head, pulling me to his chest. "I don't know how to keep you safe."

I wrap my arms tight around him, trying to hold on to the moment, but even as my heart races, the warmth inside me fades to dread.

He pulls away. "I've been thinking I might just come clean to Sheriff Wood."

I stare at him, at my empty arms. "Come clean?"

"Tell them the truth . . . about my alibi."

My stomach twists into a hundred knots. "You can't do that."

"They'll never find the real killer if they don't have all the facts."

My chest tightens. He can't realize what he's saying. "How is telling them you *could* have killed her when you didn't going to help anything?"

"I wanted Gretchen dead." His face clouds. "Sometimes that feels as bad as being her murderer."

"No." I step toward him, panicked by the hopelessness in his voice. "It's not the same, Marcus. At all."

He cups his hand to my cheek. "You're in danger as long as the real killer goes free."

I touch my fingers to his and shake my head. "It was Alex Burke."

He hesitates. "What if it wasn't?"

"It *has* to be." I pull away, pacing to the left, then the right. "We'll take that recording to the sheriff. He'll find a way to prove it."

"The sheriff does need to know the guy threatened you." Marcus sighs heavily. "But I'm not sure he killed her anymore . . . I couldn't see it in his eyes."

I stare at him. "Are you serious?"

"Don't get me wrong, he's an asshole, and if he ever comes near you—" He clenches his jaw. "But I can't just pass the buck. I wouldn't wish the situation I'm in on anyone, even him." He looks long and hard at the diptych on the wall. "Maybe it was random after all. Maybe Gretchen just ran into some psycho in the woods."

I close my eyes. "Okay, maybe it wasn't Alex Burke. I think we've established you weren't the only one who might've wanted to hurt her."

"I'm the only one the cops seem to care about. I had motive, opportunity, and no real alibi."

"No one knows the truth about your alibi but us." I slip my hand into his, anxiety and fear tangling our fingers back together. "Please, just wait, Marcus. We can figure this out."

THIRTY-SEVEN

WHEN I COME DOWNSTAIRS THURSDAY morning Uncle Noah is behind the register. It's only been five days since he was in the hospital. He looks pale and he's resting on a stool rather than standing, but his eyes are bright and alert. He cracks a wide smile when he sees me.

"There's my favorite niece."

I set my backpack on the counter and wrap my arms around his big shoulders. He hugs me back, but he feels smaller somehow, and he doesn't smell right. "I heard Aunt Elena put you on a diet."

Noah groans. "Won't let me smoke either. She's killing me trying to save me."

I pull back and study his dark wavy hair, the cleft in his chin, the twinkle in his eye. "I'm glad you're all right."

He looks out the windows at the spring leaves filling the park. "You need a ride to school today, kiddo?"

I shake my head, helping myself to a cup of coffee. "Aisha's picking me up."

A couple comes up to the register and I scan the occupied tables while Noah rings them up. It looks like a slow morning. The kind my family always complains about, but I secretly love. Sometimes on days like this, my mom and I share a crossword, filling the words in while we clean the blenders or organize pies in the display case. She's across the room now, but she probably won't be up for a puzzle. She nods solemnly, taking Mr. Moore's order, looking impossibly more tired than yesterday. The van Gendts are at a booth in the corner, there's a trucker at the counter, and by the windows sits a girl with short blue hair.

I frown. Reva doesn't come in here very often. She's vegan and likes everyone to know it. The few times I've served her, she's ordered cereal and soy milk and gone out of her way to make faces at other people's bacon and eggs. I pick up a pot of hot water and approach the booth where she's sitting with a mug and a bowl of fruit.

"More water for your tea?"

"No thanks, I'm all set." She peers up at me from a notebook. "Heard they picked up the wrong guy for Gretchen's murder. I guess that means the heat's back on Marcus."

She smirks and stabs a piece of watermelon with her fork and I just stand there holding the hot water, telling myself not to dump it on her. I cannot figure her out. I sink into the opposite side of the booth, disregarding the put-out look on her face.

"Let me ask you something . . . just call me curious. Who do *you* think killed Gretchen?"

She raises one dark eyebrow. I guess it's too much trouble dyeing them to match her head. "I don't care."

"Really? You seem kind of invested in what happens to Marcus." She ignores me.

Our last conversation plays over and over in my head until finally, one tiny detail stands out. "Last time we chatted, you were pretty adamant he never loved her."

"I know he didn't." Her voice is bitter, and a strange look flashes across her face so fast, I almost miss it.

"Oh my God." I blink. "Were you jealous of him?"

Her face reddens, but now she won't look at me at all.

"After everything she did to you?"

She sits quietly for a moment, then digs some cash out of her bag and leaves it on the table. "You're a lot stupider than I gave you credit for."

Aisha's Jeep pulls up outside and I'm about to let this go, but as Reva slides to the edge of the booth, I remember how oddly it struck me that Marcus knew so much about her. His explanation was that Gretchen had bragged about what she'd done, and I accepted that at the time. But it stands out like a red flag to me now.

"He knows what Gretchen had on you." I speak slowly, trying to figure out why Marcus would've lied. "But she would never have told him that."

Reva sets down her notebook, but doesn't seem at all surprised.

"Did *you* tell him?" I ask. "Why would you do that?"

"I couldn't very well ask you for help."

I sit straighter, chewing my lip. At least some part of this is beginning to make sense. "You asked him to get the video."

Reva exhales and gathers her things. "For the record, Marcus Perez is a liar. And pretty worthless at doing what he's asked."

My arms break out in goose bumps. "What else have you asked him to do?"

Outside, Aisha taps her horn twice. Reva stands.

"I have the video, Reva." I swallow. Right next to the one of Marcus. "I've never told anyone what's on it. I—I'm going to destroy it."

She gives me an icy smile. "*Going to.* I think those were the words Marcus used. I guess I'll just put all my faith in you now, since you're such a great person. Thanks." She picks up her bag and stands, looking down at me from a pair of high wedge heels. "You can tell Marcus I don't need him anymore. He's probably over at Evil Bean. He spends a lot of extra time there, between meeting with you and his other girlfriend."

I narrow my eyes, confused.

"Oops." She covers her mouth, making no attempt to hide her smile. "I thought you knew he was seeing Kirsten Meyer."

THIRTY-EIGHT

MARCUS ISN'T IN SCHOOL AND hasn't answered any of my texts. I can't help noticing Kirsten's absent today too. I go through the motions all day, stopping at my locker, raising my hand in class, but by last period even my teachers start to ask if I'm okay. Reva's words have smoldered inside my head to the point that I can hardly think about anything else. I don't trust her in the slightest—she's made it clear she's looking for every reason to cause trouble. But I doubt she'd make the effort without expecting some kind of payoff.

When I think of everything Marcus has said, the things we've done the last few days, my stomach turns to stone. I need to talk to him—get him to explain this so it makes sense. I just can't believe it could all be a lie.

"Aren't you supposed to be learning or something?"

The door of the guidance office clicks shut behind me. I look up to find Shelly walking toward me in uniform.

"There was some stuff I had to clear up for my scholarship." I glance around, looking for the sheriff or Amir. If Marcus turned in the recording, I expect to have half the sheriff's office and my mother down my throat. But Shelly's alone. "Is everything okay?"

"I'm just covering for Deputy Brennan. His wife had a baby last night, so I got volun-told to cover the school, and you, for a couple weeks." She winks at me.

I breathe a sigh of relief. He hasn't handed it over yet . . . though I'm not sure why he'd wait. "Thanks again for pitching in at the diner Monday. It really meant a lot."

"Glad I could help out. It was fun working with Dina again." She shakes her head. "I can't believe you're heading off to college already. We're all so proud of you."

"Thanks." I hesitate, clearing my throat. "Even my mom seems to want me to go now."

"Are you kidding? I thought she was going to freak right out when you got that scholarship. She busted in on the sheriff's meeting with the mayor, she was so excited."

I squirm. "That . . . sounds like my mother." Shelly isn't one to exaggerate, but sometimes it's hard to tell my mom's happy excitement from her panicky angst. I'm pretty sure her enthusiasm is a recent development.

"She knows it hasn't been easy, but you've worked so hard. And for you to do it all by yourself . . ."

She doesn't finish her thought, but I dig my fingernails into my palms. I'm not surprised my mom blabbed to her about the Meyers' offer to send me to college. I never want to know what strings Gretchen pulled to convince them to do it. I'm just relieved I didn't have to accept.

"Hey, I wanted to ask, is anything new happening with the case?"

She frowns, standing a little straighter. "There isn't a whole lot to report right now, but Mr. Meyer's been putting the heat on all of us. It's the top of our agenda."

"What about the other postcard?" I chew my bottom lip. "Did the sheriff make anything of that?"

"Other postcard?"

My stomach tightens at the blank look on her face.

"There's only been the one, to my knowledge." Her eyes go serious. "Unless you got another."

I don't know what to say. I was anxious that Sheriff Wood hadn't followed up with me about it yesterday, but when I saw Kirsten at school, she told me all about their conversation. She said he'd called a meeting immediately and arranged for a deputy to keep an eye on her. She seemed relieved he was taking it so seriously and I'd told her not to worry. There's no way Shelly wouldn't know about this.

Unless Kirsten was lying.

"That's just . . . weird," I say, trying to keep my cool. "Kirsten told me she got one too. I don't know why she wouldn't report it."

"Kirsten *Meyer*?" Shelly pulls her radio off her belt and eyes me suspiciously. "Sonia, if you hear stuff like this, please don't hesitate to tell me." She walks off to radio the sheriff's office.

I watch her leave, my head spinning with every reason Kirsten might have lied to me, and none of them are good. I think of her waiting in my bedroom with a postcard identical to mine. Of Gretchen slashing Marcus's painting and pointing the finger at me for their breakup. But I wasn't the one she found him with the night of the party.

I thought you knew he was seeing Kirsten Meyer.

The Evil Bean is almost empty when I walk in, though the music blares angry as ever. Marcus is behind the coffee bar cleaning one of the espresso machines with his back to the door. He doesn't look up until I bang the little steel bell on the counter.

"Hey." He turns his head, startled. "Is everything okay?"

"Is this a bad time?" My voice shakes. "You're not waiting to see someone else?"

He sets his cleaning rag down and comes around the edge of the counter. "No, did something happen?"

My face is hot. I don't even know how to start. I push up the sleeves of my hoodie, and that's when I realize it's like a sauna in here. Marcus is in a light T-shirt, the hair on his forehead damp with sweat. I look across the room and the stupid fireplace they never turn on is now blazing away with all the doors and windows wide open.

"Fireplace won't turn off, they're trying to get it fixed." He looks over his shoulder at the guy with the neck tattoo, carrying in a table-top fan. "Do you want to talk outside?"

The air is thick and suffocating, but I don't think I can force my feet to move. "Here is fine."

He leans on the back of a chair, looking perplexed, and for a second we're back in the studio, lips crushed together, his hands in my hair, and I don't—*can't*—believe that wasn't real.

"What do you know about that postcard I got?"

"What do you mean? I was there when you found it."

"Yeah, you were." I clutch my stomach. "So, whose idea was it? Were you helping Kirsten, or was she helping you?"

His face is blank. If he's playing oblivious, he deserves an award.

"Come on, Marcus. The photo was smart, and the fingerprint— it totally threw me. Even the second postcard would've been brilliant if I hadn't figured it out."

He shakes his head, his brows drawing together. "Second?"

I focus on his hands because I think I'll lose it if I meet his eyes. "Look, before anything else happens, I just want to know where we stand ... if any of what happened between us was real. Because some of the things you—"

"Sonia, what are you talking about?" Marcus steps toward me, his face patient, but bewildered.

"You've been meeting with Kirsten, in secret, just like you have with me."

He presses his lips together, his silence cutting the air between us.

I look at the paintings decorating the back wall, but the once-vibrant colors seem dull to me now. "So, is it just that I don't have thousands of dollars to dig you out of debt, or is it something more?"

His face darkens. He turns away, hand in his hair. "Okay," he says, turning to me again. "She approached me after the funeral. We talked and she offered to help me with the money, but—"

"Of course she did," I whisper.

"She's not like Gretchen. She's just trying to figure this out, like you and me." He shakes his head, clearly flustered. "There's *nothing* else going on."

When he reaches for me, I pull away. I so want to believe him, but right now even his touch feels like a lie. It would be awful enough if I thought Marcus had simply been using me, playing with my feelings while running around with Kirsten. But the photo and postcards—Marcus even said they were meant to scare me. If he and Kirsten are the ones behind them, I need to know why.

"Sonia, please. Everything I've told you was the truth."

"Including the part where you lied about Gretchen telling you all her secrets?" My fists are clutched so tight I barely notice the sweat trickling down my hairline. "Reva had a few things to say about that."

He swears under his breath. Hurt and fear vibrate through every nerve in my body. "Okay, Reva shared that with me herself, but everything I told you about it was true."

My throat feels like it's closing. "Just like that alibi of yours."

Neck tattoo guy glances our way. Marcus hunches his shoulders and lowers his voice. "Look, just tell me what this is about a second postcard."

"No." I sway on my feet, dizzy with the heat. "No more weird games or threats, I can't do this anymore."

"But I'm not—"

"Just . . . what do you guys want?" My jaw trembles. Alex Burke was a convenient distraction, but neither Kirsten's nor Marcus's whereabouts were clear the night Gretchen died. I've been careless, let my guard down—again. I think about Gretchen's memorial, tossed into the falls. If Kirsten and Marcus did that too, there's no doubt.

I'm the next bitch down.

"We all just want the truth." He balls his hands into fists. "My whole life is on the line here, Sonia. I'll do just about anything to prove I didn't kill Gretchen."

My mouth goes dry. "That's what I'm afraid of."

A breeze moves through the open door. My head clears and I step toward it, but when I look up, a blonde in a sundress blocks my path.

Kirsten stops short when she sees me, her eyes flitting over my shoulder. I think of her inviting me over, pretending she cared, and my only thought now is how right Gretchen was to hate her.

"Sonia." She smooths her dress. "I was going to call you this afternoon. The sheriff—"

"I know you didn't show him the second postcard," I cut her off.

She pauses, shifting her purse from her right arm to her left. All I want to do is run out the door, but my neck prickles as I realize I'm trapped between her and Marcus.

She glances at him and exhales. "Okay, I didn't show him. But only because—"

"Kirsten." Marcus's voice is gruff.

I look up. Her eyes flash, but her face is a mix of annoyance and uncertainty.

"We need to talk," he says.

I step away, testing to see if one of them will try to stop me. I need out of here. As much because I'm scared as I don't want to watch the two of them together. A few more feet and I'm at the door. Noah's Passat is right outside. I just need to get in and drive away. From all of this. From everything.

"Sonia—" Marcus calls.

The warm air outside hits my skin like a chill.

Kirsten speaks up behind me. "Just let her go."

THIRTY-NINE

"ONE LAST PIN AND MY masterpiece will be . . ." Haley looks up at me in the mirror. Her face falls. "What's wrong? You don't like it?"

I wipe away a tear with a shaking hand. "No, it's beautiful, thank you."

Haley spins me around in the desk chair so I'm facing her sitting on the bed. She fusses over my smearing makeup, but then squeezes my knees and looks straight into my face. "It's not going to be the same without her, huh?"

I hold a tissue in front of my face and shake my head, but I wish that was all there was to it. In a way, she's right. If Gretchen were here tonight I'd be able to focus on hair and nails and dresses and heels. If she taught me anything, it was how to compartmentalize. I'd have a whole other set of concerns getting ready at her house, wearing her dress . . . but Marcus and Kirsten wouldn't be among them.

Of course the sheriff was tight-lipped when I tried to ask about Kirsten's supposed postcard. He assured me it was part of the investigation, told me not to worry, and had Shelly take me home.

But I've barely slept the last two nights, my mind running a relay between anguish and fear. I didn't realize how much a kiss could enhance a nightmare.

Now I just feel like I'm waiting . . . for something.

If Marcus and Kirsten had wanted to hurt me, they easily could have by now. That's the part I don't understand. She knows I showed the sheriff my photo and postcard. Marcus even encouraged me to do it. The only thing they might be hesitating over is the SD card, because if something happens to me, it could still get out. Kirsten isn't even featured on it, but after seeing them together, I guess protecting Marcus might be enough for her. I used to feel that way too. I looked in my tin box last night just to make sure the little plastic card was still there. I even thought about destroying it, but it's the only leverage I have.

I'll use it if I have to.

I texted Kirsten once, but she still hasn't answered. If she doesn't by tomorrow, I'll take the card to the sheriff and do my best to explain.

Though my heart still feels sick when I think of turning Marcus in.

My mom gasps from the door. "Oh, you girls look beautiful."

I lean down to fumble with the straps on my shoes, and by the time I stand up, my face in the mirror almost passes for normal. I take a deep breath and manage a smile. It's amazing what one formal dance has done for my mother's spirits. I won't do anything to destroy that tonight. She called the school hours ago to make sure Shelly would be around, and once she was satisfied with my safety, she went off the deep end into nostalgia. I would have put my foot down about going at all if it weren't for that—and my friends refusing to take no for an answer.

Haley grabs her purse and takes my arm. "Let's get this show on the road."

My entire family is clustered in the kitchen, with the exception of Dina, who stops to whistle as we descend the stairs before she runs back out with an order.

"I'm not crying," my mom says, clicking the camera on her phone like it's going out of style. "I just have something in my eye."

Uncle Noah leans against the counter looking tired, but he winks at Haley and me. "Best-looking dates I've seen since my own prom."

"You didn't go to prom." Aunt Elena shoots him a look. "You and Roger Wood hopped a train to see The Cure, leaving me and Sarah Moore high and dry."

The corner of Uncle Noah's mouth twitches. "Oh yeah. Best concert I ever saw."

"I found this handsome guy wandering around the restaurant." Dina comes into the kitchen with a grin, pushing an uncomfortable-looking Yuji ahead of her. He's wearing a tux and carrying a yellow corsage, his Adam's apple bobbing up and down when he sees Haley in her buttercup gown.

"You look amazing," he murmurs, then glances at me. "You too, Sonia."

"Thanks, Yuji."

"You do." My mom slips behind me, tucking a stray curl of my Haley-crafted updo back into place, and I do everything I can to let this just be prom night and not an underline on my growing list of uncomfortable memories. "I can't believe no one asked you to go with them. Those boys you go to school with are the biggest morons ever." She pauses. "Sorry, Yuji."

I shrug, wondering if Kip ever found a date. Maybe he asked Brianne. "I told you, Mom, Gretchen and I were planning to go alone anyway."

"It doesn't matter. Once you get there, they'll all be wishing they'd asked."

My phone vibrates in my hand and I exhale. "Aisha and Derek are here. We'd better go."

My whole family troops out of the kitchen with us, making such a spectacle that the entire diner breaks into applause. My face must be as red as Aisha's dress, but Haley does a little twirl and blows kisses to the room.

"You kids have a wonderful night, you deserve it."

"Don't do anything I wouldn't do."

"Be safe."

"Enjoy yourselves."

"It's what Gretchen would've wanted."

I cringe at this last sentiment. Gretchen would have wanted to be here, outshining everyone in her gorgeous purple dress, getting crowned prom queen, and staying out until morning.

I move to stand between Aisha and Haley.

The five of us pose together for a few more snapshots before Tyrone pulls open the door and steps inside. "You planning to stay a while, Aisha? Should I park?"

Aisha narrows her eyes. "We've been here five whole minutes."

My mom smiles. "Are you going to prom again, Tyrone?"

Tyrone looks down at his tuxedo T-shirt and smirks. "No, ma'am, once was enough. Just driving."

Dina rushes over, getting between us and the door. "Do you all have your masks?"

Haley and Yuji hold theirs up, a yellow butterfly and one of those long-nosed Venetian masks. Aisha's is a cat, Derek's is Batman. I dig mine out of my purse. It's a black plastic Lone Ranger–style mask I found in the kids' aisle at the grocery store. Plain, but I did let Felicia help me decorate it with blue glitter.

"One more picture with masks on!" Noah hollers, wielding his phone like a paparazzo.

We pose again and Tyrone holds the door for us as we leave.

"Have a good time, but be careful," my mom says, trailing us onto the sidewalk. "Roger said there's no reason to worry. Text me if you go to the after-party, and Sonia—" She stops, turning to Tyrone and Aisha. "They might've exempted prom from curfew, but I want her home by one."

"We'll get her back safely, Ms. Feldman," Aisha says.

My mom gives her a grateful smile before Dina drags her back inside the diner.

Aisha and Derek climb in the back of Mr. Wallace's huge SUV with Yuji and Haley. I get in the front seat beside Tyrone.

"Sorry, I didn't realize my mom's insanity level went up exponentially with prom," I say.

"Aww, your whole family got into it," Haley says. "My mom lost interest after my sisters' proms. She was just glad I got a free dress."

Aisha laughs. "We all need to let loose and actually have fun tonight."

"I do charge by the hour . . ." Tyrone says.

She smirks. "Minimum wage is steep."

There isn't a hotel or event center in Hidden Falls, so our prom is put on the old-fashioned way, in the crepe paper–bedecked gymnasium. The school parking lot is already filling up when we get there, music pulsing out across the pavement like a pregraduation siren song. Principal Bova greets us at the doors in a sparkling gold skirt and matching mask, alongside Shelly Robson in her deputy sheriff uniform. They pass out purple ribbons to each of us in memory of Gretchen, then make a fuss over our masks and dresses until the next group comes in behind us. We get shuffled through the lines for raffles, prom court ballots, and the requisite photos. I watch Haley and Aisha cozy up with their boyfriends, each looking beautiful and happy. Then they drag me in front of the camera and we strike a hundred different ridiculous poses while I simultaneously laugh and try not to cry thinking what it might've been like with Gretchen here, shining in the center spotlight. Something cool and velvety brushes my skin and I jerk my head up, half expecting to see her beautiful ghost grinning down at me. I imagine her showing up later in the pictures and have to rub my arms to make the goose bumps disappear.

There are tables set up along the walls with purple, black, and yellow souvenir masks much like my own, stamped with our graduation year. Haley's current favorite song comes on and she drags Yuji onto the already busy dance floor. Aisha looks at me like she's asking for permission and I shoo her and Derek after them. I have zero desire to dance even if I had someone to do it with, so like any person alone at prom, I head for the food and drinks. They're set up by the doors, near the photos and ballot box. I grab a bottle of water, but the assemble-your-own sandwiches and chocolate fountain seem like more trouble than they're worth, and the guy lurking by the refreshment table in a *Friday the 13th* hockey mask does nothing for my appetite. I'm about to work my way around the room to find a table when a commotion at the gym doors catches my attention.

"Stunning," I hear Principal Bova say. "So glad—"

She moves to one side, allowing a late-arriving couple to make their entrance, and my hand flies to my throat.

Gretchen glides in wearing her purple prom gown and feathered mask, dazzling the room with one of her signature smiles. She moves along, casting ballots and posing for photographs, and it takes me a full minute before I'm brave enough to blink. Once I do, the scene shifts. Her piled-up hair changes from red to blond, and I realize she doesn't quite have the proportions to fill out the dress. But the way she carries herself—if you weren't 100 percent certain this had to be *Kirsten* and not Gretchen, you might think you were seeing some sort of bleach-blond specter. She glides through the crowd holding Kip Peterson's arm. He's wearing a tuxedo and a *Phantom of the Opera* mask, and he looks for the most part like he won the prom date lottery.

But why would she be here with him and not Marcus?

They see me right away, probably because I can't seem to move from the spot where I'm standing.

"Sonia, I'm so glad you came," Kirsten says as they approach. "I was going to text you, but I lost my phone."

I swallow hard.

Kip is trying not to look at me, no doubt convinced that this moment is only awkward because of him.

"I'm glad you were able to find a date, Kip," I manage to say.

He grins under the edge of his mask. "No, it's all good, it worked out." His breath smells like alcohol.

"It did." Kirsten wraps her arms around him and plasters on a smile. "I couldn't imagine missing the prom held in my sister's honor."

I can't stop staring at her. If she's wearing a purple ribbon, it's lost in the feathers.

"You remind me so much of her dressed up like that," I say.

She doesn't even blink. "Thanks. Hey, would you come outside with me for a sec?"

I step back. "I'd rather stay here. If you want to talk—"

"It won't take long, Sonia."

The hairs stand up on the back of my neck. I have no idea why she's really here—if she's simply basking in borrowed limelight, or actually trying to scare me—but I'm not going anywhere alone with her. "Actually, there's someone I need to find."

I turn away before she can speak, and cut a straight diagonal across the dance floor, getting jabbed with elbows and cutting between couples. If she comes after me, I'll call the sheriff. This can't look crazy just to me. Aisha and Derek are taking a break at one of the tables and I slump into a chair next to them, wondering if I can call Dina for a ride or if I'll have to stick this out.

"I see Kirsten decided to come after all," Aisha says quietly.

"Yeah. In Gretchen's prom dress," I mutter, taking a long drink of water.

Aisha makes a face and glances at Derek, but he's glued to his phone. "You doing okay, Sonia?"

"It's fine, I'm just . . ."

She puts her hand on my arm. "It's okay, I get it."

I press my lips into some semblance of a smile. I doubt she does, but I appreciate the thought.

I stay in my seat most of the next two hours. Through the speech by Principal Bova, Brianne and Kevin being crowned prom king and queen, and a brief video tribute to Gretchen. Every time I look at Kirsten, she's watching me. I wish the room were a little bigger just so I could move farther away. Brianne stops by our table with Jill Barkman. I congratulate her and mutter something about her tiara. She talks about the music, about being nervous for graduation, then says something about how Gretchen should've won and quickly disappears. A few more groups cycle through like this, always saying something about how unfortunate it is about Gretchen, and I start to realize I've become like some kind of human confessional, here to make everyone feel a little less guilty for having a good time without her. The music shifts to a long, slow ballad. A couple people catch my eye, start to head in my direction, and I rise from my seat. I just need a moment to myself.

I take the long way around the gym, behind the stage and sound equipment, careful to avoid wires and lights in the heels I borrowed from Dina. I'm concentrating so much on where I'm putting my feet, I don't notice someone standing in my way until I look straight up into the Jason hockey mask. I startle, losing my balance as I step back. "Jason" grabs my right arm, steadies me, and then looks over his shoulder and pulls me aside.

"Hey, what—"

He takes off his mask and I gasp, a cold ache flashing through my heart.

"Why are you here?"

"To see you." His gaze is steady, almost apologetic.

I peer over his shoulder toward the crowd. "I think you've got the wrong girl."

Marcus frowns. "You look beautiful."

"You're joking, right?"

"Not at all."

I meet his eyes and my legs weaken along with my resolve. I want to move closer, find my courage somewhere in his arms. But then I look at the mask in his hand and think of him and Kirsten together. My throat burns. I step back. "Didn't want to be recognized before you could corner me?"

He holds up his mask. "Guilty."

"So what happens if I tell Deputy Robson I feel threatened?"

"They throw me out and I lose my chance to set things straight with you."

This would be easier if I didn't badly want to believe him.

"You don't have to get thrown out for that."

His eyes flash. "So you're not going to turn me in?"

I set my jaw and push past him. "I need to go meet my frie—"

He grabs my wrist. I glare back at him.

He lets go. "Please, Sonia. Five minutes."

The music stops. The DJ announces he's taking a short break to swap out equipment. The volume around us falls to chatter. But I'm afraid if I stay, I won't want to leave.

"Move away from me and I won't scream."

He steps back.

I peer around the edge of the DJ setup. Everyone in the room is flocking back to the tables. I spot my friends in the opposite corner. Aisha scans the crowd, looking worried, but Haley's in my seat, going to town on a plate of food. I give Marcus a wary glance. We're in a quiet corner tucked behind a set of retractable wooden bleachers. It's dim, but not completely secluded.

"Give me one good reason I should listen to you."

His voice and eyes are flat. "I think I know who killed Gretchen."

My skin goes cold. The music may have paused, but the room seems louder than ever. "Five minutes."

He sets his mask down and takes a breath. "I asked Kirsten about the postcards. She showed me the one she got; it seems legit."

I grind my teeth. "Are you seriously trying to sell me that? Then why would she keep it from Sheriff Wood?"

He shakes his head. "It was Kip. He's been following her around like a lost puppy since the funeral."

"So have you." If this is his argument, I'm unimpressed. "But let me guess, you guys fought, you're upset she's here with him, so let's call him a murderer."

His jaw is hard. "Actually, she asked me to keep an eye on him. Kirsten believes I'm not guilty. She offered to do what she could if I agreed to watch her back, since she felt targeted too. But that's the *only* reason we were meeting."

He's looking straight at me, posture tense, like he needs me to believe with his entire body. My chest fills with a murky hope, wishing for him to be telling the truth. Just this once. "Nice of her to be so generous about it. That still doesn't make Kip the killer."

"No, but I got into his locker the other day and guess what I found?"

I look at the Jason mask and touch the infinity bracelet on my wrist.

"Two Hidden Falls postcards and a red Sharpie," he says. "Not only that, he had pictures of you."

320

"What?"

He nods. "Not the ones from the party—new ones. At the diner, in the halls. They're actually pretty good. Were you aware you've been doing some modeling?"

I cover my mouth, a slithering sensation creeping through my stomach.

"It makes sense when you think about it, Sonia. The guy was obsessed with Gretchen. She must've rejected him a hundred different ways, but he never got the message. Maybe after she left the party so upset, he thought he'd try again, maybe it didn't go the way he thought, *or*—" He chews his thumbnail. "She might have had something on him we don't even know about."

"No." My voice comes out unsteady. "Kip was like gum on her shoe. She wouldn't have given him that much thought."

"Maybe she should've. Whatever happened, I think he's worried you saw something."

I cross my arms in front of me, trying to imagine Kip as a killer. But when I think of the postcards in his locker, of him taking my picture, I shudder. "He . . . he asked me to prom."

Marcus's lips tighten. "Why didn't you tell me?"

I look away.

"Sonia, I'm aware you think you know the guy—"

"But why send a postcard to Kirsten? And why wouldn't she show it to the sheriff?"

"It took you forever to show him your photo. She has her reasons. She's scared." He clenches his hands into fists. "It was all I could do to get her to show me the postcard she had."

I try to ignore his defensive tone, focusing on what he said about them not being a couple. "If she's so afraid, why would she come here with him?"

A low beat issues from the nearby speakers, echoing across the gym as the music starts up.

"I warned her it was a bad idea. She said she wanted to get as close as she could to him, but I'm afraid he's starting to think of her the way he did about Gretchen."

I stare into the dark space beneath the bleachers, trying to line everything up in my head. "It just doesn't make sense. . . ."

A stack of equipment cases clatter to the floor behind me and someone stumbles toward us behind the stage.

"Hey, there you are, Sonia . . . I've been trying to find you." Kip slurs my name as he approaches. "What are you doing over—"

He stops short when he notices Marcus.

"Where's Kirsten?" Marcus growls.

Kip steps toward me, but his legs look unsteady. "What are you doing with *him*?"

"Don't come near her," Marcus says, stepping between us.

"Is he bothering you?" Kip asks. "Maybe I should go find Bova."

"Suits me. One whiff of your breath and she'll have you out on your ass with me."

Kip sneers.

"Marcus." I touch his shoulder. "I don't think—"

"So, what's it like dating the Replacement Gretchen?" Marcus asks, paying no attention to me. "Maybe if she dyed her hair red again, she'd look like the real thing."

"Fuck you, Perez."

Marcus steps forward until he's breathing in his face. "Did you scare her into coming tonight? Maybe tell her what you did to her sister?"

Kip raises his fists. "What the f—"

"Enough!" I push Kip away from Marcus. He almost falls over, he's so tipsy. "This isn't going to solve anything."

"You're right," Marcus says through his teeth. "Maybe we should ask the sheriff to take his fingerprints."

I shake my head, turning my back on Marcus so I can focus. I look into Kip's sloppy, bloodshot eyes. He does resemble a lost puppy, but I think of the threats in my locker and avoid his gaze. "I need you to answer a question, Kip—for *me*. Can you do that?"

Kip scowls over my shoulder, but he nods.

I take a deep breath. "Did you put a scratched-up photograph of me and Gretchen, and a postcard, inside my locker?"

Marcus scoffs behind me. "Do you seriously think he's going to—"

"Yeah." Kip hangs his head. "I did."

The air thins. I swallow hard. "Why would you do that?"

He slumps against the wall. "Kirsten asked me to. She seemed really angry . . . I wanted to make her feel better." He looks at me like he might be sick. "I'm sorry, Sonia."

My stomach twists. I glance at Marcus, who for once is so shocked he has nothing to say.

"I couldn't believe she even wanted to talk to me." Kip's eyes glaze. "She's so much like Gretchen."

"She is. And she isn't," I say, but the look on his face . . .

Marcus comes to stand by my side. "What else did she ask you to do?"

"That was all."

"Did she tell you what it was for?"

"No, man, and I didn't ask." Kip looks up, irritated. "You don't say no to a girl like that. Oh wait, I forgot. You just murder them."

Marcus steps forward, but I pull on his arm as Kip's words spiral through my head. I think of Kirsten being left behind after the fight at the party, then showing up at home a couple of hours later.

"Did anyone actually *see* Kirsten with that freshman she supposedly hooked up with?"

They both look at me, confused. But she's *so much like Gretchen*. I let go of Marcus and grab Kip's hand, my heart pounding in my ears because I don't have enough time to think about this, and I'm scared because it makes too much sense.

"You said she's a lot like Gretchen," I say quickly.

He nods.

"Okay." I squeeze his hand. "And Marcus just pointed out she'd look even more like her if she dyed her hair red again."

"I guess, but—"

"This is important, Kip. You told the sheriff you saw Gretchen sitting at the top of the falls the night she died, but are you *sure* it was her?"

Kip blinks at me, perplexed, but I can tell there's something going on behind his eyes.

"Kirsten's hair *was* red that night." I wet my lips. "Could it have been her?"

Seconds pass like eternity before Kip opens his mouth again.

"I guess it could have been."

"It could have, or it *was*?" I ask.

Kip slumps to the floor, resting his chin in his hands. "I didn't want to tell the sheriff how high I was that night. I was walking my bike home because I crashed and got a flat. I don't know . . . it could have been either Gretchen or Kirsten."

FORTY

MARCUS AND I PUSH OUT the side exit together, the dance beat muffled as the door clicks shut behind us. We find ourselves on the far end of the parking lot by the line of trees separating the school from the athletic fields. The air is cool and there isn't a lot of light here, but the stars are enough for me to see the conflict on his face.

"What does that mean, what he just said?"

"I . . . I'm not sure."

"Did Kip Peterson just tell us Kirsten killed Gretchen?"

My heart pounds so hard I can barely think. Is there any *other* way to interpret that?

"Marcus . . ."

"Sonia, this is important. It needs to make sense."

He holds my gaze, and I know he's right. This isn't about postcards anymore.

"Let me just try to think." I grip my head in my hands and turn a circle, gulping the night air. "Gretchen and I left the party after she and Kirsten fought, sometime before eleven o'clock. I drove her home, then ran into Haley . . ."

"I don't think Haley matters here."

"I'm just trying to get it straight in my own head, okay? *I* ran into Haley."

"Okay, fine." He backs off.

I stare at a broken chunk of asphalt lying in the grass. "I must've headed into the park a little after eleven . . ."

"Kirsten had time to make it there," he says. "It only took me fifteen minutes to walk from Brianne's to my grandmother's house. It would've taken less time than that for her to make it to the park, and any freshman at that party would jump at the chance to brag that they hooked up with her."

"So it could've been Kirsten who attacked me," I say, my voice trembling.

"If she was mad at both of you, yeah. I don't think she could've mistaken you for Gretchen."

"She was mad and drunk." I hesitate. "But that doesn't explain the phone call."

"Phone call?"

"Sheriff Wood said Gretchen called her house from her cell phone right after I dropped her off."

"Oh, right." His lip curls. "Maybe she was making sure no one was home so she could hook up with her drug dealer boyfriend."

"But someone answered."

"Maybe he was already there?"

"According to his alibi, he wasn't."

Marcus throws up his hands. "Maybe she butt-dialed and answered it herself, Sonia. Does it matter?"

"Okay, you're right, I'll figure that out later." I bite my lip. "So

Kirsten grabbed me from behind at the bridge—I struggled and got away without ever seeing her face. There was no moon that night. Then Gretchen entered the woods and . . . this time Kirsten didn't let her get away." I release a shaky breath, staring down at my hands. The scratches are healed, but I'll feel them in my skin forever. "Kip must've come by just after it was done, when Kirsten was looking down at her sister's body."

"Why wouldn't I have seen her? I showed up not long after that."

"She probably panicked when she saw Kip, and took off. There's a chance you would've missed her, even if she was just on the playground."

"I just— I can't believe it was her. She seemed so dedicated to finding the real killer. But maybe that was part of the act." He meets my gaze. "I'm sorry I didn't see it."

I look down, thinking of Mr. and Mrs. Meyer. They've dealt with so much already; this will destroy them. And Kirsten—all she ever asked for was Gretchen's love.

Everything inside me feels like it's going numb.

"Hey." He takes my hand. "What's the matter?"

"You know what it was like to be Gretchen's boyfriend, I know what it was like being her best friend. What do you think it was like to be her sister?"

"It's still murder."

I stare at the ground. "What are we going to do?"

"Go to the sheriff. Now."

"I don't think I can turn her in. . . ."

He grips my arms gently and I just wish I could sink the rest of the way into him. "Sonia, you *have* to."

"Maybe we should wait. There isn't any real evidence. It's our word against hers."

"She's planning something with these pictures and postcards. I don't want to wait to find out what it is."

"But if we call and she's arrested . . ." My stomach clenches.

"If you don't want to be the one to do it, I will." He reaches into his pocket.

"No—I'll do it."

I pull my phone out of my purse and unlock it to dial, but I'm distracted by the number of missed calls and texts on the screen. My breath hitches. All of them are from Dina and my mother. My vision clouds as I scroll through the messages. I didn't think the world could fall apart any faster.

I look up at Marcus. "I have to get home."

FORTY-ONE

MY MOTHER IS CRYING WHEN I walk in the door. One look at her face and I have to fight not to lose it too. Dina runs a mop over the floor behind the register, something we never do until after we close. There are a handful of customers scattered among the tables, most of them looking on with quiet, wide-eyed stares as if they've just seen something they'd prefer to forget.

My mom practically collapses in my arms, not speaking, just breathing. My eyes burn.

Dina drops the mop and hugs us both, squeezing me hard and fast. When she pulls away, she's composed, but her eyes are red-rimmed.

"What happened?" I whisper.

"He just collapsed. I was by the door about to seat some customers when there was this loud bang." Her face blanches. "He hit his head going down. Amir did CPR until the ambulance arrived. If he hadn't been here..." Her voice trails to a whisper. She looks down at the floor and I feel sick when I notice the mop is tinged red.

"Where's Felicia?"

"Upstairs." My mother whimpers into my hair. "I didn't want to cry in front of her, but I have to go back up—" Her voice breaks off in a sob. "The doctors aren't sure he's going to make it."

"Do you need to go to the hospital?" My voice shakes. "What can I do to help?"

"Elena said he's going to be in surgery for several hours. We suggested closing the diner, but she insisted Noah would want it to stay open." Dina frowns. "She's probably right."

"Then we'll keep it open." I steel myself, reaching for an apron under the counter.

My mom touches my arm, looking at me with huge eyes. "Felicia was asking for you. She said you made her feel better last time."

I set down the apron.

"Sonia?" She stops me before I can head for the kitchen stairs. "I'm sorry your prom was ruined."

I flinch, looking down at my dress, and think of Kirsten. "Don't be, Mom. It wasn't anything you did."

By the time I get Felicia to sleep in my mother's bed, the diner is mostly empty. I texted Aisha when I left prom to let her know where I went. My mom, Dina, and I don't talk much except to the customers. We haven't had any more word from Aunt Elena and I guess we're each preparing for the worst in our own ways.

I keep an eye on my phone, but it stays silent. Marcus and I parted in such a hurry, I'm afraid he'll move forward without me. And as the hours tick forward, I don't feel any better about what to do. I actually catch myself wishing I could ask Gretchen for help. Every time I think of Kirsten, it's like the earth falls away beneath my feet.

Dina reluctantly drives herself home around ten thirty, only because my mom's already asleep on the couch and my bed's a twin. I check on Felicia before dragging down the hall to my room, but when I turn on the light, there's something on my bedspread.

It's a small padded envelope with my name blazing up at me in red Sharpie. There's no return address. My skin flares hot at the familiar writing. Kip swore he hadn't done anything else for Kirsten, but he doesn't exactly top my list of people to trust. I rip open the end of the envelope, and a silver object on a leather strap slides out with a small, folded piece of paper.

I pick up the bracelet, just like the one on my wrist, only the clasp is broken.

My mouth goes dry.

My hand trembles as I reach for the note.

Meet me on the playground, 11pm

My knees are ready to buckle, but I look at the clock on my phone and quickly change into my Penn hoodie, jeans, and big black boots. Maybe I can reason with Kirsten—work with her. Something. I want to run down the hall, take the stairs two at a time, but I force myself to creep over the floorboards on tiptoe. I can't afford for my cousin or my mom to wake up and find me leaving.

I text Marcus as I slip out the security door into the alley.

Meeting with Kirsten, think I can figure this out.

A car rolls by as I peek out of the alley, but it isn't the deputy on patrol and the road is dark as soon as it passes. I dart across the pavement and suddenly it's like hundreds of spring nights, my boots crunching through pine needles and leaves as my feet find purchase on the path. I haven't set foot in Hidden Falls Park at night for three weeks, but I could find my way to the little playground in my sleep. The air is warm tonight, carrying all the earthy plant and soil scents that go with spring. I race once more through the trees, only this time instead of clenching with terror, my stomach twists with anxious hope.

There's a shadow sitting on the merry-go-round as I approach. It's a creaking, rusted relic of our parents' childhoods located between an equally aged jungle gym and a boring plastic slide the town put in to replace the good one. A castle of sorts stands in the middle with bridges and turrets to hide in. Black River Creek bubbles audibly beyond the play equipment, but it's much quieter here than by the rush of falls downstream. There's usually a light over the playground at night, but I guess no one thought to replace the bulb the last time it burned out. The merry-go-round squeaks softly, making a slow rotation until I near. The hooded figure puts their feet down, grinding the whole thing to a halt. They don't move or speak at first and a flash of trepidation shoots through me, wondering if I should've told someone else, maybe Aisha or Haley, where I was going.

"Kirsten?"

The figure stands and the hood falls back, revealing Marcus frowning at me in the moonlight.

I cup my hand over my mouth, my heart racing. There's only one reason Marcus would be here instead of Kirsten, and now I'm more terrified than I've been in weeks.

I scan the darkness, trying to decide if I should run, if I even could. But I've been here before and I know the woods can close in and swallow me just as easily as they could set me free. I clear my throat because I didn't give up before and I'm not about to now.

"Thank God, you got my text." My voice squeaks with false emotion. I force myself to pause, take a breath, before I throw my arms around him. He stiffens, but after a second he reaches a hesitant arm around me, resting his hand on my back. "You were right, she's planning something. I got home and found this." I pull away, digging the bracelet out of my pocket. "There was a note saying to meet her. She could be here any minute."

Marcus doesn't say anything, but takes the bracelet and looks at it.

"Gretchen got us each one for our birthdays. I lost mine the night she died." I put my hands on his chest, showing him the other bracelet. "I don't know what to do."

He traces his thumb over the infinity symbol, then clasps it inside his fist, his eyebrows drawn together. "I don't either."

My pulse surges. I touch his hand, glancing again into the dark. I just need to get out of these woods. "Maybe we can figure it out, but we should go."

He looks down at me for the first time and there's something wounded and sad that I've never seen in his eyes before.

"Come on." My voice quavers.

"The video of me." He takes a step back. "Were you going to show it to the sheriff?"

"What?"

"You could've done it by now. Why haven't you?"

"Marcus, we should really go." I touch the zipper of his hoodie, but he takes another step away.

"Real evidence—that's what you said we needed to tie Kirsten to the murder. Is that what you were looking for?"

"I don't understand." My heart is so far in my throat, my words come out a whisper.

"I'm just confused, Sonia. But I guess I've always cared about you when I shouldn't." His voice is hoarse. "Just be straight with me, for once. Are you trying to pin Gretchen's murder on me?"

My eyes widen. "Marcus, I don't—"

He pulls his phone out of his pocket and touches the screen.

"You bitch."

A shriek.

"Out of my face, Gretchen—God, I wish you were dead."

"Wouldn't that be convenient?" I close my eyes at the sound of her voice. *"You could declare your love for—"*

Marcus stops the video. "I think that's enough."

I open my eyes, trying not to panic, to find the right words. "How did you get that?"

"How did *you* get it, might be the more relevant question."

I swallow hard. If I explain, I might buy myself a little time. I need to stay a step ahead of him. I have to somehow.

"It was on Gretchen's phone."

"Her phone was found in the water."

"There was an SD card. I took it out, but—"

"So all this time, you've had it. You looked me straight in the face and said you'd *seen* it, but never bothered saying you knew exactly where it was."

A hard lump rises in my throat. I thought I was protecting him; I never wanted him to know. "I wasn't going to show anyone—"

"Then why keep it?" He glares at the phone screen. "There's a bunch of ugly shit on here, but I'm the guiltiest-looking one. Was it as simple as that?"

"Marcus, I—"

"Why *me*?" he yells.

I close my eyes, unsure who I could possibly explain this to—the Marcus I thought used to hate me, the boy I kissed three nights ago, or the Marcus in front of me now. I guess I've lost him no matter what.

I was stupid to believe this would ever work.

My thoughts shift to my mom, Sheriff Wood, Dina, Uncle Noah—my family. My future. The one without Gretchen. Beside me, the creek ripples peacefully with no hint of the drop-off downstream.

"It was insurance, that's all. Everyone was already saying it was you. I thought for a while I could just run from it, look the other way. I thought you hated me." I bite my lip and look at him, my vision blurring with tears. "I didn't expect what happened between us. The more we spent time together—I've never felt that way before."

My lip trembles. I blink so I can see his eyes clearly.

"I can't let you go down for Gretchen's murder, because I'm the one who killed her."

FORTY-TWO

I'VE IMAGINED THIS LOOK ON Marcus's face a hundred times, but I hoped I'd never actually see it. His gaze is stony, his posture rigid. He looks like he wants to throw me over the falls, and I lower my head, waiting to see if he does, because I deserve it. When nothing happens, I open my mouth. One of us has to.

"It was an accident—I didn't mean to." My heart hammers in my chest, but I keep my eyes on the ground. "She'd been toying with me, pulling one string at a time. She kept hinting that I'd regret my decision to go to Penn, that she'd find a way to get my scholarship revoked, and I was terrified because I knew she would. I didn't even realize how close she came until a week ago. She'd set up an entire website and posted *my* actual essays for sale. All I knew at the time was that I'd pissed her off. It never occurred to me there might be more to it than school. I mean, she showed me the video, but it didn't make sense then. I didn't *get* it till you told me . . . till I saw your painting the other day." I chew my lip. "I know it's not your fault, but I had been so careful to stay on her good side. I can only imagine what went through her head when she saw it."

I steal a glance at Marcus, my stomach clenching when his

expression hasn't changed.

"If I lost that scholarship, there was no way I could turn down her parents' money for college, and she knew it. I was looking for something—anything—I could use to make her leave me alone, and then you and Kirsten pissed her off just enough." A strong breeze moves through the trees, pushing the empty swings back and forth like they're haunted.

"The only reason Gretchen would have let Kirsten come to Brianne's party was for the chance to humiliate her. She was clearly trying to get her drunk when we got there, watching her do stupid things, but I don't think she ever expected to find her with you. I'd never seen her so furious. I was barely speaking to Gretchen that night, but I drove her home and dropped her off after they fought, just like I've always said.

"She was usually careful never to let me touch her phone, but she was so angry, she dropped it on the seat of the car when she went inside. I grabbed it—I'd known her passcode for months—but then I ran into Haley walking her dog just as I shut the door of the Mercedes. I was so nervous Gretchen would come looking for the phone while we were talking, but she never did. *I* called her house from it, after I went into the woods. I wanted to bargain, but you can guess how much she liked that."

My voice shakes, I curl my hands into fists.

Marcus doesn't say anything, but he's still here, he's listening.

I need him to understand.

"It wasn't just that I had her SD card, her powerful little black book. Some of that stuff—people's passwords, nude pictures—could've gotten her in serious trouble. We agreed to meet at the top of the falls. She must have thought it wouldn't take long to deal with me if she left her purse with your money in the car on the way. We were both in the clearing just after eleven. I promised to send the memory card back to her after my first semester at Penn, but that just pissed her off more. I couldn't tell if she was more enraged that I tried to defy her, or that I actually succeeded. No one ever managed to get the upper hand with Gretchen. She threatened to keep me from going to school altogether. When I didn't give in, she said she'd call the health department on the diner, have it shut down to make my family pay for what I was trying to do. At first I was shocked that she'd go that far, but I guess I shouldn't have been. It wasn't even about Penn or Stanford anymore; she just wanted to regain control. I decided to leave. I thought maybe she'd settle down overnight and we could talk. I got to the bridge, but that's when—" I stop, running my fingers over my arms.

Cold hands close around my throat and drag me backward. My heart races, my ears fill with the sound of rushing water, my own ragged gasps. I wait for her to stop—let go, but she doesn't. I scratch and pry at her fingers until finally I scream.

She drops me facedown in the dirt and for a second I think she's gone. I roll to my side to get up, but then her foot comes crushing into my rib cage and my breath leaves my body in a gush of fire. She's on top of me then, shoving my face into the earth, fingers twisted through my hair. I push and scratch at her, and for just a moment, shove her off. I scramble backward, my hand flying to my pocket.

"Just take it! I'm sorry, Gretchen, please!"

I hold the phone between us like a weapon. Her eyes graze over it, her mouth twitching. And then she lunges, knocking it out of my hand.

I manage to get my boots under me before I'm pulled sideways. The world spins, a tree rushes toward my head. A shower of stars erupts across my vision, and then I'm on the ground again. I want to give in, just lie here and let it end, but she shoves me with her foot.

"Come on, Sonia. Run.*"*

I do what I'm told.

I crash through bushes and trees, unsure how I got to my feet or where I'm headed—I just go. I don't know if she's behind me or in front of me or where I'm even going until I realize how loud the water is and that the way I've gone was wrong. I stumble back, and she's on me, and then we're in the dirt and it's hands and trees and sky and a rock digs into my side. One of us screams, but it's lost under the roar, and we're out on that rock, the water spray like ice, and she's scratching and I'm shoving and—

"Gretchen!"

Tears stream down my face. I gasp for breath.

It's a minute before I see anything but the empty darkness where she was.

I can't bear to look at Marcus.

"I ran home because I'm a coward and I didn't know what else to do. When my family saw what I looked like, they called the cops, and I panicked—I couldn't tell them what really happened. The reports came in that Gretchen was missing, then dead. Someone suggested we were both attacked in the woods and I just went with it. I was too scared to do anything else."

I hold my hands in front of me, staring at them as if they belong to someone else. "But I provoked her—then I *pushed* her. It was my fault."

340

I take the first honest breath I've taken in weeks, and raise my head. Marcus's eyes are deep and black and sad. I wish he'd say something—yell at me, lash out. He has more reason to hate me than anyone else.

"I've waited every day for the sheriff to figure it out, for *someone* to put it together. If it had to be anyone . . . I'm glad it was you."

Marcus exhales, looks at the ground. He shifts his feet and for a moment it seems like he's going to reach for me, and I allow myself to breathe . . . but then he turns his head to one side and speaks into the darkness.

"Are you satisfied?"

My head whips around in time to see a second shadowy figure climbing down from the nearest turret of the castle. My blood goes cold, and for a moment, it's like I'm seeing a ghost all over again. She's changed out of the feathery purple gown into black leggings and a sweater, but her platinum hair is still piled elaborately on her head. She walks toward us with a big smile, takes the phone out of Marcus's hand, and replays the last few seconds of me talking.

"That should do nicely."

I shake my head, looking from Kirsten to Marcus and back. Blood roars through my ears. I scan the rest of the woods in a panic as the setup sinks in. I haven't just confessed. I've been caught.

"You were in my room," I say slowly. "But the memory card—"

"I figured you probably didn't get your kicks looking at it every night, so I left you a blank one." Her eyes are flat. "You know, at first I just *wanted* you to be guilty. Gretchen treated you more like a sister than she ever did me. I kept the bracelet they found with her

341

body as a kind of memento. But when my mom pulled the matching one out of Gretchen's jewelry box, I got suspicious. I just never thought he'd actually get you to say it."

I turn to Marcus, my voice shaking. "You knew?"

He looks away.

"Cut the guy a little slack, I only told him the truth an hour ago." Kirsten frowns. "I don't think you broke his heart until you said it yourself."

My chest feels like it's caving in. I look at the phone in her hand, the implications of every word I said buzzing through my head. Admitting the truth to Marcus was awful, but it felt safe somehow. It was almost a relief. But if I'd known I was confessing to the sheriff, the town . . . Gretchen's family. It can't be like this—I need more time. I plead with my eyes, begging Marcus to look at me, but he stares past me like I'm not even here.

Kirsten folds her arms. "So, do you want to call the sheriff and turn yourself in, or should I?"

I drag my gaze back to her.

"It'll be such a shock to him." Her lip curls. "This isn't going to make him look good in the next election."

My mouth tastes of metal. "Kirsten, please. I—I can't do that to my family."

"You had no trouble doing it to mine."

I lower my head, my face flooding with shame. "Gretchen tried to kill me."

"But you killed her first."

"It was self-defense."

She holds up her phone and starts dialing. "Why don't we let the justice system decide."

I glance at Marcus, but he just turns away, looking broken.

"Kirsten, think about it." I struggle to breathe. "Gretchen was horrible to you too, just in a different way. She knew what you wanted most in the world and she never let you have it."

"You don't know what I wanted," she says, but her voice hitches.

I cup my hands together, trying to hold on to whatever nerve I hit. "I used to wonder what it was like to have a sister. I don't think it's supposed to be like that."

Her lips pull back into a sneer. "She *was* my sister."

"She was my best friend. She was crazy, she was scary, and I *still* miss her." I gasp. Kirsten finishes dialing, her thumb hovering over Call. "Please, there must be another way."

She lowers the phone, her eyes uncertain. She studies me for what feels like an age, and as she does I see the face of a little girl sitting outside a closed door listening to tea parties she wasn't invited to; a preteen who would take insult and injury from her big sister just because it meant a moment of her attention; a young woman so lost in the shadow of someone else, she hardly knows herself.

"Maybe you should just jump." Her voice is dull.

I blink at her, unsure I truly heard what she said. Marcus stands next to her, openmouthed, and all I can do is stare, but then I think of the sheriff listening to that recording and a heavy sickness twists in my gut.

"If—if I did, would you still tell everyone the truth?"

Marcus's gaze snaps to me, but I keep my focus on Kirsten.

Her eyes widen, like she can't quite process what's happening either, but she answers, slowly. "I wouldn't have to. . . ."

I nearly choke thinking of my mother waking up to that—my frozen body pulled from the water after all; just when I'd fooled her into thinking I'd be safe. But wouldn't it be worse if she woke to find out I'm a murderer?

"How can I be sure?"

"I guess you'd just have to trust me," she says, but there's something Gretchen-like in her eye that convinces me. She'll keep it secret if I do this.

"What the—are you both out of your minds?" Marcus asks.

A lump rises in my throat, but I don't look at him. I can't. "What about Marcus? If I don't turn myself in, what happens to him?"

Kirsten puts her arm through his and rests her head on his shoulder. "Marcus and I have an arrangement. He does what I ask and he gets what he needs."

He yanks out of her grasp. "No way. I want no part of this."

She regards him coolly. "You're already in. It's too late."

I look at the creek, running briskly downstream, and my eyes burn. I take a few slow steps toward the falls, then a few more. Each time I pick up a foot it seems heavier than the last, my big black boots weighing down my steps rather than making me feel secure. Kirsten doesn't say anything, she just matches my pace.

Marcus shuffles behind us. "Just call the sheriff, Kirsten. This is fucked up."

"It's her choice," Kirsten growls.

The air is warm as we move along the creek, filled with the scents of springtime and promise I'll never taste again. I have to bite back tears when I think of all the nevers. Never college, never dreams . . . never again my mother's face. I feel Marcus at my back, bearing witness to all of it. But he's just one more piece I've already lost. And then Kirsten's word echoes in my mind, and I know she's right. I *have* chosen. I chose this fate the day I applied for a scholarship. I chose it every time I fought with Gretchen. I chose it again when I dared to challenge her the night of the party. Gretchen didn't succeed in pushing me into the falls then, but she might as well have. I was stupid to think it could end any other way.

We reach the rocks above Hidden Falls before I'm ready. People have laid new flowers and trinkets in place of the old memorial, but even in the dark I can make out where the graffiti used to be.

The second bitch is going down.

Kirsten hardly glances at it, but I guess I knew it wasn't hers. Aisha was right, there were a lot of people Gretchen pissed off.

I turn in a circle and everything else is so much like it was three weeks ago, I stumble, my mind flashing visions of Gretchen in the shadows. I guess this is fitting, to never escape her. She's probably watching from wherever she is and laughing, waiting to pull me under the icy water.

"Last chance to back out," Kirsten says over the gush of the falls. It's loud, but not like it was the last night I was here. My heart pounds. If I scream, someone might hear.

I look at her, then at the phone. She's holding it up again, nine-one-one punched in on the screen. I try to imagine my mother's eyes when she finds out what I've done.

What I did.

I step a shaking foot onto the ledge where I last saw my best friend alive. The place where the good things we had got all mixed up and destroyed with everything else. I get lost for a moment, trying to remember some of them. The time she spent teaching me how to drive. How the two of us could go days quoting lines from our favorite movies. How she really did *listen*, whatever her motive, anytime I was sad or hurting.

With nothing but air and water at my back, I raise my head and try to think carefully what to say. "I am sorry. If I could bring her back—"

"You can't," Kirsten says.

I open my mouth again, but the look on her face tells me not to waste my last breath. No amount of words can make up for what I did. I turn to Marcus. His face is a black cloud, his hands opening and closing. Our eyes meet and I see a glimmer of something— maybe just something that could've been. My heart comes to pieces thinking of everything we never had because of Gretchen. And because of me.

"I meant what I said before . . . about how I feel. I never could have turned you in."

His jaw is tight. "This is wrong. Don't do this."

"No, it's okay." I shake my head, blinking back tears I hope will be lost in the spray. "It's what I want," I tell myself. "It's best this way."

I close my eyes, the rush of water drowning everything out until I almost feel like I'm alone. I take a moment to appreciate the solidity of the limestone beneath my feet, the cool humid air. But one by one my family steps into my thoughts, coming to join me. My throat closes. I don't even know what's happened to my uncle Noah. Will my mother wake up tomorrow without a daughter or a brother? How will she explain that to my cousin? Will she and Dina accept that I took my own life? Will any of them forgive me?

Suddenly, that seems worse, never having any answers. My mom could live the rest of her life above the diner, looking out into the park, wondering and never knowing. A sharp pang shoots through my chest. That's probably how Gretchen's parents feel now. I've taken my knowledge of what happened to her for granted.

I open my eyes.

"What are you doing?" Kirsten asks.

I purse my lips. I can't convey to her how much watching Gretchen die has haunted me. How if I back off this ledge now, I'd be shifting that weight to her instead of easing her burden.

"I changed my mind. Call the sheriff."

I take a step forward, on trembling legs, but onto solid ground. Marcus seems to exhale with his whole body, but Kirsten's eyes blaze in an unnerving, familiar way.

"No, *I* changed my mind. You deserve what happened to her."

"Kirsten, I don't—"

She slams into me. I don't have time to process what happens next. The wind gets knocked out of my chest, her hands close around my neck. But then Marcus is there, locking his grip around my wrist. Kirsten's fingers scrape over my shirt, and then flail; she's too close to the edge with nothing to hang on to. I reach for her, but Marcus yanks on my arm. I swing sideways, landing hard on the ground.

There's a flash of blond hair.

I scream.

Kirsten plunges down.

FORTY-THREE

SOMEONE IS STILL SCREAMING. A hand closes over my mouth and it stops.

Marcus hauls me to my feet. "Sonia, come on!"

He nearly yanks my arm out of its socket dragging me through the woods like we're on the run. Like we could ever get away. The darkness and branches blur the way they did the last time I ran like this. Running from an attacker I left dead, drowned. But then I notice the slope shifting beneath us. We're headed downhill.

Marcus pulls me onto the wooden stairs built along the side of the gorge, leading down to the pool of water below the falls. I've never been here when it was so dark. The water level is higher than I ever remember; the familiar rocks and boulders we used to perch on along the shore are knee deep. The waterfall is lit by the glow of the moon. As is the lifeless body floating facedown at the center of the pool.

Arctic water splashes my face as Marcus dives in, snapping me back to my senses. He has Kirsten's head above water in four strokes. Moments later, he's hauling her to shore.

"I don't think she's breathing. Do you know CPR?"

My eyes widen and I nod, rushing to his side. I took a CPR class once for gym credit. My mom always said it was important to know stuff like the Heimlich working in the diner, but I've never actually had to use what I learned. Kirsten's left arm is twisted at a sick angle. There's blood coming out of her nose. I listen to her chest and don't hear breathing or a heartbeat, but it's almost impossible to hear anything over the roar of water at my back or the pounding in my ears. I start chest compressions, looking at Marcus's soaking clothes as I count. Pieces of his phone lie dashed across the rocks.

"Take my phone out of my pocket. Call nine-one-one."

Marcus follows my directions while I check Kirsten's airway, tilt her head back, breathe into her mouth. I hear him shouting to the dispatcher, but I don't catch the words.

I stare at Kirsten's face, crash my hands into her chest, and plead to Gretchen—*Please bring her back.*

Nothing happens. I keep my rhythm, counting, pumping, breathing, but she's motionless beneath me. Marcus asks a question I can't hear. I can barely see through my tears. After an eternity, the first of many sirens wails faintly over the crash of water, and at the moment we're joined by the first EMT, Kirsten coughs beneath me and breathes.

We're surrounded by police and firefighters. Kirsten was rushed away ten minutes ago, but the place is still a zoo of first responders. I sit out of the way on a large rock, watching the water pour down endlessly from above. Marcus huddles under a blanket on the stairs. He's done most of the talking since the cops arrived, since the sounds coming out of my mouth stopped forming actual words. No one comes near me but Sheriff Wood, who is way too kind. I wish he'd just arrest me and get this over with.

"Sonia? Sonia!" My head snaps up at my mother's voice, even while my stomach drops. There's no way to keep it from her now. She comes down the steps two at a time, still wearing the clothes she wore to work yesterday. I stand when she reaches the bottom, and she wraps me in her arms. "Oh thank God, are you all right? Roger said Kirsten's in the hospital."

I press my face into her neck, breathing in her scent—her warmth—horrified I almost chose to never see her again. "I'm sorry, Mom, I'm so sorry."

She strokes my hair. Her tears wet my cheek.

Sheriff Wood comes over, looking haggard and overtired. "I'm sorry about this, Marlene."

I close my eyes, bracing for the handcuffs, but he puts a gentle hand on my shoulder.

"I've got a statement from Marcus, but I'll need yours too. Why don't you go home and get cleaned up. I'll come by in a little while, once I hear how Kirsten's doing." He gives my shoulder a squeeze. "Just try to calm down, Sonia."

I look up, confused. Marcus catches my eye and gives me a subtle nod.

My lips part. Didn't he tell them what I did?

"Thank you, Roger. So much." My mom gives Marcus a wary look and then leads me back up the stairs and along the path that takes us closest to the diner. "Felicia is still sleeping," she says, trying to sound like she isn't terrified and furious and relieved. "I don't want her to wake up without us there."

My breath cuts short. "Uncle Noah?"

"Elena texted twenty minutes ago. He pulled through the surgery. It's still touch and go, but she says the worst part is over."

I exhale.

"What were you *doing* out here, Sonia?" She takes a measured breath. "With that boy."

I can't tell her. I open my mouth, but it's just like before. I have no words to tell her what I've done.

What I almost did.

At home, I shower and change clothes. My mom makes me a cup of tea and asks if I want to talk, but I tell her I need to lie down. It's still more night than it is morning as I close the door to my room. I set the tea on my desk and turn my closet light on, running my fingers over the names carved in the floor. The little tin box is tucked away at the back, hidden under the clothes like no one's ever disturbed it. I drop my bracelet inside and lay Gretchen's gently next to it.

If someone had suggested what would happen to us a month ago, I think we both might've laughed. If one of us was a killer, it was never going to be me. It's too late for apologies or wishing none of this ever happened, but I take a moment now to whisper a quiet good-bye. I'm not proud of who I was with Gretchen, but I don't know who I would be without her either.

My Penn hoodie lies at the foot of the bed. I pick it up, hold it to my face, breathe into the fabric. It smells of coffee and the woods. My finger traces slowly around the outside of each red letter—because I came that close. I fold the sleeves carefully, tucking it to the back of my bottom dresser drawer. Then I sit on the floor of my bedroom and finish my tea, trying to get the words right in my head.

My mom sits forward on the couch where she waits with a cup of coffee. "Did you get some sleep?"

I shake my head and snuggle in next to her, resting my head on her shoulder. The sky outside is beginning to lighten. My cousin will wake soon. Dina will get here. The diner will open. These are the few things I'm certain of.

"Roger checked in, but I told him you were sleeping. Kirsten's going to be all right. Her parents are with her."

I clasp my hands in my lap and let out a relieved breath, trying to imagine how Mr. and Mrs. Meyer felt getting a call like that. Again.

My mom brushes my hair away from my face. "Do you want to talk about it now?"

I nod, slowly, but then a minute passes. And another. "Can I just sit with you?"

Minutes tick by. The sky brightens.

The doorbell rings downstairs.

"I'll go let him in," I say, the words like cement on my tongue.

My feet are heavy on the stairs, though I'm only in slippers, not my boots. I walk through the empty diner, touching the chrome-edged countertops and worn vinyl booths. Everything my grandfather built and my family has worked to keep.

I take a deep breath, turning the key in the door, but the person waiting for me is Marcus, not Sheriff Wood. The tension leaves his face when he steps inside.

"You're here."

"For the moment."

His eyes flash distressed. "I didn't tell them anything, Sonia. I mean, I kept it to the bare facts. Kirsten was upset about Gretchen, you got into an argument, and she fell."

I give a weak smile. "You're almost as good at this as me."

He hesitates. "Maybe you won't have to tell. There's a chance Kirsten won't remember. Or if she does—"

"I have to, Marcus."

He doesn't speak.

"I've hurt too many people." I lean into his chest. "More than I would've if I'd told the truth from the start."

He runs his hand gently over my back. "It just doesn't seem fair. It's like she won after all."

I frown up at him and shake my head. "Gretchen didn't win anything."

There's a heavy rap on the door and I turn my head to see Sheriff Wood peering at us through the glass. I start to pull away, but Marcus draws me back. He stares at me for half a second and then leans down, pressing his lips, warm and gentle, against mine. My body surges with an instant of bliss, before it fades to sadness, and finally relief.

"For whatever happens next," Marcus says.

My head swims as I move for the door, but not just about this night, this moment. I know none of this is what Gretchen would've planned, but in the weeks since her death, sometimes it's still felt like she was pulling the strings. I guess it's time I spoke for myself.

The sheriff steps inside, fixing us both with a dubious stare. Marcus takes my hand. My heart aches as I think of the anger and disappointment, explanations and apologies, knowing none of it will ever make this right. Sheriff Wood might try to help, if not for me, then for my mother. But he's been too blind, too kind. Those aren't popular qualities in a sheriff. I swallow, wondering what will happen to my family once everyone knows what I did. My aunt and uncle and cousin are dealing with so much already.

I close my eyes.

I made a decision at the top of the falls and I'm here to follow through.

"Sonia?" My mom wanders into the room.

I open my mouth, and my voice finds the truth.

ACKNOWLEDGMENTS

This book would never have reached publication without the generous time, love, and support of my family. Special thanks to Diane and Reed Hainsworth, Stefan, Nova, and Felix.

Courtney Summers and Tiffany Schmidt, it hardly feels like enough, but as always, thank you for being absolutely essential. Brenna Yovanoff and Linda Grimes—your early input and honest opinions helped get this idea off the ground.

Very special thanks (on so many levels) to Jennifer Laughran. And to Andrea Brown, Mary Kole, Taryn Fagerness, and Michelle Weiner.

Kristin Rens, thank you for taking this book on, for asking all the right questions, for your kindness and patience. Additional huge thanks to Kelsey Murphy, Alessandra Balzer, Donna Bray, and everyone at Balzer + Bray/HarperCollins, including Caroline Sun, Nellie Kurtzman, Sarah Creech, Alison Donalty, and Bethany Reis.

Thank you to Charlotte Hainsworth Moore in the best possible way, Amy Burnett and Moca (you don't know this, but the first grain of this idea came to me in your entryway), Meghan Sharron,

Matt Lowery, Louise Martorano, Jodi Bova, Gillian Maynard, Eva Barkman, Jennifer Wettstein, Jill DeRaad, Christina MacDonald, and the Park County sheriff's office.

Last, but never least, thank you to my readers.